Praise for

Patricia Potter

and her bestselling novels

"Patricia Potter looks deeply into the human soul and finds the best and brightest in each character. This is what romance is all about." —Kathe Robin, *Romantic Times*

"Pat Potter proves herself a gifted writer as artisan, creating a rich fabric of strong characters whose wit and intellect will enthrall even as their adventures entertain."
—*BookPage*

"Patricia Potter has a special gift for giving an audience a first-class romantic story line." —*Affaire de Coeur*

"When a historical romance [gets] the Potter treatment, the story line is pure action and excitement, and the characters are wonderful." —Harriet Klausner

continued on next page . . .

The Heart Queen

"Potter knows how to play on the heartstrings and she makes marvelous music in this poignant, tender, yet action-packed romance. The complexities of relationships, secrets, betrayal and murderous plots blend well in this spin-off from *The Black Knave*."

—*Romantic Times* (Top Pick)

"This is a book that is difficult to put down for any reason. Simply enjoy."

—*Rendezvous*

"Exciting . . . powerful . . . charming . . . [a] pleasant page-turner."

—Harriet Klausner

"Potter is a very talented author . . . If you are craving excitement, danger, and a hero to die for, you won't want to miss this one."

—*All About Romance*

"Potter's story gives us action and pure excitement. Her characters are strong and intelligent, and she tells a truly romantic tale. This is what romance is all about . . . Terrific . . . You'll be thoroughly satisfied and wanting more. Truly delightful."

—*Old Book Barn Gazette*

The Perfect Family

"The reader loses all sense of time as they become entangled in a web of mystery Ms. Potter spins in *The Perfect Family* . . . Flawless characterizations . . . You are holding a work of art when you pick up a book by Patricia Potter."

—*Rendezvous*

"This is a novel that will long be remembered by those who read it."

—Harriet Klausner

The Black Knave

"Well-drawn, memorable characters, compelling action, and Machiavellian political intrigue add to a story that Potter's many fans will be waiting for." —*Library Journal*

"Patricia Potter has taken a classic plotline and added something fresh, making her story ring with authenticity, color, exciting action, her special humor, and deep emotions. *The Black Knave* is *The Scarlet Pimpernel* with twists and turns that make an old story new."
—*Romantic Times* (Top Pick)

"I couldn't put it down! This one's a keeper! Pat Potter writes romantic adventure like nobody else."
—Joan Johnston

"A fabulous romantic tale of intrigue and daring . . . will keep the reader spellbound through each twist and turn."
—*Rendezvous*

"A rousing tale of intrigue, danger, and forbidden romance that engaged my interest from first to last page . . . a most satisfying read." —*All About Romance*

Starcatcher

"Patricia Potter has created a lively Scottish tale that has just the right amount of intrigue, romance, and conflict."
—*Literary Journal*

"Once again, Pat Potter demonstrates why she is considered one of the best writers of historical novels on the market today . . . Ms. Potter scores big time with this fabulously fine fiction that will be devoured by fans of this genre."
—Harriet Klausner

THE DIAMOND KING

PATRICIA POTTER

JOVE BOOKS, NEW YORK

This is a work of fiction. Names, characters, places, and incidents either are the product of the author's imagination or are used fictitiously, and any resemblance to actual persons, living or dead, business establishments, events, or locales is entirely coincidental.

THE DIAMOND KING

A Jove Book / published by arrangement with
the author

PRINTING HISTORY
Jove edition / July 2002

Copyright © 2002 by Patricia Potter.
Cover art by Bruce Emmett.

Visit our website at
www.penguinputnam.com

ISBN: 0-515-13332-9

A JOVE BOOK®
Jove Books are published by The Berkley Publishing Group,
a division of Penguin Putnam Inc.,
375 Hudson Street, New York, New York 10014.
JOVE and the "J" design
are trademarks belonging to Penguin Putnam Inc.

PRINTED IN THE UNITED STATES OF AMERICA

10   9   8   7   6   5   4   3   2   1

Prologue

Scotland, 1747

Alex Leslie rode hard. He wished he could ride a hell of a lot faster. But how could he do that with ten children, and only five tired horses among them?

He knew their pursuers could not be far behind. Soldiers of the Duke of Cumberland, the man known among Jacobites as "the butcher," the man bent on destroying each one of them just as he had systematically destroyed the finest families in Scotland.

Alex had doubled back at one point of their journey and found a small patrol sniffing around their trail. It would not take long for them to gather more troopers and follow them.

He could only urge his small band to a faster pace. He knew it would be a miracle if he and this group of children made it to the coast, and to the French smuggler who was to take them to safety in France.

Bloody hell, he didn't want to go. He would just as soon stay here in Scotland and make life miserable for the British who had brutally slaughtered so many Highland families. But he had responsibilities to the orphaned children with him.

'Twas the greatest of ironies. He was a man who disliked responsibilities. He'd been a man who loved adventure and women and song. But that was two years ago. It felt like centuries ago.

Now he was the unwilling—and unlikely—guardian of children. Children who had found him like some infernal Pied Piper. A more unlikely one probably never existed. But he could not leave them to the not-so-tender mercies of the Duke of Cumberland, the English king's brother. Once they reached France, Alex intended to find Scottish refugee families willing to take them in, and go on about his business of retribution.

Mist was falling. He usually liked the Scottish mist. It had helped cloak him and his activities. But now he had children ranging from five to twelve, and the bairn in his arms was cold, his too-thin body shivering under the damp blanket.

What hurt as much as anything was that the child didn't cry. He had no more tears. He was a stoic little soldier, his childhood destroyed when he saw his mother killed by a British soldier.

So were the childhoods of the others. They no longer knew how to laugh or smile or giggle. He didn't have to worry about their crying or complaining. Or laughing. They never laughed, never chattered, never played children's games.

Alex wanted to give them safety. Safety and security. And laughter. And that meant a family.

He wished he could stop and rest, but that was a luxury they couldn't afford. They had to be at the coast at midnight, or miss what could be their last chance for rescue.

They had been traveling all day through the mountains, staying off the patrolled roads, traveling faint hunting paths that few knew about. But the trails were so overgrown, branches stung their bodies and wearied the horses.

He led the way, one young lad in front of him in the saddle, then Robin—the oldest lad—followed on the second mount with one of the younger children. Ewan and Colm rode a third. Meg, the oldest lass at eleven, led a horse with three children in the saddle. Burke—his fellow thief—rode at the rear of their ragtag procession. He carried the youngest child, a small lass whose mother died a month ago of cold and hunger and fever, making a total of ten orphans in Alex's care and Burke's.

Burke, strangely enough, was good with the bairns despite the fact he was a rogue through and through. Like Alex, he had turned thief and murderer after Culloden. Alex believed he acted in the name of justice, in the name of the innocents killed by Cumberland, in revenge for the decimation of the Highland clans.

Burke just liked being an outlaw.

So of the two of them, who was the more honest man?

A question he didn't wish to ponder, and an answer he relished even less.

But Burke was immensely loyal to the children. And they to him. Alex had never quite understood why.

He moved up to Alex. "The pass is near, my lord. Cumberland's men may be guarding it. I'll go ahead on foot if you can take this wee one and lead my horse," Burke said. "As you know I am a bit clumsy wi' tha' beast." He gave Alex a fierce grin.

Alex nodded. He stopped the small procession and dismounted from his horse. He placed the child riding with Burke on his own horse with the lad who'd been sharing his saddle and took the reins of both his and Burke's mounts. The lighter loads would rest the poor beasts.

He would have to see that the horses were returned to Neil Forbes, who would see to their care. Just as the man was seeing to his sister's well-being. It was an unlikely match, a Leslie and a damned Scot turncoat. Still, the man had saved his sister's life and most likely Alex's and that of his charges. For the former and the children, he was grateful. For himself, he did not care.

He watched as Burke disappeared into the mist. As

large and clumsy as he was on a horse, he was a born foot-pad.

A sense of urgency filled him. They didn't have time to waste. Still, he couldn't ride into a British patrol with ten children, several of them members of outlawed clans. It wouldn't matter that they were but five and twelve.

Dark was descending quickly. Time was running out. The ship would appear at midnight. It wouldn't wait.

Shots rang out, then silence. The children and their mounts melted into the trees. The older ones held hands over the mouths of the horses, soothing them in almost soundless whispers.

He handed the reins of his horse to Robin. "Stay here," he said. "If I don't come back, go back to the cave. Wait a few days, then send Meg to Braemoor. It's two days away to the east. You can find help there."

Just then he heard a whistle. Burke's whistle. *It was safe.* He nodded to Robin, who went back and reassured the other children. Alex led Burke's mount and his own.

In minutes, they passed two bodies. A fire was hissing—sputtering—in the mist, a makeshift oilskin cover apparently torn by a falling body. Then they passed two more bodies. One was moaning.

Alex hesitated. Burke started toward the injured man, dirk in hand.

"Tie him," Alex said. He cared not about another British soldier, but the children had seen enough violence.

Burke frowned but did what he was told. He used the dirk to cut the soldier's britches into strips, then tied him securely. Alex found a lantern the soldiers were using, thanking the saints that it was lit. Then they started again, ignoring the carnage his comrade had wrought. He had not time to hide the bodies.

They started down the steep trail. How much time did they have? No more than four hours.

He quickened his pace, ignoring the pain in his leg. He was all too used to it. He wanted to mount but he feared wearing out the beasts. There was no place between here and the coast to steal fresh ones. Night closed around them. The clouds and mist shrouded the moon; despite the light from the lantern, the path was treacherous, particularly for his own awkward gait, the weakness of his leg. He cursed the British yet again.

He tried to ignore the pain and watch the ground carefully to keep from stumbling. Finally they reached the bottom of the trail. He knew this land. There would be hills ahead but nothing like the area they'd just traversed. And now they should be able to avoid a British patrol.

The pain in his leg was excruciating. It had never healed properly after being split open by a musket ball. It did well enough when not overly strained but now . . .

His throat tightened as he remembered how he used to walk ten miles with ease. Strange how a man never appreciated something until he lost it.

Burke caught up with him. "You should ride, my lord. You do not want to slow us up."

Alex nodded. It would be foolish to risk all now because of pride. He swung up on Burke's mount, tightened his hands around little Elizabeth. Burke started into a slow, steady run, moving ahead to scout out the road.

Three hours later they reached the coast. Dark figures surrounded them at the appointed spot. He and Burke were searched, and he was relieved of a purse of gold the Marquis of Braemoor had given him. He had another purse sewn into his clothes.

A light shone through the mist. A lantern on the beach responded. He held young Elizabeth. Patrick Macleod, once meant to be the chief of the Macleods and now an orphan and refugee, clung to his leg. Burke held another child. The other seven stayed together, the older ones taking care of the smaller ones.

A boat appeared out of the mist just as they heard a shout down the beach. The men with them disappeared into the shadows, and he and Burke took their charges into the cold sea to meet the approaching longboat.

A shot. Then another.

The boat approached. One of the children cried out.

Hands reached for them. Alex practically threw Patrick inside, then lifted Elizabeth to waiting hands. Burke was also loading children. Finally the last of them was inside. He vaulted inside with the help of two strong hands, then Burke did the same.

Oars moved with a steady but hurried rhythm. He heard the sounds of shouts, of spurs, of English curses. Then the mist closed in around them.

He heard a small whimper and found the source. *Elizabeth.* Her cloak was wet not only with water but with a thicker substance. Blood.

"I'll see you safe, lass," he said, finding the wound and wrapping it tight to stem the bleeding. He prayed the Frenchmen had a surgeon aboard. "I swear it," he added, trying to convince himself.

He felt her body relax against his. She trusted him.

'Twas a terrible burden, that trust. He was not a worthy recipient of that trust. Not with his current plans. Still, his arms tightened protectively around her.

Chapter One

Scotland, 1748

Jeanette Campbell stared at the letter in her hands.

"It is a solution to our problem," her father said.

"*My* problem," she corrected.

"Nay," her father said. "Our problem. We are also . . . tainted. You know there have even been hints of witchcraft."

Jeanette rubbed her arm. It was well covered. Even her hand was gloved. She was accustomed to hiding both. "Does he know?" she said in a low voice. "Does he know about the mark?"

"Aye."

"And he still makes an offer?"

Her father fidgeted with the ink bottle on his desk. He couldn't quite meet her gaze.

"He is a man of fine family. I am told he is of good disposition. But he lost his wife and he cannot leave Barbados to find a new one. He has children and needs a mother for them."

"In other words, he is as desperate as you are," Jeanette said dryly.

"And you, Jenna. You are twenty-five. You have no chance of obtaining a husband here."

Loneliness overwhelmed her. She had never felt loved in this house. She had always been a burden. Nay, worse than that. She was an embarrassment to them. She was the devil's child. Would she be that to the man offering marriage? Had her father really explained the extent of her . . . disfigurement?

Could anything be worse than this cold house and a father—and family—who embraced barbarism toward other Scots? She knew of the slaughter following Culloden. And the bloody aftermath when women and children were killed as well as wounded men. She'd heard British officers laugh about it.

Still, she couldn't resist one last challenge. "You offered my hand without even asking me?"

"I thought you would be pleased. A husband at last."

"Does he know I am considered a bluestocking as well?"

"That, Jenna, is something you *can* change. We all know why you've been hiding in those bloody books of yours."

"And if I refuse?"

"Then you can leave this house," he said.

"Does my mother feel the same way?"

"Aye."

The despair deepened inside her. The aloneness. She couldn't remember ever receiving a gentle gesture from either of her parents. Her sisters had taunted her unmercifully at first, then complained bitterly as they grew older. Jenna was ruining their chances for good marriages. Her blood was tainted. Maybe suitors would think their blood—and that of prospective children—would be, too.

Barbados. She knew it was an island in the Caribbean. Furthermore, she knew that some Jacobites had been shipped there as bond servants to plantations.

A chance to escape what had become intolerable here in

Scotland. The Campbell clan was hated by most of the Highland clans, even those who had sided with the English at Culloden. None had forgotten the massacre of the Macdonalds at Glencoe decades earlier.

Still, she tried to be loyal to her family. It was the only family she had, even if they cared little about her.

She wanted to weep, but she wouldn't give her father the power of knowing how much he'd just hurt her. Perhaps Barbados would be a good place to go. A new start. A family of her own. She only wished she believed her father when he said the planter knew about the marks. What if she sailed across the seas, only to be rejected once again? She didn't know whether she could bear that.

It might be the only chance she had. Despite a large dowry, every man feared "the mark of the devil," afraid it might be passed to any children.

And if the Honorable David Murray did not want her, perhaps she could find a position as governess. Surely if the colonies were so scarce of women that a man would offer for a wife he did not know, then there must be a shortage of governesses as well.

"I agree, Papa," she finally said. As always, she hoped for some slight sign of approval for succumbing to his will. There was none, only a fleeting look of relief.

"We will answer him then and make the necessary financial arrangements. It will be three months or more before all can be completed. You will leave for Barbados from London."

Grief mixed with anticipation. Grief that she would leave, and no one would mourn her. Anticipation that she would leave this place on an adventure. She had taken many adventures through her books, and she had always hungered to see more of the world. Because of the "taint," she had never been taken to Edinburgh, although her sisters had gone there in search of husbands.

Now she would see Edinburgh and London and travel on a ship across oceans. And maybe at the journey's end she would find peace and contentment and, if God was with her, a gentle man.

Paris, France

Alex found homes for his charges—one after another.

Only Meg and Robin had not found permanent homes, mainly because they had refused every overture. There was a strong Scottish Jacobite community in Paris. They had readily offered homes to the younger children. But Meg at eleven and Robin at twelve had dodged British patrols for nearly eighteen months. They had gone hungry and cold and had seen the people they loved killed in cold blood and their homes forfeited to the men who had done it. They were rebellious and independent and trusted only Alex and Burke.

They made it clear they wanted to stay with Alex, though he'd tried to make it equally clear he had no way of keeping them. He had found them temporary refuge with a French count and his wife who had three children of their own, yet still they appeared at his door at the oddest of hours.

He would have to work harder at finding them a permanent home.

Letting the children go had been far more difficult than he'd thought. That surprised him. He'd thought he would be filled with relief.

Yet he had protected some of them for months. He had tried to care for the mother of two of them and had ended up watching her die. He had shared their hardships, and their grief. At some point the children had carved out a piece of heart he hadn't thought he still retained.

He had not been alone when he'd had them with him. They had given him a reason to live. Now he had to find another one.

Alex looked in the mirror in his rented room. A scar ran

up to the right side of his face, giving him a permanent
smile. It wasn't a particularly pleasant expression. Men
looked at him with curiosity, women with either fear or a
perverse fascination that sickened him. He remembered
when he could have his pick of lasses.

He'd even considered marriage in the days before Culloden. Now he had no idea where Mary Ferguson was, or
whether she still lived. He had no future, no land. Where
once he'd worn the finest clothes and played cards without
a thought of stakes, he now hoarded every coin.

The former Lord Alex Leslie had no title, prospects, future, not even his real name. It might well reflect on his sister, and on his most unexpected benefactor, the Marquis of
Braemoor, if the British knew he still lived. Not only lived
but had made his way robbing from them. He had taken the
name of Will then, and he kept it now, along with the last
name of Malfour. Although some in the refugee community in Paris knew his identity, or at least knew he'd been
a Scottish noble, they accepted his new name without
question. They knew from the children what he had done
for them, how he had harassed the British for over a year.
Some even speculated he might be the infamous Black
Knave.

He didn't care about acceptance. He'd only wanted to
be rid of responsibility and indulge a burning desire to
avenge himself on those who had destroyed his country.
But that would be difficult without funds. He would cheat
and lie and gamble to achieve his goals but he could not do
that with children at his heels.

Alex sat down in a chair at a table and took out the deck
of cards he'd carried during his escape from Scotland. A
game of solitaire might serve to focus his thoughts. He
studied the first card he laid down. The jack of spades—
the black knave. He hesitated, then searched the cards for
the heart queen.

The two cards were his only links to family and country. The legend known as the Black Knave had helped him

escape Scotland. And his sister had been called the heart queen by her husband, a man Alex had once hated but now respected. They had made a life together despite the aftermath of Culloden and their conflict of loyalties. He didn't think he could ever forgive or forget the horror of Culloden.

A knock at the door interrupted his bleak thoughts.

Burke rose from his chair to answer it. He was acting as butler, manservant, bodyguard. He was not an elegant one. He still looked like a footpad. But there was no questioning his loyalty.

An elegantly dressed and wigged gentleman stood at the door. Alex recognized him. They had met at a soiree hosted by a friend of Prince Charles, who had returned to Paris after hiding for months on the Isle of Skye.

Comte Etienne de Rochemont. A gambler, he'd been told, who won and lost fortunes.

"Monsieur Malfour?" the comte asked.

"Aye," Alex said. "Welcome to my rooms, such as they are."

The comte, a man of thirty-five years or so, took off his gloves. His hands had the pampered look of someone who had never worked with them. But his smile was warm, even as he studied the poor rooms. His gaze lingered on Burke, who looked more like what he was—a thief and murderer—then a gentleman's gentleman.

"I have some brandy," Alex said. "It is better than the room would indicate. A gift from a sea captain."

"Smuggler, you mean."

Alex shrugged.

"I have been told you once captained a ship."

"More than once," Alex said. "My family had a share in a shipping business. My father wanted to make sure he would not be cheated and I took a liking to it, much to his chagrin."

"Where did you sail?"

"Philadelphia. Virginia."

"The Caribbean?"

"Not as a captain, but I went as first mate."

"How many years did you sail?"

"One as an owner's representative, two as first officer, and three as captain."

"Ever fire on another ship?"

"No, but I practiced with cannon."

The comte looked disappointed. "I can find you men who have," he said, almost to himself.

Puzzled, Alex regarded him. "Why?"

"What do you know about privateering, monsieur?"

"That it can be a very dangerous profession," Alex said dryly. "If a peace treaty comes, a privateer can be tried as a pirate, even if he's unaware of the newfound cordiality between nations."

The comte grinned at him. "I had hoped you were not aware of that small problem."

"I'm not sure why that should concern me," Alex said, though indeed he was beginning to understand exactly why it would concern him. Excitement stirred inside him. Still, it was wise to play the unsuspecting observer.

"I have been told you are honorable. And have courage. Or is it, perhaps, recklessness?" the comte asked.

"I ran from the British, if that is what you consider valor," Alex said wryly. "As for honor, I lost that too at Culloden."

"You tricked them for over a year. Anyone who can elude Cumberland interests me."

"A forest is far different than the sea," Alex said.

The comte nodded. "I need funds, and privateering is the fastest way to improve a disastrous financial situation." He paused, watching Alex, assessing him. "I have a ship. I need a captain."

"Why don't *you* captain the ship?"

"I am not a sailor. Neither do I like the odds of being personally involved," his visitor said honestly. "France and England may make peace at any time. I do not want to be a fugitive from my own country. You, on the other hand, have already lost your country. Your need of funds is obvious. I also suspect you would like to meet the British on, shall we say, more equal terms."

The comte's honesty was disarming. Alex suspected it was calculated to do exactly that. "And the split?" he said.

"Forty-forty of the profits. Twenty percent goes to the French government. Your share includes the crew."

"Guns?"

"Adequate."

"I would want to see them," Alex said. "And I would need a crew."

"You can find them. There's any number of unemployed Scottish and French sailors who would welcome a chance to earn more than a seaman's pay. The trick is finding capable men with some sense of loyalty."

"And supplies?" Alex said. "You would pay for them, of course. From your share."

"*Oui,* monsieur. Does that mean you will accept my offer?"

"I have little to lose," Alex admitted.

"We all have much to lose, monsieur. Life is precious."

Alex could have debated him on that philosophical view, but didn't. "I also suspect you couldn't find anyone else."

"That too is correct," the comte said with a smile.

"And how do I know that I can trust you?" Alex said.

The comte shrugged. "You can ask your friends."

"I don't have any friends."

"Then you can ask your fellow Scots. I am usually in need of money, but I pay my debts."

"How did you get the ship if you are usually in need of money?"

"A game of chance," the Comte de Rochemont said.

"You could sell it."

"*Oui,* but there are other ships for sale now that the war is drawing to an end, and I would not get a good price. I would rather double or triple what a sale would bring."

The ship probably needed repairs before it could be sold but Alex didn't say that. Instead, he raised an eyebrow. "Any necessary repairs would also come from your pocketbook."

The comte shrugged. "As much as I can afford."

Which probably meant very little. Still, the offer appealed to him. A chance to strike at British shipping and improve his financial position at the same time.

It didn't require much thought. He no longer had a country. If he ever returned to Scotland, he would be condemned as a traitor. His face and leg prevented much of a future as a gentleman. He had no family.

"I will make a decision once I see the ship," he said.

The Frenchman's face broke into a wide smile. He held out his hand. "Monsieur Malfour, or is it 'my lord'?"

"Will is agreeable," Alex said. "If I agree, I do want a legally drawn contract as well as letters of marque."

"That will be no problem. This government has no love for the English. They continue to try to usurp us in the Americas. And the government will, of course, welcome a percentage of the prizes." He hesitated, then added, "Please call me Etienne."

Alex turned to Burke. "What think you?"

"I don't like the sea," the man said sullenly.

"You didn't like horses either, but you rode throughout the Highlands on one."

"Reluctantly, my—" He stopped suddenly with a sideways glance.

"But you will come with me?"

"Aye," he said.

"I have my first seaman," Alex said cheerfully. In truth, he felt better than he had in years, despite the prospect of sailing what would probably be a wreck with outdated gunnery and an inexperienced crew and inadequate supplies.

For the first time in two years, he would be master of his own destiny.

It mattered little if it ended in disaster.

Le Havre, France

Alex was pleased to see that the comte's vessel was a frigate, a long, low ship that was swift in the sea. It looked as if it had once served as a warship, then had been sold and refitted as a merchantman. Most of the guns had been stripped from her, though some had been retained, probably as minimal protection against pirates.

As a privateer, the ship needed at least twenty-eight guns capable of firing twelve- and eighteen-pound shot. This one had only fourteen guns capable of firing twelve-pound shot.

It also needed other repairs, but on the whole looked sound, better than he'd expected. If he obtained additional guns, he could have it ready in three, maybe four weeks. Time, he knew, was vital. He would not receive his letters of marque nor be allowed to leave France if the ongoing peace talks between France and England succeeded. After that, he would take his chances of being charged as a pirate. God knew England would hang him fast enough in any event if they ever captured him.

He looked over the remaining guns carefully. He was familiar enough with artillery, since some of the merchant ships in which he'd sailed had traveled over sea-lanes inhabited by pirates and had been lightly armed. He knew how to direct fire. He'd practiced gunnery, though he'd never been on a ship that had actually fired at an enemy.

He knew his first acquisition had to be an experienced naval artillery officer. Then a first mate. With those two in place, they could then help him select a crew and the armor and supplies they would need.

Etienne waited on deck as Alex prowled through the ship. Alex wondered how much his partner—if they concluded the deal—could put into the vessel. As much as he wanted the ship, he would not risk the lives of those recruited to sail it.

Alex had always loved the sea. He had in instinct for sailing that he did not have for agriculture. There was something exhilarating about testing his skill against the sea and wind, a freedom he didn't find on land. He wanted this. He wanted it very badly.

He went back on the main deck where the comte was waiting.

"You said it was adequately armed. It is not. We will need at least fourteen additional cannon."

Etienne shook his head. "The most I can afford is ten."

"Then the arrangement is off. I will not ask men to commit suicide. I do not really fancy it myself."

The Frenchman's expression did not change.

Alex waited.

Etienne finally nodded. "I will see what I can do." He hesitated. "There is something else, *mon ami.* I have learned that diamonds have been discovered in Brazil. If you take several prizes, you can use the money to then go to Brazil and purchase diamonds for very little."

"Very little?"

"They are all over the country. Portugal is trying to control their production, but the natives believe the diamonds are theirs. If you can make contact with them, we can purchase them for a small piece of their real value."

"Diamonds? I thought they were found only in India. I know there was some news about Brazil, but then I heard the stones found there were not really diamonds."

"You were meant to hear that," Etienne said. "The world was meant to hear that. It is a lie told by the diamond merchants to hold down the price. They're being shipped to Goa in India, then sold as Indian diamonds."

Alex stared at him. "How—"

"The cards, Will. A year ago, I played with a diamond merchant. He drank too much wine, and when he lost, he did not have the money to pay. He told me this instead. I have been waiting for an opportunity ever since. He said he will buy any diamonds from that country and authenticate them as coming from India."

"How can you believe such a story?"

"I know when a man lies . . . and when he doesn't."

"Why tell me now?"

"For some reason I trust you. Perhaps because you endangered yourself to save children that are not your own. I also wanted to know if you were reckless. You are not, or you would have accepted this ship as it is."

Alex did not know whether to feel challenged or insulted.

He decided to feel neither. Instead, he relished the knot of excitement that continued to grow. The thought of using British cargoes to steal Portugal's diamonds intrigued him.

"We can begin interviewing prospective officers on the morrow," Alex said. "When can you have the cannon?"

Etienne smiled. "Next week."

The two men returned to the inn where they were staying. Alex would then return to Paris to put his affairs in order, write his sister, and leave what money he had with the families that had taken in his children.

His children. He had tried not to become emotionally involved with them. They were a responsibility, one last duty to the country he had loved. Nothing more. But now he knew it wasn't true. They had gone hungry together, shivered together, eluded the British together. They'd had a courage that few men had.

He would miss them.

Chapter Two

Paris, Two Weeks Later

The farewells were even more difficult than Alex had anticipated.

He had planned to leave at midday for Le Havre, where he would supervise the installation of the cannon and await additional supplies being shipped by barge from Paris. He hoped to sail at the week's end.

He had visited each of the children. The most troubling visit had been with Meg and Robin, the oldest of his small flock. The other children seemed to have been enveloped happily enough into the families of refugees. But Meg and Robin had stared at him with the eyes of the betrayed.

"I will be back," he'd told them.

"We want to go with you."

"That is impossible," he said. "It is too dangerous."

"I'm not afraid of danger," Meg replied.

"I did not think you were, lass. You do not have a fearful bone in your body, and I worry about that. But a privateer is no place for children. I could not concentrate, worrying about you."

Robin looked skeptical. "You would not have to worry about us. Ships have cabin boys far younger than me."

"Not my ships," he said. He had never approved of the practice. He put a hand on Robin's shoulder. "You need an education."

"You can teach us," Robin pleaded. "And we can learn about the sea."

"You've had enough danger in your life," he said. "Now is the time to be children."

"I will never be a child again," Meg said, drawing herself up to her full eleven-year-old height.

And she would not, he feared. Neither would Robin. But he wanted them to have a chance. He wanted them to have enough food, enough warmth, enough schooling. He wanted them to play.

"Nay," he said. "I will return. I swear."

It was not a promise he'd expected to make. But the hollowed look in their eyes, the expectancy that faded back into hopelessness had prompted it. Perhaps by the time he did return, they would be in a secure home.

He tried not to think that he might never make it back. "I must go, and Burke, too," he said. "I'll bring back something very special for each of you."

He wanted to turn away from the pain in their faces. Leaving them hurt more than any wound he'd suffered. They had lost everyone they had loved. Everything they'd once had.

But he could not stay, and he would not put them in danger's way again.

"I need you here to make sure all the others are safe," he said. "Can you do that?"

Meg looked indignant. "*They* have found homes."

"So have you."

"They do not really want us," Robin said.

The two had been the most difficult to place. Robin would have been a marquis, had his family's title and estates not been ripped from him, but Meg did not come from society. She had been the daughter of a blacksmith who had fought alongside Robin's father; she and her mother had accompanied him to Culloden as so many families had. After her father's death, the two had fled into the hills, and Meg's mother had died of pneumonia in the caves several months ago.

The lass knew little about manners although Robin's influence had helped her speech. They were so close, though, that they refused to be separated, and that had not aided Alex in placing them with a family.

"Etienne has agreed to visit you," Alex said. Etienne had taken them for an outing in his carriage, and they had liked him immediately. Perhaps because they recognized the fact that he, too, was a rogue.

Robin's eyes looked brighter. "He can teach me to be a gambler."

That wasn't what Alex had had in mind. Robin should have other opportunities. But then he himself wasn't exactly a model. For the last year, he'd been a thief and a highwayman. "I want you to have an education," he said. "Both of you."

The two exchanged looks. Alex didn't trust that look.

But he had to go. Burke was waiting with the horses. He stood awkwardly for a moment. He'd provided for their needs, and little more. He hadn't wanted to get close to them; it hurt too much to lose people he loved. And it would hurt them if they lost him. They had already lost too much.

He did not fool himself. He was embarking on a dangerous journey. Even with the letters of marque, he doubted whether he would survive a British capture. And from what Etienne had told him, the natives in Brazil could be less than friendly.

He held back, holding out his hand to Robin in a manly farewell, then patting Meg on her shoulder.

He tried to turn his thoughts to other business as he walked away. He and Etienne had found a first mate, Claude Torbeau, who had helped them find the cannon. He was a former French naval officer who apparently had been discharged as the war against Austria had subsided. Alex hoped it was not because of incompetency. But Claude appeared to know his cannon and he knew of seamen who would join them. Alex thought it a good sign that sailors who knew him would willingly sign with them.

He wondered how Burke and Claude would fare together. Burke had no sea skills and would have to be satisfied with working as an apprentice, though he was not pleased about it.

Alex had given Burke a choice. He could stay in France, and Alex would give him what personal money he had left. Or he could accompany Alex. But he would have to obey the first mate. Burke didn't like to obey anyone, including Alex.

"A Frenchie," Burke said with disgust as Alex joined him outside Rob and Meg's home.

"I plan to follow his orders myself," Alex said. "I know what I dinna know. I know the sea, but I've never even seen a sea battle. We need him, and a crew must have discipline."

Burke grumbled, "A sea battle is no different than any other, yer lordship. But you will need someone to play the pipes."

"You?" Alex stared at him. The greatest cutpurse in Scotland was a musician? Well, that was no more strange than the fact that he was becoming a pirate.

"I lost them during the battle," Burke said. "I saw no reason to moan the loss when there was naught to do about it. But if I could have that bit of coin you mentioned, I know someone who has pipes to sell."

Alex nodded. "Purchase them. I will meet you in two hours, and we ride to Le Havre. The comte is already there." He started to turn away, then looked back. "And no more 'my lord,' Burke."

Burke just shrugged.

Damn the man. Alex should leave him in Paris.

"Burke?"

"Aye . . . sir." Insolence dripped all over the words.

Better to give up. Alex turned his mind to the hundred things left to do. But no matter how hard he tried to concentrate on them, he couldn't shake the look of desolation on the faces of Robin and Meg.

London

London was exciting and stimulating. And dirty.

The filth was one of the first things Jenna noticed. And the odors.

Still, she couldn't resist peering out of the window as the rented carriage clattered down the Strand, London's principal shopping street. She was entranced by the contrasts: the fish and fruit vendors, the beggars and the well-dressed ladies and gentlemen, the fine homes and dirty streets.

She was used to country life. She had always thought the city would be a beckoning place. It was not that. Yet she couldn't deny a fascination with the fashionably dressed men and women strolling about without deigning to notice the beggars crowding the streets.

She gave the beggars what she could, but she also knew she had to keep some coin for herself. Fifty guineas and a pouch of jewels her father had given her were all she had. If her prospective husband refused her . . .

She could never return to Scotland. She knew that much. She couldn't forget the relieved looks on the faces of her parents, even her sisters. She wasn't wanted there. She would never again go where she wasn't wanted.

"Jeanette, it is unseemly to peer so," her companion said. The thought of Maisie Campbell, a hefty lady of dour disposition, as her chaperone for the next few months was daunting even as she was grateful for the company of Celia, her maid.

Yet her quiet soul exulted.

Perhaps something miraculous would happen. Perhaps she would find someone who wanted—or needed—her. Perhaps someone could accept what her family could not.

The ship would sail in two and a half weeks. In the meantime, her father was providing funds for a trousseau. Lightweight garments, she was advised. Her future home had a far different climate than that of the cold and windy Highlands.

A different climate. A different hemisphere. A different world.

Jenna had ventured out twice, both times with Celia and without the knowledge of Maisie. To be in London and not see anything was a crime, in Jenna's eyes. But they could not venture far without escort or carriage. Today, then, was a treat even with Maisie's company.

Their destination was the dressmaker. Jenna had never been to such an establishment before. A seamstress had always come and stayed at their manor near Fort William while fashioning gowns for Jenna.

Jenna regretted that her new gowns would not have short sleeves unless they were accompanied by long, matching gloves. The latter might well appear odd in a warm climate and would most certainly be uncomfortable. She told herself again she had to live with what was, and make the best of it.

Ignoring Mrs. Campbell, she looked back out at the streets. They passed a row of fine homes, then a park. The carriage finally rolled to a stop in front of a line of shops.

The coachman stepped down, and a man standing at the establishment's door rushed over to help her out, then the other two women, and led them inside.

The shop was filled with mannequins dressed in elegant gowns and tables piled with bolts of cloth.

When the older woman saw the arrivals, she hurried over to them. "My lady," she said. "You must be Lady Jeanette Campbell. We have been expecting you. Perhaps you would like to look over some patterns and materials I have selected. A complete trousseau, I am told. No expense to be spared. And the journey, my lady, it is so exciting, so romantic. I am honored to be of service to you."

She gushed on for a few moments and Jenna could imagine the order that had been sent to her through the advice of a British officer. It was probably due to her father's guilt—or relief—over her departure from Scotland.

Within minutes she was looking over the mannequins and selections of materials. The dresses were all very elaborate with huge hoop skirts and panniers. She thought of the temperatures in the Caribbean and described to the dressmaker the designs she wanted. Only one gown with a hoop skirt. The others were to have simple lines. All either had long sleeves or gloves of matching material.

Mrs. Coyle, the dressmaker, merely nodded.

She suggested that Jenna undress to her chemise so she could get precise measurements. Jenna accompanied her and the girl who had been working on the dress in the main room to a private dressing area. Celia helped her off with her dress and corset until only her chemise and stockings remained.

When Mrs. Coyle turned to her, her smile disappeared as she saw the wine-colored birthmark, but it returned quickly. The girl beside her released an exclamation. Mrs. Coyle frowned at her, and took the measurements herself. "You have a fine figure, my lady," she said. "It will be a pleasure dressing you."

The joy of the visit faded. It was all Jenna could do to stand there, her birthmark evident for all to see, until the final measurement was made.

Celia dressed her again in silence, her glance sympathetic.

Jenna pulled on her gloves.

"We should have a fitting next week," Mrs. Coyle said.

Jenna nodded as several women were ushered into the establishment. Their arms were bare. Envy washed over her.

Would anyone ever look at her without seeing the wine-colored mark that ran from the back of her hand up her arm?

Would the man who had asked her to be his wife see beyond the mark? Or would he, too, gasp and look away?

She looked straight ahead as they returned to the carriage.

At Sea

Alex stood on the deck of the *Ami* and looked out over the sea.

It had been four days now. They had slipped from the Le Havre docks under a moonless dark sky. In the days since, they had passed three British merchants but no warship, though he knew that the British often patrolled around the harbor. He had elaborately disguised the cannon, piling up supplies next to them and covering them all with tarps. As an extra precaution, he flew the British flag. He would do his hunting in the Caribbean, not in seaways where his presence would soon become known.

He was pleased with the crew, a mixture of Scots, Irishmen, and Frenchmen, plus a Portuguese sailor and a few seamen from the American colonies who had left a brutal captain when their ship reached Le Havre. He had questioned the latter to discover whether they were merely malcontents but their stories matched too well. All wanted the prospect of prize money rather than the beggarly wages they'd received as simple seamen.

Five of the total crew had been gunners in various navies, and once out of busy sea-lanes, Claude intended to conduct drills.

The crew members seemed to get along well together, all united in a universal dislike—if not pure hatred—of the English, although the colonials less so.

They should reach the Caribbean in less than three

weeks. The *Ami* was swift, a quality necessary for a privateer. They needed speed, friendly ports, and targets: British
ships loaded with goods from their colonies or sugar and
molasses from the West Indies. Just the idea of extracting
even a small price from the British for Culloden filled him
with anticipation.

At the moment he just enjoyed the wind and the sun and
the sky. It was a moderately warm day with a brisk wind,
the kind of day every sailor relished. The sun brushed his
cheek, and he savored the sense of freedom, of control,
that had been missing from his life for the past two years.
He could forget the scar and the way that his leg gave out
far too often. Here, none of that mattered.

The sound of yelling interrupted the relative satisfaction of the moment.

"Captain," one of the crewmen shouted.

Then he heard a loud curse by a young female voice,
and a "Let me go," uttered by a young male voice.

He uttered a curse of his own.

He turned to the hatchway. A sailor had two short figures in tow, both wriggling in his hold. "Stowaways, sir.
Found them in the munitions storage in the afterhold," he
added with disapproval.

Alex tipped the cap Meg was wearing and saw that she
had cut the long red hair that had been her best feature. Her
face was smudged and her lad's clothes were filthy.

Robin didn't look any better. Though he tried to draw
himself up into a position of dignity, he looked like a chim-
ney sweep. He appeared small and defiant and uncertain
all at the same time.

"How in the bloody hell did you get here?" Alex asked.

Meg stuck out her lower lip and remained silent.

"The barge, sir," Robin said.

"The barge?"

"We heard you talking about the supply barge from
Paris. We went to the riverfront and found out which was
going to your ship and we, ah, we went aboard."

"You stowed away on the barge?" Alex said.

"Aye."

Alex glowered. It was all he could do. He had been a thief, and the children knew it. It did not matter that he had done it for them. And, perhaps, a little for himself. He'd wanted to live long enough to hurt the British. So he hadn't exactly been a great example for children. He seized on the only reasonable argument. "You promised to do as I said."

"That was a year ago," an obviously unrepentant Meg pointed out.

"A promise is a promise," Alex said, finding it very hard to be a figure of authority. He had been that—of sorts—for a year, but he'd always thought of it as a temporary condition to be ended shortly. He'd never really known children before, had not thought to have any of his own for years, and he'd steered away from trying to be any kind of father to them. He had simply provided—usually not very well—for their basic needs until he found someone who could give them the security they needed.

He didn't have any love left inside him. There was only anger. The children had enough anger of their own without being even more infected with his. He didn't know how to comfort. He definitely did not know how to teach values when he had been without them these last few years.

He certainly didn't want them to be identified with pirates. It was fine for him. He had nothing else. He had no future. No woman would marry him with his physical wounds or the other less visible ones.

Burke came up from below deck and stopped at the sight of the children. "Bloody hell," he muttered. "How—"

"The barge," Alex said. "Though how they got aboard the *Ami* is another matter."

Robin shifted his gaze to Meg, then to the deck.

"Robin?"

"It was not difficult," he said. "We saw you leave. We

took some fruit aboard and sold it to the sailors. When no one was looking, we hid in the hold."

"If a ship had fired at us . . ." Alex closed his eyes. He couldn't bear thinking of what might have happened.

"But it did not, my lord." He shifted again. "Meg and I are thirsty."

"And hungry," Meg said. "We ate all our fruit."

"When were you going to make yourselves known?" Alex asked.

"When you were far enough away that you couldn't send us back," Robin said, "but Meg was hungry . . . and . . ."

Meg turned on him. "You were hungry, too."

Four days in the dark. Four days with little food and probably less water. But then their stomachs had known hunger before.

Still, it hurt the heart he'd believed shielded against such feelings. He'd thought once he reached Paris, he would be relieved of those nettlesome feelings that sometimes made him wonder whether he had guarded his heart well enough.

Claude, his first mate, joined the growing circle of seamen, all of whom eyed the stowaways curiously. "Stowaways?" he asked.

"Aye," Alex replied.

Claude was a frightening figure, standing two inches over Alex's own substantial height. He had the girth that Alex did not. Nearly two years of healing and being on the run had made Alex lean. He still didn't eat as he once had. Some of the children had stuffed themselves on the ship that took them from Scotland to France, but others—including himself—continued to chew food extensively to take away some of the hunger. It was a habit he'd been unable to break. Neither had Meg, who was far too thin.

"We can throw them overboard," Claude offered, but Alex saw a twinkle in his eyes. Claude was a disciplinarian aboard the ship, but in the weeks Alex had known the first mate, he had also seen a patience and even humor that had already made him a favorite with the men. Alex had remained aloof. Distant. He didn't want to know men he might well get killed.

Now each looked at Claude with concern on their faces, obviously wondering whether the formidable man was serious.

"That's an idea," Alex said.

"Wouldn't take much effort, puny as they are," Burke observed.

"We do not have enough food for another hand," Claude said severely. "Especially not for two."

"We might be able to keep one," Alex said seriously.

Meg moved closer to Robin, but Robin looked up and grinned.

Claude shook his head in despair. "Captain, you lack a fierce glare." He turned his gaze to Alex. "I assume you know these two . . . miscreants."

"Unfortunately," Alex said in a cool voice. "Right now, I think they need something to drink and eat. Then we will discuss their immediate futures."

Claude's threat had not had the intended impact on Robin and Meg, but his own cold words obviously did.

"They should know no' to go where they are no' wanted," Burke said.

A look of despair filled Meg's eyes and Robin tightened his hold on her hand. They both had been attached to Burke despite his rough ways.

Burke apparently saw their dejection, too. His expression softened. "Come along," he said roughly, "before one of these Frenchies decides to take the mate's suggestion." He grinned suddenly. "Then I would have to fight them, and you know how much I would hate that."

Robin's lips twitched. Burke liked nothing better than a good fight. But then the boy looked again at Alex. "We wanted to be with you," he tried to explain.

Alex closed his eyes for a moment. "Get along with you,"

he said softly. "Wash first, then eat. We'll decide your fate then."

Robin stared up at him expectantly.

"The barge was very ingenious," Alex added.

"You were a good teacher, sir." The good manners under the cloak of dirt were infectious. So was the mischief behind the words. Robin disappeared down the hatchway before Alex could retort.

What in the hell was he going to do with two children? He couldn't go back. There were British ships all over the bloody sea, their crews keeping an eye out for ships leaving the French port. He'd covered his guns and tried to look innocent, but that would not always work. If they did return and the peace talks looked successful, he would never be allowed to leave again.

"Captain," Claude said, "do we turn back?"

"Nay," Alex replied. "That would be even more dangerous. The area was crawling with British patrol ships. They would be pleased to grab that lad."

"Lads a lot younger than that one have gone to sea," Claude said. "We don't have any powder monkeys."

"We still do not," Alex said. "They can work in the cabins and galley but not in the munitions hold. I did not steal—and kill—to keep them alive to see them blown to bits."

Claude's eyes sparked with interest at the comment, but he didn't say anything. That had been one thing Alex admired about him: his lack of curiosity. The man, a former French naval officer, had wanted the job of first mate—and the five percent share of any prize that accompanied it—and he'd obviously trusted Etienne. That was all Alex knew, although he and Claude had dined together for the last four days. They had talked of little but the crew they were beginning to know.

He had probed Alex's experiences at sea, obviously weighing his knowledge, but he apparently had withheld judgment on Alex's taste for battle. But now Claude grinned, and Alex knew he'd probably had reservations of his own at taking a berth with a captain about whom he knew nothing. For some reason, a reprehensible past seemed to reassure him.

That didn't matter now. What did matter were two children who'd had too short a childhood, too little security, too much tragedy. Alex had not the slightest idea of how to make them safe.

Returning to Le Havre was dangerous. Taking them with him was just as dangerous. But the simple fact was they would probably not stay in France, even if he tried and succeeded in getting them there. They would find some way of getting back aboard.

Four black days in the munitions room. He didn't think he could abide that.

And all to be with him.

Bloody hell.

London

It was her final fitting.

Jenna dreaded it, dreaded standing for hours and suffering the occasional pinprick, all for a trousseau that might never be used.

Still, it was good to leave their lodgings. Maisie had refused every effort to leave them, even for meals. According to her, London was filled with ruffians and footpads. Her person was not safe. But the trousseau was part of her duties, and she had very reluctantly left the safety of the inn.

As the sailing date approached, she'd become more and more silent, muttering about pirates and leaving civilized society. It was obvious that the voyage ahead held little interest for her. She had been asked to serve as chaperone by Jenna's father. One dependent on his goodwill did not question such "requests."

Strangely enough, Jenna's mother had taken a liking to

the widow, or perhaps she had enjoyed lording her position over Maisie, and the woman had been brought into the house as a sort of companion/secretary to Jenna's mother. She was considered neither servant nor relative, and she worked hard to make herself valuable and therefore secure.

Yet her complaints were unceasing, and Jenna dreaded the thought of spending nearly a month in close quarters with her.

She and Celia often left when Maisie retreated to her room and took one of her naps. They would walk to a market or through a park, always sure to return before Maisie awakened or there would be hours of recriminations and threats of letters about her lewd conduct to her father.

But, oh, how she wished to visit the restaurants or visit St. James Park, or go to the Covent Garden Theater.

Although she dreaded the actual fitting, it did feel good to be outside even with the fog this morning and a light rain.

As before, a man stepped up to help them out of the coach, then opened the door of the dressmaker's. As Jenna entered the establishment, she heard a terrible scream followed by a thump. She spun around.

Maisie Campbell lay on the street—apparently from a stumble on the cobbles. A leg stuck out at an odd angle from the voluminous skirt and petticoats she wore. Maisie tried to move it and screamed again. The usher who had helped them out of the carriage took one look and frowned. "I'll go for a physician," he said, and started to run down the street.

Maisie wailed. Two men carried her inside the dressmaker's establishment. Tears streamed down the older woman's pinched face as Jenna hovered nearby, uncertain as to how to comfort her. Celia wrung her hands.

The physician arrived and diagnosed what everyone else had known.

"Mrs. Campbell has a broken leg. I'll set it but she must be kept still in bed for several weeks."

"We were to go on a voyage in three days," Jenna said.

"To Barbados," added the dressmaker helpfully.

"Not this lady," the physician said. "Not if she wishes to walk again."

Maisie Campbell grimaced, but still Jenna saw a note of relief in her chaperone's eyes. Jenna knew her companion had never wanted to take the long voyage and had been terrified of pirates. She had been more afraid, though, to refuse the head of the Campbell clan.

"We will have to go home," she stated, trying to restore her lost dignity and authority.

"No," Jenna said. "Celia and I will go on. Mr. Murray is expecting me."

Maisie looked at her in horror. "You cannot go alone. It would be scandalous."

Scandal, Jenna knew, was the worst possible thing that could happen to someone in charge of her good name.

"The fare has already been paid," Jenna reasoned aloud, desperate now not to return to her life in Scotland. "I doubt if we could get it back, and the next ship to Barbados is weeks away. I do not believe my father would regard the delay kindly. He has given his word to David Murray."

Maisie frowned, obviously unconvinced. "Your father—"

"My father wants me out of Scotland," Jenna said bluntly, not caring if anyone else heard. The hurt still pierced deeply. She knew she could not return home.

Maisie's gaze fell. It was something she could not deny. "You will be disgraced," she protested weakly.

"Is that any worse than what I am now?" Jenna asked. "Because I carry a birthmark, I am considered damaged, tainted, even evil. Perhaps society in Barbados is not so condemning."

Maisie flushed. "Then I accept no responsibility," she said.

"You have none. I am twenty-five," Jenna said. "From now on, I will see to myself."

Her mind was already wrapping itself around the fact

that her father had paid for three passages and two cabins. Now she would need only one. If she could get a refund on the second, then she would have the money to leave Barbados if necessary. Perhaps to the American colonies, where she'd heard people were judged on their merit, not on their position or appearance.

Her heart lightened. The journey now held more than one ray of hope. If David Murray did not want her, she would be off on another adventure.

With the assistance of the dressmaker, she made arrangements for Mrs. Campbell to stay in a private residence where she would be cared for until she could return to Scotland. A letter was sent by coach to inform her father what had happened and her own plans to continue on. It would arrive well after her ship had left London.

That accomplished in her usual efficient manner, she stood for the final fitting. She didn't even mind the long sleeves as her mind bubbled over with new enthusiasm. No Maisie Campbell. And she would have extra funds from an unneeded cabin that had already been engaged and paid for.

It was a good omen. She knew it.

Chapter Three

The Caribbean, One Month Later

Alex took his first English prize with only a shot across the bow. The ship had no guns, and Alex's *Ami* had far more speed. It did not take long to convince the English captain to surrender.

He decided to send the rich prize of rum and sugar back to France. The prize should recompense Etienne for the bills they'd incurred in refitting the ship. It could also carry Meg and Robin back to France. Alex thought that would be the safest place for them. The English crew was put ashore a French island with little access to the shipping lanes. News of the ship's capture would take months to reach England, making its voyage to France safe. At least safer than his own ship that bristled with guns.

His next prize would be sold in Martinique, the largest French island in the Caribbean. Etienne had assured him there was an active market there for captured vessels. He knew he would get more in France if he could sail the ship there, but he could spare no more of the crew. Although the monies would be less, the sale should provide him with enough gold to turn toward South America . . . and search for the diamonds.

The smuggling of diamonds, he and Etienne had agreed in Paris, would be a safer endeavor now that an English and French peace treaty seemed more likely each day.

Alex sent a skeleton crew under the second mate—a highly qualified and loyal man, according to Claude—to sail the English ship back to France.

But when the last quarter boat was ready to leave, the children had disappeared again. A search of the ship found nothing.

He guessed they were somewhere in the hold, but bloody hell if he could find them. He rather suspected that one or more of the crew was helping the two. They had become favorites in the past month, both of them working as hard as any of the sailors and doing jobs that the seamen preferred not to do, such as scrubbing decks, working in the galley, and cleaning the heads. They'd charmed every member of the crew.

Alex's threats accomplished nothing.

Finally, he could tarry no longer. It was too dangerous for both the *Ami* and their prize. The ships could not be found together.

After their prize had sailed, Meg and Rob appeared silently, solemn expressions on their faces, both unrepentant and ready for the lecture they would receive.

Alex was at a loss again. How could he punish two scamps for using everything he'd taught them? He was in a conundrum of his own making. Next time, he secretly vowed, he would lock them in a cabin.

"You need us," Meg said, sticking her lower lip out.

"You do," Robin quietly insisted. "We peel potatoes better than anyone. Mickey says so."

The thought of the aristocratic young lad happily peeling potatoes under their Irish cook only briefly amused Alex. He did not like being manipulated, even by Meg and Robin. He did not like the prospect of even more danger.

They had been lucky thus far, and that, he feared, gave them a false sense of security. They'd encountered no

British warships, and their first capture had been blood-less. One shot and the ship had lowered its colors. He wondered whether Burke's pipes had anything to do with it. He'd stood on deck, blowing away as if he'd been on a battlefield. The sound carried across the sea and probably sounded frighteningly eerie to the British crew. Sailors the world over were a superstitious lot.

But not every ship's crew would be intimidated by his limited number of guns or Burke's pipes.

"You can stay," he said. "For now." In truth, he had no choice. He could hardly dump them in the sea. He *could* take them to Martinique, but what then? He could not leave them there alone, and now he needed every man jack he had.

The two children grinned and then slipped away before he could change his mind.

Aboard the Charlotte

Jenna took a deep breath of tangy night air on the quarter-deck as the ship bucked in the heavy seas.

Celia was in their cabin, praying for the voyage to end. She had weathered the first days nicely, but rougher seas had brought on illness five days ago. She now looked dreadful, her face pale and her eyes dull. The mistress had become maid.

That did not bother Jenna. It was good to do something, to be useful. To be needed.

It also felt wonderful to be out of the stifling air of the cabin. Although it was the largest of six passenger cabins, it was still small and cramped, and she had given up her privacy to share the cabin with Celia. She was grateful, though. The captain at first had been reluctant to take them as passengers without a chaperone, but then had relented when a gentleman agreed to book Maisie's unused cabin at a higher fare.

Captain Talbot had turned into a guardian of sorts, taking it upon himself to look out for her, and also for Celia when she'd been accosted by a member of the crew. He was greedy but he also seemed to be a gentleman. Meals were delivered to her cabin except for those rare occasions when she agreed to eat at his table with the other eight passengers. Celia, as a servant, was not invited. Despite years of being served, Jenna's view had changed; Celia had become her friend and ally, and she didn't want to leave her to eat alone in the cabin.

At least now she had enough money to pay for her and Celia's fare if they had to leave Barbados.

She wore the customary long-sleeved gown and gloves, but as the large ship reached warmer waters, she longed to go without them, to feel the wind touch her arms, her hands. But concealment had become a way of life to her and she knew she would have to become used to the warm temperatures and bright sun after the cold, biting winds and mist and rain of the Highlands.

Despite the heaving of the ship, she enjoyed the voyage. She had the instincts and feel of a natural sailor, the captain had remarked.

The observation had pleased her. If she were a man, she might well pick sailing as a way of life. She didn't even mind the storms. In truth, she had reveled in them, while poor Celia had lain gasping in her bed.

The captain joined her at the rail. "A brisk wind, and we'll be docking in Barbados in two days."

"I will miss the sea," she said.

"Ah, you will probably be seeing it every day," he said. "Barbados is not a large island. I don't know where your Mr. Murray lives, but you will not be far from the sea."

"Tell me about Barbados."

"It's a paradise, my lady. The water is a hundred shades of blue and green. You will like it there."

She had not told him she had never seen her prospective husband. It was humiliating that the only way she could get a husband was to accept one who had never seen her, who was apparently as desperate for a wife as her parents had been to lose a daughter.

Be honest. You wanted it, too.

She bit her lip as she stared at the sky. It looked like a bolt of midnight blue velvet spread across a surface and decorated with a giant ball of gold and sprinkled with diamonds. She felt small, very small. Very unimportant. And yet it awed her, too.

"How is your Celia?"

"She will be very happy to put her feet on the ground."

"You might warn her that the land will rock, too, for a while."

She turned and looked at him.

"Aye, my lady. It will probably rock harder than this old lady has."

She looked out at the darkness again, the sea illuminated by the moon. "Do you ever see any other ships out here?"

"No. Most of the pirates plying these seas have been caught."

She shivered in the warm air. "I've heard of them. Are there none left?"

"A few who call themselves privateers," he said with distaste. "But they are nothing more than pirates. British warships have cleared out most of them."

She wondered what kind of man would turn to piracy. They were all said to be murderers as well as thieves, barbarous men who enjoyed killing their victims. She shivered although the air was warm.

"But you carry guns," she said.

"Just four old ones," he said. "We just never took them off when the waters became safer."

The ship plunged into a wave and water sprayed over them.

"You'd best go inside, my lady. The wind is increasing

and we might well have a storm tonight. It will be best if you stay in your cabin."

She nodded. Celia might need her. She started to turn back toward the hatchway, then looked back. "Thank you for being so kind."

"It was easy, my lady. I was not happy to have unattached and unaccompanied ladies with me and I almost turned you away. But you have been no trouble."

"Thank you," she said wryly. "I'm glad I was no trouble."

She could feel his embarrassment. "I meant—"

"I know what you meant," she said gently. "And I am grateful for your protection."

"In truth," he said, "I will miss you. So will the crew."

The words pleased her. Although the other passengers ignored the crew, she had found them intriguing. She had soaked up their stories of ports and storms and adventures. One even claimed to have been captured by pirates. They had killed those who would not join them, he'd said. So he joined them, then escaped as soon as he could.

"I love the sea," she said. "There's a freedom here I did not find at home."

"You're a good sailor. Every other passenger has taken to their bed."

She'd known that. In fact, she had been on the receiving end of glares because she did not share the misery of the others. Her fellow passengers included one husband and wife headed back to their plantation in Antigua, another one of the ship's ports of call. Two were government officials being sent from England to Antigua. Another was a bookkeeper who had been hired by a shipping company on Barbados. He was the one who had purchased her cabin.

The men had all been attentive at first, even though they were quickly informed she was to meet her intended husband. As the seas became rougher, they had succumbed to mal de mer. During the last two days, she'd seen no one but the crew.

The captain turned and went back to the wheel. Jenna lingered for another few moments, reluctant to return to the stifling cabin.

Just a few more days. Her sense of freedom was gradually evolving into apprehension, even dread as she considered meeting her prospective husband, anticipated the disappointment, even distaste, when he saw her birthmark. She shivered in the warm tropical air, then headed toward the companionway.

"Sail ho."

Alex heard the call of the lookout and looked toward the east.

"Bonne chance," said Claude, who stood next to him at the wheel.

Alex put the spyglass to his eye and stared in the direction pointed out by the sailor in the crow's nest far above him. "Where away?" he shouted upward.

"Broad on the starboard bow," the lookout cried down.

Alex found the sail, and blessed the seaman's good eyes.

A merchantman flying the British flag.

He hesitated. He had been shorthanded since he'd sent a prize crew to return the one ship to France. They'd captured a second and sold it—with all its goods—in Martinique.

Alex believed the sale had produced enough gold to trade for diamonds. He had not lingered on the island. The governor of Martinique had been nervous. He too knew a peace treaty was near. He'd advised Alex and Claude to end their privateering.

Alex had intended to follow that advice until he saw the large merchant ship and its English flag.

"Should we take it, Captain?" Claude asked. "It would not hurt to have more coin."

It would not. Alex had no idea how much he would have to pay for the diamonds in Brazil, how many bribes would be required.

The merchant ship looked fat and benign. It looked like prey, and Alex was still hungry for prey.

Thus far, they had been lucky. Neither merchant ship had fought back. He'd had no injuries among his crew or the enemies' crews. But it wouldn't be long before the news spread from island to island, then to England, that a privateer was attacking English vessels in the Caribbean. He did not believe it wise to hover in the area.

He planned to change the name of the ship, forge a new logbook, and sail for Brazil.

"We can claim it," Claude said, the edges of his mouth turning upward.

Alex wasn't sure why Claude hated the English, but he knew his first mate's fury equaled his own, though neither had talked about their backgrounds, or what had turned them into hunters.

Robin appeared beside him, his eyes squinting, trying to see the distant ship.

"I want you and Meg to go down to my cabin," Alex said. His cabin was on the other side of the ship from the powder magazine.

"I can help take powder to the cannon," the boy said. He'd never looked less the lord he'd been born to be. He had discarded shoes long ago, and his trousers were torn. His shirt was stained with dirt and sweat.

But the boy's eyes gleamed. His skin had been darkened by the sun, and his hair was overlong. Meg had cut her hair with a knife until it was shorter than Robin's. She looked as much lad as lass.

After the first captured ship had sailed to France and the second was taken to Martinique, Alex had given up trying to return them. They'd made it clear they were not going to be returned, and they would steal, cheat, and starve to get their way.

"No," he said. "You will not go anywhere near those cannon." He paused. "Swear it." The one thing Robin did not do was lie. Not to him.

Robin was silent.

"Swear it," Alex said again, "or I'll keep you two locked in my cabin until I find you passage to France."

Meg crept up to them. She had obviously been listening. She nodded. After a moment, Robin did, too.

"Say it," he insisted.

"I swear," they said in unison.

"Now go to my cabin," he said.

Both gave a reluctant nod, but Robin kept turning his gaze toward the British ship.

Once they were gone, Alex ordered his crew to fly the British flag, then called for more sail. Although he'd picked up several crewmen in Martinique, he knew the ship was woefully undermanned, yet there was not one complaint as they went to battle stations.

The sun hovered on the horizon, spreading trails of gold along the sparkling emerald and cerulean blue of this most beautiful of all seas. His gaze swept the horizon, the interweaving of blues and greens, and the merchantman in the distance. Once more, he hesitated. Perhaps he was pressing his luck. Perhaps he should just turn away and head toward Brazil as he had planned.

He looked in the spyglass again. Four guns. Small ones.

Arrogance. The confidence of Britain. Bitterness boiled up inside him again. He touched the scar on his cheek and felt the pain that never went away in his leg. In his mind, he heard Cumberland's order over and over again: "No quarter." He heard the moans of the wounded and the prayers they uttered as the English and their Scottish allies went from man to man, finishing them.

He'd held his breath when they came to him. He thought he would die of holding it in. Then they'd left and gone to the next wounded man. He would never forget those moments. . . .

He wanted to puncture that arrogance.

"They have guns," he said.

Claude took the eyeglass from him and looked. "They are nothing."

"There's the children."

"The guns are nothing," Claude said again. "They probably will not even fire."

Claude's assurance wiped away his last reservation.

"Claude, set the royals. We're going to take it."

"Aye, aye, sir," his first mate said with a gleam in his eyes. He bellowed out orders, and the seamen started climbing the rigging, piling on more sail. Others went down to the gun deck to man and load the cannon.

Alex reached the quarterdeck and took the wheel, reveling in the way the ship responded to him, and the sails to the brisk wind. He had more sail, more maneuverability than the English ship.

This should be easy.

Jenna couldn't sleep. Celia remained sick, unable to keep food down. Despite the fact that the pitching had lessened, the maid did not seem to improve. Jenna feared the land would be the only cure. It would be Celia's salvation and her own confinement. Jenna wished she could stay aboard forever.

First light filtered through the porthole. She rose and dressed. There would be coffee available. She had become used to the bitter brew, and found she liked it better than tea. She was discovering a great deal about herself, exploring feelings—even sensations—she'd never dared to entertain before. The wind was like a caress, the sea sometimes like a cradle, sometimes heaving with rage. She liked both equally, calmed by one, exhilarated by the other.

Swaying with the rhythm of the ship, she made her way down the companionway to the galley for a cup of coffee. Then balancing carefully, she took it up to the main deck. She loved to watch the sun rise over the Caribbean waters.

Seamen were piling on sail and with each pull she could feel the ship give a little kick as if delighted at the chance of dancing across the ocean.

Dancing, of course, was an exaggeration. The ship was more a lumbering laggard, but still she liked the image.

"Sail ho," cried a sailor above her.

She strained to see, but though she had excellent eyesight, she saw nothing of a ship.

She felt something though. The seamen moved a little faster, and their faces tensed. She walked over to where the captain stood next to a helmsman.

His lips turned up in a smile as he saw her. "First one up again this morning, I see," he said. "How is Miss Celia?"

"She will never be a sailor," Jenna said.

"Not like you," he agreed. "If you were a man I would hire you straightaway."

"I could always cook," she said, only half in jest.

"Ah, but you would have the crew in a twist," he said. "It is no job for a lady."

Being a lady was a bore, she thought, but instead of arguing, she turned back to where the phantom sail had been sighted.

"Is there really a ship out there? I can't see it."

"Williams has the best eyes on the sea," Captain Talbot said.

"Another merchantman?"

"Most likely," he said, but she could see little lines of worry dart away from his eyes.

She sipped the coffee as they both strained to see the distant ship. The sun rose, detaching itself from the sea. Against its background, she saw a sail.

"It's coming toward us," cried the lookout.

The worry on the captain's face deepened. "Can you make out a flag?"

"Nay," came the answer.

The captain turned to the helmsman. "Helm a'weather," he said, ordering a turn. "Let's see if she follows us."

She stood, listening to the calls, the new urgency among the crew. Why? They had passed other ships along the way.

But she didn't want to interrupt the captain, who was conferring with his first mate and helmsman. Instead, she went over to the rail and stared out at the sea.

The sun had risen farther, and they seemed to be sailing away from it, fleeing from the streams of light it sent cascading into the sea. The sail had disappeared again.

She breathed easier.

But the deck was still busy, and she decided to fetch tea and crackers for Celia. The rhythm of the ship had increased, as had the voices. She had hoped Celia would get some sleep while she was gone, but now she doubted it.

The cook, an east Indian, gave her a grin full of teeth as she collected more coffee, bread, salted fish, and cheese for herself, and crackers for Celia, along with hot tea, then made her way to the cabin.

When she opened the door, she found Celia asleep. She set the tray down on a table bolted to the floor.

Quietly, she sipped her coffee, nibbled on the bread and cheese, and picked up a book of poetry she had brought with her.

She'd read for perhaps an hour when she heard a loud voice outside the cabin. Celia jerked awake, looking bewildered. "What . . . ?"

Jenna opened the door. A sailor was knocking on each of the doors.

"What is it?" she asked.

"A ship is closing on us," he said. "The captain fears it might be hostile."

"Hostile?" Celia's trembling voice came from behind her.

"Yes, ma'am. The captain wants the passengers to stay in their cabins."

Jenna glanced over her shoulder to see Celia sink back

on her bed. When she turned back, the sailor was down the companionway, knocking on another door. "Stay here," she told Celia. "I'm going to see—"

"But he told us to stay here."

"I will be right back," she said, slipping out the door before Celia said any more and before the sailor turned around. She sped through the ship, out to the quarterdeck, seeing no sailors along the way. *They must all be at their posts.* The captain had turned the ship; she knew that from the position of the sun.

She looked around and this time she did see sails of another ship. She saw its graceful outline, and it really did seem to dance across the water. It was nothing like the thick, heavily laden merchantman.

Why did the captain believe it hostile? Because it appeared to be following the *Charlotte*?

She wondered how something so beautiful could be deadly, then she remembered the tales of pirates. Breath caught in her throat even as she watched the ship approach ever so slowly, its guns highlighted by the sun.

She stood transfixed, shadowed by the longboat near where she stood.

"A French flag," shouted the lookout.

She heard curses, then a boom that echoed out over the water.

The *Charlotte* was being fired upon.

Chapter Four

The sluggish English vessel tried to make a run for it but it was like a tortoise trying to outrun a fox.

Alex waited until they were well within firing range and ordered a shot fired over its bow. His crew had improved considerably and the shot landed just beyond the ship. The *Charlotte,* he saw from the writing on the side.

A good English name. It whetted his appetite.

He ordered the French flag hoisted. That had been enough, with the sight of his guns, to cause the surrender of the other two ships.

Instead, the ship turned again. It was making for Antigua, hoping, he thought, to find help.

There would be none for the Englishman. The ship he'd sent to France wouldn't yet be close to that country, and news of the one he'd sold in Martinique would take weeks to travel to an English port, then on to London.

He'd become so deadened to violence, he felt little sympathy. Still, a small glimmer of admiration stirred in him. This captain, like him, obviously believed in hopeless causes.

He ordered the gun crew to send another ball across the ship's bow.

The aim was nearly perfect, splashing about twenty-five feet past the fleeing ship.

Still, the merchantman didn't stop.

Because of valuable cargo? He hoped so.

Through the telescope, he saw men manning the four guns on deck.

"That captain must be insane," he said to Claude, who stood nearby.

"Oui," he said. "What do you want to do?"

"He must have something valuable, to risk his neck," Alex said. "Aim for their masts."

They were closing rapidly.

One cannon roared, then another. The deck lurched as the cannon recoiled beneath them. One shot fell short. Another smashed into the mizzen topsail.

He expected the ship to surrender then. Instead, he saw men working the enemy ship's guns. A ball ended fifty feet short of the *Ami*. The next splintered the deck.

He spun around at the shouts of his crewmen. None looked seriously injured other than several minor wounds from wood splinters.

"I want that ship," he said, his anger vibrating in his voice. A rolling round of thunder responded. One ball tore into the *Charlotte*'s mainmast. Another hit the deck. Smoke enveloped the ship.

Yet it fired back, this time the ball falling five feet short of the *Ami*.

He ordered another round of cannon fire, this time over the bow. Despite his angry words, he did not want to destroy the ship. He wanted its cargo and wanted to get that cargo to a French port. A destroyed ship with no sailing power would not suit his purposes. The volley of all his guns should show they meant business.

In minutes, the English flag dipped. They were surrendering.

He assigned a prize crew, then decided that he himself would go over. The captain was a fool, but a brave one. He also wanted to see the cargo that had been protected at such risk.

As the boat was being lowered, Francois, one of his youngest sailors, ran over to him. "Captain, come quick."

He followed the sailor to find Meg lying on the deck, a large splinter from the deck rammed halfway through her shoulder. Robin was kneeling next to her, holding her hand.

Her lips were clenched in pain but she didn't make a sound.

Alex glared at Robin. "So this is how you keep your word," he said, to defuse his own fear for the lass.

Robin looked down at the deck.

" 'Twasn't his fault," Meg said. "He tried to keep me from coming up, but I darted out and he came after me."

"Find Hamish," Alex said. Hamish was the closest thing they had to a doctor when he wasn't serving as sailmaker. They had not been able to find a physician before sailing, but then Alex had never had much faith in them anyway. He'd always objected to the principle of bleeding someone who had already lost a lot of blood.

He tore away the cloth around the wound. Some of the material had been driven into the wound by a three-inch wide splinter that had gone nearly through Meg's arm. He swallowed hard. His own wounds had not been as hard to bear as this one. He felt every moment of the pain, knowing the burning, tearing agony Meg must be feeling. He only hoped the splinter had missed the muscles.

Meg looked at him with huge eyes the deep blue of a Scottish loch. She would be very pretty someday with her dark red hair and vivid eyes. But now her hair was hacked off, and she had the usual smudge across her face. Her front teeth were biting her lower lip as she tried to contain her pain.

She was a gallant little soul, although he would love to strangle her at the moment. He should have locked them in the first mate's room, or his own. Or he should have taken them back to France.

But now he suffered with her.

Hamish came through the hatchway door. "Wha's wi' the lass?" He knelt next to Meg. "Ah, lass, I have to be taking this out of you."

She nodded.

"Hold tight tae the lad," he said.

Alex inwardly flinched as Hamish took out a clean cloth from the bag he'd brought and told Robin to hold it with his spare hand. Then he pulled the large piece of wood from her arm; blood poured from the wound. Meg paled yet still didn't utter a word.

Hamish stanched the bleeding with the cloth, then studied the wound. "I must fish around for the cloth that was driven in," he said. "It could cause putrefaction."

Alex saw her small hand grip Robin's even tighter. He wanted to take the other one that was knotted in a tight fist, but there was no place for him. Pain ripped through his body as she gave a small, brave nod. " 'Twas my fault," she said. "Will told us . . ."

Alex wanted to say nay, but he couldn't afford the sentiment. They had to learn to obey. The consequences were too disastrous otherwise.

Burke crowded in. "How's the lass? I heard she was—" He looked down and the tough outlaw swallowed hard as he too watched every move Hamish made.

"Sir?" Claude was playing with his hat. "The boarding party is ready. Do you wish to go with us?"

"Aye," Alex said. He really did not want to go. He wanted to stay and comfort brave young Meg, but Robin seemed to be filling that function.

Keep your distance. He had tried to do that these last months. One day they would leave him. They would be on their own.

Robin looked up at him with wounded eyes. "I'm sorry," he said. "I should have been quicker."

Alex did not trust himself to speak.

Instead, he turned and made his way to the boat that was ready to be hauled away. He sat down at the stern and tried to concentrate on the matter before him. They were all armed, in the event that all the fight wasn't quite gone on the part of English captain. Still, he couldn't get Meg off his mind, or the way she'd tried so hard to be brave. She'd always been brave. She'd also always been reckless.

They reached the other ship and climbed up the ladder. They were met by a man in a blue uniform. His eyes were fierce with anger.

"How dare you fire on an English ship?"

"By the authority of the French government," Alex said. "I sail under a letter of marque."

"You are nothing but a bloody pirate," he said. "Our navy will hunt you down, and I'll watch you hang."

"Perhaps," Alex said. "In the meantime I would like your log and bill of lading." He paused. "Whom am I addressing?"

"Captain John Talbot. And who will I be watching hang?"

"Captain Malfour," Alex said. "But if you are this foolish again, I doubt you will ever watch anyone hang."

Talbot's lips pressed tightly together, and a muscle leapt in his throat. He was furious that someone would accost a British vessel. Typical English arrogance, Alex thought.

"Your cargo?"

"Wines, flour, lard, candles, tools, furniture."

"Nothing so grand as to risk destruction of the ship. And the lives of your crew," Alex said.

"You are Scottish." Talbot uttered the words as if they were an accusation.

"How astute of you."

"A damned Jacobite."

"Who is now your captor. You might remember that. Why did you fire those shells? Surely you knew you were outgunned."

Talbot's face grew red. "I didn't know your intentions. You might well have killed us in any event. A civilized crew does not fire on another."

"There we are again," Alex said lazily. "Talking about who is, and who is not, civilized."

"Damn you. What *do* you plan to do?"

"My prize crew will take over your ship and sell it in Martinique. You and your seamen will join us on my ship. I am afraid I will have to confine all but the officers until we arrive."

A pause. "I have passengers."

"They will not be physically harmed." He stressed the word "physically." He would not guarantee their property. Not until he knew who and what they were.

Talbot clamped his lips together as if he wanted to say more.

"Have all your crew and passengers come up on deck. I want your mate to show this man your weapons closet." He nodded toward Burke. "My first mate will want your log, lading, and ownership papers," Alex said. "As soon as we've secured the weapons and log, we will transport you to the *Ami*."

Another hesitation. Then, "I have several ladies aboard. I want to be assured that they will be treated with respect, that they will not be harmed."

Alex suddenly knew why the merchantman had hazarded firing shells. Perhaps they had thought him a true pirate and had not wanted to risk the ladies. Alex's respect for the English captain rose a notch.

"I do not hurt women," Alex said. "Unlike the English."

"I take offense at that."

"Then you were not in Scotland after Culloden."

The captain looked offended. "You lie, sir. The English honor women."

Alex balled his fists. "Unless they are Scots. Or Irish."

The captain flushed. "I want your oath that you will not harm the ladies," he persisted.

"And you are asking that of a liar? That is not the way to gain a favor."

"I will not move from this deck, from this spot, until I have your oath."

"You have it. We have no interest in pale English-women."

"Two of them are Scottish. One is a lady." The captain hesitated again.

"The name, Captain?"

The man's reluctance warned him. "I imagine her name is in your log," Alex prompted lazily.

"Lady Jeanette Campbell," the captain finally said.

"Campbell?" His fists had relaxed. Now they tightened again. If there was one family in Scotland that he held responsible for the destruction of many clans, it was the Campbells. His sister had married one who'd turned out to be a rotter of the worst sort.

He hated the Campbells with every fiber of his being.

The captain must have seen his reaction, or even felt the enmity radiating from him.

"Your oath," he demanded again.

"You get nothing, Captain Talbot," he said coldly. He turned away from his prisoner. "Burke, find the weapons storage and place three of our men there. Then flush the passengers from the cabins. Mr. Torbeau, you will search the captain's cabin for his log and for any instruments you think we can use."

"Aye, sir," Claude said.

Alex stood there, watching as his men rounded up the crew and isolated them on the bow. Then the passengers were brought on deck.

There were ten in all, including three women. He identified the Campbell immediately by her dress. Though simple, its quality was evident. So was the way she held herself, even as she had an arm around another slender woman.

One of the prisoners came up to him, blustering as the captain had about being an Englishman.

"I would not brag about tha' in this company," Alex said, deepening his Scottish burr. "There is no love for your kind on my ship."

His gaze did not move from the woman. *A Campbell.* She would bring a good ransom if he could bear the presence of her long enough to collect it.

She was not a particularly comely lady. Or perhaps that was his prejudice speaking. She was slight and her light brown hair was untidy. Her face was unusually darkened by the sun, which meant she seldom wore a hat, but oddly enough she wore gloves up to her elbows despite short sleeves of a simple gown that had no hoops.

Her eyes—a blue green, almost the color of the Caribbean sea—were her best feature. They were sparking with outrage.

Well, he had his own outrage.

"My lady," he said in a mocking tone. "I understand I have the . . . dubious honor of addressing a member of the Campbell clan."

She drew herself up to her full height, which was considerably less than his own. "I am Jeanette Campbell," she said, her gaze sweeping over him with contemptuous dismissal. It did not hesitate on his scar, though, as the gazes of so many did.

She had spirit, if little else.

"Campbells are a plague upon Scotland," he said, turning to the pale woman beside her. She was obviously suffering from mal de mer. She looked as though she could barely stand. "And this is . . . ?"

"Celia, my companion," the Campbell woman said. "If you harm her, I'll see you hang."

"My, but you are a bloodthirsty bunch," he said. "'Tis to be expected of a Campbell."

"And you are?" she asked with more courage than the others apparently had.

He bowed. "Will Malfour at your service." His mocking gesture belied his words. "Gather what possessions you wish to take. Only what you can carry. One of my men will go with you to collect them."

"What about the rest of my belongings?"

"I'll decide that later," he said.

"I'm not going anywhere without them," she said.

"Yes, you will. The question is whether you will go with something or with nothing," he said, making his voice harsh. "My men are more than capable of bringing you over."

She blanched. "Why can I not stay on *this* ship? What are you going to do with it?"

"It will be sold. With all contents." The warning was clear. "All prisoners will be on my ship where they can be watched. I want a minimum crew on the *Charlotte,*" he said, "though I don't believe it necessary to make any explanations. That, my lady, will be my last one."

Her face darkened with anger. She wanted to retort. Alex could see that. He watched the struggle in her face before she composed herself.

He looked toward two of his sailors. "Go with her."

She stared at him defiantly. "Where are you taking us?"

"Martinique."

"I am expected in Barbados."

"So, I imagine, is your good captain. Unfortunately both of you will be disappointed."

"But I must get there."

"And why is that, my lady?"

"I am to be married. My betrothed—"

"Your betrothed will have to wait," Alex said. At least *she* had the opportunity for marriage. The English had ensured that he would not.

He turned around as if she no longer existed for him. "Start transferring the prisoners," he said. "The crew first."

Out of the corner of his left eye, though, he saw her take her companion's hand in hers and disappear down the companionway, two of his men behind them. Ah, someone who followed directions. That was a promising turn after his young charges' disobedience.

An older man stepped up to him, his arm around his wife. He was pale but obviously determined. "I want assurance that none of the women will be . . . harmed."

The woman was quaking.

Alex did not change his expression. "Your name?"

"Geoffrey Carrefour," the man said. "My wife, Mrs. Carrefour. I have a plantation in Antigua."

He stared at them for a moment. He wondered whether they had any Scots as bond slaves. He'd heard that some had been shipped to English possessions.

"The women will not be harmed," he said. "You can find passage from Martinique to a neutral island, then passage to Antigua. I suggest you get your belongings quickly. One of my men will go with you. Any attempt to take a knife or firearm and you will take nothing."

He turned to the captain. "That applies to you and your men," he said. "Any attempt to smuggle a weapon onto the *Ami* will result in my putting all your men in irons for the remainder of the journey."

He turned to the next passenger, the youngest of the men. "And who are you?"

"David Edwards. I'm also bound for Barbados."

"With Jeanette Campbell?" He purposely omitted the courtesy title.

"No. I just received a position with a shipping company."

Alex turned to the last two men. They were obviously nervous. Neither of them said anything. "Have neither of you a tongue?"

The shorter of the two stepped forward. "Jonathon Pruitt. I . . . have been sent to Antigua."

"Sent?"

"I . . . work for the government."

"The British government?"

Pruitt trembled. He had obviously heard part of the other conversations.

Alex turned to the last passenger, a large man with a bulbous face and a skewed wig. It was obvious he had thrown it on in a moment of haste. "And you?"

"Thomas Turvey. I—I . . . also work for the government."

Alex glared at him. "Take what you can carry yourself. No more. Remember what I said about weapons. I won't guarantee your safety if you try to smuggle a weapon on my ship."

There were three more men, none of whom posed a threat. He turned away. Claude was approaching with the logbook and bill of lading. "A fine cargo," he said. "Poor wine compared to ours, but . . ."

"You've tried it then?"

"*Oui,*" Claude said with a quick smile. "To see what we had."

"Now that you've attended to that, let's start getting the crew over to our ship. I don't want to stay here like this any longer than necessary."

Claude nodded, and started barking orders. The first members of the *Charlotte*'s crew climbed down the ladder under the prompting of guns. When the boat was full, the sailors were pressed into rowing.

One by one the passengers appeared. Captain Talbot stood by, obviously determined to stay by the side of his passengers.

Alex's admiration for him increased, though he continued to frown. Martinique was a few days' sail from here. He did not want any trouble during the voyage. Fear was one way to insure there would be none.

The quarter boat disgorged its occupants, and returned. Again it was loaded. The process took one more trip to finish the transfer of crew.

The passengers were back on deck. Fear was still written on their faces, all but on that of Lady Jeanette. She was

all outraged dignity. She now wore a bonnet that did nothing at all for her. She still wore the gloves that were oddly
out of place. Her eyes sought to impale him.

A moment of admiration ran through him. *She's a
Campbell with all the Campbell arrogance.* And she was
looking at him as if he were the devil himself.

Well maybe he was.

And maybe that impression was the best possible thing
that could happen.

When the longboat returned, the male passengers hung
back. "Lady Jeanette," he said, wondering whether she
would be as brave climbing over the rail and scrambling
down a ladder in her skirts.

"Oh no, my lady," her maid said. "I canna do that. I will
fall to my death, I will."

"I will go first," she said. "You will see how easy it is."

To Alex's surprise, Claude appeared out of nowhere and
offered his hand.

She ignored it and climbed over the barrier, then very
carefully took one step after another. She almost slipped at
one point, and he found himself holding his breath. She
might be a Campbell, but he'd always liked spirit in a
woman. His sister . . . well, his sister had had more than
he'd ever expected.

Two sailors reached for her as she took a final step to the
bobbing boat. Alex caught a glimpse of petticoats and even
a leg. Her face turned rosy as she looked up and her gaze
found his as she regained her balance on the rocking boat.

She quickly looked away, her eyes obviously searching
for her companion. "You see, Celia, no one is going to let
you fall."

The woman named Celia gave a little cry.

"I'll take her, Captain." Alex glanced up at hearing
Burke's voice.

So apparently did Celia.

She quickly moved over the railing to avoid him and

started climbing down, terror in her face. She stilled, her hands seemingly frozen to the rope ladder.

A wave broke over the bow of the quarter boat, and the maid to the Campbell wench screamed. The boat bobbed and Alex knew that if she fell, she might land between the ship and the quarter boat and be crushed.

He didn't wait. Ignoring the pain and awkwardness of his leg, he climbed down the net to where she clung. "It's all right," he said in a voice he barely remembered. Soothing. Reassuring. "You've done very well. I'll be in back of you. You cannot fall."

She hung there for another moment, sighed as if she'd been holding all her breath inside. Then she let one hand go and grabbed another piece of rope. Alex moved behind her, ready to catch her if she fell. Then they waited until the longboat moved back into position.

"Let go," he said, moving to the side. "The seamen will catch you."

She turned, frightened cornflower blue eyes staring at him, stared at him for a moment, then she did as she was told and toppled backward into the hands of two sailors.

He climbed back up without looking behind him.

"Mrs. Carrefour," he said.

She too looked frightened. But she looked even more offended. "My husband can go down first. He can help me onto the . . . the boat."

"As you wish. You have two minutes to get in, or all your belongings will be heaved into the ocean."

Geoffrey Carrefour moved faster than Alex thought possible. He climbed down the ladder as well as any monkey. Alex decided to check the couple's belongings. He would not, as he promised, allow harm to come to them, but he was bloody hell ready to relieve a slave-owning plantation owner of some of his ill-gotten gains. In his eagerness, Correfour almost missed the boat as it bobbed and weaved again. One leg went into the ocean, the other into the boat, and the seamen clasped his waistcoat, hauling him inside.

He muttered audibly about Scottish bastards, then found a more secure perch in which he awaited his wife's descent.

After that, the other passengers descended one by one without comment. Their belongings were thrown into the boat. Finally there were only Captain Talbot, Claude, and the second mate, who would sail the *Charlotte* to Martinique.

"I leave it with you, Marcel," Alex said. "You have enough sail to make it to Martinique. You'd better keep flying the British flag. We will catch up to you."

"Aye, sir." The second mate's eyes glowed at the chance.

Alex turned to Talbot. "Your turn, Captain."

Talbot didn't say anything but climbed down. Alex and Claude followed him.

As the oarsmen rowed away, Alex sat in the back of the boat and examined his passengers. The Carrefours had their hands on a valise. The two government servants looked as if they were going to their deaths. Captain Talbot stared at his ship.

Alex's gaze lingered on Miss Campbell, who sat next to her companion, eyes fixed on the ship they were leaving. For the first time, he saw uncertainty in her face, even as she sat primly, her hands clasped in front of her.

Still, she reached over and patted her companion and whispered something to her. Something, he was sure, reassuring.

Bloody hell, he didn't want to admire her, but he did. Not a word of complaint, not like the others.

Just outrage.

She wasn't afraid of him. Nor had she looked away from his face.

Those two facts intrigued him. Far more than they should.

Chapter Five

Her skirts soaked and leaden and her hair coming loose from the knot she'd forced it into before donning a bonnet, Jenna climbed up onto the *Ami* without help.

The *Ami*. What a deceptive name for a ship with so many guns and fierce-looking seamen. One offered her a hand, but she refused it.

She'd tried to hide her fear in anger. She was certainly not going to let the pirate captain think she feared him, even when she did. She did take satisfaction in the fact she'd sewn her finest jewels in the hem of her dress just before the ship was boarded.

He looked like the devil with the scar across his face, and the smile that was no smile at all but a permanent twist of his lips, and dark blue eyes that seemed to burn all the way through a person. She struggled to hide the chill that danced down her spine despite the late afternoon sun.

Her captor's speech was that of a gentleman even as his actions were that of a bully and brigand and thief and only God knew what else.

His scar itself did not repel her. Surface appearances had nothing to do with character. But his ruthless and contemptuous manner along with his actions definitely marked him as a very dangerous man.

A dangerous man was often an unpredictable man.

She waited until poor Celia climbed the rope and held her hand out to her. Her maid's face was even paler than it had been this morning. The faces of the other passengers ascending were the same. Despite the pirate's words, none of them really believed he meant them no harm. He had fired on a peaceful merchant ship. They had been fortunate that no one had been wounded.

She watched as the others clambored aboard, the pirate captain being among the last of them.

She didn't see any of the seamen from the *Charlotte*. They must have all been taken below. Captain Talbot stood near her, as if offering what protection he could.

As the privateer captain gained the deck, his gaze bored into hers as if he were looking into her soul and finding every piece of it. She shivered in the warmth of the day, aware of how she must look with her wet clothes and flying hair and probably a hat as crooked as Mr. Turvey's wig.

It wasn't that she cared about impressing the villain, but neither did she want to be at a disadvantage. It was more than a little difficult to maintain dignity when one looked like a half-drowned chicken.

But she tried. She drew herself up to her full height, the top of her head barely coming to his chin. She held on to Celia's hand, ready to do battle for her if needed.

She glanced around the deck. It was badly splintered near the hatchway. Splotches of blood darkened the wood. Someone on the ship had been hurt in the exchange of fire. What would that mean for Captain Talbot?

The pirate captain was talking to a member of his crew. Suddenly, he turned back to the small huddle of passengers, his gaze colliding with hers as if her thoughts had summoned his attention. Just as abruptly, he turned away, seeming to dismiss her as unimportant.

"We do not have space for females," he said. "The three

ladies will share my mate's room. The other passengers can sleep in the same quarters as the crew. The *Charlotte*'s crewmen will be quartered in the brig."

"I object to those arrangements. I want my wife with me," the plantation owner complained.

"You object?" the captain said softly, even gently.

Despite the tone of his voice, Jenna wished the man had not challenged their captor. Even she knew it wasn't wise.

"Yes," said Geoffrey Carrefour, obviously emboldened by living through the first encounter and oblivious to a sudden tension among the nearby crew members.

The captain turned to a sailor beside him, a man that looked as much the brigand as his captain. "Burke, you can show Mr. Carrefour to the brig with the crewmen."

The planter's face paled. "Surely you would not—"

"Surely I would," the captain said. "Anyone else wish to complain about their accommodations?"

Any objections—or requests—Jenna might have had died at that moment. She certainly didn't look forward to sharing a cabin with Blanche Carrefour, who had avoided her since the beginning of the voyage, making it clear that she thought Scots, even Scots loyal to the English king, were beneath her. Now her life depended on the whims of a Scottish renegade.

"Our possessions?" the plantation owner continued, plowing, it seemed to Jenna, a path to his own destruction.

The pirate looked at him curiously, as if he were a particularly obnoxious insect. Jenna expected an outburst. Instead, he spoke rather mildly. "They will be delivered to you in due course."

"But—"

The rough-looking sailor named Burke put his hand on the planter. "Come with me."

The planter resisted until the seaman fingered his knife. Then his face fell and he nodded, casting a forlorn look at his wife.

Their belongings had piled up on the deck. Jenna

looked longingly at hers, but she was not going to challenge the captain now, not after what had happened to Mr. Carrefour.

No one said anything. Not even Captain Talbot, who looked as if he had lost a beloved friend as his gaze continually went back to his ship. The torn sails were being taken down and other sails hoisted on the existing masts.

Unfortunately, the pirate turned his attention back to her. His gaze pinned her like an insect to a board. "And you, Lady Jeanette, do you have a complaint?"

"I have many of them," she said, "but not about the accommodations. More about piracy."

A strange glint came into his eyes. But the perpetual smile caused by the scar made her unable to read his expression. That made him truly frightening.

Yet when he turned the scarred cheek away, he was uncommonly handsome. He also walked with a limp. She wondered whether it was a recent wound. But any sympathy she might have had had long seeped from her. He had probably been trying to kill whoever had injured him.

Instead, she tried to look directly into his eyes without flinching. They were dark blue, as cold and enigmatic as the North Atlantic they had left behind.

He turned to one of his men, an officer. "Take them to their quarters. Search the men for weapons. Check through their belongings to see whether there's anything valuable. I'm going to check on Meg."

"*Oui,*" the officer said. Unlike the man called Burke, he looked every inch a disciplined seaman. He was a large man, neatly dressed, despite his hefty build.

Still, she noted a silent exchange between the two, just as there had been between the captain and the sailors left on the *Ami*. It contrasted with the disciplined crew on the *Charlotte*. Although Captain Talbot was not a martinet, he had expected formality from his crew. Perhaps there was a different kind of bond between pirates.

She absorbed everything. She wanted to remember

everything. There would be a trial someday. In the meantime, she intended to keep herself and Celia alive—and untouched.

There had been no physical threat yet, but that didn't mean there would continue to be none. The fact that the women were being put together could bode well or ill. They would be alone without male protection.

At the last minute before they were captured, she had taken a knife from a plate of cheese in her cabin on the *Charlotte*. She'd managed to wrap it in a scarf and tuck it into her corset. She was eager now to get it out, before it worked its way out of the cloth.

So she allowed herself to be led along with the other two women. And she watched every turn as they traveled down the next deck and passed several doors. Memorizing the ship probably would not help, but then again it might.

She wondered who Meg was. It must be a woman and, if so, that fact was encouraging. Surely one woman would not look away if . . .

She decided not to think about the "ifs."

Their escort stopped at a door and opened it, indicating that they should enter. It was far smaller than the cabin she and Celia had had on the *Charlotte*. There was only one small bed. They would have to take turns sleeping or else sleep on the floor.

She turned to the officer who had brought them here. He looked straight back at her without apology. She wondered if he disliked the English as much as his captain did. "Who is Meg?" she asked, the name lingering in her mind.

"La jeune fille," their escort said in French. "Hurt by a splinter caused by the shell your captain fired."

He looked around the room, at the neat chest and clothes hung on pegs on the door. "This is my cabin." Obviously disgruntled at being dispossessed, he went through it, taking a pistol from a drawer, a knife from another, and then his clothes. He turned at the door. "You will stay here unless told otherwise. I'll send more blankets." Then he left, closing the door loudly behind him.

Blanche Carrefour sat on the only bed.

"Celia has been ill," Jenna said to Blanche.

"So have I. And she's a maid."

"She has been far more ill than you," Jenna said.

Blanche glared at her.

"*I* outrank you," Jenna said. "Celia gets the bed until she is better."

" 'Tis all right," Celia said. "I cannot take your bed, my lady."

"Indeed you can," Jenna replied. "I dinna expect more than anyone else has." She hesitated. "We must get along together. And protect one another." She unbuttoned the dress she was wearing and reached inside, pulling out the wrapped knife.

A tear slid down Blanche's face. "What will they do to Geoffrey? What will they do to *me*?"

Jenna sat next to Blanche and put an arm around her. "He will be fine. Just as we will be."

"But you took a knife. *He* said he would . . . punish us if they found a weapon."

"No one must know," Jenna said past the rock that had just lodged in her throat. She wondered whether she had made a mistake. She remembered exactly what the pirate captain had said. Anyone found with a weapon would be locked away and their belongings forfeit. Her entire trousseau was in the trunk on deck, and even some minor jewels she'd not had time to sew into her hem.

She thought again about what the seaman had said about Meg. A child. Why was a child sailing on a privateer? Exactly how old was she? And how badly had she been wounded? Had she been taken from another merchantman?

She had always loved children. It was the main reason she had agreed to marry someone she'd never met. Just the possibility of having children of her own had been irresistible.

The captain had said the child's name with a softness that had not been apparent in any of his other words. Could it be his child?

She doubted that.

Blanche lapsed into sobbing.

It was going to be a very long voyage.

Meg tried to hide her pain that must have been severe even with the laudanum. The wound was covered with some kind of solution Hamish had produced from a box of medicines and herbs. Alex had watched him the first several occasions when a seaman had incurred wounds. He hadn't lost any of them. For someone without formal training, he was very good. He had gentle and steady hands, perhaps from sewing sails for so many years.

Alex had been lucky in finding him, just as he had been lucky with Claude.

"I'm sorry," Meg said again.

"I know." Alex sat down in a chair next to the cot.

"I really will not do it again."

There could not be a next time. He would search the entire island of Martinique to find someone responsible to take Robin and Meg back to France.

He reached out and put a hand on Meg's shoulder. "I promised myself I would keep you safe. I dinna keep that promise." He heard the burr in his voice deepen. It always did when he felt something deeply. And, God help him, he felt this. He wished he had taken the splinter.

She was so young and had already suffered so much. Two brothers killed by the English. Then her father. Her mother dying of a wasting disease in a cave in the Highlands. No bed. No doctor other than Alex.

Meg tried to smile at him, but it was more a grimace.

"Here," Hamish said, thrusting a cup at Alex. "Gi' her

this. It's water with just a bit of laudanum. She should not have too much, but she needs sleep."

Alex hesitated, then gently lifted her head and held the cup to her lips. She drank it in huge gulps and he realized she was in more pain than he'd thought.

"It wasna Robin's fault," Meg said with a note of urgency.

"I know," Alex said soothingly. No one could stop Meg when she was determined. Some fierce avenger he was when he couldn't control two children.

He waited until she drifted off, then went back up on deck to make sure all their prisoners were secured. He didn't think they would present any problems, but it was the largest group of prisoners he'd taken. They now numbered as many as his own crew.

He found Robin sitting on a coil of rope, staring out at sea. He looked up at Alex, tears in his eyes.

"I'm sorry," he said.

"She'll be all right. Hamish's a fine doctor." Alex hoped that he was right. Putrefaction was always a threat, particularly in a wound such as Meg had suffered. He could not even consider the possibility of young Meg not surviving. She had such a great will to live. "Go sit with her," he said.

Robin looked at him for a long moment, then nodded and rose, disappearing belowdecks.

Alex tried to concentrate on the problems ahead. He looked around the deck. The prisoners were all secured. His crew was piling on sail. He saw a sail not far away and knew the *Charlotte* was under way. If only they could make it to Martinique without meeting a warship, there would be a chance of making a great deal of money. He planned to avoid the main shipping lanes, but then he would risk grounding the ship on reefs.

Claude was at the wheel with the helmsman, studying maps they had taken from their last prize.

"How is Mademoiselle Meg?"

"Hurting."

Claude frowned. "She is going to be formidable when she becomes a woman."

"She already is," Alex said dryly.

"She needs a strong woman's hand."

"Aye. But there is none."

"There are the ladies from the ship."

"I do not want her learning English manners. And she would have none of it."

"The Scottish lady?"

"She is a Campbell." Alex said it with finality.

Claude shrugged. "You are captain." But he looked as if he disagreed.

A Campbell would be worse than no woman's influence at all, Alex reassured himself. "Robin will be with her," he said finally. "Send for me when Meg's awake."

Claude nodded, his eyes seeing more, Alex suspected, than he wanted the mate to see. "It was not your fault," Claude said after a moment's silence.

"It was," Alex said. "It *is*. It is my fault she is on this ship. I allowed her to become too . . . dependent on me. I will not make that mistake again."

"More than dependent, Captain. She cares for you." Claude shrugged. "Not even you can control feelings."

Alex could damn well try, though. He was trying hard at the moment. He hurt every time he thought of Meg, the way her face had looked so pale and she had bitten her lips to keep from crying out. Damn the *Charlotte*. Damn himself. He should never have risked it. He wanted to change the subject. "Did you find any instruments on the *Charlotte*?"

"*Oui*. An excellent chronometer and a telescope that is finer than ours."

"They didn't see *us*."

"That was not the telescope's fault," Claude explained logically. "I placed it in your cabin. I also sent down the belongings of our guests." He grinned wickedly at that.

"Their crew presented no problems?"

"*Non,* except for their captain who protested every inch of the way."

"Try to keep in proximity with the *Charlotte,*" he said. "I'll be down in my cabin." He hesitated, then added, "And call me—"

"I know. When Meg is awake," Claude finished.

Alex went through the hatchway, taking companionway steps two at a time, then quickly walked past Claude's cabin, where the women passengers were being quartered. His first mate would claim the second mate's quarters.

He reached his cabin. It had a larger bed than the other cabins in the ship. He was infinitely grateful for that. The cabin also included a table and chairs, a desk, bookcases, and a chest. As elsewhere in the ship, the furniture was either bolted down or made to swing with the rhythm of the ship.

He usually kept it scrupulously neat, not wanting objects scattering during bad weather, but now it was piled high with belongings. This was his job. He might seize goods for the ship, but he wanted no individual pilfering.

He started with the belongings of the plantation couple. They had annoyed him even more than the timid government officials. His greatest irritation, though, was the foolishly brave Campbell.

A Campbell in his hands, but the fact she *was* a woman kept him from doing anything about it. If the captive had been a male, Alex would have been tempted to kill him, or certainly hold him hostage.

Instead he had a Campbell female who apparently had to sail thousands of miles for a husband, a lady who was going to be trouble. He felt it in his bones.

He shoved away the odd notion, then dug into the first of Blanche Carrefour's trunks. She obviously believed in traveling like royalty. A compartment in her trunk revealed a drawer full of jewelry.

It was, he told himself, no different from robbing the

coaches he'd once stopped in the Highlands. Life or death was at stake then. He'd had to provide for the children.

What was his excuse now? A future for the children? Revenge against a country that had destroyed his? More wealth for France, which had done little for the Scots except urge them into doing their battle for them, then had deserted them when they needed assistance most?

He wondered why he hesitated. The look in the Campbell woman's eyes. The contempt. What did that mean to him? He didn't like the Carrefours. He didn't like their arrogance. He did not like slaveholders, and in the Caribbean, all the planters owned slaves.

There was nothing else of interest in their trunks, nor in the rather sparse belongings of the English officials.

He passed over the belongings of the captain of the *Charlotte*. There was a measure of respect involved there. The man had tried to protect those in his care.

He turned to the Campbell woman's trunk. Her name was written on it in tidy handwriting. Only one trunk compared to Mrs. Carrefour's three. Not in the mood to ask for a key, he broke open the lock. Dresses that looked new lay neatly in the trunk along with new petticoats and other finery. Then he found what he was seeking. A pouch of jewels. Campbell jewels.

He fingered them. He knew jewels. He'd known them when he'd been the heir to the title of marquis and his mother wore centuries-old gems. He knew good ones and bad ones.

These were not very good. He had expected better.

Yet the clothes were fine. And new. A trousseau. Light colors. Sky blue and a light pale green. Strangely enough, he tried to think of her in the green dress. He recalled those startling eyes. He'd never seen any quite that color, nor as full of emotion. Anger. Fear. Defiance. All three at once.

He looked further and found five pairs of gloves, all elbow length. Several matched the gowns. Others were white or black.

He wondered why. He had thought it strange earlier that all the others were bare-handed, even the redoubtable Mrs. Carrefour, yet the Campbell woman had kept her gloves on, even after they had been soaked in seawater.

Bloody hell, it was none of his concern. He balanced the jewels in his hands, then put them back.

He wasn't quite sure why.

Daylight faded from the cabin. Jenna paced restlessly. She hated the feeling of being confined.

She'd tried the door several times, but it had been locked.

Celia, oddly enough, had drifted off to sleep. Blanche Carrefour had finally agreed to give up the bed during the day if she could have it that night. Jenna had readily agreed. She didn't think she could sleep anyway.

She'd seen the enmity in the captain's eyes, and she had been the object of his contempt.

No doubt he was one of the Scots who had followed the Young Pretender. Though she had deplored the bitter reprisals against the Scots, she couldn't understand why they had backed the pretender against their king. Trying to take the crown had been an incredibly foolish act, made in the face of overwhelming odds.

The captain had no right to do what he'd done. She knew the English were close to signing a treaty with the French. Her father had discussed it with their English visitors.

She also recalled that the Campbell clan was not the most liked in Scotland, particularly by traitors to the throne.

What would he do in addition to starving them all?

Her stomach was complaining. She was also thirsty. If it wasn't for Celia, she would pound on the door.

Blanche was quietly weeping, convinced she was going to be robbed of all her possessions and most likely taken for sport. No amount of words convinced her otherwise.

And so Jenna had taken off her bonnet, then looked down at her wet gloves. She had no others with her. She debated taking them off. She glanced at Blanche. What difference did it make on a pirate ship? Perhaps it would even keep her person safe from violation. She pulled them off, waiting for a comment from the planter's wife, but none was forthcoming, just the slightest widening of her eyes.

It felt good, having her hands free of cloth. She ran a brush through her hair, trying to decide whether to braid it. She decided to leave it free, then found a place on the floor and tried to read a book until the light became too poor.

She felt the ship shift and gain speed. Away from Barbados and her prospective husband. Even if she did arrive, she would have little more than the jewels she had secreted in her gown. She had no doubt the pirates would take every other valuable she had.

She wished she knew something of the man who held their lives—and futures—in his hands.

Perhaps she could discover something from the crew.

For that, she had to get out.

She did not know what time it was when the door opened and a sailor brought in a tray of food. Bread and cheese and beans. There was also a pitcher of water and three mugs.

Blanche stood and looked at the offerings. "Take it away," she said royally.

"No," Jenna said. She smiled at the young sailor. "Thank you."

His gaze softened. "The cook has been pressed into other duties." It was partly an apology to her, not to Blanche Carrefour.

She decided to grab an opportunity. "Who is Meg?" she asked. "I heard someone said she had been hurt."

He shrugged. "She's a wee lass."

He had a Irish lilt to his voice. The ship seemed populated by Irish, Scottish rebels, and Frenchmen, none of whom seemed inclined toward sympathy for the English or their allies. "Is she the captain's daughter?" she asked.

"Nay. A stowaway. She and young Robin."

A stowaway.

"May I help?" she said, her heart constricting at the thought of an injured child. Particularly a stowaway who had no parent to comfort her.

"I will be asking the captain for you," he said. His gaze went to her arm, but then left it without any reaction at all.

Then he disappeared. She heard the door being locked.

She sat down, wondering about what he had said. A lass who was a stowaway. Along, apparently, with another child.

At least they were being attended.

Perhaps the captain had a soft spot.

She re-created his face in her mind, the cold eyes, the contemptuous looks he'd given each of the passengers.

The scar that made him look frightening . . . dangerous.

And unpredictable.

She tried to read again, but the light was poor and too many thoughts were rushing through her head. She was going to her marriage with a birthmark that had isolated her in England. Did David Murray truly know about it? That was bad enough, but now . . . she would be marked in another way that could bring disgrace to a potential husband. She was aboard a pirate vessel without a chaperone. If Maisie had been here . . .

Maisie probably would have died of fright.

But what would the Honorable David Murray think? It might just be the excuse he would need to reject her if her birthmark . . . offended him.

If she ever reached Barbados.

Chapter Six

Alex prowled the ship throughout the night, alternating between relieving Claude on the quarterdeck and checking on Meg below.

She was feverish and in much pain but never shed a tear. Robin would not leave her side.

Her continued bravery distressed him more than tears would have. She was but a lass. She should react as one.

As the night wore on, the sky filled with clouds and the wind grew fierce. He and Claude had to pace the *Ami* with their new prize, and they seemed to plow through the heavy seas. That meant more men had to be on deck working the sails and fewer watching their prisoners.

"We are in for a squall," Claude said, eyeing the dark scudding clouds.

Alex nodded.

Claude hesitated. "Sean said the Scottish mademoiselle offered to help Meg. It would relieve Hamish."

Alex's first impulse was to say no. But Hamish was one of the most experienced sailors among them.

And he wanted someone with Meg, someone other than Robin, who hadn't had any rest in far too long. Perhaps

Claude was right. Perhaps Meg did need a woman's help. But a Campbell's help?

"I'll think about it," he conceded.

He went down to the area Hamish had turned into a sick bay. Hamish was looking at the still-seeping wound. Meg's eyes were wide open but they were red and dull.

Robin stood nearby.

"She keeps knocking the poultice off," Hamish said.

The ship plunged then, sending Robin stumbling backward.

"The Campbell woman offered to help nurse her," Alex said, his voice neither approving nor disapproving.

"I should go up on deck," Hamish said.

"I do not want her here alone with the lass."

"Ye think she might hurt Miss Meg?"

He remembered the woman's eyes. There had been fear, but more defiance. And yet he did not think there had been cruelty in them. "Robin can stay in here with her," he said. "I'll send Sean as soon as he can be spared." Sean had never been to sea, but had been desperate for a berth. He was still unsteady on a storm-tossed deck, and Alex feared for him every time he went up into the rigging. Yet he couldn't seem to favor him or others in the crew would resent it.

Hamish lifted an eyebrow but his expression approved. "I'll return as soon as I can."

Alex reluctantly walked to the cabin where the women were being kept. He did not like the idea of asking a favor of a Campbell.

He knocked and then waited a moment before unlocking the door. The last thing he wanted were hysterical undressed women prisoners on his ship.

As he turned the lock and opened the door, he came face-to-face with the Campbell woman. He was surprised—not pleasantly—by the jolt of awareness that suddenly ran through his body.

When he'd seen her before, she'd been swallowed in

clothes and her hair had been secured under a modest bonnet. Now it flowed down her back and framed eyes that looked at him with both surprise and wariness. Her hair was brown with golden streaks lighted by the glow of a lantern.

For once she wore no gloves. His gaze caught the hands that had opened the door, the dark purple splotch that ran from the back of her hand up her arm. He understood now why she had been wearing gloves halfway up her arms while the other women wore none in the heat of the Caribbean sun.

He looked up and met her challenging gaze.

Not that he was one to cast stones at physical imperfections. God knew no one would swoon at his face.

But neither did he feel like offering niceties or apologies. "One of my men said you offered to help with a young lass who was injured."

"Aye," she said. "I have nursed many times."

"She needs a woman's care," he said, "but she is not fond of the English."

"I am not English."

He raised an eyebrow. "But the Campbells do the English bidding, which is worse."

She didn't turn away, but neither did she reply or attempt to hide the blemish on her arm.

"Come with me," he said shortly. He did not want to feel anything for her. Certainly not sympathy. Or admiration.

"I have to tell my companion." She ducked back inside for a moment, then returned. "I'm ready."

She had not put on the gloves again. She obviously didn't care what pirates thought. That was fine with him.

"You trust me?" she asked, obviously unable to hold her tongue.

"Only because whatever happens to her happens to you." His voice was purposefully cold, yet she didn't flinch. Her composure disconcerted him.

He led the way to the sick bay, where Hamish was leaning over Meg.

An involuntary cry ripped from her mouth, then her lips clamped together when she saw him.

Pain speared through him at her attempt to be strong and courageous. She was already the bravest young lass he'd ever met. She'd never complained during those long, cold, and often hungry months spent hiding in Highland caves. Nor had she cried when her mother died. She'd continued to be the core of their little band, taking over the position of mother to the younger ones. Without her and Robin, he never would have been able to keep the others alive.

"Ah, lass, you would try the patience of a saint," he said, not wanting her to see the agony he felt.

Meg grimaced, though he knew it was meant to be a smile. Bravado. She was full of it.

"This is Lady Jeanette," he said, purposely neglecting to provide his prisoner's last name. Meg knew the Campbell name well, as did every Jacobite in Scotland. "She has offered to stay with you."

Meg's lip stuck out. "I dinna need anyone," she said.

"Hamish is needed elsewhere, and I want someone to say with you. Robin needs some rest."

Her lip did not recede. "Who is *she?*"

"She was on the ship we took."

"It shot at me," she said sullenly.

"We shot at *it*," he explained.

"The other ships dinna shoot at us." She glared at her feminine visitor.

The logic was undeniable, if not entirely fair.

"I have to go above," he said with a warning note in his voice. Sometimes she heeded it; sometimes she didn't. Most recently, it had been the latter.

He turned and left before she could mount any more arguments.

For the first time he felt sorry for a Campbell.

• • •

Jenna regarded the young patient thoughtfully. She had not missed the fact that he had not mentioned her last name.

The lass looked to be about eight or nine years, and was one of the thinnest children she'd ever seen. Her hair had been cut short and ragged tufts stuck out all over her head. She looked more lad than lass, and the rebellious look on her face did nothing to change that impression.

The lass's gaze focused on Jenna's arm. "What's that?" she asked with a child's honest curiosity.

"It's a birthmark," Jenna said.

"Does it hurt?"

Aye, but not in the way she meant. "Nay. But your wound looks like it hurts."

"Nay," said the child, echoing her own response.

"Your name is Meg?"

The girl looked at her suspiciously as she nodded.

"How old are you?"

"Eleven."

She was three years older than she'd thought. Anger and sympathy coursed through her. The child had obviously been starved. God only knew what she'd gone through.

She took a stool next to the cot. A poultice covered the wound. She wondered what was in it.

"Can I do anything for you?" she asked. "Would you like some water?"

Meg looked at her suspiciously. "Robin will get it."

"Who is Robin?"

A voice came from the doorway, and it conveyed even more suspicion than Meg's eyes. "I'm Robin."

She whirled around. A boy of around twelve stood in the doorway, contempt on his face. "I heard you are a Campbell," he said. There was as much loathing in his voice as there had been in the captain's.

Captain Malfour had obviously passed along his hatred.

"Campbell?" Meg said.

"Aye," Robin said.

Meg turned her head. "Go away."

"The captain asked me to stay," Jenna said, disconcerted. She had no experience being rejected because of something other than her deformity. Certainly not because of her name, a name respected—and feared—in Scotland.

"He wouldn't," the boy said. "We don't need a Campbell."

"I cannot help my name," she said softly, "but I do want to help your . . . sister?"

"She is not my sister."

"Your friend, then."

The lad's speech was better than Meg's, his manner no less imperious, yet unlike hers it had an innate arrogance that she suspected came from the gentry. So, for that matter, did the captain of this ship. She would wager her last crown that both once held or were heirs to titles.

Her heart went out to the children, even if she had only contempt for a man who would put children in danger.

She had always been good with children. But she didn't quite know what to do with the hostility of these children who obviously detested her for something not of her own doing.

She wanted to help. She wanted to help more than she could possibly ever let them know. She wanted to make them safe.

"We hate Campbells" the girl said.

"Sometimes I do not care for them, either," Jenna said quite honestly.

Meg's dismissive look suddenly sharpened. "You don't?" she asked dubiously.

"Not always," she replied. "I do not like some of the things they do, nor some of their friends. That's why I was on the ship."

Meg searched her face, as if seeking the truth, then turned away. "Go away."

Robin scuffed his shoes on the floor. "I suppose if Will said it was all right . . ."

"Will?" she asked, grateful for the lad's slight softening.

"The captain," Robin explained.

"Is he . . . any relation to you?" The Irish sailor had already said he was not Meg's father but surely there was some connection.

"Bloody hell, no," Meg said.

Jenna tried to hide her reaction to the child's profanity. "Then what . . . ?"

"He takes care of us," Meg said proudly.

"The English killed her mother and da," Robin said. "They killed mine, too."

"Will saved us from the butcher," Meg said, obviously not wishing to let Robin have the last word. "He killed lots of English. And Campbells," she added ominously. "He *likes* killing them."

She'd obviously decided not to give Jenna the same benefit that her friend did. Still, Jenna's heart melted. They were too young to be orphaned. Too young to stow aboard a pirate ship. Too young to depend on a pirate for survival.

"He saved our lives," Robin confirmed. "He found us in the Highlands when the English were hunting us."

"Hunting you?" she asked dubiously. "They were looking for outlaws."

Meg glared at her. "My ma was no' an outlaw. Robin was no' an outlaw, either, but he was a Macdonald. The Campbells wanted to finish killing Macdonalds."

Jenna stared at Robin.

" 'Tis true," he said. "They were hunting all of us. They locked women and bairns in a barn, and burned it. I just barely escaped, but I . . . heard . . ."

Her heart twisted. She had heard soldiers talk but they had always quieted when she approached. She knew there were patrols rounding up Jacobites who had escaped from Culloden. They wanted no more uprisings. And she'd heard of the many executions and transportations. But children? Women?

She knew her father was ruthless, but no civilized person could do such things.

She swallowed hard, not sure how to defend herself. Her family. Everything she was. Of course, she'd heard some of the stories. Campbells were accused of nearly every misdeed or trouble that occurred in the Highlands. They were also accepted and envied and respected by families loyal to the king.

Out of fear? Fear of the clan's influence with Cumberland? With the English king?

But killing women and children?

These two children believed it. She saw it in their eyes. Was that why the captain's eyes were also so cutting?

Captain Malfour?

Will?

Neither name, for some reason, seemed to fit him. Despite the fact he was a pirate, he carried himself like a lord.

Had he been at Culloden? Had he fought against her family's retainers? And how had he become "protector" to children? Or had he simply used them? An excuse for his banditry.

He was an enigma. One she cared little about solving. But in a few short moments, the children had become important to her. She wanted their trust, to feel as if she had some worth and was not just a cast-off piece of inferior clothing. Cast off by the very Campbells they hated. She'd tried not to feel that way since she'd received the offer that her family had so badly wanted her to accept.

She looked back down at the child who had—at the least—lost her home, her family, her safety, and who, despite all that, was like a wolf cub, ready to defend herself against any interloper, even someone who wanted to help.

Robin had manners that made him unlikely to spit, but there was an iron in him that would make him very unlikely to accept her. He did not even try to hide the suspicion in his eyes.

Will. Never had there been a more unlikely Will.

"Tell me about your . . . captain," she said.

Meg turned back to her. Her eyes, which had been dull with pain, then sparking with outrage, now filled with light.

Still, it was Robin who answered. "He found a way to bring us to France," he said. "He could have left us. But he risked his life over and over again to get us to France. He found us families in Paris, but—"

"We dinna like them," Meg said. "We wanted Will."

Their devotion to "Will" was, she realized, absolute. She would not help herself by saying anything against him.

"How did you come to be with him?"

Robin looked at her as if she were trying to trap him.

"We heard there were . . . fugitives in a certain area," he said. "I found my way to them first, then Meg and her mother. But her mother died not long after arriving."

"How many were there?"

"Some," he said evenly.

"How did he get you out of Scotland?"

"He robbed the likes of you," Meg spat.

Jenna saw the warning glance Robin gave Meg. "I will not say anything," she tried to reassure him.

"You are a Campbell," Meg reminded her again.

"Aye, but I am also a Scot."

Meg made a face then, and Jenna knew it was not entirely because of her comment. It was more pain than anger or resentment.

Jenna rose and went to a table bolted to the floor and found a clean cloth. Then she filled a cup from the tap of a water barrel. She poured part of the cup's contents on a cloth and went over to the child, offering the half-filled cup of water.

To her surprise, Meg drank greedily. Jenna wiped her

face with the cloth, noticing that the child's eyes were brighter than they should be.

The boy noticed it, too.

Jenna turned to him. "Will you ask if she should have more laudanum?"

Robin nodded and disappeared out the door.

Meg's eyes met hers. They were clouded with pain that she'd obviously tried to hide earlier. So much bravery in a child.

And hostility. So Jenna sat silently, fearing that any more words might upset Meg and worsen the fever. She needed rest. She needed a sense of safety.

She needed prayers, even if she did not want the prayers of a Campbell.

Jenna turned away, looking around the small sick bay. It looked very inadequate. In addition to the small bed Meg occupied, there were some hammocks, a cabinet, a bag of instruments that was wide open, and a few jars held firmly in a cabinet bolted to the wall. They were unlabeled but she could guess at the contents: cannabis, dragon's blood, rosemary, ash bark, ginger, sulphur, flaxseed, and oil.

She wondered which was the laudanum. Or opium. Both were good for pain. The poultice needed to be replaced. She wondered what had been applied. Some physicians used lint dipped in oil. Others used a bread and milk mixture.

She'd tended many small animals that she had found hurt or sick, and for a while had tended people as well. An old midwife said she had a talent for it, but her father had been horrified. News that she was a healer, combined with her birthmark, would be added proof she was a witch.

She had been strictly forbidden to even mention herbs. Still, she knew the danger of inflammation and had even seen a man die of it. She did not want that to happen to young Meg.

In minutes, the lad named Robin had returned, an older man in tow.

"She's very warm and in a lot of pain," Jenna said.

"I'm Hamish," the man said with a gentle smile. "I come as close to being a doctor as anyone onboard. I really repair sails more than people."

"Then perhaps I can help," she said with eagerness she could not contain. She wanted so much to be useful. "Can I fix a new poultice for her wound?"

He nodded. "I use lint and oil. The oil is in a green bottle in the cabinet." He turned back to measuring out several spoonfuls of a substance into a cup of something that smelled suspiciously like brandy.

She wanted to say something, but hesitated. She did not want to be sent back to the cabin.

Instead, she prepared the poultice and went over to Meg. The lass lay still, her body rigid like the tight strings of a harp, but she said nothing as Jenna lifted the soiled cloth covering the wound. Jenna barely kept from flinching when she saw the raw wound that had obviously been dilated to take out any material, then neatly sewn shut. Still, it looked angry and the skin around it was red. Jenna threw away the old bandage and gently placed the new poultice on the wound. She prayed once again, this time that it would draw the poison.

Meg never made a sound, but she gulped the mixture that the older man gave her.

"She will sleep soon," Hamish said.

Jenna looked at him curiously. "Have you been sailing long?"

"All my life," he said. "Was a cabin boy when only a lad. Learned everything I could about sails. Apprenticed with a real sailmaker, but missed the sea. Someone who knows sails and can mend them well is respected."

"Then why did you join—"

"A privateer?"

"Aye."

"The English impressed me when my merchant ship stopped in London. Four years on a British warship. It was hell. We were never allowed off for fear we might run off. Men were lashed for no reason. Maybe after a twenty-four-hour duty, they dinna move fast enough. I still have stripes on my back." His voice had lowered, reverberating with intensity. "I believe it right that they pay me back for those years."

"Does everyone on board feel that way?"

"There are a few who want the adventure, or money, but most feel they're owed something."

"Captain Malfour?"

"He'll have to tell ye his own tale."

"Will he try to ransom us?" It had been a fear of hers. If he did, her reputation would be ruined. The Honorable David Murray would withdraw his offer if it became common knowledge that she had been held by pirates. She doubted the ransom would be paid. It was truly heartbreaking to realize no one cared about her enough to secure her freedom.

She didn't want this child to ever feel that way.

Hamish apparently saw her small shiver. "You need not fear the captain. He is a hard man, but a fair one. He does not make war on women and children. No' like some." There was a familiar accusation in his voice. She wondered that so many of these strangers apparently believed her people could do the monstrous things that were attributed to them.

Her look must have been doubtful. The captain had seemed curt and indifferent to the children. She thought he had summoned her only to free one of his men for duty. "He's very hard with the children."

"Oh, we all know he dotes on them. He thinks they obey better if they fear him. Trouble is they do not. They know he would give his life for them. And almost has. More than once, according to the young lad."

"I thought they helped him steal."

Hamish grinned. "You mean you think he was training them to be thieves? Nay. He's been trying to make Meg into a lady, but to no avail. And the lad, polite as he is, hates the British as much as the captain."

"Is Malfour his real name?"

"Now that, my lady, is another question you will have to ask him. No one inquires too much into pasts on this ship."

"How many ships have you taken?"

"Yours is the third."

"Have there been women taken before?"

"Nay."

"Then you do not know what he will do?"

"You learn quickly about a man at sea," he said. "We've been wi' him three months, and there's no' one of us who wouldna die for him."

She felt a chill run down her spine. She had thought perhaps to gain allies among the crew.

It had looked like a pirate crew. The men were ill dressed, not neatly uniformed as they had been on the merchant ship. They sported fierce mustaches, and had hard eyes and faces that glared and accused. They all wore pistols at their sides, and some had cutlasses, and spoke several different tongues. She had recognized Gaelic, of course, and French. There had also been some other odd languages. Yet the crew worked together well. Even she had noticed that.

A pirate captain—she could think of him in no other way—who ruled obviously by consent of others who looked as villainous as he. Who, according to this man, doted on children while kidnapping innocent civilians.

She wondered where he'd received the scar that so changed a face that once must have been extraordinarily handsome. Strangely enough, it did not repel her. It had been the coldness in his eyes that had done that.

"I must go," Hamish said. "Rob will stay here and fetch me if you need anything." He hesitated, then added, "Do not fret about your safety, my lady. The captain will not allow any harm to come to you."

"It already has," she said bitterly. "My betrothed is waiting for me in Barbados. He may not want a bride who had been abducted by pirates."

"Then he is no' much of a mon," Hamish said.

With that, he left her alone with young Meg, who was finally resting, and Robin, who had taken up a watchful position in a chair. He'd been silent through her conversation with Hamish, but she knew he had not missed any of it.

Meg moved restlessly.

Jenna started humming a soft song, half lullaby, half love song.

Meg's eyes started to close. The tight grimace of her lips relaxed.

Jenna continued to sing softly. Her voice was one of the few attributes her father ever complimented, but she seldom sang for anyone except herself. Shyness over her plainness and the mark that covered her arm usually kept her hidden or in the shadows when guests attended the manor.

There had been a glade, however, where she would take a book and sometimes sing just for the joy of it.

Now just the sound of words she loved soothed her.

She finished the song.

Meg was asleep. She looked at the lad in the corner. He too had dozed off.

She leaned back in the chair and watched them, and her heart ached for both. Orphans who had only a pirate to look after them, a man whose chosen life would probably result in a hangman's noose. England, she knew, often did not recognize privateers, particularly now that the formal hostilities between France and England were drawing to a close.

Then what would Meg and young Robin do? Or would they too be caught in a British net? They were not too young to be sent to a prison where they might die or be transported to some country as virtual slaves.

How could she let that happen?

She started plotting.

Chapter Seven

Alex hesitated outside the sick bay. He heard the song from within and cocked his head to listen.

The Campbell lass had a lovely voice, clear and strong and sweet, and the familiar Scottish lullaby reminded him of a home that no longer existed. A sharp pang of loneliness struck him.

How could they have this gentle song in common? Her family and his? The Campbells had torn his country apart.

He did not like to admit that the Jacobites might have had something to do with that tearing apart. Poor leadership. Bad tactics. Too much confidence in French promises. Desertion by clans thought to be loyal. An arrogant prince who spoke only French.

And the greatest gallantry he'd ever seen.

All over in a few hours at Culloden Moor.

He shook his head. She was a Campbell, and Campbells had been responsible for so many of his country's sorrows. They were duplicitous, untrustworthy, traitorous.

Bloody hell.

He opened the door. The Campbell woman was sitting

beside the child. Meg's eyes were closed, her hands no longer clenched in tight balls as she tried not to cry or show how much she hurt.

The singing stopped, but he saw the woman look at Meg with such tenderness, it hurt.

She was so concentrated on Meg, she seemed unaware of his presence. Her dress was limp and soiled. She apparently had taken some time to twist her hair into a severe knot at the back of her head, and now strands fell untidily around her face. There was nothing elegant or pretty about her, and yet something . . . touched him. Perhaps the raw longing in her face.

She's a Campbell, he reminded himself. And a plain sparrow. Why then did something inside him respond to her?

She's going to her wedding.

Her voice was strong and true. No fear in it. Or was she hiding it? Did she still fear him, afraid that he might take her virtue?

As if he would touch a Campbell.

A Campbell who sang like an angel.

"Miss Campbell." Again, he deliberately ignored the courtesy title.

She jumped nearly a furlong despite his soft tone and whirled around to face him. Robin, he noted, was asleep in a chair across the room.

"How is she?" he asked.

"Hurting. She tries so hard not to show it."

"She has had a lot of practice."

"How long has she been with you?"

"More than a year."

"What are you going to do with her?"

"Find her a home. I thought—" Why in the bloody hell was he talking to the woman?

She cocked her head, just like that sparrow he'd envisioned. Her eyes were just as bright, although they weren't dark. Bloody hell, but that blue green color was intriguing.

"You thought?" she prompted.

"There was a family in France willing to take them both." For the life of him, he did not know why he was explaining anything to her. "But they showed up in the hold four days after we sailed."

Her gaze seemed to bore through him. "You wanted to get rid of them?"

"They are better off with a family," he said, amazed at the fact she turned that against him. Apparently he was damned if he found them a home, and damned if he didn't because that meant he was abandoning them. Why, for God's sake, did he care what she thought?

Yet her contemptuous look stung him. So did her gesture of turning her back to him as she sat down and gave all her attention to Meg. He was being dismissed by his own prisoner.

He found himself standing awkwardly without anything to say. He certainly was not going to defend himself to a Campbell. "We will take care of her now," he said. "You can return to your cabin."

"I would rather stay here," she said.

"There is no place to rest."

"I could not rest in a nest of vipers in any instance," she said bitterly.

"You should know about vipers," he retorted. "You've lived among them for many years."

He saw from her eyes he'd struck a nerve.

"I do not abandon children," she said.

"They were made orphans by Cumberland."

"And you turned them into outlaws?"

"Better than dying."

"Aye," she said softly, surprising him. She lightly touched Meg's face. "She is still warm. I do not want to leave her."

There was a plea in her voice, the first he had heard from her. Until now she'd been all indignation and defiance.

"You will not use the children to get what you want," he warned her, unwilling to surrender all his suspicion toward a Campbell.

"And what do I want, Captain?"

"To get to Barbados, I suppose. Or are you not eager for a wedding?"

"Of course I am," she said, but Alex saw a moment's doubt in her eyes. He wondered what the prospective husband saw in her. There were the eyes, of course. And the voice.

She was also outspoken and a nag. And she obviously did not know the place of a prisoner.

He told himself her marriage was no concern of his. "You may stay," he said, asserting his authority, though he had no idea how he could have dragged her away without waking young Meg.

Her gaze settled on him. Her eyes were clear and yet unreadable. Bloody hell, but they were striking. He had never seen eyes quite that color before.

"You can stay," he repeated, "but you will not leave this room without someone with you."

"My thanks, my lord."

His eyes narrowed.

The latter had been said with sarcasm. Did she have any idea as to his true identity? He could not allow that to happen. His sister and her husband might well suffer. Neil Forbes was believed a loyal king's man. If it were known that he had helped his brother-in-law escape Scotland, his life would be forfeit.

His hesitation sparked something in her eyes. So it had been only a guess on her part. He could not make another mistake.

She slept on and off in the chair.

She couldn't get the captain's face out of her mind. She had thrown the "my lord" at him with impudence, nothing more. But the expression that flashed in his eyes confirmed she had struck a blow of some kind.

She had wondered at his speech, even the odd grace despite his limp. Now she was sure. He had once held a title. But which one?

It was obvious he was trying to keep it a secret. If she tried to discover his identity, would he feel it necessary to get rid of her? Still, she wanted to know. Had to know.

She thought about the man waiting for her. He had three children who needed a mother. She wondered whether he had blue eyes. Kind eyes or cold, hostile ones. Would he look at her blemish with distaste, or with indifference, as had the captain of the *Ami*?

Jenna looked at the lad, who had been so protective of Meg. They must know more than they had said. She would try the children first.

Then the crew.

And finally the captain. She decided that even as her stomach knotted with apprehension.

Alex tried to get some sleep. It had been more than twenty-four hours, and he needed to keep alert.

The bloody lullaby continued to run through his head.

So did blue green eyes.

The Campbell lass had courage. He would grant her that. She'd challenged him despite the uncertainty that crossed her face. Yet except for that one slip, she was quite adept at concealing her emotions. That was unusual for a woman. They usually wore their emotions on their sleeves.

She'd obviously had experience at not doing so.

He stood and roamed the cabin, ignoring the aching pain in his leg. It always grew worse when he had been on it all day. He sometimes used it beyond what he knew it could do, just to know it was there. He had come so bloody close to losing it.

He looked at the night sky beyond the wide window

that graced the captain's cabin. Clouds concealed the moon and stars. He was grateful for that. Still, he would not relax until they made Martinique.

Another day and they would reach the island and he could sell the *Charlotte* and rid himself of the troublesome prisoners. Then he could sail toward Brazil.

Forget the prisoners. Get some rest.

How long had it been since he had slept a night through, when he hadn't had images pounding in his head and echoing in his heart of being cold and hungry, and worried sick about the orphans who had made the mistake of trusting him?

And now there was a new image haunting him: a woman with a sad, clear voice.

A Campbell.

She was nothing to him but a nuisance, and someone who could temporarily care for Meg. It was only fitting that she cared for one of England's victims.

He clumped back to the wide bed, which was the one captain's prerogative that he liked. His body was too tall for most of the bunks and even the hammocks used by the crew. He closed his eyes, though he suspected he wouldn't sleep.

Jenna woke to the soft cry of a child.

Young Meg was feverish and thrashing. Robin apparently woke when she did, for he moved swiftly to the side of the cot.

"Meg?" he asked.

Jenna wished she had some snow, some ice cold water even. Something was needed to take down the fever. Instead, she poured warm water into a cup and offered it to Meg. Feverish eyes looked at her, the misery in them deep.

Rob looked up at her frantically.

"You had best fetch Hamish," Jenna said. She wet a cloth and bathed Meg's face. The child's eyes met hers and seemed to plead. The dislike was gone. So was the defiance. There was only fear. It went straight to Jenna's heart.

When Rob left, she poured some water on the cloth and lifted Meg's shift and washed her body. It was far too thin. She knew by now the child had been a fugitive in the Highlands, but surely in the succeeding weeks she should have gained more weight.

One more mark against the ship's captain. She was having increasing trouble trying to figure out the tangled relationship between the children, the captain, and the other members of the crew. Whenever she thought the captain might have at least a small part of a heart, a new piece of information would completely destroy that vein of hope.

She moved the poultice. The wound looked even angrier than before. At least it was draining a little. She thought that a good sign.

She covered Meg and went to the cabinet, searching for the bottle of laudanum. She also needed some hot water for a new poultice, but she wanted to wait until someone was in the cabin. She did not want to leave Meg alone.

After adding a little laudanum to a cup of water, she helped Meg balance it.

"I'm cold," Meg complained.

"I know," Jenna said softly. She started crooning. She didn't know what else to do. It was another lullaby about bringing home a pony. She saw an answering light in Meg's eyes.

"Da used to sing me that," she said.

"What about your mother?"

"She said she was not much for frivolous things."

"Music is not frivolous," Jenna said.

Meg's lips compressed, and Jenna realized she'd made a mistake. In Meg's eyes, she had criticized a dead woman. A dead woman she knew nothing about. More than that, a woman whose death had been at least partly attributed to her.

"Tell me about her," she said after a moment of resentful silence.

"She worked hard," Meg said. "My da was a blacksmith who left with our laird to support the bonnie prince. Ma followed, taking me with her. She cooked and did laundry for the men.

"Da was killed, and then the English started looking for anyone who was with . . . the prince. We hid in the hills, but they just kept searching. We hid in one cave, then another. It was cold . . . so wet. She got sick."

Meg closed her eyes. Was the laudanum working or did she just not want to answer more questions? Jenna scolded herself for asking them.

Jenna leaned back. She was tired. She had needs she'd tried to repress, but were now becoming desperate. For the first time, she needed a brief respite to her cabin. But she would not leave Meg.

The door opened and the large Hamish entered. He had a pail of steaming water with him. "The lass?"

"I do not like the way the wound looks," Jenna said. "Was it part of a cannonball?"

"No, a splinter. It drove pieces of cloth into the wound. I tried to get it all out but . . ." He stopped and looked at her. "Ye need some rest, my lady."

"The captain told me to stay here," she said.

"I dinna need two patients," Hamish said roughly, but his eyes were kind.

"Where's Robin?" she asked.

"He went to fetch the captain. He would want to know about Meg."

"He would?" The doubt in her voice was obvious.

Hamish ignored the question and bent over Meg, removing the poultice from the wound.

"I would have fixed a new one but there was no hot water."

"There is now," he said.

Jenna stood. "I'll do it," she said.

He nodded. "But as soon as the captain comes, I want ye to leave and get some rest."

She was not going to argue, even though she was torn between staying with the lass who was far more child and vulnerable than she wanted anyone to know, and seeking the rest she desperately needed. She went over to the steaming water and mixed a potion, drenching a clean cloth with it.

She carried it over to Meg. "I hate to wake her. This is going to hurt."

"I'll do it," Hamish said. He leaned over. "Lass?"

After a moment, Meg opened her eyes.

"I have to replace the poultice, Meg," Hamish said.

For the briefest moment, apprehension filled Meg's eyes. She obviously hadn't been that invulnerable to pain after all. She had just kept it under tight control, too tight for a child. But now she was too tired, too weak, probably too afraid to fight it any longer. She looked at Jenna with eyes that seemed to reflect all the horrors in the world. "Will . . . you sing the song again?"

For a moment, Jenna could not do it. Her lips trembled too much, her throat was too choked.

Hamish looked at her with steady brown eyes and gave her a brief nod.

Jenna started the song again, hearing the tremor in her own voice. She wanted to reach out and take Meg's hand in her own, but she did not think it would be welcome. The song would have to do for the moment. Meg fixed her gaze on her as Hamish put the steaming hot poultice on the wound, and she heard the child's indrawn breath. She continued the song, realizing it had a haunting sadness it never had before.

Meg's world had changed nearly two years ago. So had her own. They were both venturing into new places with only their pride and determination as weapons. But Meg was still a child. Jenna had choices.

She continued as Meg's eyes closed again.

Jenna's voice trailed off as she became aware of another presence. She had not heard anything. She'd been concentrating too strongly on her words. But suddenly she knew the captain had entered the room, though he said nothing.

She turned around.

He was close. Too close. It made him appear even taller and more imposing. His dark blue eyes were as curtained as before, and his jaw was set and a muscle flexed in his cheek.

"You sing well, my lady," he said, surprising her both with the softness of the words and the compliment.

"It seems to comfort her," she explained uncomfortably.

"So I see." He studied her, and she saw every one of her imperfections in his eyes. Her arms were bare and the livid wine-colored birthmark that covered most of her right arm was open to his slow appraisal. He had seen it before, but she still felt marked.

"You look like the devil, though," he said. "You may return to your cabin. One of my men will bring you some food."

"Not much rest there," she said wryly.

"You can use mine," he said, seeming to comprehend the situation without needing an explanation. Blanche Carrefour was not a restful person.

She must have looked startled—and horrified—for he gave her a grin that was anything but warm. She had noticed how the scar turned up one side of his mouth in a perpetual half smile, but when the other side of his lips turned upward, the expression was derisive.

His eyes challenged her, too, as if he could see straight through to her soul and found the distaste in it for him. "Do not worry, lass. You are not to my taste, even if I would sink to bedding a Campbell. I have never been that desperate, nor will I be. You can use my quarters during the day and stay with Meg at night. I want someone rested to be with her. And do not suppose I am being sentimental. I simply do not want a Campbell expiring on me. It would be inconvenient . . . *at this moment.*" He stressed the last three words.

He was trying to frighten her.

He did not have to work hard at that. He did frighten her, even though she tried hard not to show it. She was only too familiar with the hard ways of men, their disregard of the feelings of others, particularly women.

She wasn't sure she could believe him now, and the thought of sharing his cabin was terrifying in the extreme.

"I would rather use my own."

"I care naught what you would rather, Miss Campbell. Rob, take her to my quarters. See that she has some food."

She turned to look at Robin standing by the door, his eyes wider than usual, his boyish face creased with puzzlement. "Aye, sir," he said, then blurted out, "Is Meg going to be all right?"

The question was to her, and the captain frowned. "We will not let anything happen to your Meg," he said quietly. And unexpectedly.

Robin's face cleared, as if words from the brigand had been those of the Almighty.

"This way, my lady," he said.

She hesitated, still uncertain about the prospect of the captain's cabin. But the boy was already halfway down the hall. In any case, she *was* totally at the mercy of Malfour in any location of the ship. From what she'd seen and heard, she doubted whether any man aboard would challenge him.

She leaned down and touched Meg gently, then followed young Robin out of the room.

The lullaby haunted Alex. So did the echo of the woman's voice even after she left the room.

Damn her.

He did not want to be reminded of gentler years. Of

family and home. Of a mother and father long gone. Of his own promising life.

He had once been an honorable man.

Now honor had no place in his life. 'Twas best to remember that.

He needed funds. He needed a great deal. He needed it for the children, to settle them safely. Then he needed enough to create a new life for himself, one in which he could bedevil the British. That had been the only thing that had kept him alive through those agonizing months of recovery.

If he had to ransom the woman to get where he wanted to be, then he would do that.

He just didn't want to see those accusing eyes, or hear a voice that brought back too many memories and made him realize she was a person like any other. He had to regard her only as a Campbell. A thing to be despised.

Not a person with sorrows of her own.

But she had them. He'd heard them in her voice as she sang so longingly of children and ponies and gifts and safety and peace.

Why couldn't she be haughty and arrogant and demanding and uncaring of Jacobite children?

Unwanted guilt niggled at him. She looked tired. Her eyes were red rimmed, and she must be hungry. Yet she hadn't complained. That made him bloody angry.

He hoped she would stay in his cabin. He could sleep anywhere. In one of the hammocks if necessary. God knew he'd had far less comfortable resting places. And the bed he'd once enjoyed now seemed more a bed of thorns. He just damn well couldn't sleep in it.

He went up on deck. Dawn was breaking. It was always his favorite time of day. The slow rising of the sun made all things seem possible. But it was a lie.

Family, children, honor, home, peace. No longer possible . . . for him.

Did the Campbell woman believe those things were no longer possible for her, either?

Hell, why did the *Charlotte* have to carry passengers?

Alex knew now he'd been lucky in the first captures. No women. Just sailors. Some of them not entirely displeased to leave an unhappy ship.

Why had he not followed his first instinct and left it alone? Meg would not be wounded and suffering. They would be on their way to Brazil, avoiding British shipping lanes. Now they might well encounter a British warship. He knew his guns would be no match for theirs. His guns were designed to intimidate unarmed merchantmen, not ships of the line.

Claude was at the wheel. "*Bonjour,* Captain. Our luck holds. No sign of sail."

"Did you get some sleep?"

"Aye. Enough. You do not look as if you had any."

Alex shrugged. "I like the dawn."

"How is *la petite?*"

"Not well."

"I am sorry to hear that. She is very brave."

"Senseless is more like it," Alex said.

"You do not fool me, Captain," Claude said with a twinkle in his eyes. "You care more than you want anyone to know."

Alex sighed. "She trusts me. That is a dangerous thing to do."

"*Non,* I do not think so."

"Then you are as senseless as she. I should have never taken that ship."

"It had a rich cargo."

"And more trouble than we need."

"Not a man aboard would agree with that."

"Go get some rest, Claude. I'll spell you and use your quarters tonight."

"You are the captain."

"I gave my quarters to the woman caring for Meg."

Claude raised an eyebrow, but shrugged. "You're the captain," he repeated. But something like amusement played in his eyes.

Alex gave him his most formidable frown.

Unfortunately, it did not seem to faze his second in command at all. He heard a chuckle as Claude ducked through the hatchway.

Chapter Eight

Jenna awakened as the afternoon sun touched her, and she rolled over in the comfortable bed before realization struck.

She was sleeping in a pirate's bed.

His presence was everywhere in the cabin. It was in his scent—sea and soap and something tangy—and in his clothes—the white linen shirts with full sleeves and breeches that she knew molded his legs well—hanging on pegs or neatly folded.

There were maps and books. The latter surprised her.

He was a freebooter. She had not expected a literary side of him, and yet he had books in both English and French. Had they belonged to an earlier owner or captain? Were they merely stolen like so many other things?

A restless energy filled in the cabin. She felt it. Despite the neatness of his belongings, something vital and indomitable still lingered in the space.

What had brought that word to her mind?

Malfour. Will. Neither name fit him. They were tame. English.

He was a wild Scot, through and through.

She looked out the wide window. When she had gone to sleep, the sky had been black with clouds. Now the sun rippled the waves.

How close were they to Barbados, where her betrothed was waiting?

How far from Martinique, where the pirate said he would release them?

But then she thought of young Meg. Could she leave the child while she was still so ill?

Unable to find an answer, she looked down at her person. She'd slept in all her clothes, finding comfort in the added protection they provided. Now she felt foolish. It was obvious Will Malfour, or whatever his name was, had no interest in her.

She turned toward a pitcher filled with water and quickly used it to wash herself. Then she saw her trunk in a corner. Sometime while she was asleep, it had been brought into the cabin. She shivered for a moment, then decided anger would do no good. She'd obviously been untouched. Instead, she leaned down and opened the trunk.

Someone had gone through it but, to her surprise, what jewelry she'd left there was untouched. Her dresses, packed so carefully, were not as carefully replaced. She chose a light green muslin, not because it favored her but because it was cooler than any of her other garments. She put on a fresh shift, ignoring her corset, the one garment she had discarded last night.

The shift settled easily over her shoulders and fell in light folds to the floor. The bodice tied in front, so she needed no help.

She brushed her hair, then twisted it into the tight knot she usually wore. She knew it was unbecoming, but it never had seemed to matter before. No one ever looked at *her*. They just looked at the wine-colored birthmark that some said made her the devil's own.

Strange, but she'd never felt like the devil's own.

She closed her eyes for a moment, letting the years of

rejection wash over her. She'd never wanted sympathy. She hated self-pity. The only thing she'd ever wanted was someone to care about her, and people for her to care about. Children.

Meg.

She looked at herself in the mirror. Her hair was heavy, and she hated the tight knot. In a moment of defiance, she allowed it to fall down her back, then plaited it in a long braid. She tied the end in a knot. It certainly wasn't fashionable, but it was comfortable.

She hesitated at the door. Should she leave the worn dress with jewelry sewn inside? But now it should be safe enough, and Meg needed her. The beat of her heart quickened as she thought of the small lass and the way she relaxed at the sound of her voice.

Summoning her courage, she opened the door. Seeing no one, she stepped outside and walked to the sick bay.

Robin sat next to Meg. Hamish was in a chair, studying a book in front of him. He looked up and smiled. "My lady. I'm glad ye are here. I am not good at reading." Then his eyes clouded. "Can you read?"

"Aye," she said, eyeing the book.

"Nothing is working," he said. "The infection is getting worse."

She picked up the book.

"We took it from the *Charlotte*." He had the grace to look embarrassed.

She looked down at the cover. It carried the name of the ship she'd been sailing. It was a medical manual describing ailments and cures.

She leafed through the book. Under "inflammation," it said to bleed the patient. That sounded rather senseless to her since Meg was pale and already weakened by loss of blood. She read on. Cool a fever. She knew that.

She wanted to throw the book against the wall.

She gave Hamish her bravest smile. Or was it merely bravado? "I do not think bleeding will do any good."

"Nor me, my lady."

"We should keep her as cool as possible and drain the wound." She hesitated, then added, "And pray."

"Does God answer the prayers of a Campbell?" The deep, now familiar rumble of the privateer captain came from the door.

She turned around. "Do you have a better idea, my lord?"

"*My lord?*" he asked, raising an eyebrow.

"Do you deny you have a title?"

"I do not have to deny anything to you," he said curtly. He walked over to Meg and knelt beside the bed, his fingers touching her cheek. Meg's eyes opened. "Will," she said.

The easy use of his name startled Jenna. She'd always heard the children refer to him as "the captain" before. He did not seem to notice, though. "Aye, it's me, lass."

"Don't leave us."

Something like anguish, naked and raw, passed over the man's face. Jenna looked away. It had not been for anyone to see. *So he does care.*

Malfour brushed back Meg's short, ragged hair, his hand lingering on her forehead. "Ah, Meg," he said. "I have need of your sharp eyes."

Meg smiled wanly. "I have the best sight of all," she said.

"Aye, you do," he assured her. "I've never seen better, especially to spy a red coat." He moved his hand. "But next time you will do as I say."

"Aye, sir," she said.

"I doubt it," he said, but there was a gentle wink connected to it, and for the first time Jenna saw what others must see in the captain: a subdued charm, a self-deprecation that emerged from under the dark, sardonic, and often harsh exterior.

He looked up at her, and the moment of whimsy fled from his face.

Meg's gaze also turned to her. There was not the hostility that had been there before. Jenna did not like the listlessness in her eyes, though.

Her gaze met Hamish's and she saw her concern reflected there.

Still, she thought a lie would do. "You look better."

Meg looked dubious.

Jenna searched her mind frantically for something she could do to help. "Perhaps a bit of soup . . . ?"

"I am not hungry," Meg said.

"Soup would be just the thing," Hamish said. "But I dinna think the cook is much good at it."

"I am," Jenna said, grateful to be of help and sure that a small lie in a good cause would be forgiven by God. She had watched Cook make soup back in Scotland, but she had never actually turned her hand to it.

The captain shrugged. "Rob will go with you."

So she still wasn't trusted, not even enough to go to the galley alone.

Rob was already at the door. "Meg and I have been helping the cook," he said. It was more than he'd said at any other time. Apparently some of his hostility was fading, too.

She so much wanted someone to value her for what she was rather than for who she was. Or how she looked.

Robin led the way into space hotter than the rest of the ship. A large pot sat on a stove, and the smells coming from it did not tempt the appetite. She'd noticed that what food she'd received consisted mostly of tasteless beans, boiled potatoes, and hard biscuits.

The man bustling around the area was small with lively eyes and a mouth that lacked some teeth. She wondered whether it was the result of his biscuits.

"Meg needs soup," Robin said.

"Whatever the lass needs," the cook said, then turned to Jenna. "Hamish said you ha' been helpin' with Meg." It was obvious he approved.

She shrugged away her approval. "I thought some hot broth might help."

He looked dubious. "We have no fresh meat."

"Potatoes?"

"Aye."

"Any herbs?"

He looked at her as if she'd grown two heads.

"Some salt pork?"

"Aye."

With his help she added some water to chunks of salt pork, along with potatoes and a poor onion she found. She longed for spices to make it more palatable but at least it would be nourishing. As it slowly boiled, she wanted to ask Rob more about him and Meg. Why had they not stayed in Paris and instead chased after a pirate?

What was it about the man that commanded that kind of loyalty and affection? And trust? Or was it just an adventure that ended badly?

While she stirred her poor concoction, Robin perched on a stool and began peeling and cutting potatoes. Still, his eyes always seemed to be on her. Watching. Judging. Weighing.

She wanted to know more about him, but she feared asking. It seemed everyone on the ship had some terrible story to tell, and blamed it all on her family.

Did her family deserve that blame?

Even in the hot galley, a shiver ran down her back. How could she answer charges she knew little about?

Why should she feel the necessity to do so?

She had been an innocent sailing on an English ship. Captain Malfour was in the wrong, not her. He was the one who had taken two children on a dangerous voyage. He was the one who had shot first.

Yet she felt terribly guilty.

It amazed her how important Meg had become to her. Despite her outward rebellion there was a vulnerability in her eyes that went straight to Jenna's heart. She knew that vulnerability, knew about steeling herself so no one could see her fears or reach inside her heart and hurt her.

"She will be all right, won't she?" Robin's question was like a thrust into her stomach.

"I think so," she said, wishing there was more confidence in her voice.

"She pretends that nothing bothers her, but she's always afraid. That's why she . . . does some of the things she does." Then his lips snapped shut.

"Trying to fool God," Jenna said. She had done the same thing too many times, tried to pretend an indifference when her heart was breaking.

Robin ducked his head, obviously feeling as if he'd betrayed a confidence.

"It is nothing to be ashamed of," she said. "You want to help her, and she has nothing to be ashamed of, either. It takes much more courage to do something when you are afraid than if you have no fear at all."

"I tried to tell her that, but I do not think she believes it. Maybe you—"

"I don't think she wishes to hear that from a Campbell."

"You are not like the others. They would not sing to a Jacobite," Robin said, then added a little shyly, "You have a bonny voice."

"Thank you." She hesitated, then added, "'Tis fine when someone enjoys it."

"They did not enjoy it in Scotland?"

He was far too perceptive.

"I was not . . . favored."

His steady gaze met hers. He seemed so much older than his years. "Why?" he asked.

"The marks on my arm," she said. "Some believe they are marks of the devil."

His brows drew together. "I do not think that at all. I had a brother with a birthmark. It was not quite as—" He stopped suddenly as if he feared saying something hurtful.

"As large," she finished for him. She found talking

about it not as painful as usual. He had accepted it as part of her, not something for which to shun her. Her family's name did that.

There was an odd kind of comfort to that.

"I did not even notice," he said diplomatically. In thinking back, she realized he had not once stared. Neither had the girl or Hamish or the captain. Because they had larger grudges against her?

Still, despite being a prisoner, she felt freer than she had in years, ever since she had realized her family intended to hide her away from visitors and that they never expected a good marriage for her. And that, for the Campbells, was the only value women had.

Being as she was had had one advantage, though. While her sisters were paraded in front of Scottish and English families, and taught all the manners expected of a young woman, she'd learned to read. She took her pleasure in books, in faraway places and in the adventures of others.

She had thought the journey to Barbados would be an adventure, but there had always been the specter at the end, the meeting with someone who might well reject her.

And now she was in a different kind of adventure altogether.

She'd read a few romances that young women had brought to the manor. The hero had always been noble, beset by evil men who wanted to take away what he had.

The hero was never a man who admitted to stealing, who did not seem to mind a murder or two in the process. She could have been killed in the bombardment of her ship. A child might have died because of it.

Malfour—whoever he was—did not have a single heroic bone in his body. And he could well destroy any chance she had for a normal life.

Anger welled inside her again. She had been foolish to believe, even for a few moments, that a few soft words belied what the man was.

She stirred the broth. She did not expect much from it, but at least it would be warm.

An hour had gone by. Perhaps even two. Robin continued to peel potatoes. He did it extraordinarily well. His well-formed features were tight with concentration. *A young lord.* Although he had never mentioned a title, it was written all over him. He had a natural grace and air of confidence, even command, that couldn't be dimmed, no matter what he was today. He wasn't "just" a Macdonald.

"Tell me about your family," she said.

His eyes lost their friendliness, becoming wary. "I have none left."

Still no trust. Not in a Campbell. Did he think that she would inform on him once she was released? But then why wouldn't he believe that?

Could they even afford to let her go?

She looked at the knife in Robin's hands. His gaze followed hers. She read his thoughts as his hand tightened on it.

Jenna looked back at the cook, at the crooked teeth with its gaps, and was surprised by a slight smile. She remembered when she first came aboard the *Ami.* Everyone had looked like brigands, as if they would kill if she so much as sneezed. Now she saw how much they cared for Meg, how they treated Robin. Not as a young lord but as a lad doing a job. They showed respect for that.

They care for their own. The observation caused a pang of loneliness. No one cared for her.

She finally decided the broth would do. The cook offered a bowl, and she filled it.

Robin took it. "I am used to the roll of the ship," he said.

She was too, after three weeks at sea. But there was nothing to gain by arguing with him.

She turned to the cook. "Thank you."

He nodded, the smallest glint of approval in his eyes. She wondered then what they knew about her. How many

cared that she was a Campbell, or Scottish? Were there allies among the crew?

But then she remembered again the respect they all
showed the captain.

She followed Rob back to the sick bay. The captain was
still there, pacing back and forth with a restlessness that
balked at the small confines of the space. Meg's eyes were
closed, but they were closed too tightly. She was awake.

Jenna took the bowl from Rob and sat down next to her.
"Meg."

Meg did not move.

Jenna looked at the anxious faces around Meg. No
wonder the child was pretending to be asleep. "Go," she
said. "All of you."

The captain gave her a disbelieving look and started to
say something. Hamish shook his head and led the way
out. Robin followed. After a pause, so did the captain.

"They are all gone, Meg."

The lass opened her eyes. They were filled with pain
and also urgency. "Miss . . . I need—"

"I know," Jenna said. She looked around and finally
found an object she could use. Then she helped Meg per-
form the necessities. Each movement cost the lass.

When Meg had finished, she fell exhausted back onto
the cot.

Jenna waited patiently, aware that Meg wrapped independence and pride around her as protection.

Finally, Meg gave her a faltering smile.

"Can you take some food?" Jenna asked.

"I dinna know."

"You must," Jenna said. "You have to keep your
strength."

Pale blue eyes stared at her. "Why do you care?"

"I just do." She put all the feeling she had into those
words. All her fear for the child, for herself, for the circumstances. All the hope she had for children of her own.
For children everywhere. Jenna had never linked them al-

together like that before. She should have. She should have fought for those who could not fight for themselves. She did not know how, but she should have made the attempt.

She'd had enough food, enough clothing. She'd had maids. Now it all seemed wicked as she pictured children hungry and alone in forests and caves with only a bandit to look after them.

She lifted a spoon of the broth to Meg's mouth, and the child obediently opened her mouth and drank it. Then another and another until nearly the entire bowl was gone.

Finally, Meg turned away. Jenna looked at the wound. It was still red and ugly, still secreting fluids. The poultice, though, had obviously been newly placed.

There was little more she could do. She took a cloth and poured water onto it, then washed Meg's face and thin chest.

Meg's lashes were fluttering.

"Go to sleep, love," Jenna said, saying the last word so softly she didn't believe the child heard.

"Will you sing to me again?"

"Of course."

"The same song," Meg demanded.

"Aye," Jenna said. She started to hum, then sang the words she knew so well. Her nanny had sung them to her. Mary had been her name, and she had been the one person who had been kind, who had told Jenna she was pretty. And special. God's chosen, she'd said about the mark. Not the devil's handiwork, but God's.

She had tried to remember that.

Jenna soon saw Meg's tense little body relax. Her hand reached out and clutched Jenna's.

As she sang softly, she felt tears flow down her face, tears that she knew had been there for years but had never been shed. Tears for every child that had been wounded, orphaned, killed.

She sang until Meg's eyes closed, and even then she continued.

• • •

"What does the likes of her know about children?" Alex strode up and down the area outside the sick bay.

"She is a woman," Hamish said. "The most likely of the group. The lass needs a female touch."

Alex glared at him. "She has never been shy before."

"Has Meg ever been hurt like this before?"

"Her mother died," Alex said flatly.

"And what did you do?"

Walked away. He had walked away and let Robin comfort her. He had seen too much death. He could not force himself to say all would be all right. Scotland would never be right again. And so he had stepped out into the freezing mist of a Scottish storm and mourned in his own way. No, not mourned. He'd raged. He'd raged against God, and against Cumberland and all who assisted him, especially the Scots who cold-bloodedly killed their fellow Scots.

She had not been a part of that.

But her family had been.

The argument warred in his head. He knew he was being unfair. Women in this world had little say in political matters and none in the conduct of war. Yet every time he looked at her he saw the men wearing Campbell colors systematically killing the wounded.

He heard the melody coming through the door. A lullaby was always lyrical, sometimes sad, always wistful, usually hopeful. But this one reverberated with loneliness and sadness, and every note hurt.

"Sail ho!"

Even down here, he heard the call.

He took the steep stairs two at a time and emerged through the hatchway onto the quarterdeck.

Claude stood next to the sailor at the wheel, and the lookout clung to rigging far above.

"An English man-o-war," Claude said.

"Has she spotted us yet?"

"*Non.* I ordered the British flag hoisted."

"What about the *Charlotte?*"

"She's far enough ahead to escape notice," Claude said.

Alex looked to the west. Clouds billowed across the sky, some dark purple, full of rain.

And cover for an escape.

"Change course," he said. "Westward."

"It looks like a strong squall," Claude said.

"I hope to God so."

"And Mademoiselle Meg?"

"She will have no life at all if we are taken," Alex said. "Neither Rob nor Meg. Change course now."

"Oui," Claude replied. He shouted orders, and the seamen scurried over the deck, putting on more sail.

Alex took the spyglass and looked through it. The British ship had obviously just seen them. He saw activity on their decks.

They were out of firing range. Would be for several more hours. But the British ship had both more speed and more gun power than the *Ami*. Their only chance was losing the warship in the storm.

Then take an easterly course to reach Martinique. He would lose a day but that was preferable to losing to the British.

The question was whether the *Ami* could make it to the squall in time.

Chapter Nine

Jenna felt the sudden surges of speed as more sail was added. The ship kicked more, and she said a brief prayer of thanks that she was not prone to seasickness. She worried about Celia, though.

She wanted to see, make sure she was not being mistreated by Blanche Carrefour. In fact, she'd thought earlier that she would ask the captain whether Celia could stay with her, but she'd been so concerned with Meg.

Sleep, she willed the child. Sleep. It was the best thing for her now.

She heard the noises above: the snap of sails, the footfalls of sailors, the shouted orders.

What was happening?

Another ship to capture? Or an English warship ready to take the *Ami?*

The thought inspired mixed emotions.

Rescue?

At what price?

What would England do to the sailors—and children—of the *Ami?* She now knew the children and the captain and probably others had run for their lives from Scotland, had experienced great hardships to escape the country.

She found it hard to believe that England—and her country—would execute children. But the fear was there in them. It was alive. She'd felt it.

And the captain? He most certainly was wanted by the English, whether for piracy or treason.

But *she* would be safe.

Oddly enough, the idea held little comfort.

Robin had left with the captain at the warning. Now he returned, opening the door quietly and closing it in the same way. He walked soundlessly to the cot and peered down at Meg.

"She's sleeping," Jenna mouthed soundlessly.

He nodded.

Jenna rose and went over to the other side of the room. Robin followed.

"What's happening?"

"An English warship," he said. "The captain is trying to outrun it into a squall where we can lose them."

"They have seen us?"

"Aye. It turned in our direction. The captain wanted me to tell you it might get rough." He looked over toward Meg, his brows gathering together in the same way she had seen the captain's do. "I will be staying with you to help."

She looked at the lad, realizing that many of his mannerisms were modeled after Malfour's. He must be a hero to Robin.

Her heart jerked at the thought. What chance would Robin ever have if he followed the thieving ways of his mentor? And what would become of Meg, who obviously worshiped both of them?

Somehow she would have to get them safely off this ship.

What would David Murray say if he were confronted with two small Jacobites as well as a woman who many said carried the devil's mark?

She walked around the room and secured what she could, placing medicines back in the cabinet and blowing out the lantern. It threw the cabin into gloom, and she knew they were heading toward evening.

"Do you think she will be all right?" Robin asked, uncertainty and a need to be reassured once more in his voice.

"I think she is a very stubborn and braw lass," she said. "And that is very important."

Robin, who until now had seemed more man than child, gazed into her eyes as if he were seeking her heart in them, and the truth.

Then he looked away.

"What do you plan to do after this journey?" she asked.

"We are going with Will to Brazil," he said.

She raised an eyebrow. "To Brazil?"

He suddenly clamped his lips together. She knew he'd forgotten for a moment she was the enemy. A Campbell.

The ship rose, then shuddered as it plunged into a trough. She leaned down and held Meg as firmly as she could without waking her.

A huge roar blasted through the room, and she thought they were being fired upon until she realized it was thunder. Lightning erupted in an explosion of light outside. The whole sky must have been alight to illuminate the cabin through the small portholes. The ship shook, then settled back down into another trough before rising again.

The cabin went dark again.

"I'm going above," Rob said. "I will be right back."

"Is it safe for you?" she asked, thinking that the last place she wanted to be now was on deck. She wanted to be below only slightly more.

"Yes," he said. "There are safety lines. I want to see how long . . ." She heard worry in his voice and knew instinctively the concern was for Meg rather than himself.

She wanted to stop him, but she could not do that and hold Meg safely at the same time. She did not think he would take advice from her even if she had the right or authority to do so. Still, she wanted to reach out and stop him.

"Robin . . ."

"*Lord* Robin," he said bitterly, then dodged out the door before she could do anything else. So she had been right. He did come from the aristocracy. And he evidently regretted those few moments in which he'd lowered his guard.

For the first time since she'd been at sea, Jenna felt real fear. Even more than when the *Charlotte* had been fired upon. She felt it more for Meg and Robin than for herself.

The ship rolled.

Meg woke with a small scream.

Jenna leaned over, protecting and holding the child's body with her own. "It is all right," she said. " 'Tis only a storm."

But in the dim light of the cabin, she saw the fear in the child's face. "Cannon," Meg said.

"Nay, 'tis only thunder."

"Da," she cried, her voice contorted with terror.

Jenna's heart skipped several beats as she took Meg's hands in her own.

"Where's Da?" Meg was delirious, obviously back in other places that were full of terror.

Jenna's heart lurched. She'd believed her past was filled with sorrow. It was nothing like that experienced by Meg.

She wet a cloth and bathed Meg's face, now dry and hot from fever. "It's all right, love. You are safe. Everyone is safe."

But the lass obviously did not hear her.

"Da," she kept saying. "Please, please don't die."

The door slammed open, and Rob appeared at her side. She felt droplets of water and realized he was shaking.

"Are you all right?" she asked.

"Yes." But his voice didn't seem so sure. His teeth chattered.

He stationed himself on the other side of the cot, kneeling on the floor since there was no chair, and when light crackled through the portholes again, she saw that he clutched Meg's other hand.

Meg cried out again. "Da. Please, please don't die."

Stricken, Jenna looked toward Rob. "She was not . . . there?"

"Aye, she was. After the battle, her mother and she went looking for her father. They found him as he was dying. Then the Sassenach came. They . . . abused her mother. Meg hid, but heard everything. Later she got her mother to the woods, but she was never the same and she died when we were with Will."

Dear God. Jenna struggled to hold back tears. It would not do Meg any good. Only toughness would.

She suddenly understood Captain Malfour, or Will, or whoever he was, and why he was what he was.

You could drown in these children's stories.

But what Malfour was doing was disastrous. He was turning their loss into hatred, into a path that would eventually lead to more violence and death.

Lightning snaked into the room again, and she saw the pinched faces of the children. Thunder roared overhead, and the ship bounced like a cork in the sea. Fear surged through her again. Stronger. This was nature. She could at least try to reason with human beings. You could not reason with nature.

And she wanted these children to live, even more than she wanted to live. She wanted them to have joy and happiness and security and love. Everything they needed so badly.

Thunder boomed again.

A cry escaped Meg's lips.

" 'Tis nothing but a wee storm," Jenna whispered.

Meg only tossed more wildly. Her fingers were still in tight fists, the knuckles white with strain.

Light exploded into the room again, and the ship seemed to roll all the way to the side.

Jenna leaned over and caught Meg. The cot was bolted to the floor, but Meg was not bolted to the cot.

It was all Jenna could do to keep from letting out a scream of her own, but that would only terrify Meg more. She grasped Meg's hand even tighter as the ship groaned and creaked and fought her way through the waves. Jenna heard the shattering of glass as bottles broke loose from their moorings and the sound of doors swinging back and forth as their latches gave way. The lanterns, their contents emptied for safety, swung wildly as the floor heaved.

During another flash of lightning that illuminated the cabin, she saw Robin's white face. Yet he, like Meg, displayed a courage that would humble most men.

"It's all right, my lady," he said. "The captain is a fine sailor. He can do anything."

Jenna wasn't so sure. The captain was apparently a successful brigand, but could he do anything else? Such as steer this ship through these seas?

She prayed he and his men were competent seamen. She had encountered other storms in the past weeks, but nothing like this. It was as if the ship were being tumbled over the fingers of God.

She prayed silently over and over again. She did not want Meg—or Robin—to know how afraid she was.

Meg whimpered. Her body was rigid, her lips clamped in pain. Her nails had pierced Jenna's skin as she'd clutched her hand ever tighter.

"It's all right if you yell," Jenna whispered.

"Nay," Meg whispered. "The English will hear us."

Fear ran through her. The child was somewhere else. A dark place full of terror. Her heart broke.

"What can we do?" Rob's voice was full of fear. She could feel his anxiety.

She wished she had an answer. How did one stop a plunging ship in a storm, or cool a raging fever, or cure an infection? How did one prevent war, or banish evil? She had never felt so helpless in her entire life.

"Talk to her," she said. "Hold on to her hand. Let her know you are here."

"It's not enough."

Nay, it wasn't enough. But she had nothing else to offer at the moment, except her prayers.

"You can pray," she said.

"God doesn't listen," Robin said bitterly. "If there is a God."

She was shocked for a moment. She knew that many Jacobites were Catholic, while her family was Protestant, but she had never met anyone who did not at least proclaim themselves believers. To do otherwise was heresy.

She knew about heresy. When she was a child, she had a way with animals as well as healing. It had only added to the rumors associated with her birthmark. Children had taunted her with the accusations of witchcraft. So had people in the nearby village. It was a fear that had infected her parents and had turned them away from her, not because of superstition but because they felt it cast suspicions on the entire family.

Was heresy worse than being a Jacobite child in today's Scotland?

Jenna was beginning to hate what she was, what she had been. She didn't know if she could have done anything had she been more aware. But she should have seen. She should have tried to help.

Captain Malfour had tried.

She did not want to think well of the pirate.

He hated her, hated everything she was. *She* hated what *he* was. You did not fight violence with violence. You did not defeat enemies by becoming a thief and murderer. You did not kidnap women or other helpless civilians. You did not take children on perilous voyages.

They stowed away. He could have sent them back. One side of her argued with another, even as she realized neither was helpful.

She was where she was, and she had to make the best of

it. At least no one had attacked her person. But that was of little comfort as she tried to ease the agony—both present and past—of a young lass.

Meg!

With every great heave of the ship, Alex could almost feel what it did to Meg's thin body.

The storm had been the only escape. But he had not realized how bad a storm it would be.

He tried not to think of Meg. There was nothing he could do now. He could only hope that the Campbell lass had common sense. And Rob should be with her now. The lad had come on deck until Alex had told him he needed to stay with Meg. They could not be trusting a Campbell.

Mainly, though, he wanted the lad to be safe below-decks.

If there was any place safe in this squall . . . Squall, bloody hell. It was closer to a typhoon.

More than ever, he wished he'd taken the children back to Paris.

Lightning seemed to leap from cloud to cloud, and Claude's shouted orders were barely audible through the noise of driving rain and pounding thunder. The decks were dark except when the occasional flash of lightning lit the entire sky.

Lifelines had been rove fore and aft the decks to prevent the crew from being washed overboard, and the sails were being furled. He'd given Claude command. The first mate had more experience with storms than he did, and Alex knew enough to admit what he didn't know. Instead, he worked to furl the sails with the other seamen, hearing their oaths, their prayers to the saint of seamen.

He was drenched through and through, and more tired than he believed possible, when a furled sail broke loose, flapping in the wind and threatening to tear away the main-yard. He climbed up the mast; he wouldn't ask another man to do it.

As he perched above the sea, the *Ami* plunged through waves twice its height. He held on for dear life as he cut the halyards and barely avoided being swept away as the sail flapped against him. Then it was gone, carried out of sight by the wind.

He hung there for a moment, fascinated by the majesty of the storm, then carefully climbed down. His hands were swollen from the burn of the ropes and the irritation of salt water. His bad leg ached from the strain he'd placed on it.

Claude gave him a nod of approval as he landed back on the deck. Despite the fact that he was the captain, he felt a sense of accomplishment that had eluded him most of his life. He'd had an easy, comfortable existence until he joined Prince Charlie. He'd had a good education and had followed a childhood dream to go to sea, but with his father's fortune behind it, he hadn't had to work at it.

All that had disappeared at Culloden. Since then he'd lost much of his confidence and certainly the arrogance. Defeat and hunger did that to a man. Thieving did it, too.

He'd seen the contempt in the Campbell lass's eyes. It had hurt, even coming from that quarter, or perhaps even more coming from that quarter.

Burke awaited him below, muttering to himself about bloody fools.

Only another damn fool Scot, and one who hated the sea, would stand out there in the gale and worry about a worse fool. Alex had sent him down earlier to see to the prisoners. But now he'd been enlisted to handle the sheets as had every other man jack.

"What?" he yelled to Burke as the man continued to mutter.

Burke's reply was lost in the scream of the wind.

Alex moved around the deck, working the sails and grabbing a sailor as he almost plunged into the sea when a huge wave washed over the deck. He, along with the other sailors, cowered under the bulwarks and held on to the belaying pins or whatever they could find to keep from being swept overboard.

The rain battered the decks, and the wind continued to howl like a banshee.

It seemed forever before the winds gradually grew less fierce, and the ship righted ever so slightly.

Claude ordered some sail, enough to steady the vessel, and directed the helmsman to turn the ship southwest with the wind. Waves still washed over the decks, keeping him from opening the hatches, and Alex could only wonder what was happening below, only pray to whoever might be listening that the Campbell woman and Rob were protecting little Meg. Hamish's knowledge of the sails had required his presence abovedecks.

The ship seemed tiny in the whirlwind of the sea, and the clouds still twisted and writhed so low he felt he could reach out and touch them.

Like the others, he braced himself as the ship continued to roll, then finally steadied slightly as the sky seemed to lighten. The waves were not as vicious, and finally the crew could move without help rather than lurching from one fixed object to another.

When the water no longer crashed over the deck, Alex and another seaman opened the hatchway. He climbed down awkwardly, his leg paining him more than usual. He tired to ignore it as he reached the sick bay, opening the door.

The floor still moved with the heavy seas. The cabin was dark. As his eyes adjusted to the darkness, he could see the Campbell wench. She had her arm held across Meg, and the other fixed to the bolted cot. Rob's hand clutched Meg's and the other kept her legs steady. A blanket had been cut and tied around her but apparently both the Campbell and Rob had thought that was not enough.

He wondered how long they both had held those positions.

"It's lessening," he said, and he felt, rather than saw, two sets of eyes on him. "How is she?"

"Delirious," the Campbell lass said. "She kept talking about her da."

He approached her and stared at her fingers curled around the iron leg of the cot. They seemed anchored there and he had to open her fingers one by one.

"It's all right," he said gently. "You can let go."

He noticed then that she was shivering.

The ship was still tossing too much for him to light a candle or a lantern. "Rob, take . . . the lady to her cabin."

"I would rather stay with Meg," she said.

He started to say he did not care what she would rather do. She was a prisoner, and her well-being was his responsibility. Or so he told himself.

"Why?" he asked harshly. "She's just Jacobite refuse."

"She needs me," the woman said stubbornly.

He did not want to admire a Campbell, but that insidious feeling crept through to a heart he thought well shielded. He could hear the weariness in her voice, almost feel the pain of muscles too long strained in one position.

"You will do her no good if you drop from exhaustion," he said. He was aware of her eyes on him.

"You must be exhausted, too," she said, still contrary. He wondered whether she was always that way, or just to him.

"I am used to it, my lady. I spent a year evading the English and their turncoat allies. There was little sleep."

"You think I have no heart," she said.

"I do not question your heart," he replied. "I do not know you that well. I do question the endurance of your body. I'll send someone to watch over her."

Still, she did not move.

"Please let her stay." Surprisingly, the weak, barely audible words came from Meg.

"Oh, Meg," the Campbell said. Then she looked at

Alex. Even in the gloom, her eyes looked misty, as if tears hovered there. Tears for Meg.

Alex tried to ignore them. Instead, he leaned down and felt Meg's cheek. Still hot. But perhaps not as hot as it had been. Or was that merely wishful thinking? He had given up on hope and prayers long ago, but perhaps . . .

He swallowed hard, then knelt next to Rob. "Meg?" His fingers touched her cheek.

"I want her to stay."

He was too startled to react. She had been the fiercest of them all against their enemies. "Whatever you wish, little one," he said finally.

Her hand took his. So small. So fragile.

"How do you feel?" he said.

"Bloody well," Meg said gamely.

He heard the Campbell wench's indrawn breath at the oath. Meg, he thought, had probably been with Burke and himself too long.

Just then, Meg moved and gasped. He checked the poultice. It was wet and sticky. Blood. "Has she had any laudanum lately?"

He made out the negative shake of her head.

"I was afraid to leave her. We tied her down, but she still rolled and I did not want the bonds to hurt her."

He stood silently as seconds turned to minutes. The ship still rolled but the tumbling had ended. "You can untie her," he said finally. "The worst is over." He went to the porthole. Minutes earlier it would have been awash with waves. The storm had passed.

He stanched the bleeding as best he could. Meg clenched her teeth as he did so. Then he returned to the cabinet to fetch her some laudanum. He was careful about its use, knowing it was addictive and could be dangerous.

He poured just a small portion from the bottle into a cup. Thank God the cabinet had protected what few medicines they had. Then he looked for water. The pitcher had been fitted into a slot, but the tossing of the ship had apparently spilled it.

"Rob," he said. "Go to the gallery and fetch some water."

"Aye, sir," he said.

Rob had always been far more polite than Meg. To Rob, Alex had simply been "Will" until he'd become captain of the *Ami*. Now he was "sir." Even Rob did not know Alex's true name, or if he did, he never mentioned it. Only Burke knew exactly who he was. And Burke was not a confiding man.

Keeping the cup steady, Alex returned to Meg's side. The ship plunged and immediately the Campbell leaned over to protect her. It was not, Alex had to admit, out of duty but out of true concern. True caring.

That Meg did not want her to leave put truth to that observation. He remembered the soft lullaby she'd sung earlier, the loneliness and longing in her voice.

How long since Meg had known gentleness? Certainly not in the past year. Probably not before that. Meg's mother had not been a demonstrative women. Alex had seen that firsthand. She'd been a dutiful wife and mother, yet not an affectionate one, and definitely not one to sing lullabies.

Meg had cared for her in the caves, but the woman had just given up. She'd not had her daughter's will to live.

He still remembered Meg's tearless face when he had buried her mother. No sign of emotion as if she had turned off everything inside herself.

But now she looked very much the vulnerable child with her hair hacked off, and her thin face, and the need for a woman.

Even a Campbell.

That was the most telling of all.

The door to the cabin opened, and Rob lurched toward him with a keg in his arms. Alex tapped it while Rob held the cup. Alex filled it and mixed the water with a small amount of laudanum, then went to the cot.

"Drink this, Meg."

She took tiny little sips. No protestations. No rebellion. It was not like Meg.

He waited until her breath grew easier.

The Campbell lass said nothing, merely kept her hand on Meg's, occasionally leaning down to protect her when the ship bucked. She said nothing to Alex, and he found himself wishing she would.

When he was sure Meg felt no more pain, he went to the tinderbox and took out the flint, steel, and tinder. Even as experienced as he was, he had trouble striking a light. Then the linen tender flamed and he finally got the bloody candle lit.

The Campbell woman rose and retrieved a piece of cloth from the cabinet. He watched as she carefully washed Meg's wound. Some of the stitches had torn away. The wound looked raw and ugly.

"We need some milk," Jeanette Campbell said.

"There is none."

"A milk poultice is best for a wound."

"Hamish does not seem to think so," he said coolly.

"The oil is not working," she said just as coldly.

"Do you have any way of conjuring a goat or cow?"

In a sudden flare of the candle, he saw her flinch. For a moment, she looked as vulnerable as young Meg.

Surprised, he felt a moment's regret. She had, after all, helped Meg and had done far more than he'd expected.

"Go to your cabin and get some rest," he said again. "You will be needed in the morning."

"And you?"

"I'll sleep then."

"If there's not another British ship."

His gaze met hers. "Aye."

"Will you then find another storm and to bloody hell with Meg?"

He did not know if he were more surprised at the oath or the accusation.

"And what would happen to her if the ship was taken by the English?" he asked. "Just what do you think would become of her then?"

Her hand trembled. "Certainly it could be no worse than this."

"Then you do not know them, my lady."

"You merely want to save yourself."

"Aye, I do," he said. "I have a few debts to repay."

He saw from the sudden flare in her eyes that she knew exactly what he meant.

She ignored him and looked at Meg's wound. "I can sew that."

"I'll wait for Hamish." He knew he sounded churlish. But she was reaching some part of him he did not want touched. "Leave," he said again. "She's sleeping. She doesn't need you."

"You are an ass, Captain," she said flatly as she rose and left the room with regal dignity.

Chapter Ten

Jenna tried to keep her temper intact. No matter who he was, no matter how he carried himself, he had the manners and demeanor of a ruffian.

She would not have left, had the child not been asleep. She hadn't wanted the tension to somehow affect her. But she was indeed tired, and she was glad to be free of the captain's presence.

For a moment, when he had touched Meg, she thought she possibly might have been wrong about him, that he did have some decency and humanity left inside. But then he had growled at her yet again and glowered as if he hated her.

Well, 'twas obvious he did. And oddly enough because of her name and not because of the mark she bore. Perhaps because he considered her so poorly, he cared little about it. Perhaps he had not even noticed it.

How could he not notice her mark? Except hers was of God's making. Or the devil's, as so many claimed.

Yet he had never thrown it at her.

He has not yet had time.

And what did she care in any event?

She could not get the picture of Meg out of her mind, or the ugly wound. Neither could she dismiss the image of the captain. He had been soaked to the skin, his dark hair plastered to his head, lines crinkling around tired eyes. Perhaps because his face had been etched with weariness, the scar had been more visible as it turned up his lips. Only it had been more grimace than the curious half smile that usually hid his emotions.

When he'd touched Meg with gentleness, she'd felt an odd tug in her heart. Would a murderer and thief have a tender touch?

Even a tiger had a care for its young as it devoured other more helpless beasts, she told herself.

She was determined not to be a more helpless beast.

She made her way back to her cabin, but it was locked, and there was no crewman there to open it. She knocked and heard a wailing inside.

"Celia," she yelled through the door. "Are you all right?"

"Aye, my lady," came a weak voice.

"Is that you crying out?"

"Nay, it is Lady Blanche," Celia said. "She is ill."

"And you?"

"Not as badly," Celia said, but she sounded awful. "And you, my lady?"

"I am well. Unhurt. I'll try to get the captain to let you stay with me."

Another wail.

Poor Celia. Jenna expected her maid's cabin mate—Blanche—was worse than the seasickness.

She debated whether to return to the sick bay to make her request, or wait until later. When would she have more chance of success?

She turned back toward the sick bay and opened the door. The interior was dark but so had been the rest of the bowels of the ship. Rob was asleep on the chair. Then she saw the captain. He was next to Meg's bed, his long legs folded, his head slumped on his chest. For a moment, she did not know whether it was in defeat or sleep.

Then he slowly moved and raised his head. She knew then it had been sleep, and she regretted her decision. She did not care about his welfare, she told herself, but she did about the ship and the people on board. At least some of them.

He rose, and his limp was even more pronounced. Something deep inside responded to the man who looked so utterly tired and, for the first time, vulnerable. He came to the door, held out a hand to direct her back outside, and then closed it behind him.

"Aye?" he said.

No title. No courtesy. Only an abrupt, irritated question.

"Celia . . . my companion . . . I would like her to stay with me. She's been ill and—"

"And you need a maid?" He turned back to the door in dismissal. "Well, this is one Campbell who will have to go without."

The area was dark, and she could not see his eyes or even much of his face. But his voice was rude and presumptive.

"I want to look after her, not the other way around," Jenna said, her anger now equal to his. For a moment earlier, their joint concern over a child had united them in a common cause, or so she had thought. He made it clear now there had been no common cause, no temporary truce.

He turned and stared at her. She wondered if he could see more of her face than she could of his. He seemed cat-like in his movements, uncanny in his ability to see in the dark.

He didn't say anything, but she still felt his enmity like a palpable thing. She was a Campbell. She suspected whatever she did, or said, was not going to make up for that. And it was one thing she could not change.

She waited, refusing to be cowed or intimidated.

He hesitated, then nodded his head once. "Go. I'll have one of my men bring her."

"Thank you," she said through clenched teeth. If nothing else, she was a pragmatist. Anger over his rudeness and unfairness accomplished nothing.

"And you will stay there until I say otherwise," he said. "I do not want you wandering the ship."

"I would be delighted if that means I will not see you," she said with the same contempt he'd put in his voice. So much for holding back her anger.

"Then we are agreed on that point," he said. She felt his gaze on her again. "Go," he said.

She turned around, afraid her defiance might prod him to change his mind.

Why had she said anything at all?

Because she had wondered for a split second whether there was more to the man than she'd first thought.

There was not.

He would get some rest in Claude's cabin.

Damn, but he hated to give up his own quarters, with the only bed on the ship large enough to accommodate him.

Still, the infernal Campbell wench needed sleep of her own, and she would never get it with the bawling Carrefour woman.

He rubbed the corner of his left eye. He had not meant to go to sleep. That he had dozed meant he needed it badly. He woke Rob. "I am going above to see whether Hamish can join you. If not, I'll send Burke to relieve you. Then you get some sleep. I will be in Claude's cabin."

Rob nodded, his gaze going over the still form on the bed. "Is she . . . ?"

Alex shook his head.

"Miss . . . Lady Jeanette was . . . kind." The lad's words were tentative, unsure.

"She wants to stay alive," he said curtly.

Rob did not say anything else, and Alex left him. Damn, but his leg hurt. If he weren't careful, it would give way at any time. As it was, every step was agony.

Hamish was seeing to the repair of the hauling of sail. A sliver of light peeked through distant clouds, though rain still fell steadily. The waves had diminished in strength. So had the wind.

The lifelines were still in place, though, and the ship still leapt through heavy seas.

He approached Claude, who was next to the wheel. "See anything of the *Charlotte*?"

"*Non.* I hope it avoided most of the storm."

"Burke?"

"Here."

Alex spun around. Burke was indeed next to him. It was uncanny the way he always appeared at the right moment.

"Stay with Rob and Meg in the sick bay," he said.

"Aye."

"And get that Campbell lass's maid. I want her sent to my cabin."

Burke raised a surprised eyebrow. "I thought ye would be using it."

"Just do it," Alex said.

Claude turned and gave him a searching look. "Ahhh," he said.

Alex glared at him. "I'll use your cabin for the next two hours to get some rest, then I'll relieve you."

"*Oui,* whatever you say, Captain," Claude said with an amused look.

Alex was damned if he was going to explain himself. Instead, he left the quarterdeck, trying not to hear Claude's chuckle.

He was not softening toward the Campbell wench. She would be no good to Meg if she too did not get some rest, and she obviously would not do that if she were worried about her maid.

Worried about her maid? A Campbell?

Campbells were a devious lot. Dishonor ran in their blood. She would be no different from any of them.

Damn her anyway.

A few more days and she would be off his ship.

Celia was pitiably grateful for her new quarters. Dawn's light was now creeping into the captain's cabin, and it must have looked very grand to her after the tiny quarters she'd been assigned to earlier.

The maid's face was white. Her dress was soiled, and her hair looked as if it had not been combed in a week. "Oh, miss, I did so worry about ye," she said.

"No more than I of you," Jenna said.

"You look tired, my lady," Celia said.

"And you look ill."

"I will no' be sorry to see land," Celia said, her pale face looking even more pinched. "They will let us go?"

"Aye," Jenna said, not nearly as sure as she hoped she sounded. But Celia needed the reassurance.

"They did not lock the door here," Celia noted.

"An oversight, no doubt," Jenna replied dryly. "Or else they know we are no threat."

She put a hand on Celia's shoulder. "Let me help you with your dress, then you can help me with mine."

She undid the buttons down the front of Celia's dress and tugged it down. Celia did the same with hers. Then they both stood in their shifts. "You take the bed, my lady," Celia said.

"Nay, it is large enough for both of us."

They looked at each other as a knock sounded at the door.

She did not have a key. For a moment, fear returned. Then for some reason it faded. The captain might despise her, yet she knew deep down he would do her no physical harm, nor allow it to happen by someone else's hand.

She went to the door and opened it a crack. A young

sailor stood there, a jug in one hand and a basket in another. "The captain sent this."

"What . . . ?"

"Some wine, miss, and some bread and crackers and cheese."

She reached out and took the offerings, handing the jug to Celia. "Thank you."

"Yer welcome," the sailor said, then turned and disappeared.

Jenna stared at the gifts, for surely they could be nothing else from captor to captive, and wondered at the paradox that was both gentleman and pirate.

Alex woke with a huge ache in his head, a leg that did not want to respond, and a glowering discontent.

He did not want to deal with the Campbell woman.

Meg. How was Meg? Someone would have wakened him if she were worse, but still . . .

He hurriedly dressed. Shaving could wait until later.

He looked out the porthole. Blue sky, by God. The ship still rolled, which meant the seas were running high.

He left the cabin and strode straight to the sick bay. Meg was awake. Both Burke and Rob were with her.

"How do you feel?" He felt her face. He would swear the fever was lessening.

"*You* look terrible," Meg said.

"We are not talking about me."

"Are you worried about me?" She looked pleased even if her smile seemed more like a grimace in her too-pale face. She was definitely a female. And definitely getting better.

"Aye. It would be inconvenient if anything happened to you," he said.

"Why?"

He grinned at her. It had been a long time since he had done that. "I would miss you," he admitted wryly.

"Really?"

"Aye. But I would have preferred missing you if you'd stayed in Paris."

"They dinna care about me."

"They did, or they would not have offered to take you in."

"I dinna need charity," she said belligerently.

Now he knew she was feeling better.

He understood. Dear God, he understood. But what to do with a lass of eleven years whose manners and speech were atrocious and who did not know the meaning of obedience? Her one goal in life seemed to be to vex him.

He would have missed Rob and her, had they not stowed away. But the last few hours had proved just how dangerous it was for them.

Yet there was little he could do about it now. In the past hours he'd considered leaving them on Martinique or another French island, but he knew no one he could trust to care for them. If he left money, who was to say the children would not be abandoned and the money stolen? As dangerous as the *Ami* might be, it probably was no more so than the alternatives.

It strengthened his resolve to end his privateering for the immediate future and try the diamond business. It had, after all, been the original plan.

After selling the captured *Charlotte,* he would change the name of the *Ami* and sail to Brazil.

What about the woman?

He would leave her and her maid with enough money to get to Barbados. The rest they could manage on their own.

He owed it to her. As much as he disliked acknowledging it, she had helped Meg. He paid his debts, particularly when owed to the Campbells and their English allies.

The sun streamed into the captain's cabin, waking Jenna.

Celia was still sleeping next to the wall.

Leaving her maid to rest, Jenna rolled off the bed and

stood. The ship seemed to be skimming over the sea now, rather than rolling or floundering in it.

She chose a dress she could don without help, then looked for something to use to transfer the jewelry from the stained dress she'd worn when captured to the one she was wearing. Jenna wanted her jewels with her. They were her only safety now, her only means of escape and survival. At best, she would have to pay passage to Barbados for herself and Celia.

She should have arrived today. Would her prospective husband worry when she did not arrive today, or tomorrow, or even weeks from now?

She found her sewing kit intact and quickly sewed the jewels into the dress she intended to wear. Then she stepped into the dress and laced up the front, trying to be as quiet as possible. Like most of her dresses, this one had long sleeves. After a moment's thought, she discarded the matching gloves. What difference did it make if anyone here saw her birthmark? Many had already seen it. Word of the devil's mark had probably already traveled throughout the ship.

She tried the door. To her surprise it was unlocked.

She'd been warned last night—or was it this morning— not to leave the cabin without permission. But she had to know how Meg was doing, and she had no idea when someone would remember—or care about—her existence. Opening the door a bit wider, she looked in both directions, seeing no one.

She cautiously made her way to the area used as a sick bay, fearing that any moment the captain would appear.

Light streamed through the passageways, which meant all the hatches were open. The warmth felt good after the chill of last night. She reached the door of the sick bay and hesitated, listening for voices. When she heard none, she knocked lightly, then went inside.

The man called Burke was trying to spoon some food into Meg's mouth. The girl was sitting up, and her face looked far better than it had earlier. Serious blue eyes regarded her cautiously.

"Hello," Jenna said. "I came to see how you are."

"Burke says I am better."

"You look much better." She leaned over and lifted the poultice. Some of the inflammation had subsided. Maybe the oil worked as well as the milk she always used in poultices.

She felt Meg's cheek. It was warm still but not like early this morning, and the lass's obvious appetite was a good sign.

Rob stood in a corner. He swallowed, then approached her. "Thank you for looking after Meg last night," he finally said, the words obviously difficult for him.

"You helped just as much," Jenna said. "You are a good friend." She hesitated, then asked, "Did you get any sleep?"

"Aye, I did."

They faced one another awkwardly, a woman and lad separated by a war, by a battle, by prejudice, by so many things. They had worked together last night, yet in the glow of day, that bond had frayed. His eyes were cool. It was clear that her name was a major obstacle, even with these children.

"I want to help," she said.

"Why?" he asked bluntly.

"Is it so impossible to think a Campbell might want to help?"

"Aye," he said.

"I like . . ." She started to say children, but these two were no longer children. "To be useful," she finally finished.

"We no longer need ye," Burke said roughly.

Surprisingly, tears gathered behind her eyes. She had not cried since she was a very small child. She had always felt alone, but that had been all she had known. But now this particular rebuff was especially painful, perhaps when delivered by children.

She backed out, then turned and walked down the passageway. She stopped at the hatch. She could go back to the captain's cabin and possibly wake Celia, or she could go up on deck and breathe in the fresh air.

She proceeded carefully. She was not up to meeting with the captain, though she supposed he was probably asleep.

On deck, a number of sailors were sewing and repairing sails under the watchful eyes of Hamish. A carpenter was repairing a quarter boat that had been ripped from its moorings. Four men were up in the rigging.

No one paid her any mind.

She found a secluded place out of sight of most of the crew and sat on a coil of rope. It was damp, but she did not care. The rain-washed sky was as pure a blue as she had ever seen. Heavy dark clouds roiled in the distance, but the few above scudded across the sky like balls being kicked by a child.

Why did she keep thinking of children?

She breathed deeply. The air was cool with a tangy and fresh scent. Overhead, a seagull circled with a lonely cry that seemed to echo across the endless sea.

They must be close to land if seagulls reached them.

Land that belonged to the French, or the English, or the Dutch?

It was strange how attached she had become to young Meg in the past days. Would she feel that way about David Murray's children?

But somehow that seemed a long way, a long time, from this ship and the man who had captured her.

She took another deep breath of air as she rose. How she would like to drink a cup of tea out here as the wind blew free!

A gust of wind hit her, taking with it the ribbon securing her hair at the nape of her neck. Jenna pushed her hair back, plaiting it roughly, knowing it would soon blow free again, yet not caring to return to the captain's cabin. The sea wind had, from the day they left England, awakened something inside her, giving her a sense of freedom she'd never had before.

As she finished braiding her hair, she took several more steps away from the forecastle and halted to stare at the man who seemed to dominate sea and sky alike.

He was at the wheel of the ship, the unscarred side of his face toward her. It was stubbled, but that seemed to add a dash of intrigue to him. From this side, he looked uncommonly handsome, his face all angles and strength. He easily handled the wheel, which she knew required enormous strength, as if it weighed little more than a pound.

He wore an open-necked white linen shirt with flowing sleeves and tight breeches that gloved his long legs. His eyes were fixed on the distance as if seeing something no one else could see.

He looked powerful and wild and free.

Magnificent.

The impression hit her so strongly, she reached out to catch a corner of the forecastle to keep from falling.

In that instant, she knew she would always think of him this way. Not with the frown, or the limp, or even the scar. But as someone free and grand.

Her heart suddenly jerked. How could she feel that way about a pirate? A thief? Possibly a murderer?

A man who hated everything she was?

Chapter Eleven

Alex treasured the spectacular hours that often followed a storm. The sea was still restless, the wind brisk, filling the sails and sending the *Ami* skimming across the waves. The sky seemed especially blue, the air fresher.

He'd traded places with Claude, who had accepted relief gratefully. They had gone over the maps and navigation and decided they were within a day's sail of Martinique. There they could make repairs, replenish supplies, and be rid of their unwanted passengers.

The last should have elated him. Unaccountably it did not.

He kept hearing the Campbell's soft voice in his mind, even as he willed the wind to carry it away. The melody of the lullaby would not leave him.

The memory brought back visions of Janet, the smile on her face the last time he had seen her. Her husband had turned out to be a far better man than Alex thought possible of a Scot turncoat.

But Neil Forbes was an exception.

Where there was one, were there others?

He should stop making judgments.

Against anyone but a Campbell.

He saw a slash of red carried by the wind and his gaze searched the deck, settling on the slim figure standing next to the forecastle. Hair with the sheen of gold flew around a lightly tanned face.

Strange he had not noticed that before. His first impression had been of mousy brown hair under a bonnet, but now as the sun's rays touched and caressed it, it looked bewitching. She did not look mousy, either, though there was an uncertainty in her eyes, even in the way she stood. And yet there was spirit in the way she braced herself against the wind, the color in her cheeks.

He recognized her own pleasure in the day, even in the ship. It seemed to echo his own.

She had been told not to leave his cabin.

For some reason he could not find it within him to order her back. Not after she had spent the night caring for Meg in a way that went beyond what he had expected.

He turned to the helmsman behind him. "Take the wheel."

"Aye, sir."

He approached the Campbell. He saw her flinch as he neared but she did not give ground. She had courage, at least. He'd noted that last night. She hadn't screamed or pleaded or surrendered in fear to the storm. Instead, she'd held steady.

"I wanted some fresh air," she said defiantly.

"It's a fine morning after a poor night," he said mildly. He saw surprise flicker in her eyes.

"Aye," she said carefully.

"How is your maid?"

"My friend and companion," she corrected.

He raised an eyebrow.

"You probably do not know much about friends," she said. "I suppose a cutthroat rarely does."

"I have lost enough of them to know their worth," he

replied. He did not have to say more. The thrust had hit its mark.

She turned away and looked back at the sea.

"You appear to like the sea," he said after a moment's hesitation.

"Aye."

The short answer dismissed him effectively. The prisoner dismissing her captor. He thought he should be offended, but strangely enough he was not. He'd always liked heart, even in a Campbell.

"You can come and go as you like," he said, then turned and left, as startled by his surrender as she was.

Having permission to remain made the top deck just a little less attractive, Jenna admitted to herself. Especially since, in the past few seconds, she thought the storm winds were approaching again.

The air had become dense, thick, electric.

She would almost swear lightning had leapt from the captain to her.

She did not want to think that he was the cause of such sudden heat. 'Twas the sun's rays and her imagination. Instead, she tried to tell herself that she had won one small battle, one of the few she'd won in her life.

But it was dimmed by the overwhelming presence of the man, a presence that lingered just like clouds often lingered after a blow. She realized her arms crossed each other, fingers clasped around her arms in a self-protective pose. When had she done that?

Had he seen it?

She did not want him to think she feared him, or had any other emotions concerning him. But her legs were shaky. How could a man—particularly this one—affect her so?

Maybe she was far more tired than she thought.

She tried not to look toward the wheel. He had returned there, she knew. She did not want to see that quiet power, the authority with which he mastered the helm. She did not want her eyes to meet his dark blue gaze again. Nor did she want to feel the heat rushing through her blood.

She hesitated. He could *not* know he affected her in such a way. In any way.

She remained, trying to regain the brief pleasure she'd felt earlier. She did not want the new uncertainty, nor the sudden instability of her legs. How could she—for a moment—believe the pirate was appealing in any way?

He'd been unshaven, his lips pulled up in that mocking half smile. But there had been something in those dark blue eyes that had caught her off guard, a small, self-deprecating apology that had inexplicably warmed her through and through.

Her breath caught in her throat. For the first time in her life, she had felt the warm rush of lust. She hadn't known what it was until now, and she was sure her face went red when her analytical mind finally identified it.

Abruptly, she turned and headed toward the sick bay, trying to keep her legs steady enough so she wouldn't fall to the bottom of the stairs.

Perhaps Meg would like a story. Or a song. Anything to take away the awareness that had taken over her mind. Her body. Her very soul.

The door was open. Rob was sitting in a chair, reading the medical manual. He looked up when he saw her, then went back to the book. Meg's eyes were closed. No help there. She took the chair where Hamish sat when he was present and looked at the children.

"Les enfants," the first mate had called them. But they weren't. They were short adults who had no one but a pirate to care for them. It was still difficult to understand, or even envision.

She wanted to look at the wound, but did not want to wake Meg. Rest was by far the best thing for her. Jenna's eyes started to close, then flew back open. Every time she closed them, she saw the infernal pirate. How long before she could leave the ship?

And Meg?

As if the child heard her thoughts, she moved, then cried out in pain.

Jenna flew to her. "Meg?"

"It hurts."

It was the first complaint she'd heard from Meg. She felt the child's forehead again. It was still warm, but she did not think it as hot as earlier. Then she checked the wound. The poultice needed replacement again. The wound had been torn last night, and evidently Hamish had not had time to sew it closed.

It needed to be done. She thought about calling Hamish, then hesitated. He was busy, and she had sewn wounds in both people and animal.

"Will you allow me to fix it?" she asked softly.

Meg looked at her with big eyes full of pain and uncertainty. She had given up some of her dislike and hostility yesterday, but Jenna saw lingering distrust. "Aye," the girl finally said in a low voice. "I do not want to bother Hamish."

"I do not believe you bother anyone," Jenna said. "Everyone, including the captain, is very concerned about you."

"He will leave me," Meg said despondently.

"He will make sure you are safe," Jenna said in a soft voice.

"I do not want to be safe. I want to be with Will."

Will again.

She wanted to ask the lass whether she knew Will's real last name, but that would be taking advantage of a sick child and she was not ready to do that.

She knew where Hamish kept the needle and thread. But first she wanted to give the lass something to relieve the pain. More laudanum? How much had she had?

"Have you had a draft of anything this morning?" she asked.

"Nay," Meg said. "And I don't need anything." But her lips quivered. Bravery apparently went only so far.

Rob woke up then, blinking his eyes. He wiped them with the back of his hand, looking his age for the first time. "Meg?"

"I should sew up her wound," Jenna said. "Can you convince her to take a draft of laudanum?"

"Rather have rum," Meg said.

Jenna tried to suppress her surprise. She wasn't sure whether Meg was saying it for effect or was serious. And if she was? A lass?

A glass of sherry or wine at supper was permissible for a young lady. But a child? And rum?

She hesitated.

"It's all right," Rob said. "We sneaked some when we stowed away."

At least the captain hadn't given it to him. Still she hesitated. She had no idea where the rum was.

"I'll get it," Robin said, and was out the door before she could say nay.

She sat down next to Meg. She was not the child's mother or guardian. Not even a friend. Not yet, though she hoped to be. She had no right to correct or criticize. Still, she would love to find a proper dress for Meg, and see her hair grow. She could be quite lovely, Jenna thought. Her hair, now darkened by dirt, looked as if it might be light brown. Her eyes were large and expressive, though expressively suspicious at the moment.

Jenna knew her observations would not be welcomed, might even destroy what little headway she had made.

A bit of rum to take the pain from the stitches would not be a sin.

She started humming a song, and Meg's eyes were rapt on her. "Sing it," Meg demanded.

Jenna knew she should not. It was a song she'd heard a servant sing and soon after, that servant had been dismissed. But she loved the melody, and she loved the optimism, and it was a song she'd secretly harbored in her soul.

> *"The Gypsy rover come over the hill,*
> *Bound through the valley so shady.*
> *He whistled and he sang till the green woods rang,*
> *   and*
> *He won the heart of a lady . . ."*

Meg listened intently until she finished.

"I know a song, too," she said. "I learned it in Paris."

"Sing it," Jenna said, hoping it would take her mind off the pain.

> *"Charlie is my darling, my darling, my darling . . .*
> *Charlie is my darling, the young chevalier . . ."*

Jenna knew immediately the song was meant to provoke her. Charlie was obviously the prince now in France, the man most despised by the English and the Campbells.

But not Jenna. She had always been fascinated by the man. He was said to have great charisma. Unfortunately his military ability, according to her father, had not been as impressive.

"You have a good voice," Jenna said mildly. And she did. Weak and thin now, but it had a purity that was God's gift.

Meg looked disappointed. She seemed to alternate between wanting to start a fight and wanting comfort. A small war waged in a heart badly damaged. Everything was a small test. Jenna was not sure whether she had won this one or not.

Then Rob was back with a mug of foul-smelling rum.

Meg downed it as well as any sailor.

Jenna got a needle and thread from a chest she'd seen Hamish use, and started sewing.

• • •

"Land ho!"

Alex looked west, where the island of Martinique should be, then relinquished the wheel to Claude, who had returned looking far better than when he'd left the quarterdeck. He'd even shaved.

Alex had made no comment. Instead, he peered through the spyglass, looking for both land and enemy ships. Or, for that matter, friendly ones. He wanted to hear the latest news on the possible treaty between England and France.

Blazes. He should never have let that British merchantman tempt him. He would be halfway to Brazil. That damned flag always had a way of making him do foolish things.

Now he not only had passengers he did not want, but he had a wounded child.

He dared not linger in Martinique. The moment a peace treaty was signed, British ships would be hunting any privateers, and the *Ami* would not have the protection of letters of marque.

The lone bird had been joined by others circling overhead. Alex squinted against the sun and saw the land in the distance, a dark green jewel resting on a background of sapphire and emerald. Nothing, he thought, was as beautiful as these waters and these islands.

But they would be as dangerous for him as Scotland once a peace treaty was signed. They were small, and word traveled among them. He would be a marked man.

His only hope for a future lay in the interior of America, a vast land where a man could lose himself and his past.

He searched the seas around the *Ami*, and wondered about the *Charlotte* and those aboard her. Had they made it through the storm? Had the British seen her? Hopefully, they were already in Fort Royal.

He put down the spyglass. He would tell the Campbell woman she would soon be safe. It was the least he could do. He frowned, startled by the jump in his heart at the thought, and the sense of loss where relief should be.

• • •

Alex stopped at the door of the sick bay. He heard female voices singing.

Two female voices.

He pushed the door open. Meg's gaze was on the face of the woman above her. He saw that much. Her voice followed the Campbell's melody. One mature and strong and lovely, the other weak and sweet.

Meg was singing! Hell, he hadn't known she could sing.

That realization hurt, though he couldn't quite understand why. He hadn't wanted to get close to the children. He'd known he could not keep them, not with the future he'd planned, nor the price on his head if anyone discovered Alex Leslie was still alive. His bad leg and the scar on his face marked him forever. His options were limited. There was no place for children with him. No safe place.

He swallowed hard as he listened to the two voices. The one sounded so weak. Should Meg be expending her energy that way?

And the other voice lowered her own as not to overshadow it. Or so it sounded.

Although he was already half inside the door, he knocked, and the singing stopped. He felt an inexplicable sense of loss. He stepped inside. There was no time for personal indulgences.

Meg and the Campbell lass turned to face him.

"We've reached Martinique," he said. "I'll talk to the royal governor and make arrangements for your passage to Barbados."

"What about Meg?" the Campbell asked.

"I'll find a doctor for her. She is no longer your concern."

"Will you leave her there?"

He truly did not know what he was going to do. He went over to the bed. "How are you, Meggy?"

"She threw my arm," she said, slurring her words. As he leaned down, a decided odor of rum met him.

"Rum?" he asked.

Robin had been sitting, watching. "Meg did not want laudanum," he said. "She asked for some rum." He hesitated, looked at the Campbell lass. "I fetched it. She didn't have anything to do with it."

Now Rob was defending the damn woman. It did not make him feel better that he too had had raised his opinion of the lass. Reluctantly. "It's all right," he finally said. "Go get some rest. It will be several hours before we anchor."

Rob still hesitated.

Alex glanced from Lady Jeanette to each of his two charges. He felt oddly betrayed.

"Rob," he said in a tone that he hoped would spur the lad's departure.

The lad cast an apologetic look at Lady Jeanette, then plodded to the door and left.

"Do you have packing to do, Lady Jeanette?" he asked. At least he could put some distance between them with her title. Since his own had been taken by King George, that put her a step above him. In that aspect, anyway.

"Nay," she said equably, though her back stiffened.

He saw the gleam of battle in her eyes, and perhaps something else.

"How is your companion?" he asked.

Her gaze faltered at the courtesy. "Better," she said, then nodded toward Meg. "I want to know what you plan for the children," she said steadily.

"I will do what is best for them," he replied curtly.

"Like go to war with the English navy?"

"What would you suggest?"

"I could take them with me. At least Meg," she pleaded.

"Nay," Meg said. "I want to stay with Will and Robin."

Alex glared at the Campbell. He was back to thinking of her as that now. "We will talk outside," he said. Then he leaned down and touched Meg's cheek. Still too warm. "Get some sleep if you can," he said.

Then he went to the door and held it open. The Campbell did not move. He moved back into the room rather than stand in the doorway like a helpless fool.

"My lady," he said in the same tone he used to issue orders to his men. It didn't seem to faze Jeanette Campbell. "I don't want to have to carry you out," he said after another moment passed.

She hesitated, then took a rigid stance. "You cannot think of keeping that child with you," she said.

"I cannot think of abandoning her, either," he said.

"You are a pirate. They will hang you and probably these two children, too."

"Then you admit your English friends are barbarians."

"No more than the person I am looking at now."

"What would you do with a Jacobite child?" he asked sarcastically. "Would your betrothed approve?"

"I do not care what he thinks," she said after the briefest of pauses.

"You think I would let her be raised by an English sympathizer?"

"I do not know that he is," she said.

"Oh, you do not?" he said.

Her chin came up. "His . . . politics have never come up."

"You do not aim to be a dutiful wife, do you?" he observed with cynicism. "I doubt he will appreciate being presented with orphaned fugitives."

"They are *children.*"

"That has never mattered to the English—or Campbells—before," he said.

"They . . . we . . . are not all villains."

He did not deign to answer that. "Get yourself and your companion ready," he said, dismissing her. But despite the impossibility of her suggestion, he admired her for making the offer. Even if her interest lasted only as long as most English promises.

He would not put Meg back in English hands. He would never forget, nor forgive, the systematic slaughter of Jaco-

bite women and children following the battle at Culloden
Moor. He would never trust the rulers who condoned such
actions.

He looked at Meg's wound. The new stitches. He knew
Hamish had been on deck all night and day, supervising the
repair of sail. It could mean their lives. So the Campbell
had sewed Meg's wound.

The stitches were well done. Even he could see that. Unlike many highborn ladies he knew, this one had skills other
than singing and comforting.

Again, a reluctant admiration tugged at him. For a fleeting moment, he considered the possibility of keeping her
aboard the *Ami* for Meg's sake. But then he would be no
better than the English he hated. It was one thing when she
was a passenger in a ship he'd taken; it was far different to
detain her after arriving at a safe port.

But Meg needed a woman's presence. She was turning
into a hoyden, or perhaps she had always been one. It
would not be long before she reached marriageable age,
and he wanted her to have a happy and contented life. She
needed to learn manners and womanly skills.

And she had unexpectedly responded to Jeanette Campbell.

Nay, he warned himself. *You cannot even consider such
a thing. She's a Campbell. Have you lost what wits you
have?*

Even worse, he wondered whether there was a part of
him that wanted her to stay for reasons other than Meg's
well-being. It was that accursed honest streak that he'd
never quite been able to quiet.

She was the first woman who didn't appear to notice his
scar or his limp. She detested him for other reasons, mainly
for the lack of character she attributed to him.

He couldn't dispute that assessment. In the last two
years, he'd forgone every bit of honor he'd ever possessed.
He doubted whether he could get it back. Or even wanted it
back, if it meant giving up his hatred of his enemies. It had

been the only thing that kept him alive in the months after Culloden. It was who and what he was.

Ignoring the Campbell lass, he sat with Meg until her eyes closed. Part exhaustion, part rum, he thought. In this matter, at least, he could not disagree with the use of rum as a sedative. He knew how addictive laudanum could become.

Now what? The woman had asked a very good question. What would he do with Meg and Rob?

What you've always intended. Find them homes in France. You just have to try a little harder to find the right people. After this trip, there will be enough money to provide the very best.

After Brazil.

Then he would no longer have the responsibility.

He stood. Jeanette Campbell would leave with the other passengers. He would have peace again. At least as much peace as his memories would allow.

Blazes, why did that thought disturb him so?

Chapter Twelve

Ever since the capture of the *Charlotte*, Jenna had wanted her freedom back. She hadn't liked being told what to do by a pirate.

When had she realized she'd had no freedom even before her ship was captured? She had been caged by people who judged her by her mark, and by her own self-doubts.

And now . . .

There was something seductive about the *Ami*, and its occupants. Even its captain.

There was also something very seductive about the freedom she'd felt today.

It was strange to lose freedom to gain some.

But as contradictory as that fact was, it was true. Hamish, Meg, and even Robin had accepted her to some extent. She had been useful. She had even been wanted. Her mark had been accepted also as a part of her, neither good nor bad. It just was. And that was the greatest gift she'd ever had.

She had come alive in the past several days. Perhaps the past several weeks. She loved the sea and the wind and the sun. She loved being free of the darting looks and the unguarded shame in her parents' eyes.

She only knew that she felt strangely at home on this ship, even more so than on the *Charlotte*, where she'd been loath to let the other passengers know about the mark. She knew her excess of clothes had made her appear eccentric. She had tried not to care, just as she had tried all her life not to care.

In truth, she'd come to care very deeply about Meg. Perhaps because of Meg's vulnerability, one that Jenna knew only too well. How could she leave Meg, or Robin with his too-old bravado and cynicism? Whether the captain or Robin or even Meg knew it, the children needed her as much as she needed them.

How could she leave them in the company of pirates? On a ship that could be taken at any time by the English? If the captain was correct, the children would be at risk, both because they were Jacobites and because they were aboard a privateer that could—at the stroke of a pen—be labeled a pirate ship.

And as unwise as it was, as completely foolish that she knew she was, she did not want to go ashore. She did not want to go to an uncertain future with a man she had never met.

Her stomach tied into knots at the very thought. Far more now than it had in Scotland. Then marriage had seemed her only escape. Now she wondered if she were going to an even worse situation where she'd have no protection, no alternatives, no escape.

The simple—and devastating—fact was that she did not want to leave any of them. Meg. Robin. And worse, she did not want to leave the captain.

He cared nothing for her. She cared nothing for him. But he . . . intrigued her as no other man ever had. Not, she admitted, that she had known many men well, or even slightly. She had always been hidden away.

And now she wanted—nay, needed—to explore all the

contradictions of this particular man: the roughness and tenderness that seemed to be a part of him, the cynicism in his eyes and the loyalty he inspired in his crew. Her father had never had that kind of loyalty from his soldiers. They obeyed out of fear or for monetary rewards. Not out of affection. And affection was what this crew gave their captain. She saw it in the way they responded to him.

She could not stop thinking about the man who was her captor, and how different he was from her first impression. Or was he?

Had he just known how to use her?

But even more important, she did not want to leave the ship without Meg. She wanted Robin, too, but Meg was in more jeopardy. She was a lass who did not belong with a crew of men, while Robin was twelve, old enough to be a cabin lad.

In the past few minutes, though, the idea had taken root in her heart.

Something in the child had struck a chord in her. She recognized the loneliness, the quiet desperation, the fear. They had different causes. Hers came from nature, and a family who never accepted imperfection. Meg's came from cruelty and fear.

But how to keep her when the captain was so adamantly opposed?

She doubted she could smuggle the child off the ship, even if Meg would go willingly, which she doubted. And if she did, what then would happen to Robin? She wanted to keep them together, to keep them both safe.

She reached the captain's cabin and opened the door. Celia was inside, moving around, which was progress. A tray of food was on the table.

Her maid looked up and smiled. "I heard them saying we will reach land soon."

"Aye, today, it seems," Jenna said.

"Bless the angels," Celia said thankfully. "I will no' be

sad to see the last of this ship. I've been living in mortal fear."

"No one . . . has harmed you?" She had thought Celia safe, under the protection of the captain, and had certainly checked on her.

"Oh, nay, my lady, but that is not to say they would not. Black-hearted villains they be." She looked at Jenna for approval of her assessment. When one was not immediately forthcoming, she added, "It was a gentlemanly thing he did, giving ye his cabin. That Mrs. Carrefour . . ."

"He may be many things, but I would not include gentleman among them," Jenna said dryly.

"Without that terrible scar, he would be fair handsome," Celia ventured.

"I have not noticed," Jenna said. It was a lie but a small one. Attractiveness came from the inside, not the outside.

"How *is* the lass?"

"Still very ill," Jenna said. She went over to the windows and looked out. She could see land now. A great dark green mound seemed to rise straight out of the sea, contrasting with the emerald sea.

"Well, I for one will be pleased to be on dry land," Celia said as she stood beside her. "My, but it does look fine." Then she turned to Jenna. "We will stay awhile?"

"I am not sure," Jenna said.

"I do not like the sea, my lady."

"I am expected in Barbados." Her voice held no conviction and she knew it.

From the expression on Celia's face, she had realized it, too. "Ye *are* going to Barbados?" Celia asked.

"I am not sure Mr. Murray will still want me." *Or the children,* she added silently.

"But of course he would. 'Tis not your fault that the ship was seized."

"He has never seen me. My father says he knows about the birthmark, but what if my father lied?"

Celia did not say anything. It was obvious that she would not put that beyond her father.

"The child is very ill," Jenna repeated.

Celia's lips turned downward and panic widened her eyes. "My lady . . ."

"I will take care of you," she assured Celia.

Celia did not look reassured.

"I do not know exactly what I will do," Jenna added. "I wanted to keep the child with me, but the captain—"

"Would never give her care to a Campbell," Celia said with the familiarity of years of serving Jenna. "I have heard the insults. They are not fit to wipe your shoes."

"They have reason, Celia."

"You did nothing to them," Celia said.

"They believe my family did, and I fear they may be right."

"Ye are not responsible for that," Celia said indignantly.

"I canna blame them, though. Meg's father was killed at Culloden Moor; her mother was abused and later died. Robin's father was also killed, and—"

"Nay, ye cannot blame yourself," Celia said, her voice softened with sympathy.

"I have to find a way to help Meg. And Robin if possible. If they are taken by the English . . ."

"What can ye do?"

"I do not know yet, but there must be something."

"I cannot go back to sea," Celia said, her hands twisting together. "I would do anything for ye, but—"

"I know," Jenna said. Celia had lost much weight and her face was pale. She had been better this past day, but she would never be a sailor.

"What are you planning?"

"I am going to try again to have her stay with me."

"And Mr. Murray? Would he accept the bairn?"

"If he does not, I will not stay."

"Then . . ."

"I could become a governess. I have some jewels that I could sell."

"But you are a lady," Celia said in a horrified voice.

"Someone useless, you mean." Jenna fixed her gaze on the land ahead. Martinique. A part of France. Her country's enemy.

Needing something to do, she started to fold the dress that had nearly been destroyed and placed it in her small trunk.

"My lady, I will do that."

"Nay, you are still feeling ill. I am not useless, Celia." The words were more snappish than she'd intended. She felt so helpless at the moment. For a few hours, anyway, she had felt needed and wanted. Then she had been so lightly dismissed by the captain, her offer so easily rebuffed.

But she had idea.

The question was whether she dared.

Alex saw the *Charlotte* at anchor as the *Ami* sailed into the harbor at Martinique. So the ship had made it. He made a note to give the second mate, Marcel, an added bonus. It looked battered, but not nearly as badly as the *Ami*. It had probably avoided the heart of the storm.

Still, the blow had taken its toll.

Marcel was obviously alerted to his arrival. He stood on the *Charlotte*'s deck as the *Ami* anchored next to it.

"Pleased to see you, Cap'n," he yelled. "We was worried about you."

"And I you," Alex said. "Did you see the British frigate?"

"Nay."

"We had to go into the storm to lose it."

"No sign of the Sassenach around here."

"Have you been into town?"

"Nay, I was going to wait until you appeared." He grinned. "I knew you would."

"Good lad. Let some of the crew go into town now. They deserve it. And give them each a guinea."

"Aye, sir."

Alex turned back to his own crew as the anchor was lowered. He wanted to see the French governor first to hear whether there was any news—or changes regarding their welcome since the last time they visited the island.

"Hamish," he said. "You are in command while Claude and I go ashore. I'll try to find a doctor."

"And the prisoners, sir? They are a sorry lot after the last day."

"They can come on deck," Alex said, "but I want them guarded. Hopefully we can release them in a few hours."

"And the Campbell lass, too?"

"And why not?" Alex said shortly, even as he realized the Campbell had charmed the old grizzled Scotsman who hated as much as he did.

Hamish shrugged yet continued to watch Alex steadily.

"She has been . . . useful," Alex admitted. "But she was a passenger on the *Charlotte*. We cannot keep her. She is to be married on Barbados."

"I dinna think she is that eager to go."

"Every lass is eager for marriage." But he knew that was not right. Many women married because they were forced to make a good alliance, or because they simply found that to be preferable to being the barely tolerated spinster of the family.

For some unfathomable reason, Alex did not want to see that happen to Jeanette Campbell.

He watched as the anchor was lowered.

"Should we lower the quarter boat?" Hamish asked.

Alex felt a rare moment of indecision. "In thirty minutes. I want to check on Meg."

He saw a twinkle in Hamish's eyes and silently damned the man. He was not going to see the Campbell lass. It was a matter of supreme indifference to him that she would soon be leaving the *Ami*.

Good riddance.

But first he needed to know how Meg felt.

He went down the companionway, hesitated at the passage that led to his cabin, then turned in the opposite direction to where Meg received care.

Robin was, as usual, at Meg's side. She was clutching his hand as if it meant her life. Alex saw pain in her eyes.

"Meg?"

"I am better," she said.

But she was not. He knew it. He had thought the fever had gone down, but now he wondered. Fever spots reddened her cheeks and her eyes were far too bright.

"I see," he lied.

Robin looked up at him with real fear in his eyes. Alex had seen fear in his eyes before, but never like this.

"Where is Lady Jenna?" Meg asked.

"Jenna?"

"She asked me to call her that," Meg replied.

Jenna. The name seemed to fit her far more than Jeanette did. Jeanette was formal, aristocratic. Not the lass who obviously loved the sea, stood up to privateers, and had a way with children.

"We have reached Martinique. She is leaving."

"Nay," Meg said.

"There will be a doctor there."

"I want her."

Alex was stunned. He knew that Meg had been drawn to Jeanette Campbell. Perhaps because of the songs or the softness so long denied her. He had no idea how important that connection had become. "She is a Campbell."

"She is not like them," Meg said.

He wanted to say the Campbell lass had been trying to save her own life. But that would not be the entire truth. He had seen the tenderness in the woman's eyes, something she could not disguise.

"She is going to get married. She could not stay, even if she wanted to."

"Will you ask her?" Meg's eyes were pleading.

"Why?"

"She makes me feel better, as if she really . . ."

Alex ran a rough, calloused finger along her cheek. "A lot of people love you, Meggy," he said. He surprised even himself with the words. He had never used the word before with the children.

Meggy's eyes filled with tears. An ache filled his heart. He could help her. He could demand that the Campbell lass—he could not think of her in any other way—stay aboard. Hell, his life would be forfeit anyway if he were captured.

He had nothing to lose.

But could he destroy Jeanette Campbell's life, no matter how much he hated her clan? She *was* to be married. And if she stayed aboard the ship, she would be in as much danger as the rest of them.

For Meggy's sake. Why did he think that would mean more to the Campbell lass than her own wedding?

Perhaps because he never would have thought that even he would put this child before his own goals. Because he now knew it was possible to care beyond revenge and hatred, even unwillingly.

"I will talk to her," he said, his fingers clenching into fists. "I cannot make her stay if she wishes another life."

Meggy looked up with big, luminous eyes as if he were God.

If he were, he would cure her with a touch.

Since he was not, he had to approach a Campbell. *God help him.*

Jenna had been told to stay in the cabin. But she wanted to see Meg. By the saints above, she was going to do just that. She could not leave the wee lass without at least a good-bye. She hoped it would be only a temporary good-bye.

She planned to appeal to the governor. Surely he would understand the need for a child to be in a woman's care.

Meg was no relative of the captain's. If that tactic failed, well then, she'd heard the ship was looking for new hands. Even at her short height, she was as tall as some of the sailors.

If an eleven-year-old lass and twelve-year-old lad could stow aboard, then so could she.

She would lose her reputation forever. She did not care.

She paused at the mirror. She had changed into a clean dress, a green one she knew turned her eyes to a shade of aqua. She thought about putting on a pair of gloves, but to what purpose now? Everyone had already seen her mark. She did pin a cap over her hair to keep it from flying wild. How she wished to wash it.

She turned to Celia. "Stay here. I will be back."

She tried the door. It was unlocked. She went through the empty passageway. She supposed most of the hands were abovedecks. She quietly opened the door to the sick bay, not wanting to wake Meg if she were sleeping. Instead, she saw the captain sitting next to her, Meg's small hand in his large one. Neither of them saw her at first, and she was startled at the strength of the bond between them, the tenderness in the captain's face.

Until he turned around and glowered at her.

Her fingers curled around the edges of the door. "I want to say good-bye to Meg," she said.

He rose, his height dwarfing her. He had always been impressive in stature, but he was intimidating in other ways as well: his cool eyes, the grim set of lips permanently hovering on the edge of a smile. It made him look dangerous and wicked and oddly appealing.

"How is she?" she asked softly, refusing to retreat.

"The same. I hope to find a doctor in Martinique."

"Can he do anything more than Hamish?"

He shrugged helplessly. It was difficult to imagine the man being helpless about anything.

Then he caught her gaze and held it. "Are you anxious for your marriage?"

Stunned, she could only stare for a moment. "That, sir, is none of your business."

"Nay," he agreed. "It is not. Except . . ."

She blinked. The intimidation had been replaced by an uncertainty. A rare uncertainty, she was certain.

"She has been asking for you," he said reluctantly.

Jenna felt her heart beat rapidly. Meg wanted her. Someone wanted her.

Remember your duty. Your promise.

No one would really care. Probably not even her intended husband. He could send away for another wife, one who would probably please him more. But then what would she do when Meg was better and she was put ashore?

And she would be put ashore. She had no doubt about that. She was being tolerated only because the child had asked for her. "I can stay on board until you leave Martinique," she said.

"You did not answer my question," he said.

"What difference does it make?"

"I would not want to be responsible for destroying your future."

"A Campbell's future?"

"Perhaps just one Campbell," he said.

There were other comments she could make. She saw by his clenched jaw that every word was difficult for him.

"I will stay as long as Meg needs me," she said instead. "But I want Celia to be put ashore and made safe and comfortable."

"It will be done, Lady Jeanette," he said stiffly. He was standing close. Very close, and she felt the heat from his body, fancied, even, that she could hear his heart beat. For a moment, her breath seemed to leave her, and she thought . . . for the barest moment . . .

He moved away, leaving her to stand alone. "Jenna," she said, somehow feeling it necessary that she say something. "My name is Jenna."

● ● ●

It would have been easier, Alex supposed as she stepped down into the quarter boat, if the woman had refused. If she had even protested. It was only now that he realized she had not answered his question about her forthcoming marriage.

She'd simply looked . . . relieved. He did not want to like her. He did not want to admire her spirit, her willingness to remain among enemies for the sake of a child.

In truth, for a moment, she had looked uncommonly appealing with the white cap holding long golden brown tresses in place and those expressive eyes wide with surprise. He'd been stunned to realize he wanted to kiss her. And even more so at how much he wanted to do it.

It had taken all his strength to take a step backward. She was a Campbell. She was on her way to wed another. She was, he'd reluctantly realized, an innocent even if she had Campbell blood.

And he was the devil.

He told himself it would be just for a few days here in port. Then he could rid himself of her as planned.

Claude looked at him curiously. Alex said little to him as they discussed what they would tell the French governor and how much of a bribe they would offer him to allow them to drop off the passengers and sell the *Charlotte* here. He would grumble that it might provoke the English, and that right at this moment there might be a peace treaty.

Then he would claim a substantial percentage of the prize in the name of the French government, which would receive damned little of it. Alex had already played this game a month earlier. It was one reason he'd sent the first prize back to France, but he simply could not do that again. His crew was already too small.

"When do we take the *Charlotte*'s crew in?" Claude asked.

"This afternoon, I hope."

"And the Campbell mademoiselle?"

"She will be staying a few days."

Claude's brow furrowed, but he wisely said nothing

more about the Campbell lass. "What about the personal belongings?"

"Lady Jeanette can keep hers. The others will be allowed only enough to get them to where they are going."

Claude nodded.

Alex's attention turned to the small group on the docks awaiting their arrival. Among them were several uniformed officers and a patrol of blue-coated soldiers.

Alex and Claude exchanged glances.

As they stepped on the dock, the patrol surrounded them, and the officer addressed them. "The governor wishes to see you."

Alex nodded. He leaned down and told the senior crew member in the quarter boat to row to the *Charlotte* and tell its master that he was not to let any of his men leave the ship at the moment. He said the words in Gaelic.

"What are you saying?" the officer demanded.

"Just that they should stay aboard."

The officer looked at him suspiciously. "Any attempt to leave will be considered an act of war."

A chill ran down Alex's back. Had a peace treaty been finalized? And if so, was one of the conditions the seizure of his ship? And his crew?

He nodded to the quarter boat crew to return to the ship, then turned and with Claude and the escort strode toward the governor's house, wondering whether this would be the last time he knew freedom.

And, bless all the saints, what of Meg and Robin and his crew?

And the Campbell lass?

Chapter Thirteen

Jenna stood on deck and watched with endless fascination the small but active port of Fort Royal.

Several large ships, most flying French flags, were anchored in the natural harbor. A number of small fishing boats rocked at their moorings.

The town itself was colorful, with whitewashed buildings set against the rich, dark green of the foliage.

She looked for a glimpse of the captain, who had dressed for the occasion in dark blue breeches and waistcoat over a linen shirt. The color emphasized the Atlantic blue of his eyes and his dark hair.

He had been gone for hours.

She still felt the electricity that had darted between them in the hallway, still knew the urge that had made her look up at him, still experienced the heat that had flooded her at the glint in his eyes. He had wanted to kiss her. He had come very close to it.

She had come close to willing him to do it.

No man had ever looked at her with desire in his eyes. It was a new and intoxicating feeling.

But she knew it would come to nothing. He would

never consider an alliance with a Campbell. He'd made that clear.

She could never consider an alliance with a man of violence.

A man without a country. A man who was wanted by at least one country. *Her* country.

She wanted peace and contentment and family.

And yet . . .

She could not get his face from her mind, nor the almost chagrined offer he had made. She could tell how much he cared about the children, when he'd asked her to stay. Not demanded. Requested. He had even voiced concern over her marriage. The expression on his face had told her it was one of the most difficult things she'd ever done.

He had done it for Meg. And that touched her heart. No true villain would be capable of such an act to one he considered an enemy.

She glanced back at the hatchway leading below. At least Meg was resting. But the lingering fever worried Jenna. After months of hiding in the Scottish mountains, Meg simply did not have the strength to resist it. She had the will, though.

Jenna had come up to get some fresh air. She had, she knew, also hoped to catch a glimpse of her enigmatic captor. But she soon discovered he had not yet returned and that the crew was getting restless, even nervous.

Probably because they were under the guns of Fort Royal.

She wondered whether she too should be nervous.

Why did he not return?

"Do you see him?" Robin appeared beside her.

"Who?" she said, not liking that sudden moment of guile. But she didn't want anyone to realize she was actually watching for the captain.

"The captain. Will," Robin explained.

"I was looking at the mountain," she said.

"It's a volcano," Robin offered. "Will told me about it the last time we were here."

"Did you know Will before . . ."

"Culloden Moor?" Robin finished.

"Aye."

"Nay," Robin said shortly.

Jenna knew from his tone that she should not persist or she would break down the small trust she had already established with him. "The crew likes him," she observed, choosing a less sensitive topic.

"Aye," Robin said unhelpfully.

"He must have been at sea before."

"He would have to tell you that," Robin said, turning his gaze from her and searching the wharf.

Another hour went by, then another. She continually went down to check on Meg. She was awake the second time, and Jenna sat with her, trying to make conversation without saying anything that might upset her. She certainly was not going to ask any questions about "Will."

"How do you like the sea?" she asked. That seemed a fairly innocuous question.

But Meg's lips turned down in a frown. It took several moments before she mumbled, "I like it."

But could she really? The only lass among so many men. No female to talk with. No one to answer questions. No mothering. Little gentleness. What was her past life like, or had the horror of the last eighteen months completely clouded the past?

"I like it, too," Jenna finally said. "There is something liberating about it."

"Lib-erating?"

"Making you feel free," she explained.

"Did you not feel free before?"

Meg was asking her questions now. Jenna hoped that talking and thinking of something other·than her wound would be good for her.

"Nay," she said.

"Why?"

"Because of the birthmark on my arm," she said frankly. "A lot of people believed it is the mark of the devil. They feared me. And my parents thought it best if I did not appear in—"

"But that is no' your fault," Meg said with indignation. "And I did no' even notice," she added.

Of course she had. Everyone did. No one could help but notice. But pleasure flooded Jenna at the heated defense. She could not remember when anyone had defended her. That it came from a badly injured eleven-year-old lass made it even more . . . touching.

"Thank you," Jenna said.

"But ye are to be wed," Meg said. "He must not care, either."

Jenna could not say anything. It was terribly humiliating that she was wedding someone who had never seen her, who possibly did not even know about the birthmark. She flinched at the idea that people would believe she was so desperate that she would travel half the way around the world to wed a man she'd never met.

People? No. The captain.

"He says not," she said. She did not know whether that was true, but it was what her father had told her.

"I think you are bonny," Meg said in a vehement defense.

"Thank you."

"But you are, Jenna," Meg protested.

A warmth enveloped her at the use of her name combined with the child's protectiveness. How ironic that a child not yet twelve sensed something that Jenna had never expressed before, not even to herself.

"So are you," she said with a smile.

"Nay, I am plain. My ma used to say so. She said I was too much a hoyden to ever get a husband." Meg tried to sit, and she grimaced, but still she did not cry out.

"You can say something," Jenna said. "Scream, cry, yell."

"That would no' do any good," Meg said with the certainty of one who knew.

Jenna wondered if Meg would ever cease touching her in so many ways.

Meg was still too warm, the wound still too raw for Jenna's satisfaction. The pain was also still too intense.

"Where's Will?" Meg asked as she shifted her position, then sat back with a little sigh of relief.

"He's gone ashore."

"And Robin?"

"He's watching for the captain."

A flicker of worry passed over Meg's face. Jenna wondered whether the lass would always worry about people leaving her, or being taken away. "It is a French island," she said. "He will be fine." *Selling English goods.*

"Will you see if he has come back?" Meg asked.

"Aye, if you wish it."

Meg nodded, her eyes huge and red-rimmed. Fear was very much in them. For the captain? For Will? The two were the same yet Jenna sometimes had problems uniting the two. The captain was ruthless, reckless, emotionless. Will was the man who had touched Meg so gently.

She stood. "I will be back." She wanted to tell her to get some rest, but Meg would not do that now. Something was bothering her. Some instinct told Meg all was not well.

Jenna hurried up the companionway to the top deck. The number of men watching had grown. The tension had become palpable. One of them particularly seemed agitated. Burke, she remembered. He had been down to see Meg several times, though he never directly addressed Jenna. It was obvious that he held her Campbell heritage against her as much as his captain did.

"What is wrong?" she asked Robin, who seemingly had not moved from the place he'd been earlier.

"The captain cancelled orders for the crew to go ashore. That is unusual. And there has been no sign of him."

"Perhaps someone should go into town and—"

"He said to wait."

"And everyone does what he says?" It was a ridiculous question. Of course they did. He was the captain, but he was more than that to many of them. She'd learned that, though she did not yet entirely understand why.

"Aye," Robin said. "Most of the time," he added honestly, and she was reminded that he and Meg had stolen aboard.

"We need a doctor," she said. "Cannot someone go ashore and ask for one, and perhaps ask about the captain at the same time?"

Robin's face brightened. He turned to Hamish who'd apparently taken over command of the ship "Should we send a boat for a doctor?"

Hamish frowned, then nodded. "The captain did say he'd be seeking a doctor."

She did not say more. She had planted a seed, and now she had to let it grow. If she pressed, then they would be suspicious.

She was doing it, she told herself, only for Meg's peace of mind, certainly not for her own.

In minutes, Hamish was calling for volunteers to go in the longboat into town to find a doctor and see what they could find out about the captain.

Burke stepped forward, but Hamish shook his head. "The captain wants you here." Another man, and then a third volunteered. Jenna wanted to go, but she knew that was out of the question. They might have become more tolerant of her, but she was still a prisoner on board.

Still, she could tell Meg that they would have news soon.

Alex fumed in the handsome prison to which he and Claude had been relegated.

The interview with the governor had not been productive. Apparently he'd been intimidated by English threats. The island had been attacked—and taken—more than once by the British.

He'd learned that a neutral ship had visited Martinique with a warning from the British authorities in Barbados. It was known that a pirate was operating in the Caribbean, and if the French in Martinique helped the pirates in any way, they would pay a price for it. Since the peace treaty between the two countries was apparently nearly completed, the governor himself could be charged with crimes.

The governor obviously believed the threats. He was a timorous man who was greedy. Alex suspected he feared an investigation of the large sums he took to expedite the sale of British goods on the island.

He and Claude were prisoners while the governor vacillated between greed and fear. Louis Richárd did not want to return the *Charlotte* to the British and lose all the commissions and bribes. He could, of course, seize the *Ami,* but he was not quite sure of the importance of Alex's backers in France.

The governor obviously had not expected Alex and the *Ami* to return, much less with an English prize and English passengers. So he dithered, insisting in the meantime that Alex and Claude stay as his guests in his residence. Well-guarded guests.

Alex had tried to tell the governor they needed a doctor. The man had not listened. He obviously had not wanted to give Alex a chance to send a message to the ship and allow it out of the harbor until he'd made a decision.

Alex paced up and down the room, as Claude drank from the bottle of wine provided by the governor along with a platter of roasted chicken, cheese, and fruits.

"You should try this wine," he said. "Our host has good taste."

"Probably from the last ship I brought in," Alex replied.

"His greed knows no end. He wants the *Ami*. He wants to soothe the British by giving them the *Charlotte*."

"And your head," Claude added helpfully.

"We have got to get the hell out of here," Alex said. "If that treaty . . ."

"Oui," Claude said cheerfully. "We will all hang at the end of an English yardarm."

Gallic insouciance. It drove Alex mad. "Just think of a way out."

"Without killing some Frenchmen and becoming hunted men in France and every one of its possessions as well as every English one?"

"Aye."

"That might be more . . . *difficile.*"

Alex went to the window. There were two soldiers outside that, too. He looked out at the ships in the harbor. "Do you think he is acting on orders from France?"

"Non. He has his own problems here. Too little protection from France and a very big threat by the English. And he is greedy. He knows a peace treaty is likely and is using that excuse to seize our ship for himself and pacify the English with the *Charlotte*."

Alex cursed under his breath. He'd not liked the governor from the moment he met him. "What if we escaped and went to sea?"

Claude shrugged. "If we make it out under the guns, there is little he can do. I do not believe the French government would appreciate his greed. That could be one of the problems. He might like the idea of our being taken by the English. There would never be tales of bribes. For every dollar the governor takes in bribes, the French government loses."

"We will have no safe haven."

"We have none now, Captain."

"Then let us find a way out of here."

Claude took a sip of his wine. "Without killing too many of my fellow countrymen, I hope."

• • •

The quarter boat returned to the ship. Robin climbed up the ladder like a monkey. "The doctor will not come on board, but we were given permission to take Meg to him," he said to Jenna, who was waiting.

"Where is the captain?"

Robin frowned. "They just said he was meeting with the governor. But he's been gone eight hours, and there have never been soldiers on the dock before. They will not let anyone come ashore except Meg and whoever comes with her."

"I would like to go with her," Jenna said.

He frowned. "I don't think the captain would like that."

"He was going to release me here anyway," she said.

Hamish stood beside them. "I donna like this," he said. "Any of it."

Robin swallowed hard. "If we get ashore, maybe we can find out something about the captain."

Hamish brightened slightly at that. In her brief observations, Jenna thought he was a man who was competent when told what to do but unwilling to make decisions on his own.

Jenna wanted to say something, but she was still viewed suspiciously if not with the original hostility. But she too wanted to know where the captain was and whether there were problems, or perhaps if the peace treaty had been completed. She did not care about the captain's fate, she told herself, but she did care about Meg and Robin and Hamish and some other members of the crew.

"I'll tell Meg," Jenna said.

Robin nodded as he looked at Hamish.

"Aye," Hamish said, "Robin can go. He knows that Frenchie talk."

"I'll get Meg ready," Jenna said. "How can we get her down?"

"Hamish can carry her," Robin said.

Jenna nodded, then went down the companionway to

the sick bay. Meg was awake, her face clammy. Still, she summoned a piece of smile. "Is Will back?"

"Nay, not yet. But we are taking you on shore to see the physician."

"A real one," Hamish added.

"I want Will." Now she looked like the child she still was. Her lips trembled.

"I know you do, Meggy," she said, using Robin's pet name for her. "But perhaps Robin can find out something when you go ashore."

Like Robin's face had lit earlier, Meg's did now. "Oh, miss, do you really think so?"

"Aye."

"You like him, too." It was a statement, not a question.

"I want him safe for your sake," Jenna said cautiously.

But Meg ignored the reason. Instead, she nodded solemnly. "Will is very handsome. I will marry him someday."

"What about Robin?"

"Well, Robin, too."

"You cannot marry them both."

"Nay, I suppose not," Meg said with a quick grin.

"Now come, I will help you dress. Then we will go out on deck. Hamish will carry you down to the quarter boat."

"I want you to go, too," Meg said, surprising her.

"I do not—"

Meg stuck out her lower lip in a stubborn expression Jenna was beginning to recognize. "I will no' go unless you do."

"You must go and have your arm mended," Jenna said.

"Will it get better?" The child was back. Uncertain. Afraid.

"Aye, it will. The doctor ashore may have medicines we do not have."

"I did not mean to go on deck," Meg said.

"I know, love." She leaned over and put her hand on

Meg's forehead. Still too warm. "I would have done the same thing."

"You would?" Meg said doubtfully.

"Aye; now we must get you ready. I have a clean shift you can wear. It will be much too big but I understand you stole away with very little."

"I wish I were a lad."

How many times had Jenna wished that she had been born a man with choices?

She would not have chosen to be a warrior. She would have liked to be a doctor, or even a farmer. She would have liked to sail to many places. She would have liked to have some control over her life.

"Then," she said logically, "you could not marry either Will or Robin."

Meg's mouth screwed up in consternation. She evidently had not considered that before.

"I'll be back soon," Jenna said.

She went up to the quarterdeck with Robin, who pressed her case. "Meg will not go unless Lady Jeanette does," he told Hamish.

Hamish looked as if he were being plagued by all the demons in hell. "All right then," he said reluctantly. "Mickey can go with them."

She tried not to smile as she hurried to her cabin. Celia was not there. She wondered where she had gone, then felt relief that her friend was well enough to leave the cabin.

Her dress would be suitable, but she hunted in her trunk for the old armor of gloves. She found a pale green pair which would match her dress and started to pull them on. She stared down at the glove that covered a mark that had ruled her life.

No one on the ship seemed to care about it. The captain's gaze never lingered on it. Neither had Hamish's nor Meg's nor Rob's. If they did not care, why did she? Why did she worry about what a stranger might think?

Or her intended husband?

She had feared his reaction ever since she had stepped on board the *Charlotte*. She had carefully kept her birthmark secret from the other passengers on that ship. It was only when she had started to care for Meg that she'd almost forgotten about the birthmark.

She pulled the glove back off. She would not hide any longer. It seemed she had spent her life hiding.

With a bravado that was new, she gathered up Meg's clothes. She had not been able to get rid of all the blood. A pink stain lingered on the rough wool shirt Meg had been wearing.

She riffled through the trunk to try to find something that might be altered. Celia was wonderful with a needle and thread.

She was surprised to find the pouch of jewelry she'd not had time to sew into a dress, nor had searched for until now. So the captain had not taken it as she had expected.

Jenna sat on the bed and regarded the trunk, the pouch, the gloves.

The prospect of an unknown, unmet husband.

The long absence of the captain.

She should welcome the thought that he might be having difficulties. That he might be stopped. That he might be held for the British. That he might hang.

Her heart skipped every time she considered such a possibility.

Because of the children, she told herself. For no other reason.

She took the clothes she had set aside for Meg and left the cabin. She could not linger or the French authorities might change their minds. The physician may have nothing more than Hamish, but the ship's stock of medicines seemed pitifully small to her.

She hurried back to Meg with the clothes in hand and helped her dress. Then she called in Hamish, who was waiting outside with Robin. Hamish picked Meg up and cradled her as Rob led the way up the companionway.

Day had faded into dusk. A few stars were barely visible, and a cool breeze wafted over the ship. The sails had been furled and the deck seemed strangely silent.

The quarter boat below was already manned by oarsmen. Jenna did not look forward to climbing down the ladder in her skirts and petticoat and wondered briefly if Meg had not had the better idea.

Hands reached out and helped her into the boat. Robin clambored down like a monkey. Then came Mickey, Meg holding on to his neck as he carried her down and lowered her to a seat. Dressed in the shirt and trousers, and with her cropped hair, she looked every bit the lad she'd wanted to be. Her face was pale, her lips locked in a grimace, and the smallest sigh escaped her lips as she leaned against Robin.

In minutes they reached the wharf. The seamen tied the boat up and helped Jenna out, then Meg. A platoon of soldiers made no effort to help.

The man seemingly in command stepped forward.

"Docteur?" Jenna asked in French.

The soldier in command just stared at him

"Aye," Mickey said. "And where is our captain?"

The man shrugged. He turned and said something to one of his men, and the soldier gestured for them to follow. Robin followed with the rest, then seemed to disappear down a street.

The lad spoke French. So did she, since it was a fashion among Scottish and English aristocracy. She had always loved the language, the beauty of its sounds, and hoped it would serve her well now. She wondered whether Captain Malfour spoke French. Most likely, if he had been part of Scottish aristocracy.

They arrived at a white building, and the soldier led the way up some stairs to a second-floor door and knocked. It was opened by an older man, who apparently had been alerted to their visit.

Mickey carried Meg inside, while the soldier hovered in the doorway. *"Qù est le garçon?"*

"He went back to the quarter boat to wait," she said in French.

The soldier looked dubious, but said nothing else.

The doctor clucked as he unwrapped the dressing on Meg's shoulder.

"What have you been doing for her?" he asked in broken English.

"Lint dipped in oil," Jenna said. "I cleaned it first."

"It looks as if the wound has been stitched several times."

"Aye. They were torn out during a storm."

The doctor nodded. "She should be bled every few hours," he said. "And given bark for pain."

"I have given her laudanum."

The Frenchman grimaced. "It is addictive," he said. "Bark is preferable. And the poultice should be of bread and milk."

"We had no milk," Mickey replied.

"It is inflamed," the physician said, "but there is not yet gangrene. She should be bled."

"Nay," Mickey said. "She is too weak already."

Jenna nodded in agreement. She had never seen the advantage of bleeding an injured person. Many had already lost too much blood. The theory, she knew, was to rid the body of "bad" or diseased blood, but it had always seemed foolish to her. Still . . .

"It is the course of treatment for such wounds," the physician said in French. "That and bark. The bark relieves pain by tightening the vessels, and thickens the matter."

Jenna translated for both Mickey and Meg.

"Nay," Mickey said again.

The physician's face reddened. "You came to me," he said to Jenna.

"I know," Jenna said, "and we were told you were a very fine physician, but Meg has already lost a great deal of blood. Is there not anything else you can do for her?"

The physician's eyes softened. "I will give her bark and

give you enough to see her through this. Give her the bark mixture every four hours. No more laudanum. Use poultices of milk and bread. I will give you some plasters to bind the wound so it will not tear again. The arm should also be splinted. I will do that for you. That is all anyone can do. Just pray the inflammation does not move into gangrene."

Again, Jenna translated but left off the last sentence.

"Is she well enough to travel?" she asked.

He shook his head. "I am not sure whether staying here would change anything."

Jenna had been prepared to stay here, if the captain would allow it. Perhaps even secret the girl away. But . . . after seeing how Meg looked every time Robin came into the room or the captain's name was mentioned, she knew she could not do that.

"Merci," she said as the physician prepared a drink of bark.

Meg looked at it suspiciously.

"It will make you feel better," Jenna explained, holding Meg's head and urging her to drink it. The mixture looked dreadful.

Meg swallowed once. Her body shuddered, then she gulped it down.

"She can stay here tonight," the physician said.

Mickey shook his head.

"Nay," Jenna said, "but if she gets worse we will call you."

The physician put an adhesive plaster on the wound, then rigged a sling. He gave them a bottle of bark.

"Milk?" she said.

"You will have to get that in the morning," he said.

She nodded.

Mickey leaned down, picked up Meg, and carried her to the door. The soldier was outside.

They made their way down to the wharf. Suddenly, Robin appeared at her side.

"They are keeping the captain prisoner," he whispered.
"Why?"

"The British have threatened the island."

An unexpected ache settled in her heart.

Will. The captain. Whoever he was would unquestionably hang if the British caught him.

They couldn't let that happen.

For Meg's sake.

Chapter Fourteen

Under the eyes of the French soldiers, the quarter boat returned to the *Ami*. Jenna climbed aboard with little trouble this time. Then she waited for Meg, who was half slung over Mickey's shoulder, her good arm around his neck.

Once aboard, Meg stood on her own legs, though she swayed a little. She took some deep breaths of air. Then Jenna helped her to her cabin—the captain's cabin. Jenna thought the bed would be far more comfortable than the sick bay cot, and she would use a pallet. She and Celia could take turns looking after her.

Celia was more than agreeable. Still, she searched Jenna's face. "When will we leave the ship?"

"I do not know," Jenna said. "The French are holding the captain and will not let anyone leave the ship."

"Not even us?" Celia said.

"Nay."

Meg eyed them anxiously from the captain's bed.

"I will not leave you," Jenna promised, knowing that she had already made that decision earlier. Wherever Meg went, she would go. Whether it was to this island or on the ship. If the captain or the French did not like it, she would find a way.

"You get some rest," she said, pulling a blanket over Meg. Then she gestured Celia outside. She had to tell Celia what she planned.

"I may remain. If you wish to go home, I will leave you with enough money for your passage to Barbados, and then back to Scotland, or you can stay here or in Barbados. You are good with children, and Mr. Murray may wish you to stay. You can take a letter for me."

"I cannot leave ye, my lady."

Guilt ate at Jenna. She wanted to give Celia every opportunity to change her mind. "I know the sea does not agree with you, and one of the other passengers can help you find passage to Barbados and a position if you wish. I am so sorry I dragged you from Scotland."

"You did not drag me. I thought it would be a glorious adventure. And it would have been if I had not gotten so sick."

Jenna gave her a quick embrace. "You have been as dear as a sister. I want what is best for you."

"It is staying with you, my lady."

"Even if we stay aboard this ship?"

"Even if," Celia confirmed. "And," she added, "there is a gentleman—"

"A gentleman?" Jenna didn't think Celia had been well enough to see any of the prisoners from the *Charlotte*.

"A crew member," Celia said. "A man named . . . Burke. He has been bringing me food while ye have been with Meg."

"Burke?" Jenna had seen him several times. He seemed closer to the captain than any of the others, despite the fact that he did not appear to be an officer. A burly man with little grace, yet when he had been in to see Meg several times, Jenna had noticed a certain rough tenderness in him.

"Aye, my lady. He has been bringing me concoctions to

help my sickness. He said he had the same illness, but that he no longer does. Ye can get used to it, he says."

Celia was slight, pretty, and timid. Jenna could barely imagine her with the rough, gruff Burke who looked like the worst kind of brigand. She wondered how many times the two had been together.

"We will talk later," she said with a smile. "Stay with Meg until I return." She meant to talk with Mickey and Hamish and Burke as to what they intended. She had been invisible most of her life. She did not intend to be invisible any longer.

She planned to fight for Meg. And for herself.

Alex paced his prison while Claude watched him. He cursed, plotted, raged. He had to get released without setting the entire French government against him.

If possible, he would sell the entire contents of the *Charlotte* at a very low price, and get the bloody hell out of these waters. At this point, he was inclined to give the governor whatever he wanted, even if it included the *Charlotte*. Just as long as it did not include his head, the *Ami,* his crew, and the children. The latter was the most important.

In the meantime, the governor had sent the best brandy and food found on the island, obviously in hopes of mollifying him if he decided to let Alex go.

He was no better than the Scots who wavered between one side and another, weighing who might be the winner. That brought Alex's thoughts back to the Campbell, and how he had wanted to touch her, to kiss her. He would be betraying everything he believed. To trust a Campbell was akin to trusting a scorpion.

She did not fit his image of a Campbell. And she was so much prettier than he'd first thought. Perhaps because then he'd just seen a Campbell, not a person who had thoughts and feelings and emotions. Or compassion.

But with her hair free from the tight knot at the back of

her head and the dreadful gloves left off, she was a remarkably attractive woman. Particularly when defiance and challenge set her eyes aglow like the Caribbean sea when the sun hit it.

He had never felt such an attraction before—sharp and deep and so damned unexpected. He'd felt a tingling before with her, even perhaps a stray bolt of awareness, but he'd attributed that to being without a woman for so long.

But that last encounter . . .

Every nerve in his body had responded. More disturbing, his emotions had also been affected. He had wanted to see her eyes brighten. He'd wanted her customary guardedness to fade. He'd ached to touch her face and soothe away the worry.

And he'd wanted to tell her the birthmark meant nothing, less than nothing. He'd sensed her sensitivity to it by the way she protected it, the way wariness entered her eyes when a glance might linger there or when she met someone new. He knew how he felt about his own scar, how he'd had to adjust to the new face and the limp. But those occurred because of decisions he himself had made, not the accident of birth.

She did not seem to realize that she could be a lovely woman, particularly with those fine eyes and hair that glimmered with gold.

She remained a Campbell, though. The rage and hopelessness he'd felt after the wanton destruction of all he felt was good and true about Scotland was deep inside. He'd lost his heart during the bleak days and weeks and months after Culloden, and later his soul. If it had not been for his sister and her new husband, he might have become as cold a killer as Cumberland.

He wondered what she was thinking now. Had she left the ship to try to get passage to Barbados—and her intended husband? And why did that thought hurt? He should be pleased to have her out of his presence.

Don't think about that. Think about getting out of here.

Burke, he knew, would be chafing to storm the town. Unfortunately there were a lot more French soldiers than there were members of his crew. At least Hamish was a cautious man and not one to disobey orders. Alex had left orders that everyone was to remain on board until he returned.

No, he would have to do this on his own.

He might as well have the French navy after him as well as the English. It was better than sitting here, waiting for the English to take his head.

He went to the window. It couldn't be long until dark. If he did not get an audience tomorrow, then he and Claude would fight their way out. Though he had no bloody idea how since they had no weapons.

"I have orders," Hamish said stubbornly.

Burke bristled. "I dinna care what orders you have. We must fetch our captain."

Jenna stood in the shadow of one of the longboats, listening. No one paid any attention to her. In the past few days, she had gone from being treated like a prisoner to being one of the crew because of her care of Meg.

Jenna wondered about her shy maid's words about Burke. He seemed the opposite of everything Celia was and admired. Except, perhaps, for his sense of loyalty.

"No one steps off this ship again until I get word from the captain," Hamish said. "I knew he wanted a doctor to see the bairn, but he said nothing about you."

Burke made a threatening step toward him.

Mickey stepped in between. "Hamish is right. The crew is already short. If more are taken by the damned French, we can never sail from here."

"Then I will go alone," Burke said. "I ain't no sailor, anyway."

"That's obvious," Hamish said acidly.

"I'll go, too," Robin said, stepping forward.

Jenna moved from out of the shadows. "I think it is the captain's decision as to what you should do."

"But they willna let us in to see him, to know what he wants," Hamish said.

"They might let him see his wife."

Everyone stared at her as if she were mad.

"A Frenchman most certainly would let his wife see him. *If* he is a true Frenchman," she added.

Mickey's eyes narrowed. "How do we know we can trust you?"

She shrugged. "How could I betray you? Or him? The English and French are still at war. Captain Malfour was planning to put me ashore anyway. He meant to put all of us ashore. You know that."

"But why would you be helping us?"

"I care about Meg," she said simply. "And she cares about the captain. I would not want her life—or Robin's— at risk."

Burke, Hamish, and Mickey all exchanged glances.

"I do not think—" Mickey started.

"I do," Hamish said. "They willna let us see him. But the lass is right. There is a chance that she could get in to see him. He can tell us what needs to be done."

"They are not letting anyone ashore," Mickey reminded them.

"We can at least try," Hamish said. "The lass can take a pistol under her skirts."

They were talking as if she were not even present. But at the moment she did not mind. Anxiety eddied in her stomach. She had never . . . lied, at least not in a major way. She had never even been in the company of men, other than her family, until this voyage. What if the governor refused to believe she was the captain's wife? She was certainly plain, and who would wed someone with her birthmark? What if the governor discovered who she really was? What if the captain blurted out her name? Then her future would indeed be ruined. Pretending to be the wife of a pirate captain voluntarily was far different than being a captive.

And would the captain even want the assistance of a Campbell?

Heat rose in her as she remembered that electricity between them, then the way he had stalked off as if she were a viper.

"'Tis the best thing. We can do nothing withou' him." Hamish's voice broke into her thoughts, and she straightened, trying to look more confident than she did. "And the lass is right," he continued. "There is no way she could betray us, particularly with Burke and the lad wi' her."

"Why would they let Burke ashore?"

"He can be my servant," Jenna said, surprising even herself.

Burke glared at her.

"Surely they would not expect a lady to go ashore without protection," she added.

Doubt filled the eyes around her. She had been a captive. Robin was a boy. And Burke did not seem to be exactly trusted by the other crew members.

"I say aye," Robin said.

Mickey looked around. "They will never let ye ashore."

"Then no harm done," Hamish said.

"Will they not wonder why the cap'n never mentioned a wife before?"

Hamish shrugged. "The captain is not a talkative man."

"But she went to the doctor's," Mickey said. "Did she mention her name then?"

"Nay," she said, obviously startling them. Despite the fact they were talking about her, none seemed to remember she was there in their presence.

They all turned to stare at her, appraising her. Studying her.

"I can do it," she said. "And I will not betray anyone. Particularly not Meg."

Hamish shrugged. "Ye can try."

It was dark. Late.

"Should we try tonight or in the morning?" she asked.

"Tonight," Hamish said. "The cap'n's wife will be frantic." He looked once again at Jenna. "I do not think my lady is good at panic," he said with a gentle smile. "Do ye think you can feign it?"

"I'll try."

Hamish's approval was clear. So was Robin's. Neither Burke nor Mickey had quite that much faith. That much was obvious.

"I will look in on Meg, then change clothes."

Hamish looked at her plain dress. "Do you have something more . . . lively?"

Her trunk was in the captain's room with her trousseau. There was her wedding dress, then a sea green dress intended for evening events. She had an emerald necklace to match it. And gloves of the same fabric as the dress.

She had never worn the necklace. The dress had been a last-minute addition to her trousseau, but it was the richest-looking garment she had and by far the most flattering. She hoped Celia was well enough to dress her hair. She could pull it into a knot and brush it, but she'd been kept out of sight for so long that she was inexperienced at dressing her hair. So, she feared, was Celia.

Celia was with Meg in the captain's cabin. Meg gave her a small, tired smile. She was still feverish, though.

Was she doing the right thing? Would Meg be better in Fort Royal with a physician whose best advice was to bleed a patient? Was she risking the child's life?

She had no answer. Only instinct. And instinct told her the child was better off with Robin and the captain and Hamish. People who cared about her and whom she cared about. As much as Jenna wanted her, reality had an ugly way of rearing its head. Meg tolerated her, might even like her, but Malfour was the one who had saved her life, had taken in her mother, had provided for her over God knew how long.

"Can you help me dress, and do something with my hair?" Jenna asked Celia.

"Aye, my lady. Which dress?"

"The green one."

Celia's eyes lit. "Oh, miss, ye do look wonderful in that."

In moments, Celia had helped her with a corset, under-petticoat, then the hooped petticoat. Jenna was not quite sure how she would get in the quarter boat with the hoops but the dress required it.

Once dressed, she sat and Celia brushed her hair until it crackled. She pulled it back, leaving one curl to fall down Jenna's back. Then she helped Jenna with the necklace and adjusted a hat with a green ribbon that tied under her chin.

Lastly, Jenna pulled on the gloves.

Celia used just a touch of rose petal to color her cheeks, then stepped back and viewed her critically. "Oh, my lady, ye look so bonny."

"I have never looked bonny," Jenna said, but she glanced in the mirror just the same. A stranger looked back at her. Her eyes, which she always thought pale, sparkled in the mirror and looked larger and deeper in a face that glowed from its exposure to sun. The green of her dress complemented both her eyes and light brown hair.

"Be careful, my lady," Celia whispered.

Jenna had told her the reason for the transformation while Celia was helping her. "There is no danger."

"If anyone knows wha' ye are doing, ye will be ruined."

"No one will know," Jenna said, though that familiar apprehension fluttered in her stomach again. "I must do it."

"I wish I could go with ye."

Guilt rushed through Jenna. She should have known that Celia would think first of her.

In the past month, her entire life had been turned inside out. All her life, she'd felt inconsequential. It was only when she boarded the *Charlotte* that she began to feel the heady sense of freedom, and then on the *Ami* she'd learned what it was to feel being of worth.

But Celia looked at her with fear in her eyes, and apprehension, and something like real affection.

Jenna hugged Celia. "Thank you," she said. "Thank you for being my friend."

Celia's cheeks reddened.

"I will be back soon," she said.

"Godspeed, my lady."

Jenna glanced once more at Meg, then went out the door and down the corridor to the companionway. She had to go up sideways to accommodate her hoop and even then it swayed upward, revealing much of her stockinged leg. She feared it would show much more when she descended into the quarter boat.

On deck, Burke dropped a coil of rope as she emerged. Mickey looked stunned. Robin's jaw dropped open.

A small smile played across Hamish's face. "My lady," he said with a courtly bow.

Jenna wasn't sure whether she should be gratified or insulted. Did she really look so terrible the rest of the time?

A frisson of pleasure shot through her despite her nervousness about the impending descent. She would truly hate to dispel those looks of admiration by falling into the sea, something entirely possible in these skirts.

Hamish eyed them cautiously as if he had the same thought. "Do ye think ye can hide a pistol under all those skirts?" he asked.

"Aye," she said in a steady voice. At least, she hoped it was steady.

"I have a double-barreled flintlock pistol," he said. " 'Tis only six inches."

She thought about it. "We can tie it to my leg, but it would have to be high and—" She suddenly realized she was discussing things no lady should discuss. She had intended to say under her stockings.

Hamish, strangely enough, looked discomfitted. Robin

looked interested. Burke leered, or perhaps it was his natural expression.

"Just bring it to me with some bandage."

"Aye, my lady," Hamish said, moving faster than she'd ever seen him. No one seemed to think it strange that she was giving orders. Except, possibly, her.

He was back within minutes. She took the pistol from him and balanced it in her hands. Heavy. Then she took the bandage and disappeared around the forecastle out of sight of the men. With no little difficulty, she pulled up her skirt and petticoat with its hoop, but she needed two hands to tie the pistol to her thigh and one to hold the voluminous skirt out of the way.

Unfortunately, she had only two.

She plopped down on the deck, grateful that it was kept fairly clean and tried again. She could not ask one of the sailors to do it. Nor Robin.

She finally took off the hooped petticoat, pulled up the underpetticoat, tied the pistol to her thigh with a bandage, smoothed the underpetticoat, and fought with the hooped petticoat, finally emerging triumphant.

How she'd loved her simple dresses that required no corset, no hoop.

She stood, very aware of the extra weight attached to her leg. She checked to see that her dress covered the hooped petticoat, then stepped out to find rows and rows of seamen watching her. Word must have traveled.

They looked at her curiously. Then they all doffed their caps in something that looked like a salute.

She was embarrassed. She had never been the center of attention before, at least not in a good way. And she had not done anything. Not yet. Except, mayhap, make a total fool of herself.

Hamish stepped up to her. "We appreciate this, my lady." Then before she could reply, he turned to Burke. "You go first and help her at the bottom."

The taciturn seaman did so without comment, climbing

down the net with the agility of a monkey. She looked over the rope railing and saw him join the eight seamen already in the boat below, all of whom were going to see a lot more than was proper.

Robin was next. Then she found herself in Hamish's arms, her skirt and hoop sailing upward for all to see as he swung her over the railing and held her until she found her footing on the ladder.

There was nothing to be done for it. She stepped down carefully, then stood about four feet above the lightly swaying boat, her dress ballooning outward. She also knew her face must be a flaming red.

"Let's go," Burke called. "I'll catch you."

She was not sure whether she trusted him that much, but then she did not trust herself, either.

She let go.

Burke caught her and in a rustle of skirts helped her to a seat in the quarter boat.

She wasn't sure how she would step up on the wharf.

But she would meet that obstacle as she had met the one climbing down.

She suspected the greatest obstacle would be Captain Malfour. He would not be pleased to know he had married a Campbell.

Chapter Fifteen

"Your excellency," Jenna said in French as she was led into Governor Louis Richards' presence. She curtsied. "It was very good of you to see me."

"I did not realize Captain Malfour had a wife," the governor said, his dark eyes devouring her like a shark might a fish.

"He is a jealous man, your excellency. He may feel that you might be a threat to him. A powerful and handsome man like you."

He visibly preened. He was not an unattractive man, and would even be handsome if he did not have such an obvious love for food and wine. His face had a red splotchy look of a man who liked the latter too much.

"I have worried about him," she said. "We have not been married long, and you, a man of the world, must know how . . . sad it is to be parted."

"*Oui, madame,*" he acknowledged with a gleam in his eyes. "You speak French very well."

"*Merci.* My husband has taught me."

"You are Scottish?"

"*Oui.*"

"One of the refugees?"

"*Non,* your excellency. Not refugees. Not in your fine country. We were befriended by the Duc d'Estaige, who helped finance our voyage," she said, remembering a name she'd heard mentioned—and cursed—by her father and his British friends. It was, she knew, an influential French name, and a man who had financially supported Prince Charles. "He will be most appreciative of all the help you have given us. But then we share much, do we not? We have a common enemy. But I feel my husband has lingered too long. 'Tis the grape, I am sure. He does have a tendency to indulge too much. So I came to ask for your help." She had said her little speech without a pause, thus denying him the opportunity to interrupt.

"We too enjoy his company," the governor said, his gaze darting away from hers. "We did not realize we would be detaining him from such a lovely wife."

"You are too kind," she said. "I shall report back to the duc that you have been ever so kind and helpful. I am sure he will find a way to express his gratitude. And in the meantime, may I see my husband? I do wish to scold him for not bringing me ashore to meet you."

He looked uncertain.

"Are you married, your excellency?" She was babbling. But she had no idea what to say to him.

Still, he was listening. *"Oui."*

"Then you know a wife would miss her husband. And feel safe with him, and . . . and . ." She hesitated. "Will you convince him to return to the ship, that his duty lies there . . . with me?" She fingered the emerald necklace. "I would be ever so grateful."

She was trying to give him a way to retreat from keeping the captain prisoner while indicating she had far more influence than, of course, she had. In truth, she had absolutely none.

He dithered, but his gaze did not leave her necklace. "That is a fine emerald," he said.

"An admirer in France gave it to me." Again, she left the impression that it was someone with sufficient money and power to give her such a gift. In reality, it was a family heirloom. At least her family was proud enough not to want to send her to Barbados with nothing.

She saw the intended worry flit across his face. Had he made a mistake in holding the captain? She could almost see him weigh the possibilities: trouble with the English or the ruination of his career.

"May I just see my husband?" she pleaded. "I know he might feel that I will scold him for his neglect, but you are a sophisticated man and . . ." She allowed tears to form in her eyes. It was not difficult. She was terrified. Was she overplaying? Would she make it worse?

Jenna dismissed the persistent fear of losing everything—her future, her reputation, what little regard her family had for her. She had gone this far.

For the children. And oddly, for a man who had shown her more acceptance and compassion as an enemy than her family ever had.

That was the most frightening thought of all.

The governor hesitated, then brightened. "You and your husband can join us for supper. I will inform my wife."

"May I see him first?" she said, not sure at all how the captain would react to being informed he suddenly had a wife. "I have . . . news to tell him."

His eyes widened. There was no mistaking her meaning.

"I have been waiting," she said, "but now I think it is time." Jenna wondered again if she was going too far. And yet she felt as though she was succeeding.

Was it just wishful thinking? A desperation to be useful?

"Ah, but you can do that later. First I would like you to meet my wife. You and she have something in common. Especially now."

Common? Her heart sank. Obviously he meant children. Also obviously he had not yet decided a course of action. Giving him time to think was not in her plan.

"You will have pity on a poor wife," she said desperately, afraid of what might happen if she did not first warn the captain. "I am so anxious . . ."

The governor regarded her for a moment, then went to the door and opened it. He said something almost inaudible to one of the soldiers standing outside, then returned. "Will you join me for a small refreshment, Madame Malfour?"

The lingering fear turned to sheer panic. What if the captain had been summoned? What would be his reaction?

But she tried her best to hide it. "You are very kind, your excellency."

"I have some magnificent sherry," he said.

She had never had anything but watered wine. She certainly did not want to befuddle her mind now. "Thank you," she said, "but I have been ill. . . ."

"Of course," the governor said as he poured himself a large glass of what looked like brandy from the top of a buffet.

"You must tell me of Paris," he said. "It has been a long time."

She tried not to blanch. She had never been to Paris. She had never been anyplace outside her home in Scotland until she had journeyed to London. She tried to remember the books she'd read, even as she kept an eye on the door.

The Holy Ghost, what had she done?

"It is very grand." She started with something she thought innocuous. Every city was grand to her.

"And the salons? Which did you visit?"

She hoped her face did not go white as her heart stopped pumping. "La, so many," she said. "With the prince in residence, the city was lively." She hesitated, then added, "Perhaps I will have a small taste of that sherry."

That, at least, would occupy him for a few moments.

"I miss it," he said, as he went back to the buffet. "The colonials, well—"

A knock at the door, then it opened.

The pirate captain stood in the doorway, his expression glowering, the perpetual smile on his face turned into a frown. She watched as his gaze went from the governor to her, and back again.

She ran over to him and threw her arms around his neck. "Darling," she said. "I have missed you so much, you naughty man."

She felt his hesitation as she looked up at him. His eyes were cloaked as he glanced from her to the governor and back. Then his arms went around her waist and he squashed her to him. She felt the tension in his body, then the quick reaction as part of his anatomy pressed into her.

He bent his head and his lips touched hers. Touched, then scorched. They devoured hers, just as his arms drew her even closer. For a moment, she was senseless, even drugged with sensations that were dizzying. His lips ground fiercely against hers, and against all reason she melted against him. She knew he was playing her game, pretending when he despised her, yet a warm, honeyed feeling flowed through her as she responded in a way that was terribly wanton. Her hands went to the back of his neck as she returned kiss for kiss.

He broke the kiss and raised his head, his eyes unguarded and smoldering for a small second in time. She saw something else in his expression.

Curiosity.

Admiration?

He slowly released his grip on her as if he were reluctant to allow even air between them.

"I told the governor I must see you," she said in soft ragged tones she didn't have to pretend. Her body was singing from his touch, every part of her echoing with sensation from the encounter. "I did not tell you before, husband, but we are to have a child, and you . . ." She stopped, and allowed tears to come to her eyes. It was not difficult.

Not so much as a flicker of surprise crossed his expression. Instead, he bent and kissed her forehead. "What wondrous news," he said.

"Now will you come back to the ship? A pox with business. I have missed you so."

"Ah, sweetling. If only I had known," he said, his arm still around her.

Dear God, but he was quick. Far quicker than she would have been. But then he was a thief and a murderer, and duplicitous.

"Will you come with me, tonight?"

Malfour looked away. This time at the governor.

"I have asked Madame Malfour—and you—to sup with me tonight. You did not tell me you had such a beautiful wife."

Jenna saw the captain's gaze turn back to her, saw the surprise in his eyes at the governor's description. A part of her cringed inside. He had seen her imperfections. He had obviously been acting the part every bit as much as she.

"She *is* beautiful," he answered carefully.

"She tells me you have important friends in Paris. You did not share that information with me."

"I do not brag, your excellency, nor trade on friendships."

"Perhaps you should, or we would not have unfortunate misunderstandings."

She felt him tense.

"I too would like to avoid such unpleasant circumstances," the captain said. "I wish to keep your friendship."

"I—we—have enjoyed your company today and are pleased that you agreed to accept our hospitality."

"It has been . . . quite informative," the captain said.

Jenna looked at the governor. He was suddenly nervous. But still he continued. "I hope you will tell your friends at court that I provided every courtesy."

Jenna was aware of the captain's gaze moving back to her, heated and probing. She did not know whether it was of anger or approbation or something else.

"Of course," he said easily. "Especially if I can finish my business on the morrow and leave on the evening tide."

"Such a rush," the governor said. "There are a few financial matters, but we shall leave that until later. In the meantime, I would like you and your wife to join us for supper."

"I would be honored," the captain said, "but I would also like to see my wife alone."

"Of course," the governor said, all accommodation now that he'd decided that his fate rested more with the Malfours than with the English.

"My first mate would like to return to the ship."

"I will, of course, make the arrangements."

The captain bowed, then put his arm around her shoulder and guided her toward the door. She felt the weight of it and the control behind it.

"In an hour," the governor said.

Captain Malfour nodded. "It will be our pleasure," he said graciously.

He kept his arm around her as they ascended a grand stairway, then walked down a hall to a room where one man stood guard. He looked at them curiously, then stepped aside.

The captain kept one hand on her as he opened the door.

Claude sat at a table with a deck of cards in front of him. He looked up, then stood so abruptly that the chair crashed behind him.

The captain shut the door behind him, then turned to face her. "What in the hell . . . ?"

Claude too had moved to stand before her. His brows were drawn with puzzlement. "My lady—?"

"It was the only way," she started to explain. "The French would not allow anyone to see you and we thought perhaps a wife . . ." She looked up at the captain. "You did not look surprised. I feared—"

"I have stopped being surprised by anything lately," he said. "But why did you do this?"

"Meg," she said simply. "She wants you back. Robin and Burke came with me, but they kept Burke at the wharf."

"And Robin?"

"I do not know. He disappeared."

"Does the governor know who you are?" he asked.

"That I'm a Campbell?"

"Aye."

"Nay. He just believes I am your wife."

"I did not know you were such a good actress."

"Neither did I."

"You are a little fool. Do you know what this will mean if anyone learns who you really are? You will be in as much danger from England as I am, not to speak of destroying forever your chance of marriage."

His words, coldly spoken, were like daggers to her heart. She had not expected gratitude. She had, in truth, expected anger. He would not want her help. And she had been right.

She had not expected it to hurt so much.

She ignored his comment. "The crew did not know what to do. I convinced them I was the only one who had a chance to see you."

His eyes stared through her, as if piercing her very soul. "I will have Hamish's head. And Mickey's, too."

"You will have neither of them if you cannot leave here," she replied tartly, her temper beginning to emerge. She had expected him to be less than enthusiastic about her pretense, but his ingratitude toward his men was intolerable. They worshiped him. "You would prefer to hang?"

"In preference to being married to a Campbell," he replied, but this time there was no bite to the words, only puzzlement.

"And having your child," she added serenely.

He stared at her as if she had two heads. A muscle twitched in his cheek. The unmarked side. "What else did you tell him?" he finally asked.

"That I—you—have friends in powerful positions in Paris."

"And your name?"

"He simply called me madame. He did not ask my first name."

The captain muttered something under his breath. Claude regarded her with admiration. "Clever, my lady."

"I do not think you should call me that," she cautioned.

"Oh, bloody hell," the captain said.

"I have a pistol," she offered.

"You know you can be tried for treason for helping me," he said. "At the very least, it would destroy your wedding."

"It does not matter."

"It *does* matter," he said, fury returning to his voice.

"I did not do it for you," she said. "Meg needs you. So does Robin. And the others. They had no idea what to do."

"They need to sail away."

"They will not leave you."

"They are fools, just as you are." But his voice was ragged, and for the first time she suspected feeling behind the harshness. His gaze bored into her, and she felt the heat from it radiating throughout her body.

She just stood there, still feeling the sensations from his kiss, wondering how that could happen. She had never been kissed before, but she did not think it was always like this, not a world shattering moment. Her blood seemed to flow slower. She was barely aware of Claude's presence. She was very aware of the captain's, of his dark blue eyes and the lips that smiled on one side, and the way he pushed back a lock of hair that fell over his forehead.

"Do any of the other passengers know what you are doing?"

"Nay, they are locked up."

He nodded. "And Meg?"

"She still has a fever. The physician wanted to bleed her, but Hamish and I thought she was too weak."

"Did you tell the physician your name?"

"Nay. It was never mentioned."

Surprisingly, he appeared worried about her, rather than himself.

"You will not be able to stay ashore here now and try for passage to Barbados."

"I know." She found breathing difficult. The electricity between them was alive now. Alive and sizzling. Tension was compelling, almost visibly drawing her closer to him. His eyes darkened, the usually cool blue now intense.

One of his fingers touched her cheek. "How did you ever get into the quarter boat?"

She swallowed hard, only to discover a lump in the throat that had not been there before. "Hamish literally threw me."

"Does nothing frighten you?"

"A great deal frightens me."

"But not me?"

"Especially you."

"Then why . . . ?"

She did not reply. She had told him a few minutes earlier that she was doing this because of Meg, but at this moment she—and she suspected the captain also—knew it had something to do with him.

His fingers trailed fire down her cheek. Then they caught a lock of hair. "You are very bonny, Lady Jeanette."

"Jenna," she told him again.

"Jenna," he agreed with a wry twist of his lips.

"Then you are not angry?"

"I am furious."

The lump became bigger. But she tried to keep her voice steady. "I think the governor might release you. He believes you have very powerful friends."

"I will let him continue to think so," he said.

"Then you will not need the pistol."

"I have no place to hide it. Where . . . ?"

She felt her face warm. "Inside my . . . stockings."

A smile played around his lips. A true smile, not the half smile that permanently made him look sardonic and as if he were always laughing at—but not with—the world. "A little uncomfortable?"

"Aye," she agreed, heat puddling deep in her abdomen. The discomfort had faded amidst more intriguing physical reactions to him. Her pulse was throbbing much too rapidly and there was a tightening in her chest.

Suddenly, he stepped back and his fingers played with her bonnet ribbons, untying them. The bonnet came off in his hands, and he touched the hair that Celia had worked so hard to contain. A curl fell down on her face.

"You do not stop surprising me," he said.

She had not stopped surprising herself these past days, nay weeks, since she had left home. She had discovered a part of her she had never realized existed. A part that had been buried deep inside by years of being told what she could not do, rather than urged to find those things she could do.

Claude cleared his throat, dispelling the moment of magic, the impression of being totally alone in a world of their own making. Jenna forced herself to step back.

The captain looked startled, as if jerked from a dream. His smile faded, replaced by the suspicious, sardonic look she knew so well.

"Perhaps we should discuss what to do next," Claude said.

The captain nodded. "Do you know what the governor intends beyond dining with us?"

She shook her head. "No."

He muttered under his breath. "Give Claude the pistol in the event the governor changes his mind again. We can hide it in the room."

"I will require some privacy."

The captain and Claude both went over to the window, turning their backs to her. She sighed. Getting even slightly undressed in the company of men was a daunting prospect. So was the prospect of fighting with the skirt and petticoats again.

And her hands and fingers would not work right. They were still trembling from the lingering impact of that moment when the world had seemed to stop.

Alex brooded as he fixed his gaze on the ships in the harbor. The *Ami* lay at anchor. The *Charlotte* within shouting range of it.

Freedom. So close and yet so far.

He'd felt that freedom since the moment he had set sail from France. The frigate had not been in good shape, but it was fast, and Hamish had been invaluable in supervising the sails. It had sped over the waves, and the wind, once they reached the Caribbean, had been warm and welcoming, not like the cold, wet mists that had so plagued them in the Highland caves.

He did not need the warmth now. He felt on fire.

And for a Campbell.

He'd never been so startled as when the door opened and she stood there. He had seen traces of beauty in her, but he'd not been prepared for what he'd seen tonight. The bonnet had a wide brim that framed a face that had been too severe without it. The bonnet softened it, or perhaps it was the green fire in her eyes or the fact that her face had come alive with excitement. If placing her life and her future in jeopardy could bring a glow to her face and sparkling light to her eyes, he had to wonder what kind of life she'd had at her home. Life, or mere existence. Had her family robbed her of the joy and vibrancy he saw in her now? Whatever had brought it about now, it made her infernally appealing.

But his anger did not come from her being a Campbell

or attractive, or both. It came, instead, from the sacrifice she was making.

She had to know she was risking her marriage. Even her life.

That thought was devastating. He did not want that sacrifice. He wanted nothing from her. He certainly did not want to owe her.

He definitely did not want to be attracted to her.

He was. He could hear the rustling of silk behind him. He heard a soft sigh. Then frustration. He wanted to help. He could see her legs in his mind's eye. They were probably slim, most certainly attractive.

She had a pistol tied to her leg—a provocative image. He had to stop thinking about her, and start thinking about how to get through this mess. Could he rely on the governor's possible change of heart, or should he make his move now?

Unfortunately, all he could consider was the woman behind him. His enemy. A woman he had captured and treated as a prisoner rather than a lady. A woman who had stormed the governor's mansion with all the nerve of a born adventurer. A woman who was clearly uncomfortable lying, even to an enemy.

And Robin? Burke? The latter had never been hesitant in taking action. He needed to control events, not be a puppet of them.

Alex heard her voice again. Soft with just a touch of Scottish burr, and it fired something deep inside him.

"You can turn back now," she said.

Both he and Claude turned at the same time. She held out the pistol with one hand as if it burned her.

Claude took it, checked to see whether it was loaded, and found that it was.

Alex looked at the weapon, then at the woman who had smuggled it in. He wanted to reach out and touch her again.

She was everything he never thought he would find in a

woman. She loved the sea, she had cheerfully taken care of a sick child, she was intelligent and adventuresome enough to get to him when no one else had. She had obviously charmed the governor.

The plain Campbell sparrow. How he had underestimated her on all counts.

She was everything he wanted, and she was a Campbell. He was not convinced he could ever get beyond that. Even if he could, what could he offer her? The life of a fugitive. A wanted man. A scarred and crippled man.

A knock came at the door, and a servant indicated that both he and Lady Jeanette should join the party downstairs.

He nodded, then closed the door and turned to Claude. "If they let you go before I see you again, tell the crew to wait and keep the prisoners below. I want them to know nothing about Lady Jeanette."

"And if you do not return?"

"If we are not back by tomorrow night, set sail for France."

"We could not leave you."

"You can, and you will for the children. And the crew."

"And the *Charlotte?*"

"Leave it. Transfer the crew to the *Ami.* Those who can swim should do so; those who cannot go by boat, but do it at night."

"Aye, sir."

"The logs and money are in my cabin. Just make sure the children are aboard this time, and that they reach France."

"What about Burke?"

"He goes, too. Even if you have to knock him out."

Claude hesitated, then nodded.

Alex turned to the woman who had been listening intently. "How long have we been married, my lady?" he asked, trying to keep his voice low enough that no one would hear it.

"Long enough to be expecting a bairn."

He winced at the reminder. "A year?"

"Aye."

"Where?"

"Paris."

Alex nodded. "Any other details I should know?" He tried to keep his voice even. It was not easy with his body still responding to hers. He struggled to keep it in control.

"A great deal," she said, and though her voice was teasing, it also trembled just a bit. She was not nearly as at ease with this as she wanted him to believe.

A knock on the door again.

"I will agree with anything you say," he said.

She raised a dark eyebrow in an expression that was endearing. And challenging. "You will?" she asked doubtfully.

"Aye," he said. "You have trapped me neatly, my lady."

"I do not think you are so easy to trap."

He looked her straight in the eye. He wanted to agree, but it would not be true. *She* had trapped him. In more ways than one. More ways than he would ever let her understand.

"Let us go," he said.

Chapter Sixteen

Jenna could not help watching the captain, studying him, stunned by the ease with which he had accepted her deception. The memory taunted her—of how he had fallen into the role earlier with hands and mouth as intense as the storm they had weathered aboard ship.

They should not have followed each other so easily. But they did. He was a man who obviously adapted to whatever circumstances faced him. He might rebel at them, but then he used them to his advantage.

She was finding it disturbingly easy to do the same.

He rarely showed his emotions, except flashes of anger and just now a glimpse of something else, a momentary warmth and passion that he'd cloaked as quickly as it had revealed itself.

She had no idea now how he felt about her deception, other than he was willing to use it at the moment.

And then what?

Did she go to Barbados now? Had she changed too much in the past few weeks to become the wife of a man who knew nothing about her, much less had any affection for her?

Especially after the heated moments she'd shared with Captain Malfour. She'd experienced startling intimacy and attraction, a glimpse of a splendid world she was not sure she could now ignore.

She also knew, though, that this world would not include the captain, not with his contempt and even hatred for her name. Nor, she thought, could she accept his easy breaking of the law and the peace. There was a way of addressing grievances, and it was not through theft and piracy and murder.

Still, she was chastened to realize that she found a small thrill in his attentions, no matter how fleeting they may be.

For the first time, she felt shame, not for her actions but for the thoughts that followed them.

The servant opened the door to a small salon, and Captain Malfour stood back to allow her entrance. Again, she felt an odd sense of belonging, of a kind of completeness with him.

The governor greeted them effusively. She looked at the captain. He did not even raise an eyebrow, appearing to accept the new cordiality as his due. The governor's wife, Gabrielle, was a thin and pale woman who seemed to hang back from her husband. Still, she could not withhold curiosity.

"My husband said you have been in Paris. How wonderful. I do miss it. You must tell me all the news. He said you knew the Duc d'Estaige. Such a good man."

Jenna's heart sank. Having never met the duc, or been in Paris, she had no answer.

The captain broke in. "Aye, he is, and his wife is the toast of Paris. Her brother is to marry a German princess."

"And the fashions?" Gabrielle asked.

"They have not changed," Jenna said, which seemed a safe reply. Surely English fashions would not be that different from French fashions.

"Your dress would be the envy of Parisians," her erstwhile husband told the hostess, and the woman blushed with pleasure.

"Enough about fashion," her governor interrupted. He led the way into the dining room and to a large table sparkling with silver and crystal at one end. "I thought we would eat at this end," the governor said, "and Madame Malfour can tell us more of Paris."

Trying not to send a panicked look at the captain, she sat down.

"In the meantime," the captain said smoothly, "I would like my first mate returned to the ship."

"You do not enjoy our hospitality?"

Jenna held her breath. There was a trace of a threat in the question.

"My mate has particularly enjoyed it. You have good wine, your excellency, but I have an unruly crew and I would dislike them to become anxious."

The governor's lips thinned, but then parted and turned upward again. "He can go back tonight."

"And my wife and I?"

"I pray that you will stay tonight. We have business to conduct. After supper."

Jenna almost dropped the knife she was using. To stay tonight meant sharing a room with the captain. She did not think she was ready for that.

A gleam came into the captain's eyes. "Her clothes . . ."

"My wife will lend her something tonight, or you can send for something from the ship. I understand two of your crew are outside."

"That would be Burke and the cabin boy."

"Aye, one of them is a lad. They have been fed, but they will not leave."

Jenna froze. What if one of them slipped and mentioned her name?

The thought did not seem to bother the captain, though, nor did the idea of spending the night in the same room. "Then my wife would be delighted to stay here," he said.

"She has been wanting time ashore. And after supper, I'll send the boy back to the ship."

"Done then," the governor said, and started eating.

His wife kept glancing at them. Probably because of the captain's scar, and her own wearing of gloves at supper. They must appear to be an odd couple. At least the gloves hid the lack of a ring.

Jenna was barely conscious of the food, although the captain ate well. She felt like a fly snared in a web, and it did not help that the web was of her own making. How could she get through an evening with the governor's wife without exposing the fact that she had never been to Paris? And how could she get through a night in the same room as the captain?

And ever more important, if the *Ami* was allowed to sail with all aboard, then where would she be going?

She had been carried along like a feather in the wind these past weeks, ever since the letter came about the possible marriage to Mr. Murray. There had been Maisie's fall, the voyage, the capture of the ship, and Meg's illness.

Until she had taken this step earlier today, nothing had been of her own doing. In one impulsive, or perhaps not so impulsive, move, she had perhaps changed her life forever. If she allowed herself to think about it, she knew the knot of apprehension lurking inside would become enormous. Where would she go? The captain could not wait to rid himself of a Campbell's presence. He would use her well enough. But then . . .

"You did not tell me that the Duc d'Estaige was one of your backers," the governor probed.

"I have many backers," the captain replied cautiously. "Not all want their names used. It might be politically unwise for them. My wife does not understand such things."

"Women rarely understand business matters," the governor agreed.

Jenna clenched her teeth at the patronizing words. She

knew exactly why the captain said them but they grated, anyway. She looked at the governor's wife.

A flash of resentment sparked in Gabrielle's eyes, too.

A life of quiet desperation, Jenna thought. Was that what she had bargained for when she had accepted David Murray's proposal?

She turned to Gabrielle. "Do you have children?"

The woman's face brightened. *"Oui, deux garçons et deux filles."*

Jenna seized upon the opportunity to take the conversation away from herself. "Please tell me about them."

She kept Gabrielle busy talking about her children, listening with one ear to the discussion at the table, wondering how she would get through the evening.

And the night.

Alex saw the flash of discomfort in Lady Jeanette's face as their host suggested they spend the night at the governor's residence. He did not want it any more than she. He did not need the infernal attraction that seemed to rage between them every time they were together. But she had created the problem by claiming her need to be with her husband.

The quarters were luxurious and it would be an insult to refuse. He could not risk that, not when he was close to escaping. He only hoped that no British warship would appear in the bay in the meantime.

He also hoped that the governor, true to his word, would release Claude and let him return to the ship, young Robin and the impetuous Burke with him.

Regardless of his distaste at spending the night with the Campbell, he could not help glancing at her throughout the meal. She wore those bloody gloves again, and something inside him rebelled at the thought. She had been so careful to cover the birthmark when he'd first met her, and had continued to do so until it interfered with the care she'd given Meg. It was obviously hurtful to her in more ways than he had imagined.

Except for the gloves, she looked enticingly attractive. Her eyes sparkled as she spoke fluent French to their hostess, and the rose in her cheeks from the Caribbean sun emphasized her amazing eyes. And when she happened to catch his glance, her long dark lashes veiled them in a gesture both shy and seductive. It was a potent combination.

His loins hurt.

He tried to focus on what the governor was saying, even as his gaze continued to return to his . . . wife.

"Ah, the passion of the young," the governor said to him in a low voice. "I can tell yours was a love match. I envy you. She is an appealing woman."

Not beautiful. Appealing. And the governor was right. She had little of classic beauty. Her mouth was too wide, her eyes too large, her face more heart-shaped than oval. But there was something about her, an earnestness that was intriguing for its rarity, an intelligence that challenged, a vulnerability that provoked all that was protective in a man. He had never thought of a woman as a partner before, but now as they sat at this table in common cause, he knew an odd sense of comfort and even rightness.

A Campbell. Bloody hell.

Their gazes met again. A flame leapt into her eyes as the contact lingered, and he knew it most probably was every bit as unwelcome as the ache tormenting him. She had no use for him. She knew him for what he was: a thief and pirate and even worse. And yet for a child's sake, she was helping him at the risk of her own future. She must resent that unreasoning attraction as much as he.

"Oui," he finally said.

"I can tell we will have little business tonight," the governor said. "You are too . . . distracted."

Alex tried to concentrate. "I do have a proposition," he said.

The governor looked at the two women engaged in a lively conversation now. "Your wife offered me those lovely emeralds she is wearing."

Alex felt as if a piece of lumber had just crashed into his chest. "She is a generous woman," he said, "but I hope to make you a better offer."

A broad smile spread across Louis Richárd's face.

"I'll sell the contents of the *Charlotte* to Monsieur Sevier. He bought the last ship I brought here, and I think he would like these particular goods. You can keep the ship yourself to do with as you wish. If you think it best to return it to the English, then so be it. If you would rather make a profit yourself, I will not mention it to my backers. I will give them my share from the contents, instead."

He watched the governor mull over the proposal. The ship was worth far more than its contents. Greed warred with caution on his face. As well as the opportunity of exchanging the ship for England's goodwill, he would not be taking the chance of offending Alex's French backers.

On his side, Alex could leave the island, and with at least a good part of his prize.

The governor finally nodded.

"I would like to see Sevier in the morning. I want to sail tomorrow night."

"I will send someone and tell him of our agreement. He can look over the manifests and ship tonight."

"Merci," Alex said. "And may I compliment you on the wine. I believe there is some very good stock on the *Charlotte,* and I'll exclude that from Monsieur Sevier's purchase."

The governor nodded solemnly. "You are a gentleman, Captain Malfour. I hope there are no . . . misunderstandings between us."

The man was actually fawning where yesterday he had been arrogant and cold and even contemptuous.

Was the change due to the Campbell lass?

No doubt. He owed her.

Owing a Campbell was his worst nightmare.

Or would it be spending the night in the same chamber?

• • •

Jenna wanted the evening to end. She wanted it to continue forever.

As the governor conversed with the captain, she tried to keep the conversation going with the governor's wife. She had never been in society. She had kept to her room, engaged herself mostly in books.

Her governess had tried to instruct her in the conversational arts, but seeing that she was hidden from most of society, Jenna never thought it important, and neither had the governess. The conversational tidbits were mostly inane observations about the weather. A lady, the governess had said, never discussed politics or issues of the day. She would be considered a bluestocking. No man wanted a bluestocking.

But then no man had wanted her in any event, bluestocking or not.

She tried to dismiss that thought. She had been aware of it for too many years. She was unlovable. An unsuitable wife. She should be thanking her father profusely for arranging the long-distance match. That's what everyone said.

But now she found herself conversing perfectly well. Asking questions kept her from answering any awkward ones, and the governor's wife seemed to enjoy the attention of a newly arrived visitor. She wondered if her growing skills had something to do with newfound confidence. She had reached the governor, had possibly changed his mind. She had helped Meg, and had gained the friendship of both her and the lad.

Still, she had to hide the icy fingers of fear and apprehension raking up her back. Fear that the governor would change his mind about releasing the captain. Apprehension about spending time alone with him, the pretense of their marriage becoming too real for comfort, if only for one night.

What had she done?

The minutes crawled on.

Finally, the governor rose. "I understand," he said, "that my guest would enjoy spending some time with his wife. I would not be accused of keeping them apart." He turned to the captain. "My men will escort your mate to the ship as well as the others who came ashore with madame."

Madame. The title seemed strange to her. As she stood, she steadied herself. She'd had several glasses of fine wine, a rare occurrence for someone who rarely drank anything other than watered wine. She'd told herself she did it to be polite, but it was also the stuff of courage, false as it might be.

She thought she had been careful not to have too much. Now she wondered as her legs seemed uncooperative.

She thanked her hostess effusively, then the governor, afraid that she was prattling.

The captain wrapped an arm around her, putting her even more off balance. She did not know how he would react when they were alone. Oh, he had been mild enough when told of her deception, but Claude had been in the room and the governor's soldiers outside.

It did not help that the captain's arm's touch torched a path of heat that quickly radiated to every part of her body.

It did not help at all.

He turned suddenly, as if he too was burned. "I will have that cigar and brandy with you," he said to the governor. "After taking my wife upstairs. I fear she has land sickness."

She remembered Hamish warning her about that, recalled the odd feeling of being at sea when really on land. "Aye," she said softly. "I am feeling a bit . . ."

The governor bowed. "I understand. I hope you have a good night, madame."

The captain guided her out then. She felt oddly compliant. Whether it was due to the wine, the warmth of his embrace, the heady success of her mission, or just plain exhaustion, she did not know.

She ascended the stairs with him, this time with no guard escorting them. She could not doubt her success. And in achieving what she had set out to do, she had likely destroyed any chance she had for a marriage and home and children with David Murray. She had been impulsive. She had wanted an adventure, and she had let her heart rule her head.

Melancholy gripped her. Another result of wine? Or the prospect of the next few hours or the next few days or the next few years?

Too soon, they reached the room where she had been taken earlier. The captain opened the door, and both of them saw Claude sitting in a chair, a glass of wine in his hand.

"You can go now," the captain told him. "Find Burke and Robin and take them back. We sail tomorrow night. Just before we sail, you can row the passengers ashore, but I don't want any of them on deck until we are ready to release them. They cannot know what happened tonight or that Lady . . . Jenna had any part of it."

"Aye," Claude said. "And you? When will you return?" His gaze went to Jenna, who was still standing in the captain's shadow, still held close by his arm.

"In the morning. The governor wants us to accept his hospitality tonight, seeing that I have neglected my wife so badly."

Claude raised a bushy dark eyebrow.

"I do not have a choice," the captain said wearily. "Lady Jenna has convinced him she and I have friends in very high places in France, and that we are indeed husband and wife. We cannot decline his hospitality without raising questions."

"He will let us sail out?"

"Aye. I offered him the *Charlotte*. We will sell its contents. That seemed to alleviate some of his fear of the English. But he could still change his mind. If for some reason we do not make it back, I want you to set sail. It's a new moon. Done slyly, you should be able to escape the fort's guns."

"Leave you?"

"I want the children safe. And the crew."

"They will take their risks with you."

"Nay, they will not," the captain said. "Now go, before our host changes his mind."

"Aye, sir." He said it reluctantly.

"Now!" the captain snapped.

Claude disappeared out the door without another word.

The captain lowered his arm from her waist and walked over to the window. She joined him and looked outside, following the path of his gaze.

Claude emerged from the residence. He was met by Burke and Robin outside. The three walked down the walk, accompanied by one soldier.

The captain turned to her. "I should go back and have that cigar with the governor."

She could only look up at him. She was feeling steadier now, but still had a flutter in her stomach.

"Take the bed," he said curtly. "I will sleep on the floor."

He could not wait to leave her. A chill displaced the warmth that had infused her at his touch. Perversely, she was wounded. She had worried about being alone with him, but it was not because he repelled her. Just the opposite—he aroused any number of wayward feelings in her.

His rejection was devastating. He could not stand being in her presence. The brief satisfaction at accomplishing something faded. She was no more to him than she had been the day he had taken her ship.

She was a fool to even entertain such thoughts, yet they had crept up upon her and would not leave.

She turned away from him, holding herself rigid, trying to keep tears from gathering in her eyes. She remained that way until she heard the door open and close.

A knock at the door sent a jolt of expectation through her, but when she opened it, a maid stood there, her hands full.

"My mistress sent this for you," she said, spreading out a nightdress and robe across the bed. The nightdress was a fine lawn, its neck embarrassingly low, and there were no sleeves.

"*Merci,*" she said as the woman backed out the door.

Jenna slowly took off her gloves, glaring at the birthmark on her hand and arm, then stepped out of the hooped petticoat, watching as the green dress dropped to the floor.

She shed her clothes down to the chemise, then hesitated. Should she wear that, or the nightdress?

Then she realized it did not matter. The captain obviously had no interest in her. But the nightdress was lighter and would be more comfortable. She stood and looked in the mirror as she took the pins from her hair, letting it fall around her face. She should braid it, but . . .

Instead, she crawled into the large bed that dominated the room.

She pulled the coverlet over her and sank in the feather mattress.

And she had never felt so alone in her life, not even when she'd stepped foot on the *Ami*. She'd then had her anger and indignation as armor. She'd built a wall around her heart.

When had it been breeched?

She was appalled when a tear wandered down her cheek and dampened the pillow.

Alex had been stung by the effect of touching the Campbell lass. Even more stung by the vulnerability in her eyes. He had seen so many emotions in them this evening: trepidation, fear, pride. They had all touched him in ways he thought impossible.

Most painful of all was the desire that stirred in his loins. He wanted her. He could not deny that any longer.

He had tried to convince himself that his attraction toward her was nothing more than his lack of female companionship in nearly two years, that it was only the natural need of a man for any woman.

But as he'd watched her during supper, he knew it went much deeper than that. He had been stunned by the very audacity of her actions. That she was intrepid enough not only to do what she had done, but to plan it, was unbelievable. That she had been able to fool a Frenchman and his wife that they were wed was astonishing. That she had bluffed the governor into believing he—Alex—had far more important backers than he ever dreamed of was even more incredible.

That she would do it at all was beyond his comprehension.

He had also been uncomfortably aware of a stab of jealousy at the leering way the governor had looked at her.

To his surprise, he'd taken umbrage at such overt lust.

He surprised himself even more by risking everything by changing his mind and accepting the governor's invitation for brandy. It was the last thing he'd wanted to do.

Next to the last thing, he corrected himself.

The last thing was being alone in a bedchamber with her.

One brandy led to another.

"Your lady was very positive she wanted to be with you," the governor said after the second one.

"She is feeling unwell," Alex said. "She said it must be the bairn. There is a change of moods, I am told, when a woman is with child."

"Oui" the governor said gloomily. "I fear it is true."

"I will purchase something lovely for her tomorrow."

"She is a very interesting woman," the governor said.

Alex could not agree more. *"Oui,"* he said.

"You did not strike me as the marrying kind," the governor said.

"There is always a woman who can make you change your mind," Alex said. He had never quite believed it. A few of his friends had married well, but he had never seen a woman with whom he wanted to spend a lifetime.

But those friends were dead now, their wives either dead or fled to places safer than today's Scotland.

He had given up any idea of a future. He was a poor prospect indeed.

The governor stood. "I will not keep you from her any longer," he said. "My wife has sent up a nightdress and night robe."

"My thanks for your hospitality."

"I . . . apologize for the brief misunderstanding," the governor said. "But we are in a very precarious place here on the island. We are so close to the English and we do not have the French troops we need. We have only the fort, and if they attack from the other side . . ."

"I understand, your excellency. I want nothing to interfere with our mutual interests."

The governor fairly glowed with good wishes. "I too have that desire."

He started for the door, then turned around and leered again. "And say a pleasant good night to your wife on my behalf. As I said, I envy you."

If only the governor knew that the Campbell lass was here only because of two children, not for him. She had no doubt braced herself for his return to the room. She must have felt the attraction between them, but she was fighting it as bitterly as he.

The world was between them. Not just a name.

He suspected the floor was going to be only a small part of his discomfort.

Chapter Seventeen

Alex paused before the room assigned him, trying to decide whether to knock.

But surely she would be abed. Hopefully asleep. He certainly did not wish to waken her.

He opened the door. An oil lamp flickered on a table in the room. She'd apparently left it lit for his convenience.

He pulled off his boots and his waistcoat, then sprawled in a chair, looking wistfully at the large feather bed.

She was lying on her side, her hair spread over the pillow. He longed to go over and run his fingers through it.

Hell, he longed to crawl into bed next to her and sate the ache in his loins. He would not sleep this night. He knew that. Not as long as she was in this room.

Alex saw her dress and the petticoat laid neatly on a chair, the bonnet she'd worn next to it. She had been shielded by clothes earlier. He wondered what armor she wore now.

He damned himself for such thoughts. Yet they would not go away. He trod quietly to the window. Dear God, how he was tempted to leave this room now and return to his ship. But that would belie the marriage they'd claimed, and one lie would suggest another.

To want something so badly, and be in such proximity to the object of that want, was akin to walking through hell.

He suddenly realized that he had not said a kind word to her tonight. Not a compliment or even the slightest expression of gratitude. He told himself it had been his shock, then lack of opportunity. Or was it resentment because he had been thrust into the position of owing a Campbell?

She was no longer a Campbell in his mind. She had, instead, become a woman unfettered by convention and traditional code. In his estimation, that took more courage than a man doing what was expected of him and going into battle. It was that woman who so intrigued and attracted him.

The woman with eyes the color of the sea and the wide generous mouth and the soft and lovely voice.

His nerves tingled. The ache throbbed. His skin seemed to burn even in the breeze that cooled the room.

He turned and found her watching him. In those few moments she had awakened—if she had been asleep at all.

He strode to the bed and sat down beside her. She seemed to withdraw into its depths.

"I did not thank you earlier," he said softly. "I thank you now."

"A Campbell?" she asked warily.

He then saw a small trail on her face. Dried tears. In all that had happened, he had never seen her cry. And then she had cried alone.

He felt like a bastard. A man who had forsaken his sense of justice in favor of hatred of a mere name.

"Aye," he said. "A Campbell. And a brave and bonny woman."

Her eyes widened.

"I did not thank you, either, for all you've done for Meg."

"I did not do it for you."

"I know that," he said, knowing a smile was playing along his lips. How well he knew that.

"Has the governor changed his mind again?" she asked suspiciously, as if she believed he could have no other reason to be kind.

"Nay, you thoroughly charmed him with your tale of a wayward husband and bairn to be."

"I could not think of anything else," she explained, obviously unsure whether he approved or not.

"It did take me by surprise," he said.

"You did not act like it."

"I learned long ago not to react to circumstances."

"And I am a circumstance?"

"Aye, a very intriguing one."

"Why?" Her expression turned from wary to curious.

"Why would you help your captor? The man who kept you from your marriage?"

"Because . . . I did not want the children to be at risk."

"At the cost of your own future?"

He watched her swallow hard. "I have never met the man I was to marry." He saw pain in her eyes, a pain so deep that it reached out and touched a heart hardened to tragedy.

"Then why?" he asked.

"You have seen my arm," she said bitterly.

"Aye, a birthmark."

"Many do not see it that way. They believe it is the devil's mark, or that I am . . . tainted in some way. My family kept me away from others. There were no . . . suitors. Mr. Murray's wife died. He needed a wife, a mother for his children. My father also offered a . . . substantial dowry."

He closed his eyes for a moment. She was being discarded because of something over which she had no power.

He touched her cheek, gently running a finger down the trail of dried tears. "Why did you accept?" he asked.

"I want . . . children."

There was so much anguish in her words. He wondered

whether she had ever been loved for herself, ever felt the security that he had as a child. He and his sister, Janet, had lost everything, but they'd had a heritage of love.

Janet had married the first time for the same reason as Jeanette was giving. She'd lost the one man she'd ever loved, and settled, instead, for a marriage with a man who had three daughters because she loved children. It had been a marriage made, consummated, and endured in hell.

Had Jeanette been sailing toward the same fate?

Yet he had nothing to offer, either. Any woman foolish enough to care about him could soon be a widow with a traitor's name. Still, that odd attraction was more compelling than ever. He saw in her eyes a recognition of that fact, and he felt that they were both about ready to be swept into a whirlpool of currents that resisted all reason. He needed to step back, to get away from her.

Now.

Instead, he smoothed his thumb across her eyebrows, feeling the silk of them, over cheeks, feeling the heat, the softness. "Do not settle," he whispered.

She moved, her hands appearing from beneath the coverlet, revealing the nightdress and its low neck. He could see the slight swelling of her breasts, the slight movement as her heart beat. She regarded him silently, her eyes full of questions.

"My sister married someone because she fell in love with his children," he said. "He was a monster."

"What happened?" she said.

"He died," Alex said shortly, still trying to fight the urge to touch, to comfort, to savor.

"Where is she now?"

He was silent for several moments, unsure how much he wanted to tell her. There was already too much intimacy between them. He could not let her know his true name, nor his sister's, or he could put Janet in real danger, along with her new husband.

"Safe," he said more curtly than he intended.

She nodded. Accepting. For the first time, he wondered whether "safe" had meaning for her. He thought about her earlier words. *My family kept me away from others.* No self-pity. Just a statement of fact.

He had not thought he could feel empathy again. He thought it had all been crowded out of him. Too much death. Too much misery. Too much pain. But now he knew he still felt. He still wanted to right injustices. And Jeanette Campbell had obviously endured an injustice.

What an irony to think such a thing. He who had given up honor.

She asked no more questions, as if she knew she would receive no answers. Her left hand plucked at the top of the coverlet. Her right one, the one with the birthmark, was again under the cover. He turned down the coverlet and took that hand in his.

"You do not have to hide it," he said.

Her face flushed. "I am not hiding it."

"Aye, and there is no need," he said.

" 'Tis ugly."

"Nay," he said gently, surprising himself. He had not realized gentleness was still possible inside him.

He touched her arm, his fingers skimming the length of the birthmark, then back again. "You should not hide it. It is nothing of your doing, and is as natural as those eyes of yours. They are . . ."

Once pretty words had rolled easily from his lips. Once he had had the world at his feet. Once he'd had a face that had attracted lasses. A title that had made him welcome in any household.

Now he had no pretty words, because they would lead to where he could not go.

But her eyes were wide and intent on him. The light from the lamp made her hair look as if it were spun gold. His right hand left her arm and went again to her face. Then, against every grain of sense he thought he had, he leaned down and his lips touched hers.

It was a kiss that he'd never experienced before. Her response, tentative and shy, took his breath away. He had kissed many times, but never had he known the rush of emotions he felt now. A need to bring a smile to eyes that did too little of it, a desire to pull her into his arms and protect her from everything that had hurt her, every cruel word, every taunt.

Stop, he warned himself.

But her hand touched his face in a wondering kind of a way and trailed the scar as if it were something fine rather than a mark of damnation. How he'd hated that scar. It was as if it separated him forever from civilized people.

She did not seem to think so. Instead, there was a tenderness he had never known in a woman's touch before. Sweet and cleansing.

Bloody hell, but his body was tied up in knots, consumed by an ache that had spread to the empty places inside him. He hadn't realized how empty he had become until now. Yes, he had the children, but he'd kept them at a distance, afraid to once more know the same pain he'd experienced when he'd lost his family and friends. Or was it that he hadn't wanted them to know more loss? He'd known from the beginning he could not continue to care for them.

He was a fool. He had no better future today than he'd had earlier when she had intruded into his world with her tale of marriage. Until then, he'd managed to keep her at a distance, even if there had been the intense attraction between them.

Two lost souls, he thought wryly. Except he'd had a part in his own destruction. He'd made conscious choices, even knowing he was fighting for a lost cause and probably an unworthy prince, a man who claimed Scotland's throne but hadn't cared enough about the country to speak its language. It had been the aftermath that had destroyed all the good parts of him.

But her touch was bewitching. He pressed his lips

against hers once more in a deeper kiss. The yearning between them exploded. All his doubts faded in a compelling fierceness that brooked no denial. Not when her lips responded to his. Not when they parted slightly to allow his tongue entrance. His hands touched her shoulders, ran along her arms, feeling the softness, sensing the welcome.

His kiss suddenly gentled, their breath intermingling. Her fingers had left his face, but now they returned, touching with a tenderness that made him weak.

He felt the tremors in her body, but they were not of fear. He knew that because he was experiencing the same uncontrolled need. Her body moved, arching under his hands, and the nerves in his body became raw and burning.

Wrong, so wrong, and yet so completely natural. Need quickened inside him as his tongue teased her tongue, and his hands seduced her body. He slid his hands to the top of the nightdress, the low-cut neckline that allowed him entrance. He caressed her breasts and she moaned, her body going so rigid he thought it might break. He drew away, reluctantly ending his exploration.

"I'm sorry," he said.

"Don't stop," she whispered. She touched his face with a searching tenderness that made him weak.

He felt heat curl inside his loins, even as he hesitated to go further. She looked so wistful, so vulnerable, yet there was a strength in her that was even more attractive to him.

He knew she must be a virgin. Her touch was tentative, her responses shy, even as they seduced. He had never taken a virgin before. He'd always sought out experienced women who knew and accepted the ways of a wandering man. He had no right.

He had no choice. Not when she was looking at him with those wide eyes that undid him every time. Now the spectacular blue green was slightly misted with passion, her mouth swollen by his kiss. He put a hand on her left breast and felt the ragged beat of her heart and the hardening of her nipple. He felt the pounding of his own heart.

He needed her. He needed her warmth and belief in him. He needed the gentleness of her touch and the sweetness of her lips. He needed the magic in a life that had been made cold and barren.

Enough to destroy her life?

How much of a bastard was he?

He sighed, released her lips, and sat there looking at her. She stared back at him gravely, her eyes glazed with emotion. Desire. Need.

"I canna do it to you," he said. "You . . . still have your . . . wedding. I do not have much honor left, but I have tha' much."

"Nay," she said. "If I have learned one thing on this journey, it is that I will not go to a man out of necessity or pity or money. I have thought from the beginning that if we did not suit, then I would sail for America and become a governess or teacher or something of worth."

She did not add that the past week with him probably would further complicate any marriage. She would not lie. She would not say that she was forced to do anything. She would not further blacken the name of this man.

Truth be told, she had learned in these weeks that she need not depend on anyone. She had discovered she *was* of value. She would never let anyone tell her she was not again.

And she was not going to let this moment go. She was not to live her life as a spinster who had never known what it was like to be a woman. She did not care about the cost. She would have this moment.

His touch was magical. Jenna had never known she could feel like this, that every sense could come alive. That she would feel such a warm puddling wanting inside. That there could be such a yearning, such expectation, for something unknown. The sheer strength of her need frightened her, but she had to follow it. She had to finish the journey she'd started, not only the journey to a new world, but her own personal journey, and this was part of it. With her newfound courage, she wanted to meet that fear and conquer it. She must, or she would wonder her entire life what she had missed.

He had awakened her entire body. For the first time in her life, she felt wanted and she reached out for him. Her hands went to the back of his neck and her fingers tangled in the thick dark hair. Then they fell to his shirt. He had dressed for tonight and though he had discarded his waistcoat, he was still wearing his shirt and cravat. The white of the fine linen garment contrasted with his sun-bronzed face.

She sat up in the bed, unafraid now to leave her arm uncovered. She untied the cravat and the shirt fell open at the neck.

"Jeanette," he whispered. He said it with an awe that filled her with pleasure, even wonder.

He turned around and slid in next to her, though he still wore breeches and shirt. His lips trailed kisses along her cheek, starting just below her right eye and moving along the bone to her throat, searing her with a brand she knew she would carry forever, exploding greedy wildfires in her body.

His tongue found its way into her welcoming mouth, and teased and stroked until her body shuddered with unaccustomed sensations.

"You are very bonny," he said.

She had never believed it, but now she saw his eyes, the intense fire in them, and she did believe him. For now, at least. For this moment. And that was all that mattered.

He shifted his weight, and she took that opportunity to pull his shirt from his breeches, feeling wild and abandoned and wicked. And desired. For the first time in her life, she felt desired.

Her fingers touched the skin underneath the material of the shirt, and it was warm to her touch. Warm and seductive. His body was lean and muscled, and tense. Ever so tense.

He moaned slightly as her hands ran up his chest. "All

the saints in heaven," he murmured, then sat up. He unlaced his breeches and pulled them off. She watched every movement, and the want inside grew as he turned back to her.

"Are you sure, lass?" It was the first time he had called her that, and it sounded warm and intimate and loving.

"Aye," she replied. Part of her wasn't sure. She had heard both wonderful and terrible things about the act of joining, of loving. Some said it was a curse. Painful and humiliating. Because of those reports, she had dreaded marriage even while she had coveted the fruit of it.

But others had obviously reveled in it, glorying in the union between man and woman.

And how could anything that made her body sing like this be less than wondrous?

She held out her hand to him.

He gave her a crooked smile that went straight to her heart and erased the last of her doubts.

He took the coverlet completely off the bed and then slowly, lazily tugged off her nightdress, caressing her as he did so, each touch igniting new fires, sending more expectant sensations flaring through her.

Then his lips were on hers again, this time with a kiss sweet and searching and gentle all at the same time. She felt the restraint behind it, a concern that lessened any remaining apprehension. She felt like a very precious object. It was a new feeling and she relished it, knowing she would remember it always.

She touched his body, felt its tension. Then her hand moved up to his cheek and touched the scar. He flinched.

"Nay," she said. "It gives you character."

"I am truly glad something does," he replied seriously, but the half smile on his face broadened. She smiled inside. She had not realized before he had humor. He had been very good at hiding it.

His lips seized hers again, and his hands wandered down her body, touching her breasts again, then moved to the triangle of hair, his fingers soothing and searching, creating shock waves of sensations. His kiss deepened, and now there was little gentleness, just a hard, driving need that fired her own.

Her body arched in instinctive reaction and her arms went around him, drawing him to her. She felt the probe of his body at the entrance of the most secret, private part of her, and after the first stunned reaction, she knew a craving so strong and so deep that she cried out. Her body moved shamelessly against his and she savored the contrast of her soft skin against his taut, hard body.

Yet still he hesitated, even while the brush of his arousal made her moan with frustration. Then he moved slowly into her. Hot. Pulsating. A strange fullness, and then pain. Pain so sharp and unexpected that she cried out again.

He paused, did not move, and the pain gradually subsided.

She felt his taut muscles strain, and she was suddenly aware of how much self-control he had, how much he was reining in his own desire.

"Lass?"

She felt sore, but even more she still felt the craving. Her hand touched his mouth, and she arched her body once again, wanting desperately to continue this voyage of discovery, to find where all these feelings were leading.

He moved again, slowly, tentatively, and the pain waned. The fullness in her, the strangeness of it, changed into something so sensuous and beautiful that she instinctively moved with him. Heat flooded her as his rhythm increased and he ventured deeper and deeper until she thought he could go no farther. Spasms of pleasure rolled from the deepest core of her, exploding in a great storm of brilliant colors and bursts of splendor.

She heard his heavy breathing, a groan, but he did not move away and she savored the feel of his body so intimately connected to hers. Sensation continued to roll through her, like waves on a beach.

"Ah, lass," he said in a whispered exclamation.

"Hmm," was all she could reply. She had no words to express the transformation that had just taken place in her body. She had taken her voyage and found the destination far more incredible than she could ever express.

He balanced himself on one arm, and he brushed a lock of hair from her face in a gesture now intimate and even more tender than any that had gone before.

She saw him swallow hard, saw his dark blue eyes search her face.

"I am sorry for hurting you," he said in a ragged voice.

She pressed her fingers to his mouth. "Nay," she said. "The hurt has eased but the wonder will always stay."

He moved, and she lost the warmth of him. He rolled over to lie next to her, and she rested her head against his chest and heard his heartbeat.

"Jenna," he said, his arm going around her. "This should not have . . ." But despite his attempted denial, she heard a note of tenderness in the sound.

But there was also despair.

Her chest tightened.

She had known a moment of glory but it would not last. He would not let it.

He would regret it instead.

Because she was a Campbell? Or were there other reasons?

She snuggled farther into his arms, seeking his warmth even as a cold chill permeated her.

Chapter Eighteen

The night air brushed Alex's face as the sails filled, and the *Ami* left the harbor. He remained on watch until the flickering lights of the town faded from sight.

No cannon from the fort. No commands to stop.

He was free.

But he knew that was a lie. He had never been less free. Not even when hiding in the Highlands for so many months.

He wondered where *she* was. Probably with Meg. Claude said she had gone to be with Meg as soon as she'd arrived back on board. He had stayed behind to manage the sale of the contents of the *Charlotte*.

By the saints, he had made a mess of things. When she had woken this morning, 'twas plain she expected gentle words. Perhaps even an avowal of love.

He couldn't do it. He could not hurt her further.

So he had turned his mind to the next hours, to the negotiations that would take place. He had watched the disappointment, even pain, on her face before she masked it and feigned indifference. God, but it hurt, and yet he knew he could not feed her hopes. A break now was better than later.

And so he had tried not to touch her as they thanked the governor for the night's hospitality and he walked her to the wharf. Then he'd found the man he hoped would buy the contents of the *Charlotte*.

He had made the best bargain he could under the circumstances. He'd received less than half the worth of the cargo. He'd hated to turn over the *Charlotte*'s papers to the governor. But it was far preferable to what he thought he would receive the night before or to trying to sail his own ship from the harbor under the guns of the fort. During the next hours, his mind's eye kept returning to Lady Jeanette, and the way she had looked this morning. Her eyes had been sleepy but when she'd looked at him, he saw longing. He had feared guilt or regret or anger. There was none of that. Only a slow smile that was worse than anger . . .

Until he had pretended that nothing had happened, nothing had changed . . .

In the soft quiet evening with a slice of moon and thousands of stars, he wondered just what he had done, and what would be the repercussions. What if there was a child?

He had thought of nothing last night except how he had needed her. He'd been lost in that need, in the way she had made him feel. A magic had bonded them; for the first time since Culloden he'd felt whole and complete.

Now she had to sail with them. She could not stay on the island now, nor could she sail from there to another destination. The *Charlotte*'s passengers—if they heard of the captain's wife—could never find out that his "wife" was Jeanette Campbell. They would not have known that he did not have a wife aboard when they were taken.

When one had asked about Lady Jeanette, Claude had simply said she was being held as a hostage to be ransomed.

It would hopefully offer her some protection. No matter what she decided to do.

And as far as he was concerned, she could do anything she wanted, and he would help her. He owed it to her.

Anything, that was, except allow her to stay in his life. It would be a sure path to disaster. For both of them. A Leslie and a Campbell. Fire and water. Then why did they explode together as they had the night before?

It would not have mattered so much if not for the price that would be on his head. He no longer blamed the sins of the Campbell on her. She was unique. He had never met a woman like her before, except perhaps for his sister.

Jeanette Campbell had suffered at her family's hands. That much was obvious. What father would send his daughter thousands of miles away to a man she did not know?

What did matter was that he could not afford to have a lady in his life.

It would be years before he could safely settle somewhere. To do so, he would have to avoid all English colonies. He would need enough money, after seeing to the needs of his ten orphans, to go somewhere the English could never find him.

After Lady Jeanette had gone into the sick bay, the passengers had been herded up on deck and released. He had let them keep their personal property—clothes and even jewels—that seemed to mean something to them. The rest he kept.

Spoils of war, he told himself. In truth, it was defiance against a conscience that was beginning to work again. It had been sleeping since Culloden, since life and death depended on ruthlessness. Or so he thought. He had taken out his rage and sorrow and anger in the only way he thought available to him.

He was not going to change one thing, though. He was a wanderer. He had always been a wanderer, even before the British destroyed his home. He'd loved the sea then.

He'd loved coming home, knowing it was there, knowing his father and mother and sister were always there. But after a few months, he would feel restless again. He'd needed to make his own way, not just inherit land that had already been played out and could not support its people.

The *Ami* was in full sail now, skimming the waves. He loved the feel of the ship below his feet, the soft rhythm of the sea, the flap of sails, the cool night breeze, the fading lights.

It was life to him. Particularly now, when there was no other home, no anchor other than the one he could pull up at any time.

He wondered whether Jenna had second thoughts about what had happened last night. He had been no help this morning. He had been cold and distant after waking up in her arms. It had taken every bit of his control to do so. He'd wanted badly to clasp her to him and promise her a future.

It would be no service to her. The best thing he could do for her was to set her free from the *Ami*, and from him. She was strong enough to find a man worthy of her, one that did not wear a scar that marked him, nor a leg that might someday completely cripple him.

But as he looked at the sliver of the moon and the array of stars, he felt a loneliness and loss that was as vast as the sky. Only it had no light, no glitter, no promise.

Jenna watched Meg sleep. She had been gone twenty-four hours, and in those hours, Meg had improved tremendously. Whether it had been the bark, or just time, she did not know. She only knew that the child's face was cooler, more relaxed.

And she would always remember Meg's welcoming grin. "I was afraid you would not come back," Meg had said.

Surprisingly, the lass's eyes had glistened when Jenna produced the dress she had purchased on the way back to the ship. It was a summer sky blue that matched Meg's eyes, and the cloth was a fine, soft lawn.

Meg had tried at first to disdain it, but her eyes and fingers kept returning to it.

The child's reaction warmed a heart that had been damaged this morning. She still felt a throbbing inside her from last night's . . . lovemaking. She hated herself for that. Especially after she'd awakened this morning to his indifference.

Light had crept through the window then, and he was no longer in bed, but dressed and standing at the window. And when he turned to her, his eyes were impossible to read. Where last night, she had seen so many emotions, now they were as undecipherable as they had been when she'd first met him.

"I'm sorry, Jeanette," he'd said.

"Jenna," she'd corrected, obviously reaching for the intimacy they had shared the previous night.

"Jenna," he'd conceded. "I have to get you back to the ship," he said. "The governor might change his mind again."

"I don't think so," she disagreed.

"I am not willing to take that chance."

"And you?"

"I have some business. I hope to be back this evening and we will set sail then. I do not want any of the passengers to see you until we leave, and I will not be sending them ashore until we are ready to sail. I want to leave nothing to chance."

"Captain . . . Will . . ." She couldn't keep calling him captain. The children called him Will. She was sure, though, that it was not his name. She didn't know why she felt that way. Perhaps the way he'd looked the few times she had been in the area when his name was mentioned. There was always a pause.

He had that look now. For a moment, his eyes softened. "Alex," he said. "My name is Alex."

She wanted him to say the rest of it, because that would mean trust. But he did not. Still, it was a step.

But then his jaw had tightened and the softness disappeared from his eyes. "You took risks last night," he said. "I shall see that you are repaid."

Her heart froze. "I did not ask for repayment."

"All the same, I have to see to your safety," he'd said coolly.

The words broke her heart. When he'd said his name was Alex, she had seen warmth in his eyes, but it had disappeared almost immediately.

She had invited what had happened last night, but from her heart, because it felt right. His offer of reparation made her feel the whore. Had she really thought he would wake this morning and declare his undying love? That he would forget she was a Campbell? Forget that they were thousands of miles apart in their loyalties?

Except they weren't. She had no loyalties now except to Meg and him. He knew it, and yet . . . he was denying it.

"You have to see to nothing," she said, matching his coldness.

"You cannot stay here. The governor will know you lied to him."

"And you cannot go to a British island. So what do you intend to do with me?"

He looked at her with frustration burning bright in his eyes. "We are in a pretty muddle," he said.

Muddle. That was all she was to him.

She stretched, feeling an unaccustomed soreness deep inside, and yet there was something else, too. She felt sated. She had never understood the word before. She also felt a hunger she could not define with words.

A hunger she feared would haunt her forever.

Yet she still had pride. A pride that had carried her beyond small affronts, her parents' shame, her sisters' displeasure. She reached down for the nightdress that had been discarded so easily earlier and covered her nakedness, forcing herself to do it slowly, without any sign of shame or embarrassment.

She shivered. She had felt beautiful last night. Beautiful and loved and cherished. And now she felt like a fool. "I require some privacy," she said calmly, maintaining the pretense.

He left the window and turned back to her. "Jenna . . ."

"Please go," she said.

He hesitated, then walked away, through the door, shutting it too softly behind him.

She had allowed a tear or two, then had dressed and waited for his return. She had steeled herself to behave as he had, despite the ache and need and despair inside. He would never know it. Just as she had never let anyone know how their looks or comments or actions had wounded her.

Strangely enough, she never even entertained the thought he might abandon her. He had not abandoned the children. He would not abandon her. There was an odd sense of honor about him.

And he hadn't. When he had returned to take her back to the ship, she had tried to be indifferent. She'd said little, merely remarked on the fine weather.

And at the wharf, when the quarter boat came for her, she declined his outstretched hand to help her step inside and instead took that of one of the sailors.

She was torn. She wanted to disappear on the island, but he had been right about that. She could not do it. She wanted to demand to be left off at the next island, but then what of Meg and Robin?

Perhaps if he cared so little about her, he also cared that little about Meg and the lad. Perhaps if he thought she really would take care of them, he would feel relieved at ridding himself of the lot of them.

She doubted it though. His affection—even love—for the children was evident in his actions, his concern. She should be ashamed of such a churlish thought, yet she dared not. It was all she had to stiffen her resolve to care for the children.

To keep from showing the captain—Alex—how much he had hurt her that morning.

She knew she should not feel such hurt. She had known exactly what she was doing last night. She'd known then that it was a borrowed moment, not to be confused with the promise of a future.

A moment only . . . of utter joy . . . complete freedom. More than she had ever had in her life.

Knowing was not the same as accepting . . .

Turning away from such disturbing thoughts, Jenna looked down again at the sleeping Meg, remembering the child's awed face as she'd told Jenna how pretty she looked. She'd tried to brighten, finally singing a sailor's song she had heard aboard the *Charlotte*.

"Tell me how you found . . . Will," Jenna had said.

"Someone told me that there was a man in the hills with children."

"Children?"

"Aye," Meg said. "There were nine, including Robin. I made ten."

"Ten?"

"And Burke," Meg added. "He helped take care of us."

"For how long?"

"Near a year."

"In the mountains?"

"Aye. Sometimes we were cold and hungry. Sometimes we had to run from one place to another, but Will ne'er left us."

The dour captain. The man who had surprised her with the slow, lazy smile, with hands that were gentle. Even kind.

Until this morning.

So many contradictions. Who was he really? *What* was he really?

"What happened to the others?" she asked.

"He found them homes in France. He tried to find me a home, me and Robin, but we belong with Will," she said proudly. "Someone has to take care of him, too." Meg's eyes fastened on her for a moment, opening wide as if an idea had just been born.

"Perhaps ye, my lady . . . ?"

"You," Jenna corrected, then added almost desperately, "And I am betrothed."

Meg looked disappointed. "But—" she started.

"But nothing, love."

She stayed a few more moments, then stood and went to the window. The captain was coming back aboard. He would surely stop by to see Meg.

She did not want to be here when he did.

Jenna leaned down and touched one of Meg's short curls. "The captain will be here soon," she said. "And I have to change clothes. I will see you later."

Meg smiled. "I missed you last night."

It was the first time Jenna had ever been missed. After this morning, it was like being handed a gift of the finest gold. "And I missed *you,* love."

Meg's smile could have lit the room if a lantern hadn't already illuminated it. Still, it did get brighter.

Jenna pulled up the cover. The porthole was open and a fresh breeze flew into the room. She started to close it but Meg had protested.

Meg snuggled in the bed, wincing just a little. Jenna had rebandaged the wound after looking at it. There was less secretion and it looked as if it might finally be healing. Some of the painful redness had receded.

The child should sleep well, particularly after seeing Alex and being assured everything was well with her world.

But would it ever be? Regardless of his feelings for children, the captain—she was trying to think of him that way again—apparently did not want ties.

He did not want family. He did not want obligations. He

did not want any of the things that she so desperately needed.

Perhaps now that he did not feel so hostile about her, he would let her have Meg and Robin.

It was a matter of making the proposition in the right way, at the right time.

She would not have him. Or a husband. But she would have what her heart had yearned for these past years: someone to love.

She hesitated. She did not want to leave. But then she heard the sound of the anchor being pulled up, the creak of the ship as it started to move. He would be here soon.

Her thoughts drifted back to the room last night and again this morning. She feared they might for a long time.

She tried to shake the images from her mind. She had other things to do, including changing her clothes. She still wore the dress she'd worn to the governor's residence.

She heard passengers being herded through the ship, listened to their loud complaints. She stayed where she was.

Then a crewman came by and quenched the lantern. "The captain doesn't want any lights," he said. "And he wants you to return to his cabin."

Jenna took one last look at the sleeping Meg and left the sick bay for the captain's room.

The captain's cabin was dark, but she heeded the crewman's words. The captain, she'd learned, never issued orders unless he had good reason for them. It took several moments, but her eyes gradually adjusted to see shapes. Celia was not there, and she wondered what had happened to her friend.

She slipped off the hoop skirt, then twisted around until she was able to unbutton the top of her dress in back. Thankful for the low neck, she was able to twist it around and finish unfastening the buttons.

Then she sat on the bed in her chemise. She wanted to cry, but she would not. She would not give him the satisfaction, nor herself the pity. Instead, she found a simple day dress that tied in the front and put it on. She longed for the trousers and shirt that Meg wore. She could not even imagine the freedom those clothes allowed.

She looked out the two windows of the cabin. She could still see some lights from the town.

Without putting on gloves, she went to the door and opened it. She would never wear them again, at least not to cover the mark. At least the captain—Alex—had given her that. If someone could not accept it, then they were not worth knowing.

Alex. No wonder she never felt as if Will fit him.

Alex *did* fit him. *Alexander.* Her mind ran over Scottish families with sons with that name. Too many to remember.

And if she did? It would be knowledge she needed to forget. She *was* hurt, even angry, but she knew she would never do anything to hurt *him.*

The passageway was dark. If she had not become so familiar with it, she would have lost her way. She found the companionway that led up to the main deck. It did not take her long to adjust to the rhythm of the ship this time.

She reached the main deck, opened the hatch, and stepped out into the fresh breeze of a Caribbean evening. She loved the smell of the sea. She looked around. Claude was at the wheel. She did not see the captain. She did see Celia standing next to Burke. Amazingly his arm was around her.

Longing pierced her.

She turned and looked at the flickering lights of the town. One by one they faded as the ship turned away from the harbor. More sails were being hoisted. She felt the ship quicken.

Then she heard the cry of "Sail ho."

Burke's arm dropped from Celia and he pushed her toward the hatchway. Jenna ducked around to its side, trying to make herself invisible. Where was the captain?

Then she heard his voice not far from her.

"Flag?" he asked.

"British," said the sailor up the mast.

She heard curses. "They were waiting."

"The French must have known," one man muttered near her.

"Set the royals! Rig the stuns'ls." Alex's voice over-powered all the others. "Gun crews to your stations."

"Better get below," one sailor said as he brushed past her down the companionway.

Instead, she peered out to sea and saw a huge ship under full sail turning toward them. She remembered the fear she'd felt several days earlier when the British ship pursued them into the storm. There was no storm tonight, only a clear sky lit by stars and a crescent moon.

They were not moving at top speed yet. They had not set all the sails, and she watched as men grabbed lines and hauled sail. She felt the kick of the ship but she knew it would not be fast enough.

The captain left Claude and started for the hatchway, then stilled when he saw her.

She had expected to be ordered off the deck, as she had before. Instead, he touched her cheek. "The governor was more sly than I thought," he said.

"Or maybe he did not know," she said, unwilling to believe their host could be so devious.

A loud boom echoed in the night air. She saw the splash to the left of the ship. "Go to Meg," he said. "Remember, no lights."

"What about Robin?"

He hesitated. "I would tell him to go with you, but he won't. He knows we're shorthanded. I'll be looking out for him."

She did not hesitate. She went down the companionway, then to the sick bay. Meg was sitting up on the cot.

"What is going on?"

"A British ship," Jenna said. "It was apparently lurking in wait for us."

"I want to go up and help."

So did Jenna. But she realized she would be more a hindrance than a help. So would Meg.

"Everyone would be looking out for you rather than doing what they should," she said.

"Robin—" Meg started to protest.

"Robin isn't wounded," Jenna said, knowing Meg would completely reject the notion she couldn't help because she was a girl. She paused, then added, "Want to know a secret?"

"Aye," Meg replied, her eyes wide.

"I wish I were up there helping too, but I know I would be more trouble than assistance."

"But you—" Meg's lips clamped down.

"I know. I was taken from a British ship, but that does not mean I agree with everything they do."

"You . . . do not?"

"Nay," Jenna said. "I'm on your . . . Will's side."

Meg's face broke out in a broad smile. "I knew you would be."

"And now the best way we can help is to stay here until someone comes." She felt the lurch of the ship as added sail quickened the ship's movement. It was a swift ship. But swift enough to outrun the warship?

She heard the boom of cannon from their own ship and held Meg's hand tighter. Then another. It sounded just like thunder she'd heard nights ago.

Meg trembled. Despite the child's brave words about helping earlier, she must remember the day she was hurt.

The roar of cannon came every few seconds. Then she heard shouts. Exultant shouts. Something had happened. Had they hit the British ship?

But still the cannon roared. Her heart pounding, her throat dry, she waited. It was the hardest thing she'd ever done. But she could not leave Meg's side. She would not put it past Meg, no matter how frightened she was, to go topside.

She remembered a few nights ago when they were also being pursued. She wondered whether one ever got used to it, especially if one was a child.

Despite the dryness in her throat, she started a song, a funny little ditty, and before long Meg joined her in singing away the fear.

She felt the ship lurch forward again. She knew all the sail was up, and the ship felt as if it were flying through the sea.

The door opened and Celia entered, her face flushed.

"They knocked down a mast of the British ship," she said excitedly. "It's falling behind."

Jenna stared at her in disbelief. "Have you been up there?"

"Aye, for a little while," she said. "Mr. Burke, he told me to come down here, but I stayed around the hatchway and I heard them shout."

Timid, seasick Celia?

Was what she, Jenna, had catching? And what did she have? A new taste for adventure and excitement, for freedom and independence?

"You are not seasick?"

Celia looked surprised. Then she frowned, as if she had not even thought of it. "No, my lady, I guess I am not."

Jenna couldn't help but giggle at the startled tone of her voice. Maybe Celia had been sick before out of loneliness and fear. Whatever had happened, Celia looked prettier than she ever had before.

Jenna could not imagine a more unlikely choice for sweet, timid Celia than the burly, rough-speaking Burke.

Celia sat down on the floor next to Meg. "My mistress says you have a brave little soul."

Meg looked at her suspiciously just as she had regarded Jenna earlier. "I am not little," she said.

"Nay," Celia said. "I can see that. And I heard you singing. Ye have a bonny fine voice, just like my lady."

Some of the suspicion left Meg's face. "You did not leave with the others?"

"Nay, I would not be leaving my lady."

Loyalty meant something to Meg. Jenna already knew that. Otherwise she would not have followed the captain into who knew what.

She was suddenly aware that the booming had stopped.

"Will you stay with Meg?" she asked Celia.

"Aye, it would be my pleasure."

Meg smiled slightly.

Jenna gathered up her skirts and ran out the door and up the gangway. She opened the hatch cover and went out on deck. The ship was moving swiftly, kicking up water as it plowed through the seas. She saw a new scar on the bow, but no one appeared to be wounded.

One of the sailors saw her and came to her. "We hit their mainmast," he said. "We left them behind."

"No one was hurt?" She held her breath. She thought of Hamish, Mickey, and, most of all, the captain, as well as the other hands she was beginning to know.

"No one was hurt, my lady. The captain and Mr. Torbeau are plotting a new course away from the sea-lanes."

"Then we are safe?"

"For the time being, my lady."

She saw Robin then, pulling on the sheets of one of the sails. He looked earnest and full of pride.

Jenna knew boys as young as eight were often employed on ships, usually as powder monkeys. Robin was twelve and large for his age, and yet she couldn't help feeling a jerk of apprehension for him.

But she had discovered what she'd intended, and now she hurried back to Meg.

She wondered if she would ever get used to the idea of children being exposed to such danger. But where would they be safe? Robin, in particular, would be in danger in Scotland. He was a lad with a banned name.

She and Celia exchanged glances and she knew that
Celia saw the anxiety in her expression.

"It will be all right, my lady."

Jenna nodded. But she didn't think it was all right.

She knew fear now that she had never known before.

Chapter Nineteen

Jenna had no idea where the *Ami* was heading. At the moment, she didn't care. She was beginning to believe its escape was *her* escape.

They had left the warship far behind. The *Ami* was sailing swiftly in a good wind, skimming over a now quiet sea.

She went up on deck with Meg. Meg's fever had faded, and Jenna could no longer keep her below. Not even "Will" could do that. It was better, she thought, if she went with Meg in case she became dizzy or faint.

Jenna had asked whether she wanted to wear the new dress, but Meg shook her head. "It is too fine," she said.

Jenna did not argue the point. Meg would have to make up her own mind as to when she wanted to become a lass. In the meantime, it was just as well. The crew was well disciplined but still composed of men. That Meg was considered as much a cabin boy as Robin probably kept her safe.

And the trousers were probably safer for her, too. The deck was often slippery, and the wind had a way of blowing a dress against one's body, and even sweeping it upward. She felt her own garment doing that now. It was a day dress, one she'd worn in her own rooms at home. A simple white shift with a blue overdress. She usually wore a lace cap with it, but now she bound her hair with only a piece of ribbon to keep it from her eyes. She'd used precious water last night washing it, using the rose soap she'd found at the governor's house. It felt clean and fine.

She planned to wash Meg's tonight, despite the caution with which all water was used aboard ship.

But now she watched as Meg, accompanied by a protective Robin, wandered among the men, receiving warm teasing about "getting out of work." Despite her recent illness and still obvious weakness, she was as surefooted through the companionway and up on deck as the most seasoned seamen.

She grinned and made retorts, and the wind and sun colored cheeks that had become too pale.

Oddly enough, she flourished in this rough company.

But then, Jenna thought, so had she. Everyone seemed to be accepted for what they could do, not for what they were, or had been, or what their pedigree was. No one stared at her arm with distaste or fear. If she had been despised in the beginning, it had been due to her family's name, not her appearance.

She stood at the railing and watched Meg, who finally sat down on coiled rope and held court. This quite possibly was where the child belonged, among adventurers who cared for her. The thought was, she knew, indicative of the changes she'd undergone.

She looked away, across the sea. The day was beautiful, bright with a sky so blue it made her eyes hurt, glorious with the sun weaving trails of gold across the sea. The *Ami* sprayed water as she sped along the sea, doing so well what she was created to do.

And what, she wondered, was she created to do?

• • •

Alex had thought it would be far easier to stay away from Jenna Campbell on ship than it had been in the same room with one bed.

Bloody damn fool thought.

He had tried to put all his concentration on the days ahead. He had planned to sail to Rio de Janeiro, but that was a busy port these days. He couldn't risk it now.

The governor might well have told the British where he was heading. He'd made the mistake on his earlier visit of telling him. It had been foolish of him, but he'd believed the governor hated the British as much as he. He had not considered the fact that the governor feared them even more than he hated them.

He'd studied the maps. He would try Vitória, instead. It was a small dot on the map but not a great deal farther from the diamond mines than the other ports. His partner in France had told him that he should find a *bandeirante*, the term given to Brazilian explorers who discovered and exploited the diamond and gold fields. He'd been told the *bandeirantes* banded together in small groups under their own flag, usually with a priest among them. They might well know of diamonds that were not being shipped through the Portuguese government to Goa, where they were stamped as Indian diamonds.

In the meantime, he had his men repaint the name of the ship from the *Ami* to the *Isabelle*. The Portuguese flag was flying now, rather than the French one. He was trying to make other small changes as well. Not, he knew, that it would make much difference if they encountered the same British warship as before. They would recognize the sails immediately.

A week, perhaps ten days, and they should be at the port. Then what in the hell would he do with Jeanette Campbell? He doubted there would be an English ship in port. But perhaps he could find a respectable captain willing to sail her to Rio de Janeiro, where she could find passage to Barbados.

A mental image of her with the British plantation owner was like a sword thrust through his gut. Yet he had to give her that chance. He would also make sure she had enough money to go elsewhere if she wished. Enough to keep her safe.

And happy.

He wanted that now. He wanted it very badly. It no longer mattered that she carried a hated name.

He looked back toward her. Any man would be insane not to want her.

She had blossomed in the past few days. No longer was she covered from head to foot to fingers with garments that neither suited nor favored her. No longer did she keep her hair in an unattractive tight knot at the back of her head. No longer did she seem diffident and shy.

Now she stood on the deck, letting her hair flow free, her face glowing with the sun and wind, her eyes bright with the sensuous pleasure of the day, and he felt his heart softening with a need he'd never experienced before.

It wasn't lust, although lust was certainly there. Instead, it was a need to be with her, to touch her, to hear that too-rare laugh. She'd been enchanting at the governor's dinner, unlike the uncertain, though defiant, person he'd first met. She had been entranced with her own deviousness, weaving one false tale after another and enjoying their success even though a part of her, he thought, must be flinching. She was too honest to do otherwise. He had made an art of deceit these past months and yet she had been even better at it than he.

And she had been marvelous with Meg. The lass was far better physically, but also in other ways. For the first time, she was taking an interest in her appearance, making small improvements.

There were so many layers to Lady Jeanette Campbell, so many contradictions that he suspected it would take a lifetime to uncover all of them.

But he did not have a lifetime, particularly with a

woman raised as a lady, even though she'd been badly treated by her family.

This was an adventure for her now, but she was the type of woman who needed a home and family, stability and respectability.

He expected never to be respectable again.

He had to do a far better job in avoiding her.

Still, his spirits lifted when she smiled at Meg, and when her hair caught golden glints from the sun. Part of her new awareness came from him, and he couldn't help but relish that fact. Even as he knew it couldn't last.

Vitória, Brazil

The island of Vitória—one of many islands in an archipelago along the Brazilian coast—was amazingly brilliant in color. The azure blue sea faded into a long white beach. The bay and beach interrupted a rocky coastline. A scattering of buildings fronted the harbor.

Alex had seen to it that the sailor with the sharpest eyes was stationed in the crow's nest far above the main deck. He would keep someone there as long as they were anchored here.

The sun pounded down on the ship, and his men had taken off what clothes they could, considering the presence of three females. Sweat glistened on them. Most, including himself, were from countries with cold winters and mild summers and unused to the hot and humid tropical air.

He ordered the ship anchored, then silently cursed as Jenna and Meg appeared on deck. He nodded to her but did not approach.

He'd been successful in avoiding her this past week. He worked eighteen to nineteen hours a day, often doing physical work with the crew, then falling into a hammock in a cabin he shared with Claude. He realized it hurt her. Bloody hell, it hurt *him*.

He would destroy her if he allowed himself to get any closer to her. He could never marry her. It could well be a death sentence for her. At best, they would be fugitives all their lives.

Rory Forbes, the former Black Knave, had married. The Black Knave had been wanted by the British. Alex's mind turned that over, before he discarded it. Perhaps Forbes was alive. Perhaps he was not. But Rory's wife had been a fugitive from Cumberland, a Jacobite marked for death. She'd had nothing to lose.

Jenna had everything to lose.

He turned his attention back to Vitória, the capital of the state of Espírito Santo. He looked for Marco, one of the crew who was Portuguese and would act as translator. Alex knew some Spanish, and the two languages—Spanish and Portuguese—had much in common.

"You and I will go ashore alone," he said. "Claude will stay here. I want him ready to sail immediately if he sees another ship come in." He looked at Marco closely. "We may be left."

The man shrugged. "Every time I go to sea, I take risk."

"We will leave in thirty minutes," he said.

He turned back toward Jenna, who was standing with Meg. They were both looking toward the town as he approached them. Yet he knew Jenna was aware of his presence, just as he was always aware of her presence. She seemed to stiffen.

"Meg," he said, "I want to talk to Lady Jeanette. Will you find Robin and send him up here?"

Meg looked at him curiously, but left without argument. For a moment, he just stood next to Jenna, enjoying the sense of rightness and belonging her presence gave him. There seemed no resentment on her part, only a guarded interest.

"I am going ashore for a few hours," he said. "I told Claude to set sail if he sees a British ship."

She nodded without comment.

He suddenly felt as uncertain as a schoolboy. "I . . . thank you for taking such good care of Meg."

"I care about her," she said simply.

"What do *you* want to do?" he asked. "I cannot take you back to your . . . betrothed." The word stuck in his throat, even knowing as he did that she had never met the man.

She turned and looked at him then as if she had no idea how to answer. It was the first indecision he'd seen in her. There had been defiance, anger, resentment, then a passion that had stunned him.

"If you wish to go on to Barbados, I'll see if I can arrange it," he said. "I will find you a ship. And I will give you funds to go anywhere you wish . . . if it does not . . . if you do not want to stay with him."

She lifted her chin. "I have enough money."

"I saw what you had," he said.

He saw in her eyes the realization that he had admitted searching her trunks. She hesitated, then said slowly, "I sewed some jewels and money in the hem of my dress."

"The necklace you wore in Martinique. I thought I had missed it."

"Nay."

He was stunned. He hadn't thought about that, but then he hadn't had much to do with ladies' garments lately. "Are you sure you should tell me that?"

"You just offered me money. I do not think you will steal what I have."

"True," he said. "But this is all my doing. You should not have to pay for it."

"It has been an adventure," she said. "I do not regret it." She was silent for a moment, then added, "I have learned much."

"About pirates?"

"Aye, about pirates who care about children. I remember when the captain of the *Charlotte* assured me there were no more cutthroats in the Caribbean, that the Royal Navy had cleared the seas of them, and I believed him.

Then you appeared out of nowhere and I was so frightened."

"You did not look frightened. You looked angry."

Her eyes were wistful, and he wondered again how he ever thought she was plain. She attracted him as no other woman ever had, not even the bonny daughters of Jacobite lords, or the well-dressed women of Paris. The latter had smelled of too much perfume, and their hair was stiff. Jenna's hair was soft with tints of gold. He remembered how it had felt in his fingers that night. It was a memory he'd tried to shed.

And now he wanted to run his fingers through the silken strands of her hair, and take her hand, and run a finger down her cheek.

Bloody hell, he sounded like some miserable poet.

Still, he couldn't resist putting his hand on her shoulder, resting it there, reveling in the easy comfort of it. She'd thought so little of herself when they first met, though he had not realized it then. He could kill those Campbells who had made her feel that way. She was worth so much more than she had ever known.

She should have her chance.

She still had not answered his question.

"I want to stay here for a while," she said.

"Here?"

"On the *Ami*. Or the *Isabelle*," she quickly corrected herself.

"It is dangerous," he said.

"I am very aware of that after the past several weeks," she replied. "But Meg is here. And Robin. Perhaps I can go back to France and take care of the children."

"Robin no longer considers himself a child," he said, trying to hide his astonishment. She had said something like that before, but he had not taken it seriously. He would not have allowed her to take the children to the house of an Englishman.

Now she was offering to give up any life of her own for

two orphans, both of whom had been anything but pleasant to her for the first few days. She asked nothing at all from him.

He'd thought his heart had been hardened against almost everything. The children had made cracks in it, though he'd tried to patch them. But now he felt swells of tenderness inside.

He told himself there could be nothing between them, no future. And she'd never mentioned the night they had spent together, nor made demands, nor said she cared about him.

She showed you.

And he had walked away from her, making no promises except one to himself not to further endanger her.

"Captain?" Robin's voice broke his thoughts.

He turned, lowering his hand away from her shoulder, missing the feel of her.

"I'm going ashore, lad. Just Marco and myself. I want you to look after Meg and Lady Jenna," he said, slipping into the name she preferred. He took a key from his pocket and gave it to Robin. "This is a key to a box in my . . . in the lady's cabin. It is for you and the children and Lady Jenna if I am delayed."

"I want to go with you," Robin said.

"You are grown up now," Alex said. "You have responsibilities. I am entrusting Meg and Lady Jenna to you."

"What about Claude?" Robin said.

"You are family," Alex said. "I trust only you to do this for me." He had already decided this was the only way Robin would stay aboard. And keep Meg with him.

Robin drew himself up. "Aye, sir."

Jenna gave him a small smile as if she knew exactly what he was doing, but she did not say anything.

A most unusual woman.

He watched as the quarter boat was lowered. Some men manned the oars, then he and Marco climbed down the ladder and the boat started for shore.

He kept his gaze on Jenna. Meg had joined her, and Jenna had one arm around her. Robin stood on her other side, straight and sure and proud.

A large lump grew in his throat, and he turned away, toward the town that looked little more than a village.

A local drinking establishment was Alex's first stop. After, that is, a few bribes were paid to the local authorities waiting for him to land.

Bribes were beginning to deplete his prize money quickly. He had also made arrangements for supplies, the stated reason for his arrival. That, and to repair damage caused by the storm. He'd not had time to make them in Martinique.

There was canvas to purchase and sails to be repaired. He also had some possessions taken from the prize ships that he intended to trade for coffee. Diamonds were something that he had no intention of handling through official sources.

He and Marco found the most disreputable tavern they could, one they were told was patronized by a few *bandeirantes* that had been to Minas Gerais, the Brazilian state where diamonds had been found.

One of the soldiers, to whom he'd slipped several gold pieces, told him to look for a Tomas Freres. If, he added with a leer, Alex didn't care if his throat was slit.

Well, Alex had done his own share of slitting throats.

The tavern was poor indeed with dirt floors, dirty glasses, and rum that would kill most men. It was also mostly empty. The one person inside regarded them with suspicious eyes.

Alex leaned against a rickety bar and let Marco talk for him. Marco, he knew, had never been to Brazil, but he had been born in Portugal to a whore. He'd grown up on the waterfront and was as tough as any man in his crew, and that was saying a great deal.

Alex tried to look indifferent, as if the conversation was

of no import to him, and drank the rum. He'd had bloody poor liquor before, but this was about the worst. It burned all the way down his throat and settled in his stomach like molten lava.

He knew Spanish well enough to make out some of the conversation; it was close enough to Portuguese to understand meanings. He pretended otherwise, though. It suited him to act the swell. He wanted to be underestimated.

Tomas was indeed in the town. He had a wife here who was pregnant and he returned often to see her between expeditions into the interior for gold, diamonds, and other precious stones. Only God himself, though, knew when he would attend the bar, and no one was willing to tell them where he lived.

He and Marco sat at what passed as a table in chairs he feared would break under Marco's hefty weight. One rum became two, and two became three. The sun sank into the west, a ball of fiery red.

God, it was hot. He wished he were on the back of a fine horse on a Highland path, making his way across a glen with tumbling waterfalls. He longed for the heather and nettles and light brown cottages with their dark brown thatch roofs. There everything was muted: the mist, the hills, the skies, even the purple of the flowers.

Here, everything was brilliant. A sun so bright and large you felt you could reach out and touch it, green so startling it was more vivid than a polished emerald, flowers like colors in a kaleidoscope.

The heat sapped strength while the cold of Scotland invigorated him.

By all the saints in heaven, he was homesick. He even missed the smell of peat and the taste of oatcakes.

He knew he would never know any of them again. He could never return to Scotland.

The thought—or maybe the rum—made him morose.

And led to an even more dangerous image of a Scottish lass.

She had the strength of the Highlands in her. The muted beauty. The character tempered by steel. Despite her Campbell heritage, she had the attributes he loved best about his homeland.

Marco kicked him.

He realized he'd been staring down at the bloody rum. Crying in his cups, someone might say.

He looked up.

Two men in white shirts and white trousers were entering the establishment. They paused, looking cautiously around the interior, their gazes fixing on Alex and Marco. Their faces were burned brown with the sun, their eyes predatory, their stances wary. Their features indicated Indian as well as Portuguese blood, and perhaps even some African.

Their eyes were contemptuous as they regarded whom they obviously considered interlopers who did not belong.

They went to the bar. A rumble of a language not quite Portuguese ensued between the bartender and the newcomers. Then one turned toward Alex and came over to him.

"Senhor, I hear you are looking for me."

Alex understood, though the dialect made it difficult.

"Si. Bon tarde," he said in an accent he knew gave him away as something other than Portuguese. Still, one look at the man's eyes and he decided he best not play games. He doubted pretending an ignorance of speech would do him any good.

"Tomas Freres?" he asked.

The man nodded warily.

"I was told," he said in Spanish, "that you might know of diamonds I can buy."

"You can buy diamonds in São Paulo," the man said shortly, and turned back to the bar.

"But then I would have to pay taxes and send them to Goa. There is an easier way."

"Only for thieves," the man said.

"Aye," Alex said.

The two men regarded each other steadily for a moment. Marco was silent, watching. So was the second man who had entered just seconds earlier.

Slowly, the first man smiled, a wide smile with a gold tooth glinting. "I think I like you, Senhor . . . ?"

Alex hesitated, then said, "Malfour." His true name of Leslie was known only to Burke. He intended to keep it that way.

"So do you like snakes, Senhor Malfour? To reach the . . . stones, you will have to move among them."

"I've been around the two-legged kind."

Another brilliant smile. "Ah, they can be more deadly, perhaps."

"Their intentions are."

"And how much *dinheiro* can you offer for my trouble?"

"You have none to offer?"

"Senhor, no. I am but a . . . how do you English call it . . . a messenger." His look became sly. "I can take your *dinheiro* and return. . . ."

Alex smiled. "That is very kind, but I would not like you to encounter the snakes alone." He paused. "And I am not British."

Tomas raised an eyebrow in question.

"I once was a Scot, before they stole our homeland."

"Then you and I have something in common, senhor. My ancestors' land was also stolen."

"Are you interested in my proposition?"

"*Sím,* you interest me, senhor."

"You interest me, too," Alex said, turning to Marco. "This is my friend, Marco."

The man merely nodded. "How much will you risk for your prize?"

"Much."

"I know someone who might help you. But you will have to go inland, and it is risky for someone who does not know our country." He grinned again. "Of course, you could change your mind and trust me."

"Would you?" Alex asked.

The *bandeirante* grinned again. "I think I like you. We will leave this afternoon."

Chapter Twenty

Alex returned to the ship. He and Marco would go with Tomas; Burke would stay in Vitória with half of the money they had. He'd been told the journey would take a minimum of twenty days. Eight days to the meeting with a band of *bandeirantes* on the Jequitinhonha River. Four days there to bargain, eight days back.

The three of them met with Claude.

Alex and Claude pored over a map. "I want you to sail the ship north, away from the shipping lanes. Return in twenty-one days," Alex said.

"Do you trust him?" Claude asked.

"I trust no one," Alex admitted wryly. "But if all goes well, we can all leave this ship rich men."

Claude nodded.

"I want you to watch the children. And Lady Jeanette. No one is to follow us."

"Oui," Claude said.

"It probably will not be easy," Alex added with an ironic twist of his lips.

"Little is easy with you," Claude said.

Alex chuckled at that. "Aye, I think you are right." He

looked at the others. "We will leave a little before dawn. Tomas says it is easier traveling then."

"Is it safe?"

Alex shrugged. "Burke will stay in Vitória with the remainder of the money to buy the diamonds. He will take proper cautions on secreting it, then leave instructions with you, though I trust his abilities to stay alive completely. No one will know he has any funds with him. I will take enough to let them know I am serious. I am not foolish enough to take it all with me. I am hoping their greed will keep me safe."

He left then, heading to the main deck where he knew he would find Jenna and the children. She was sitting on a stair leading up to the forecastle. Both children were sitting on a step below and she was reading to them from a book.

It was a pretty picture.

He had found her unusually literate and well-read, more so than most women. She would probably be called a blue-stocking in England, but he enjoyed the company of a woman who knew more than how to organize a household and was not afraid to show it.

He walked over to them, aware somehow that she was aware of him, even before he approached. He regarded the book's title. Poetry by Thomas Gray.

Alex knew it, despite the fact that Gray was English. In truth it was his book. He had purchased it in France.

"You like it?" he asked.

"Aye, it is gentle."

"At times," he said.

Her large expressive eyes were cautious. And well they might be. He'd been cruel in order to be kind. At least, that was what he had told himself. Perhaps he had been protecting himself.

She looked down at the children. "Will you fetch me a cup of tea?"

Robin and Meg looked from one to the other knowingly, then started for the hatchway, leaving them alone.

"You came to tell me something," she said.

Her honestly never failed to startle him. He had never thought that a quality of women, but then, he chided himself, it hadn't been of men, either. Wasn't he a prime example of that?

"Aye," he said. "I will be leaving before dawn for the interior. I will be gone for three weeks or so. Claude will sail the ship north, far away from the shipping lanes, and wait."

"And what do you propose to do about me?"

"Will you stay aboard, look after the children? Make sure they do not come after me?"

"Aye."

He stared at her, astonished by the simple answer. She had said she might return to France, but he did not think she would like it. She would find Paris as he had; frenetic and superficial, a city of extravagant privilege and extreme poverty.

"And I have been thinking," she said, confirming what he was thinking. "I think I would like to go to America, to Boston or Philadelphia or Charleston, rather than France. I have been talking to one of the crew members. He said . . . people are more free there. Even women."

Her answer did not surprise him. "I will see you get there."

She looked away. He felt a loss. He wasn't sure why. He shouldn't. He was grateful, aye. She had been unexpectedly helpful. And he would repay her for that help.

She was biting her lip. She had done that at the governor's house, too, displaying an uncertainty in a woman who could be so surprisingly competent. It was that vulnerability that made her so . . .

Irresistible.

He leaned down and his lips brushed her nose now sprinkled lightly with freckles from the sun, then lowered to her lips. They were slightly salty, her face warm. She tasted good, so good that he did not care about the stares that must be directed toward them. His fingers touched her cheeks, then her hair.

He forced himself to draw away. "I had best get some sleep. I probably will not see you in the morning, but you have my thanks. And if either Burke or I are delayed in returning, Claude will have orders to get you to America with money I have set aside for you and the children."

Her eyes clouded. He wondered whether it was at the thought of his not returning. But that was foolish. He knew she was not a woman to sleep with a man lightly, and yet he understood that a night's passion could not overcome centuries of distrust and hatred, nor futures destined to follow in different paths. It had been a moment robbed from time, one caused by extraordinary circumstances.

"It should all go to the children. I told you I had means—"

"You will need more to raise them properly."

Unexpected mischief crept into her eyes. "Properly?"

He felt an odd tug at his heart. Perhaps it was because her own was so strong.

"Aye, and it will no' be easy," he said, lapsing into his Scottish burr.

She looked at him steadily, even as he saw she was trying not to show apprehension. Or something more than apprehension.

"I will be back," he said.

"Meg will be heartbroken if you are not," she said with forced cheerfulness. "She plans to marry you one day."

"I thought she had her heart set on Robin."

"She's having problems making up her mind."

"A decidedly female trait."

"That's a decidedly male opinion."

He grinned at her. He couldn't remember when last he had done that, when he'd so enjoyed an exchange with a lass. She never backed down.

"You," he admitted, "are the exception. You are stubbornly set in your actions. And opinions."

"Aye. I thought you a pirate when I met you, and you are a pirate still."

"And has your opinion changed about pirates?"

"Aye," she said softly. "I did not realize pirates cared so much about others."

He wanted to say nay to that, that he was a fraud and not at all what she thought. But the words did not come this time. He stared at her for a long moment, wondering when she had become important to him, exactly what moment, what second, had brought feeling back into his life.

But hope was gone. Dead. Buried with so many of his clansmen in a place called Culloden Moor. How could anyone who had witnessed that carnage, the brutality, the stark inhumanity to women and children, believe in God, or hope, or dreams? He had been a soldier. He had taken his chances. He would never blame what had happened to him on someone else. But what had happened to hundreds of innocents was something else.

"Thank you for caring for them," he said, then turned away and went down the hatchway. He *did* need sleep. He certainly needed his wits. And they had a way of deserting him when he was with Lady Jeanette Campbell.

Alex managed several hours of sleep. He woke sometime in the middle of the night, dressed, checked his weapons: pistol, powder, dirk, and a second knife. He had liked Tomas, but he knew a renegade when he met one.

He divided the gold to be used to purchase diamonds. The sale of the ship's contents in Martinique had given him more than enough to purchase what he wanted. He kept a small portion he could easily carry, and gave the rest to Burke, who would stay at one of the small inns in Vitória.

Alex bundled a second shirt and second pair of trousers with him, then pulled on his long boots. To the bundle, he added still another knife, and wrapped everything in a rough but warm blanket, then in a poncho, which should protect the contents from water. He'd already learned that there could be violent rain storms as well as dangerous rivers to cross.

He searched his mind to see whether he should include anything else. He knew he was placing a great deal of trust in Claude, and in Jenna. But this was the one opportunity to provide security for those he had taken under his care.

The adventure was important, too. It always had been. He'd sought it even in his youth. Yet wandering no longer provided the satisfaction it once had. He no longer wished to see the rest of the world. He wanted peace.

Satan's blood, but when had that thought formed?

He went up on the main deck. Burke was already there, but that did not surprise him. It seemed Burke never slept. His face looked rough. He had been shaving lately, probably because of Celia, but he had not bothered tonight. He looked even more fierce than he normally did.

"How is Celia?" Alex asked.

Burke looked startled, as if everyone on the ship did not know that he was paying attention to—if not courting—Jenna's maid. They made one of the most unusual combinations Alex had witnessed: the shy and timid Celia and the cutthroat Alex knew Burke to be. And yet Burke was the most steadfast of men when he gave his loyalty.

Now he growled at the question.

Alex chuckled. He felt like growling, too.

"Let us find Marco," he said. "You've brought along your weapons?"

Burke gave him a look of complete disgust in reply.

"Of course," Alex murmured to himself. Burke would *never* be that lovesick.

He looked up at the sky. Dawn was possibly two hours away. But he needed to get away from the ship. And Jenna. Before he threw everything away. Before he complicated things beyond repair.

Claude came over to him. "We leave on the morning tide."

Alex nodded. "Make sure no one else goes ashore."

"Like two children?"

"And a woman."

"I will keep a sharp lookout."

Alex looked around. He half expected to see her here, to see Meg's curious little gamin face.

He hated the disappointment he felt that they were nowhere to be seen.

He felt loss.

Jenna huddled in a chair, her arms hugging her legs to keep from going abovedecks or gazing forlornly out a porthole. Celia slept peacefully on the bunk.

She wanted to be with Meg, but there was no place to sleep there, and Meg no longer needed her as she once had.

She knew Alex was leaving. She heard the sounds of the boat being lowered. Soon, she knew, the ship would be moving away from the Brazilian coast, and from him. She knew from crew members that the interior, where he was going, was dangerous. There were fish that nibbled at people, alligators that ate people, snakes that killed instantly. She knew all that, and yet she wished she were going with him.

For some unfathomable reason, she felt safe with the pirate, safer than she had ever felt in her life.

He did not love her. He obviously did not think he could—or should—love anyone. He took great pains to make that clear to others, even tried to do that with the children, though he failed miserably. He had not failed with her. She was convenient, and willing. Nothing more.

Jenna knew she should feel bad about that. She didn't. No matter what else happened in her life, she had taken risks and experienced something she might never know again. It was worth being a fallen woman.

She waited in her cabin until she heard the boat return, heard it being hauled back up on deck. She heard the anchor being lifted, then she made her way to the sick bay where Meg still slept.

The cabin was dark, but she heard a stir when she entered and light filtered in from a lantern in the passageway outside. A flurry of movement told her Meg was not asleep. Nor was she alone.

"Robin?" she said.

The boy appeared from behind the door. Meg sat up. Both, in the dim light, looked disgruntled.

"You got left, too," Meg observed.

"Aye," she said. "We would be in the way."

Meg considered that in the serious way she had. She did not want to agree, but there was no denying that her injury had created problems.

"I was afraid you might have tried to follow," Jenna admitted.

"I promised," Meg said solemnly.

Jenna was impressed that Alex had been able to extract such a promise, and startled that Meg was observing it. Still, she saw guilty looks on both faces and wondered what they were plotting.

"He will be back," she said.

"I know," Meg said. "He can do anything."

But Robin didn't say anything, and she wondered what hid behind that expression. Should she be more worried than she was?

And why was she so worried already?

Bloody hell, but it was hot.

He tried not to struggle through the jungle, his body unaccustomed to the humid and extreme heat. His leg hurt with every step.

He could stand the pain. But he felt that at any moment, it would stop holding him upright.

He was beginning to wonder at the wisdom of this journey.

Yet he'd known in Vitória that if he did not come, he would not succeed. He had never refused a challenge. If he did now, he feared that he would do it again. He would not allow the English to win, and they would do so if they kept him from doing something he wanted to do.

He'd also thought the challenge would get Jenna out of his mind.

His mind was not so obliging.

Why did he feel such a sense of loss? Wasn't this exactly what he wanted? That she would forget him and make a more secure, safe life for herself?

He stumbled and Marco caught him. Marco, in truth, was managing far better than Alex had expected. He seemed tireless and, to his amazement, had developed an unspoken understanding with Tomas. Perhaps because they were the same kind of men.

He merely nodded, then accepted a stick from Marco. He hadn't wanted to show his weakness but neither, he hoped, was he a total fool.

One foot in front of the other. Concentrate on that. And yet it was Jenna's face that kept him going.

They stopped when it got too dark to see the trails. Tomorrow, he was told, they would travel down a river in canoes. Anything to get out of the jungle with its leeches and snakes and growth that had to be hacked through with machetes. He was learning to be as good with a machete as he had been with a sword.

Tomas disappeared into the jungle. He did that often, returning with meat of some kind. It was usually already skinned, and Alex didn't ask questions. He was quickly learning about another kind of survival than the one he'd mastered in the Scottish Highlands. He had had two enemies then: the English and hunger. Here, the dangers were exotic and he knew enough not to argue with someone who knew how to deal with them.

He slumped gratefully against a tree. His shirt was sticking to his back. So were leeches. He plucked the bloody things off, wishing for a fire. But rain had poured down during afternoon hours and everything was damp. There would be no tinder.

At least he was no longer on his leg. Damn, but it ached. Down to the bone, it ached. Every muscle that had been strained beyond tolerance screamed for relief.

The shadows closed in on him. The moon was shielded by the heavy growth. But he didn't fear those kind of shadows. He feared only the shadows of his soul, the soul he thought he had banished, the soul that cared beyond bearing when he would forsake such emotion.

He touched his face. He felt the bristle as well as the sweat. He must look like hell.

He wondered what Lady Jeanette would think if she saw him like this.

If she saw the real Alex Leslie at all.

Jenna thought the sea would comfort her, engross her, make her forget a man she should never love.

Instead, she saw him in every movement of the ship. She would come up at dawn and watch the sun rise, and look for him at the wheel, even though she knew she would not find him there.

Still, his influence was all over the ship. The crew was polite, even diffident toward her. Respectful. Because they knew she was the captain's mistress? Claude would certainly think that. How much had he said to the others?

Meg joined her. She had improved even more in the past several days. Her cheeks were glowing again with the sun.

"I wish we could have gone with him," she said.

"Aye," Jenna said. She did not pretend with the children. That would be a betrayal of the confidence they had built among one another.

Meg was wearing the trousers and boy's shirt that she usually wore. Jenna couldn't disagree that it was probably safer and more comfortable, but she longed to put her in a fine dress.

Meg didn't say anything else, but merely sat next to her

and watched the sails. The wind was strong, and the ship moved swiftly along the rich green coast.

Three weeks.

Three weeks of not knowing what was happening to him. Three weeks of worrying about him.

And three weeks of worrying where he would banish her when he returned.

Alex sat in a clearing, surrounded by the most disreputable band of miscreants he had ever seen.

He tried not to keep reaching for his dirk.

Marco, he realized, had the same urge. But one move and they would be dead. They might be dead under any circumstances.

He was already exhausted. Running from the British had been child's play compared to traveling down a river alive with alligators and hacking his way through a jungle crawling with all manner of creatures. Ten days. He had eleven days to return.

He allowed Marco to do much of the talking. Tomas had fallen back once he reached a primitive campsite and introduced him to a man named Jorge Filho. He was obviously part Indian, swarthy with straight black hair and a face more scarred than his own.

A man in priest's clothes stood at his side.

Jorge gave Alex a contemptuous look, but the priest regarded him with interest. "You are a Scot."

"Aye."

"Jacobite?"

"Aye."

He gave him a tight smile and spoke in broken English. "You do not like the English infidels."

"Nay," Alex said.

"You want diamonds."

The man named Jorge was listening intently, a scowl on his face.

"Aye."

"You have gold?"

Alex merely looked at him.

"You are a wise man, Captain . . . ?"

"Malfour, at the moment."

"Why should we sell you diamonds?"

Although the priest was asking the questions, Alex knew the authority was the scowling man next to him.

"I was hoping you hated the British as much as I do."

"Why would that make a difference? Your quarrel is none of our affair."

"I understand you cannot get a fair price for your diamonds because the market is controlled by the Portuguese, and the stones must first be shipped to India, then sold as Indian diamonds."

Neither man said anything. They just seemed to wait for further explanation.

"I have a friend in France who can sell them directly. We will pay well."

"Why should we not take your gold now and kill you?"

"Because I will come back. Because I can ensure a steady market for your gems."

The two men looked at each other.

"I do not imagine you appreciate the Portuguese taking your diamonds," Alex said.

The man named Jorge spat on the ground. "Why should I trust you?"

"We are two of a kind. We do not like authority."

Jorge spat again.

Marco looked worried.

The priest beamed at them.

Alex didn't trust that gleam. "Do you have diamonds?" he finally asked.

"I can get them," Jorge answered in guttural Portuguese. "Do you have the money?"

"Aye, here and in Vitória."

"You do not trust us?"

"Do you trust me?"

Jorge studied him. "You have courage, senhor, but I must consider this."

"I should be back in Vitória in ten days."

"That is not my problem, senhor. I did not invite you."

"Tomas did."

"Tomas did not have the right. How do I know you are not with the authorities?"

Alex pushed back the dark hair that clung to his face, showing the scar. "Do I look as if I was a dog of government?"

That reply forced a small grin. "Maybe we can do business."

The *Ami* stopped along the coast to pick up fresh water. A small coastal ship sailing a Portuguese flag was anchored nearby.

Alex had been gone fifteen days, and each one of those days seemed a lifetime.

How could she miss someone so much?

She spent much of her time with Meg and Robin, teaching the former to read. Robin already could read well, but Meg had never read a book and had seemed to have no interest in it until Jenna had told her a good sailor had to read to know navigation. Once started, Meg was insatiable. She had a curious mind that once awakened couldn't get enough.

In just a few days, Meg could already pick out words. When Jenna wasn't around, Robin took up the lessons.

Where was the captain now? Was he safe?

She stood by Claude as he yelled down at the smaller ship. "What news?" he asked in poor Spanish.

A man yelled back something she did not understand.

Claude, though, turned pale.

He turned to her. "The English and French have signed a treaty."

Chapter Twenty-one

Alex spent the next two days haggling. With the haggling came the drinking. It was, quite obviously, a necessary part of bargaining.

A man who did not drink, according to the *bandeirantes,* was not to be trusted. Jorge Filho refused to even discuss diamonds the first day. Alex tried to keep up with them, but after several drafts began to pour most of his share on a convenient plant. He needed to keep his wits about him, and the stuff offered by Jorge was as potent, and as unpalatable, a brew he'd ever tasted.

Late on the second day, Jorge disappeared with Tomas.

Alex lived the next few hours in torment, as the remaining *bandeirantes* passed out except for one cold-eyed man whose stare never left Alex and his friends, and whose hand curved menacingly around the handle of a machete.

Filho returned alone. Tomas, he explained, had business back in Vitória. Alex felt a chill run down his back, but he tried to keep any emotion from his face.

"Do not worry, senhor. The priest will accompany you back."

The idea of the priest did not comfort Alex. He appeared as sly and dangerous as the others.

"I brought some diamonds," Jorge said. "This is a sampling."

Alex studied them. Etienne, who had broached the venture to him, had taken him to a jeweler who gave him instructions as to what to look for. He'd even brought a small magnifying glass with him.

They were diamonds. Not the finest he had seen. And certainly rough, but very, very marketable once certified by a Paris merchant as Indian diamonds.

"I have seen better," he observed.

The bandit squinted at him. "Which would you value most highly?"

He looked at the diamonds in his hand. Most were black or various shades of green. There was a clear polished one, also some the shade of cinnamon, and even an orange one. His eyes kept going back to one that was pale blue.

He hesitated, wondering whether he should reveal what knowledge he had. But he was a judge of men. If he lied, or pretended to be a fool, he probably would not live another day. "The blue," he said.

"You chose correctly. That stone is worth a hundred times the value of these others."

Alex didn't say anything.

"You are unusual," the man said. "Most outsiders believe we are fools or innocents."

"Did they live to discover their mistake?"

Jorge laughed. "I do like you, senhor. I think we can do business. The government pays my people little for the gems they find. In truth, they often enslave our people to mine them. Sometimes they can secret one or two. It is worth their lives to be discovered. But with luck we can buy their freedom."

He paused, then added, "The gringos say the gems are worthless, but we are not fools. They would not be mining every river if that were so. But we have no way to get them to market." He paused, then added, "It is difficult to trust one."

"It is against the law to smuggle diamonds," Alex said. "You have to find an honorable thief."

"And have I found one?" Jorge asked.

"Would my word assure you?"

The *bandeirante* chuckled. But there was a warning in it. "I think not. You will have to prove yourself."

"And how do I do that?"

"I want a good price for these diamonds," Jorge said. "If you get a better price wherever you are taking them, we will be asking for more gold next time."

"How will you know?"

"If you return, senhor, I will know."

"If I do not?"

"We will at least have gotten more than we would from the *cão*."

Alex did not need Marco's translation. *The dog.*

Jorge poured more of the foul alcoholic brew in a rough, hollowed-out wooden mug. He saluted Alex with the drink.

Alex continued to drink carefully. He knew he needed to keep his wits about him. As Jorge did not trust him, neither did he trust Jorge. Had he brought his gold with him, he would have been dead days ago.

But they were two dangerous men with two desperate goals.

They could make a devil's bargain.

"I have to go back to Vitória," Jenna told Claude. "He has to be warned about the treaty."

"His orders were clear, mademoiselle," Claude said. "We are to stay out of sight until we return to Vitória."

She had been growing more and more restless as they finished taking on fresh water. The Portuguese coastal trader lay at anchor next to them, also taking on fresh water from an inland waterfall.

Claude had paid a call to the captain of the small trading vessel, seeking more news. He'd learned that a British warship was in Rio de Janeiro to refit, then planned to search the coast for "pirates." Other ships were hunting throughout the Caribbean.

Claude had hidden the guns earlier, and piled the decks with barrels and boxes to make the ship look like just another merchantman. Dirt had been rubbed on the newly lettered name—*Isabelle*—to make it look older. The Portuguese captain had accepted Claude's explanation that his own captain had sickened and he was serving as acting captain.

"I can pay the captain of the Portuguese ship to take me to Vitória," she said. "I can warn the captain and Burke."

"Someone else can do that, mademoiselle."

"You cannot take the ship near a main port. You cannot even stay here. You told me what he said. The British will be searching up and down the coast."

Claude was silent. He knew she was right. And if an English ship stopped at Vitória, someone was bound to remember a man with a scarred face and a limp. His captain could walk into a trap. "I will sail there myself."

"And put the children and everyone else in danger?" she asked. "I am of little importance to your captain, and I can take care of myself. I have money, jewels, and connections." She was not very sure of the latter, but she would not hesitate to use the threat of them. "The children's safety is of far more value to the captain." She let that sink in, then added, "Did not the captain mention an island south of here? You can go there and wait for us."

"I cannot put you at risk, mademoiselle."

"I will not be. I will say I have been a captive. I will escape from you, and ask the Portuguese captain to take me to Vitória where I can find a ship to take me home. I have money hidden in my dress. I can offer it to him. There I can get word to Burke. We can . . ."

She watched him struggle with his options. But he was

French and considered himself a gentleman. *"Non,"* he said finally. "I cannot risk it."

"You said the Portuguese captain seems a decent man."

"A woman alone . . ." Claude shook his head.

"There is bound to be a reward for my safe return," she said. "A reward instead of a ransom. A sum that would be more than what he makes in a year." She did not tell him there probably would be no reward from her family. "Surely he would take care if he knew that my family is close to the king's."

He shook his head in finality. *"Non,"* he said. "I will send one of my men."

"Who?" she asked. "Whom would you trust? Who could convince the captain to go out of his way?"

"Hamish."

"You need him for the sails."

"Mickey then."

"He's Irish. He doesn't know Portuguese. Or French." The Portuguese captain had replied to Claude's Spanish in a corrupted form all of his own. "But I do. I know some Spanish. I know Latin. And French. I have always been good at languages."

Claude muttered under his breath.

"I did well with the governor," she reminded him.

"Oui, you did," he admitted.

She saw him weakening. There was no one aboard who knew Spanish other than his own smattering, and none but Marco knew Portuguese. They were primarily French and Scots. Hamish had told her they had been lucky to find Marco before leaving France.

But then he stiffened. *"Non,"* he said, and turned away.

Jenna watched as the last of the water barrels were loaded. Both Meg and Robin were in the galley, helping Mickey prepare the evening meal. Robin, she suspected, was cleaning beans and Meg was helping with the baking of bread. It was best to do so at anchor when the threat of fire was less.

Jenna thought of both of them as they were earlier. Meg surprisingly had put on her new dress and shyly appeared to the grins of the crew. Robin had stared at her in amazement, then followed her around like a puppy. Later, he had helped with her reading lesson.

She had looked down at the two heads. Meg's short hair had grown out a little and, once washed, curled around her fine face. Robin had always been a young knight to Jenna, kind and smart and graced with a handsome face.

She would always think of them that way.

She would see them again. Soon. She told herself that.

But now she had to get over to the Portuguese ship. Once there, she knew she could convince the captain to take her to Vitória, the closest town of any size where she could get passage for England.

The water barrels were all loaded, and they would leave on the tide early in the morning, before first light.

She had only a few hours. And she needed an ally. She searched her mind for one; the only possibility was Mickey, who served as cook and jack of all trades. He also hated the English and would do anything to thwart them.

She watched as dusk appeared. There were some last-minute negotiations for fruit in the village; the quarter boat had been lifted aboard, but the smaller tender was still in the water.

Jenna went to the captain's cabin and searched her belongings. She would take two dresses, the undergarments she would need, and most of her jewels. Once again she started sewing them into the hem of one of her dresses.

"Claude, he is too timid. What can you expect of a Frenchman?"

Jenna thought she knew how to gain Mickey's cooperation. He did not care for anyone other than the Irish, except, she'd discovered in these past weeks, the captain.

The captain was his god, his leader, his hero. The captain had outfoxed the English, had made them pay for their arrogance, and Mickey would do anything for him. At the same time, his Irish temperament—a seemingly inborn resentment of most authority—had placed him at odds with Claude more than once.

She had waited until after supper. She read to the children, then left Meg nodding off to sleep. She put her hand next to the child's neck. "Sleep well," she whispered. "I'll be back."

Then she made sure that Robin, too, had gone to bed.

She went up to the galley where Mickey was having his one authorized cup of rum.

"Miss?" he asked, starting to rise.

She had, she knew, acquired almost sainthood status in his eyes. She had helped get the captain back to the ship. She had helped save young Meg's life.

"I need your help," she said.

His thick black Irish eyebrows shot up. "Me, miss?" Although he had softened toward her, he had never used the courtesy of "my lady."

"Aye," she said. "We must warn the captain about the peace treaty, but Claude cannot risk the ship by turning back to Vitória."

He nodded. "But what can we do?"

"I can 'escape' to the Portuguese ship," she said.

He studied her for a moment. "And what does the first mate be saying about that?"

"He does not agree."

He weighed that for a moment. "He be a cautious man."

"But you are not," she said. "Once I am aboard the Portuguese ship, he will have no choice but to let me return to Vitória. He cannot risk offending the Portuguese by trying to bring me back here."

"And you need me . . ."

"To take the tender for last-minute supplies. I can dress

as one of the men. I am as tall as some and with their clothes . . ."

"I could not leave you alone on a ship with foreigners."

"You can go with me, if you think it is necessary. I will say that you are my protector."

He snorted. "They would not believe that. Yer servant, mayhap."

"Whatever you suggest," she persisted.

"Whatever I wish?" he asked in a wondering tone, as if no one had said anything like that before.

"Your captain's life may depend on you," she prompted.

His brows knit together. "You are risking yer life, my lady."

She started at that. It was the first time he'd uttered a title he evidently loathed. "'Tis no more than he would do," she said. "I do not want to see the children left alone again."

He suddenly grinned. "Ye have a servant," he said. "I would love to see that Frenchie's face when he realizes what has happened."

Jenna felt both great relief and that odd sense of anticipation, of being alive.

"I'll need some clothes to leave in," she said. "Something a sailor would wear. The first mate cannot learn what has happened until the tender returns."

He eyed her speculatively. "I can get you some clothes, but they may be none too clean."

She nodded. "I'll put some of my own clothes in a sack. Can you get it in the tender?"

"Aye. Goods to trade."

She looked at him directly.

"Thank you," she said.

"Do not be thanking me. I owe the captain me life. I was starving in Paris when he took me in. No one else would hire an Irishman. When this voyage is finished, I can get my family out of Ireland."

For the first time, she hesitated. What was she asking of him? She had thought of him all alone. She had not known he had family. She had not known much about him at all. He had not said a word. She wondered whether he had horror stories of his own about English rule in Ireland.

She felt a sharp pain in her heart that she had been so unaware of the misery in the world.

"Perhaps . . ." she said, stricken by guilt. Guilt for humanity. Guilt for what she was asking of him. It was mutiny. A benign mutiny, but mutiny nonetheless.

"There will be few people on deck af'er dark," he said, ignoring her sudden uncertainty. "I will be bringing you some clothes close to midnight. We will leave just before the changing of lookouts. The first mate will be sleeping then."

Her heart in her throat, she nodded in agreement.

Alex feared for the first time he would not make it back. Much of the terrain was rocky, strewn with boulders and uneven ground, then it would dissolve into heavy forest. It rained frequently, the forest steaming with heat mixed with water. Leeches crawled over him and the unsteady ground caused him more than a few spills.

Tomas had not returned, and a man who never spoke led the way. He never stopped until Alex simply could not go any farther despite Marco's help. The priest, also mostly silent, accompanied them. He would finish the transaction. Alex suspected that somewhere in the flowing robes was a pile of uncut diamonds.

The pain in his leg was agonizing. His face was bearded now and caked with dirt and sweat. But in his pocket he carried the blue diamond as well as other less valuable stones. It was his future and the future of the children.

Bloody hell, but it was hot. And with each step, he felt warmer. Despite the rain, he couldn't seem to quench his thirst. The mere thought of food was repellent.

One foot in front of another. He kept telling himself

that. He kept telling himself that his . . . weakness was temporary, and yet he knew it was not true. His leg was worse. It might well become useless. The thought of being crippled or losing his ability to walk was agonizing. It had become all too real these past days.

He tried to keep going by thinking of the children, but instead, Jenna's face kept appearing. That gave him the ability to continue. *Concentrate on that. Don't think about the jungle.*

Something swung down in front of him. He swore and the *bandeirante* turned around, his machete moving as fast as a Scot's sword as it cut a snake in two, and it fell just inches from him.

He knew that one bite would have killed him. He'd learned about snakes in the past fortnight.

He nodded at the man, who nodded back, then continued to lead the way for the four of them, his arm constantly chopping at the heavy growth that seemed to have invaded the path they had taken just days ago.

Alex slapped at an insect with his free hand. How many days now? Three, four left before they reached Vitória, and the ship. He envisioned the cool green water, a fresh sea breeze against his face rather than the thick, too-sweet smell of rotting vegetation. It was difficult to breathe.

The priest fell in step with him. "Your leg is giving you pain, no? Should I tell Roberto to stop?"

"We do not have time," Alex replied. "We have a ship scheduled to pick us up. I do not want it to have to linger."

"Will you keep your word, senhor?" the priest asked suddenly.

Alex stopped. "What word?"

"You will return?"

"If I do not personally, someone will," he said. "My associates are most interested in a continuing relationship."

The priest stared at him for a long time. "We do not trust easily, senhor. Smuggling is a serious offense. But our people are poor; some are escaped slaves. We need gold.

They watch the gold mines, but we find diamonds in streams they do not know about. We cannot easily find someone to take them to market for us. The diamond merchants, they say our diamonds are no good."

"They lie," Alex said. "And there are merchants who will accept them." He hesitated. "If I am not caught, I will come back. I know what it is to be hunted."

"I believe you." The priest nodded. "It was the *bandeirantes* who opened Brazil, who found the gold and the diamonds. Now the authorities are bringing in slaves to mine the snake-infested streams and take everything for themselves. We are now often called outlaw for wanting a little of what we find."

They were silent the rest of the afternoon and into dusk. The guide finally stopped alongside a river. Alex studied it carefully and did not see any alligators. He went to the water's edge and started to step into it to wash off some of the accumulated dirt and sweat.

"Be careful," the priest said. "There are snakes."

Alex jerked his hand away.

He ate something that Roberto gave him. He'd stopped asking questions about what the food might be. Then he leaned against a tree, feeling the pain in his leg, willing it to go away. He thought about the diamonds in his pocket and those the priest was carrying. A fortune in Europe.

But his mind kept going to another image. Hair touched with gold and eyes the color of the sea.

"Go away," he mumbled, knowing as he did so that it would not.

The ship was dark when Jenna and Mickey went over the side. There were five men on watch but Mickey had already told them he was taking one last trip for some special alcoholic brew that he'd heard the Portuguese were willing to sell.

The remnants of the crew—most were asleep since they

would leave before dawn—saw nothing unusual, especially when Mickey gave them an extra dram of rum.

She'd stayed to the shadows after making sure both children were asleep. She'd left a note for both of them; she did not want them to feel she had deserted them.

Grateful for the men's clothing, but feeling very strange, she climbed down the ladder. The freedom of movement was marvelous. She made every step and jumped easily into the small boat.

Mickey rowed the tender and they quickly reached the Portuguese ship. A sleepy-eyed sailor looked at them in surprise.

"We would like to see the captain," she said in a mixture of English and Spanish. She took off her cap, letting her hair fall around her shoulders.

The man shrugged helplessly, but gestured them to come aboard. He disappeared while she waited anxiously, hoping that no one would report this trip to Claude. In minutes, she was in the captain's cabin. It was neat, just as Alex's cabin had been, but far smaller with room only for a bed and a table.

But this captain had obviously hurriedly dressed. His shirt was not tucked in, and a threadbare waistcoat barely covered a protruding stomach. His hair was messed, and his cheeks were shadowed by a heavy beard.

He was clearly puzzled as he regarded her long hair flowing down her back, then her clothes. His gaze went to Mickey, who, like so many of the *Ami*'s crew, looked like the worst kind of cutthroat.

"I need your help, senhor," she said in French. "Do you speak French?"

"*Sim,* my . . . *grandpere* was French." He bowed slightly. "But what may I do for you?" he asked.

"Take me to Vitória."

His eyes widened. "But that is impossible."

"Why?"

"I am going north."

She reached into a pouch she carried and took out a garnet necklace that glowed in the dim light of a lantern. "I will make it worth your while."

"I do not understand."

"There will be more. Much more," she said.

"But why can you not go in your own ship?"

She was ready for the question. Mickey was quiet, listening without understanding, yet ready to defend her with the knife tucked in a scabbard on his belt.

"I was taken by a pirate," she said, delivering the speech she'd rehearsed in the past few hours. She felt, rather than saw, Mickey move closer.

She hurried on. "They planned to ransom me, but I escaped when the ship was in Martinique and stole aboard the *Isabelle*. They have been kind, but they had trouble with authorities in Rio—a matter of smuggling, I think—and he will not take me to a port where there might be an official government office."

Jenna had no idea if any of this made sense. Although she had planned her story, she was now improvising the details as she watched the captain's expression. They made sense to her after all the talk of smuggling.

"I hoped," she continued, "that you would rescue me and take me to Vitória. My family will pay you very well, and you can have this necklace as well."

The captain's covetous eyes went to the necklace. "There will be more, you say?" She wondered if he was involved with a little smuggling himself.

"Aye. My family is very wealthy and influential, and would be very grateful."

She saw he was reluctant to believe that. Still, the necklace alone would be worth far more than a week of his time.

"How can I refuse such a lovely senhorita," he said.

"We should go before the crew of the *Isabelle* realize I am gone."

His eyes sharpened. "I would think they would be relieved that you would find a safe harbor."

She hesitated, then said as if reluctant, "I think they would feel they are due a reward; too, and I have nothing else of value with me. But you, sir, look like a gentleman. And you are Portuguese; you are not afraid to sail into your own ports."

He was bowing practically down to his feet now.

She looked past him to Mickey. His face was pure bewilderment. He realized she had succeeded but he did not know how.

She nodded to him with a smile, then thanked the captain.

Within the half hour, they were sailing away from a still-sleeping *Isabelle*.

Chapter Twenty-two

The letter explained things.

Though not to Claude's satisfaction.

Still, he had no choice. He even felt a small bit of relief.

One of his sailors had awakened him when the Portuguese trader sailed away, the *Ami*'s—no, *Isabelle*'s—tender with it. He went to the captain's cabin first and found the note on top of the table.

He could go after the trader, but apparently the mademoiselle had woven her magic over the Portuguese captain as she had over the governor. And the captain. And even himself. He had no doubt that she would get what she wanted: a chance to warn the captain about the peace treaty.

Claude had not been willing to disobey his captain's orders to allow that exact thing. He had been in the French navy too long, his sense of duty to the captain of his ship—even a privateer—too ingrained for him to flagrantly disobey an order.

But at the same time he realized the danger to a man he'd come to respect.

Lady Jenna had taken matters into her own hands. And

if anyone could do it, she could. She was as resilient and resourceful as anyone he had ever met.

"Bonne chance," he whispered in the night air.

Vitória was exactly as Jenna remembered it.

It had taken two days' sailing, and she prayed every minute of those two days. *Please let me make it in time.*

The sun was setting when the Portuguese trader lowered the anchor. The captain joined her at the deck. "You are not happy?" he observed. "You said you wanted to go home."

"I wanted to get away from the pirates," she corrected. "But I am to be married to someone I do not know."

"And you are afraid?" He gave her a sly smile. "I doubt that."

"I would rather go ashore tonight," she said.

He shrugged. "You have paid me well."

"I promised you more."

"Promises are easy to make. I did not depend on it. You were in need."

"You really are a gentleman," she said with a smile.

"Please do not tell anyone."

"I will see that you are repaid for all your trouble. If not from my family, then from—"

"A man escaping the British?"

She stared at him.

"I am not a fool, senhorita. You told a good tale, but I did not believe it. I did admire your courage, though."

"Are you married, Captain?"

"Sim."

"She is a fortunate woman."

"She said I am gone too much."

"Then you should take her to sea with you."

"We have six children. She must stay with them."

She digested that. "Your wife is a lucky woman to have so many children," she said. "And such a kind husband. I will not forget you."

He beamed. "If anyone discovers it was I who brought you here, then I have merely aided a woman in distress. And made a profit doing it. I do not like authorities. They take bribes and do little to protect us. I wish you well."

"Where can I find you?"

"I come from Pôrto Alegre."

"We will find you," she promised, after memorizing his name, and his wife's name.

She changed into a dress, then she and Mickey were rowed ashore. She prayed she could find Burke.

She prayed she was in time, that the British or even the French had not arrived before her.

Mickey left her at what constituted an inn in Vitória. It was the best, she was told, that the town had to offer. And, in truth, despite its simplicity, the sea breeze flowed through the windows and the bed was comfortable.

The establishment's owner, who eyed her with more than a little curiosity, could not understand her limited Spanish and knew no French or English. She did learn that no British ship had visited Vitória.

She wanted to go with Mickey to try to find Burke or one of the group of men Alex had contacted, but he said she could not go where he was going. She would only hinder his efforts; he would probably be killed defending her honor. The thought of Mickey defending anyone's honor was an interesting one, but she did not want to risk his life to make it a reality.

He would return, he added, within four hours.

So she sat at the window, watching the Portuguese ship leave the harbor.

Hours went by. More than four, she supposed.

Then she saw a new ship enter the harbor and anchor. A British frigate.

Apprehension surged through her. She started for the door, then reconsidered. Vitória was small but she knew females did not go into drinking establishments alone, particularly those of the type that adventurers patronized. She would only bring attention to herself if she left now.

She vacillated. What to do? Wait and see what happened. Perhaps the ship had stopped for water and provisions, but Rio de Janeiro would have been better for that. It was larger, with more merchants.

She continued to watch as a quarter boat was lowered and a party of soldiers led by a man in a red uniform climbed down.

Would they check with the inns? Would they ask whether the *Ami* had visited the port? It had gone under another name and flag but its size was unmistakable. Not many large ships, she'd gathered, stopped at Vitória.

She wondered whether Mickey knew the ship had arrived, whether he had found Burke or Alex, or if either of them was even here.

But then if they were, they would know. Just as their arrival weeks ago had been noted by the residents, so would be the arrival of a British frigate, especially one bristling with cannon.

She looked in the bundle she had brought with her. She still had the trousers and shirt and hat she'd used earlier, but while she might pass for a sailor at night, she doubted she would in the bright light of day.

Her heart sank an hour later when Mickey had not yet come and a detachment of British marines, accompanied by a well-dressed gentleman, approached the inn.

Burke glared at Mickey. "You disobeyed orders."

"The lass was coming with or without me. Wasn't anything going to stop her," Mickey protested at a table in a hut that served as some kind of tavern. Mickey had had terrible drinks before, but nothing that approached what he was drinking now. It had taken him hours to find this small establishment with dirt floors, a few tables, and chairs that looked as if they would break under the slightest strain. "Where's the captain?"

"He said to wait here for him. I am staying in a seamen's lodging not far from here. He has gone with the *bandeirantes*."

"*Bandeirante?*"

Burke shrugged. "Soldier of fortune, adventurer." He frowned. "But what is *she* doing here?"

Mickey turned away. They had never liked each other. Burke was Scottish, Mickey Irish: and they had been natural competitors. The fact that Burke had the captain's ear had always been a thorn in Mickey's side.

"She wanted ye to know a peace treaty has been signed between the British and France. It was signed before we took the *Charlotte*."

Burke stilled. He knew what a treaty meant, as did all the members of the crew. It did not mean so much to him personally. He was accustomed to being a fugitive. So was the captain. But now every member of the crew would be called pirates by the world. There would be no safe waters anywhere.

"When will he return?" Mickey asked.

Burke hesitated.

"I am on your side, bucko," Mickey said.

A newcomer entered and started talking rapidly, then a tall, swarthy man with a beard approached Burke. He spoke in broken English.

"English ship in harbor."

Burke stood so rapidly the chair fell and splintered. Without saying anything more, he left the room, Mickey hurrying behind him. They both arrived in time to see a quarter boat heading for shore.

"I should warn Lady Jeanette," Mickey said, starting in that direction.

Burke stopped him. "She will learn soon enough. No one must know that any of the *Ami*'s crew is here."

"But she—"

"Is a Campbell and safe from the British. She can fend for herself," Burke said. "We have to warn the captain."

Mickey hesitated. Perhaps it would be worse if he were found with her. But there was no telling what she might do if she did not know her warning had reached Burke.

"I'm going to tell her."

Burke shrugged. " 'Tis your neck."

Mickey did not wait. He almost ran down the streets, even as they seemed to roll beneath his feet. For a seaman, land was always more unsteady than the sea itself.

He reached the inn just as the British quarter boat landed. He saw an officer along with a man in civilian clothes step out of the boat, then address an officious-looking man in white who met them. He did not waste any more time. He went to the back of the inn and up the back stairs that were for the servants.

Lady Jeanette opened on his first knock.

"Mickey," she said.

"I found Burke. He's waiting for the captain. He'll warn him."

She took his hand, and surprisingly, clutched it like a lifeline. "Thank you."

Embarrassed, he merely nodded and averted his gaze.

She went to the window and looked out. He followed and saw the procession reach the inn's door. They had to know a white British woman was there.

She turned to him. "You must go. Where can I find you?"

"Come with me."

"I cannot. They know I am here. I do not want them searching for me."

He thought hard. "I'll return to the back of the inn every moonset," he finally said, and without another word, slipped out the door and started down the back steps, hearing as he left the precision steps of British soldiers.

Jenna captured a ringlet of hair that had escaped from the neat knot at the back of her head. She quickly found the lace cap that she had brought with her and placed it on her head. She smoothed down her skirts.

Who was the man without a uniform?

Maybe they just wanted lodgings. Still, her hands trembled. She could not make a mistake now. And she had no idea what to do. Should she go back with them? What excuse could she give if she did not? Would her hesitation to return send the British on a hunt for her abductor?

How could she leave him? How could she leave everything she had found?

A knock sounded at the door. She moistened her lips, then opened the door. She recognized the uniform of a navy lieutenant, several British marines, and the man in civilian clothes.

The latter turned searching eyes on her, studying her face, then the rest of her. She was suddenly conscious of the livid birthmark.

But his gaze did not remain there. And she weighed him as well. His hair was a very light brown, almost sandy. His complexion was ruddy and his eyes a light blue.

"Lady . . . Jeanette," he said.

"Aye."

"I am David Murray. Thank God, we have found you."

Alex was hot, feverish.

His leg barely held him. The pain had become so great that the leg had become numb, or had he willed his mind to ignore the agony? Just a few more hours, according to the priest. He was a Jesuit, a member of an order persecuted by both the Portuguese and the Spanish.

He would not go into Vitória, but would stay just outside and wait for Alex to return with the gold. The exchange for diamonds would then take place.

If, Alex thought, he made it. The insects were thick, the heat oppressive once they came down from the hills. They had not yet encountered the fresh breeze from the sea.

"Senhor," said the priest, "you need to rest."

He shook his head. "Have to . . . meet . . . ship."

The only thing that kept him going was the memory of Jenna's face, the way her eyes lit when she saw him. He kept remembering how she smiled, and the way she tipped her head when she was about to do something outrageous.

His fingers clutched the bag of diamonds. Those and the others he expected to collect would mean security for Meg and Robin. It would mean freedom for Jenna. Safety for himself.

What would safety mean without Jenna? Without the children?

He'd thought all he wanted was to rid himself of them. Now he knew how much he would miss them. But he also knew more than ever the limitations of his body. Until now, he'd never really accepted it.

They stopped at dusk, and this time he could not eat at all. All he wanted was water and rest.

"You should eat, senhor," the priest told him.

He just shook his head.

The priest touched his forehead. "You have the sweating disease," he said.

"What—"

But the priest was gone. His eyes closed, and the jungle closed in on him.

Jenna sat as David Murray paced the room.

"How . . . ?" she asked.

"That doesn't matter," he said. "Were you . . . injured?"

"Nay," she replied quietly. "Neither my companion nor myself."

He did not seem to comprehend the former part of her sentence. "Thank God," he said. "I was told they were the worst kind of villains." He hesitated. "How did you get here?"

"I was released at a small village north of here," she said. "A Portuguese trader brought me here. But how are you here?"

"I had heard of the peace treaty," he said. "Then you did not arrive and there were tales of pirates in the area. A British ship dropped off a planter and his wife who had been held captive along with you, and I learned that you had disappeared. I decided to go with them as they hunted this pirate. I thought you might need help, or someone to care for you."

She was astounded at the pronouncement. Even more surprised that his gaze did not linger on her arm and hand. She had started to believe it did not matter. Alex had not cared, nor had others in the crew, but then they were not like any other Scotsmen or Englishmen she'd known. Perhaps that was why she'd liked them.

But this man seemed not to care, either.

She suddenly realized neither did she any longer. She no longer tried so desperately to cover it. She'd allowed it to diminish her life far too long. She'd been made so ashamed of it that she'd seldom ventured out.

Now she was seeing the world. Perhaps not in the way she'd imagined but she was fascinated with every moment of her adventure. She had come alive in so many ways.

She looked at him more carefully. His expression was concerned. His face was not handsome but rather pleasant. The skin around his eyes crinkled, though she did not know whether it came from the sun or laughter. His lips were wide, and she imagined his smile would be quite nice.

"Your home, your children?" She started, remembering that his family was the reason he'd consented to accept a bride he had not seen.

"You are my betrothed," he said. "I could not leave you to an uncertain fate. I didn't know whether the woman they said was here could be you. My prayers were answered, as were those of your family."

"They could not know," she said, startled at the idea that her parents would care at all.

"I told them in a letter that you had not arrived."

She took a deep breath. She looked down and saw that her hands were twisting together in her lap. She tried to relax.

"Why did they release you?"

"They heard rumors of peace," she said. "I told them they could expect no ransom, that my family would be relieved to have me gone." She would not have spoken so plainly weeks ago. She probably would not even have admitted the truth.

His eyes were intent on her. He turned to the lieutenant who had accompanied him. "Will you leave us alone?"

The lieutenant nodded. He backed out, joining the marines who had been hovering in the corridor outside.

David Murray closed the door. He lowered his voice. "Is it the truth? That no one hurt you?"

"Aye," she said.

"You need not worry," he added. "It would not be your fault. I would not hold it against you."

The words surprised her. Even dismayed her. She had been so sure that he would not want her once he saw her arm, let alone if she had been compromised. Even if she had not been in the company of what he considered pirates for nearly two months.

He must have seen the doubt in her eyes. "I made an offer," he said. "I intend to keep my word."

"You did not know about my arm when you made that offer," she said.

"I did." He shrugged. "Your father wrote me about it."

She must have looked surprised.

"He also said you were kind and gentle," he said, further startling her because her father had never expressed that to her. "Those are qualities I want in the person caring for my children," he continued.

No words of love. But they would be a lie. Instead the words were a declaration from a man who seemed to like simplicity.

And he was offering what she thought she wanted most, something that she thought would be impossible.

He was offering her a family.

What if he discovered she had posed as the privateer captain's wife?

What if he knew she had spent a shameless night with him?

Why did David Murray chase over hundreds of sea miles to rescue her?

All those thoughts tumbled through her head.

"You can come with me now," he said. "I'm sure arrangements can be made to comfortably accommodate the daughter of Robert Campbell." He looked expectant.

The daughter of Robert Campbell. The sound of her father's name was like icy water thrown in her face. She wondered then how much the dowry was.

Or was she using that sudden question as an excuse? In the past few weeks, she had fallen in love. She had fallen in love with a man, two children, and the sea.

But that man had not fallen in love with her. He had made it clear that he saw no future with her.

You can still have a family.

At what price?

David Murray appeared pleasant enough but she knew surface appearances meant little. Hadn't she at first considered the *Ami*'s captain a villain of the first order?

Still, David Murray was offering her a life, a family, a future. Safety. Security.

Accept, her head said.

Do not, argued her heart.

Could she really sail away without ever seeing Meg again? Or her captain? Without knowing whether he escaped or not?

"Is the ship sailing to Barbados?"

"No," he replied. "The captain is looking for the ship that captured yours. The authorities in Martinique heard one of the crew say they were going to Brazil. This is the third city we've visited. The captain will be making some queries before we leave."

She considered that. They would discover that a frigate had stopped here three weeks earlier, probably that someone had left the ship and gone into the interior. They might also discover that a man came ashore with her yesterday. Shivers ran up and down her back. When lies begin, they were like seeds that grew and grew. "Then I . . . would like to stay here," she said. "The sea . . . the rocking . . . I get ill. I was so relieved to finally reach solid ground."

Concern immediately crossed his face. She wondered whether she had misjudged him seconds earlier when she thought about the dowry.

"Then I will stay here, too, while the ship is here," he said. "We must get to know each other better, and I can protect you."

The shivers grew stronger. She did not want him here. She wanted to know what was happening to Alex. How could Mickey get back to her? And what would they learn?

If she agreed to go with him, if they left immediately for Barbados, perhaps they would forget about the *Ami*?

She doubted the British authorities would abandon their search for a pirate just because she wanted to go home.

"That is not necessary," she said. "I have been looked after very well here."

He gave her a searching look. "Be assured, my lady, I do not think less of you because of your misadventures." He paused. "I have been looking forward to our marriage. I have been lonely, and my children need a mother."

"How old are your children?"

"A girl just a year old. Her mother died giving birth. Then there's Simon, who is four, and David, who is five."

"Who is caring for them now?"

"A housekeeper. She is a widow."

She absorbed all that information, then put a hand to her face. "I am grateful for your concern," she said. "I never thought you would want me after what has happened."

He took her right hand and brought it up to his lips. "I am grateful you survived and are unhurt. But still I will see those pirates hanged. Every last one of them." His voice hardened. Then he seemed to remember something. "Your maid. She was with you?"

Dear God. What explanation now? She bit her lip. "They did not release her."

His lips tightened. "The blackguards. Well, Lady Jeanette, we will find her for you. And I think the lieutenant will want to talk to you. You may have heard something about this pirate's plans."

She blinked rapidly. "But I did not, sir. I was locked in a cabin the entire time. I knew nothing until I was taken to the Portuguese trader."

"Did they rob you?"

She hesitated. She did not want to convict Alex and his crew any more than they already were, yet it would seem very strange indeed if the pirates had not taken her valuables.

"My coins and some poor jewelry," she said. "Someone advised me to sew most of my jewelry in the hem of my dresses, and I did that. They did not know all I had."

He looked at her with admiration. She shrank inside herself. She did not want admiration for duplicity. She didn't think she wanted his admiration at all. She did not want to like him.

Why couldn't he have been unpleasant and bullying and accusing? Why did he have to be so understanding? So trusting?

You made a promise.

Circumstances have changed.

She was no longer a virgin. She would be cheating him. Lying to him.

Her mind and heart continued to argue within her. She wondered whether the battle was obvious to David.

He will find out that not only did you help the pirates, you slept with one. Then what would a marriage be like?

Three children. A home. A family.

"Lady Jeanette?"

She looked back up at him. His brows were drawn together in consternation.

Jenna put her hand to her head. "I am sorry. It is too much. The last months . . . oh, do you understand? I cannot talk about it now."

He nodded. "I know you will need time. I just want you to know I will do everything I can to make you safe. I will ask the lieutenant if the questions can wait." He bowed. "Will you have supper with me?"

She had no reason to refuse. At the moment, she would have promised the world if he left.

She stood. "Aye. Thank you for all your kindness."

"You are welcome." He paused. "It was not entirely explained to me how . . . pretty you are."

She? The woman that no one wanted?

The very thought renewed suspicions that it may not entirely be her charms but her dowry and his need for a mother for his children that prompted his understanding. And yet, for the first time in her life, she had choices. But did she? She felt like a fly entrapped in a web and not one but several spiders were after her, one of which was her own conscience.

"I will try to fend off the lieutenant until tomorrow," David said, "and I will return at six."

"Thank you," she replied gratefully.

"I will move to the inn this afternoon. If you need anything . . ." His voice faded away, but he searched her face for a moment before quietly opening the door and leaving.

Chapter Twenty-three

Alex knew when the sun rose. He knew it by the heat. But when he tried to move, he could not. His face was drenched in sweat, but his body was shaking with chills.

He couldn't remember ever being this sick, even after Culloden when he was wounded so severely. He'd been weak from loss of blood, from infection, but this . . . Whatever it was blurred the world and racked his entire body with tremors.

He heard the priest mutter something he did not understand.

He tried to sit but could not. He was shaking too badly. He curled up into a ball, trying to find warmth in his own body.

A blanket covered him, then another.

"Malaria," he heard the priest say in Spanish.

Alex heard the word. It seemed hollow, far away, but it penetrated somewhere deep inside. Men died of malaria. He had heard of it, but had never known anyone who had it. He fought the chills, tried to move and rise to his feet. He had to get somewhere. He had to keep moving. . . .

"Must . . . leave . . ." His teeth were chattering so hard, he could not make out his own words.

He heard the priest say something to the guide, but then he was seized by more shaking, and he could no longer concentrate on what the priest was saying, or even what he himself intended to say.

Mickey slunk among the shadows, trying to make himself invisible. The bloody British were all over Vitória and particularly at the inn. The fellow in the fine clothes, in truth, had not left and a detachment of marines had made it their headquarters as they searched Vitória.

They were knocking on every door, asking questions. He had pulled a cap far down on his head to hide his red hair and had folded his body against a wall as if drunk. He had been passed once, but he did not know how much longer he could fool these bloody English. His hand rested on his dagger, but he was loath to use it. Not for any moral reasons, but because he realized a death would prompt an even greater search.

He wondered what was happening with Miss Jenna. At least she had not been taken from the inn. She was shrewd enough to outsmart the bloody soldiers, but she was still only a woman. If they wanted to take her, they could.

Mickey waited until nightfall, then, using the shadows for cover, he made his way back to the tavern. Burke was gone.

No one else understood English or even his poor attempts at a few words of Spanish. Three people were there. Three faces looked at him with blank expressions. Then he heard English voices outside.

One man gestured to him, and he followed the man to a door in the back, down a dirt road, and then into a forest. The man he'd followed was dark complected with black hair and a dark beard. His eyes were like pieces of coal.

"Where's Burke?" he asked.

The man shrugged. "Follow me," he said.

• • •

Jenna looked over her poor bedraggled wardrobe. She had the simple day dress she had worn from the ship, the sailor's clothes, and one afternoon dress. Her trunk with her trousseau was still on the *Ami*.

She glanced down at her arm. The wine-colored birthmark was still there, but it was no longer the whole of her. She realized for the first time how she had allowed it to rule her life.

She would never wear a glove again. Unless, of course, she was disguising herself.

The thought startled her. Where had it come from? Why would she disguise herself unless she became a fugitive? Or choose to be one? Jenna looked longingly at the sailor's clothes she'd worn the night before. How free she had felt.

And now she was trapped.

Or freed?

How strange that after a lifetime of never having choices, she had too many now.

She looked in the steel mirror over the table and tried to see herself objectively, to see what David Murray had seen.

A stranger looked back at her. Not a mouse with her plain brown hair pulled back in a knot. Her face glowed with the sun. Her hair was touched by gold as it cascaded down her shoulders. Her mouth was still too wide, her nose too stubbed. But now she saw life in them rather than the pallor of one confined and without hope.

Was it love that had changed her face?

She left the mirror—a foolish exercise in vanity. But still, to one who had never had reason to have vanity, it was seductive.

She sat in front of the window and watched quarter boats and tenders go back and forth. Her gaze followed the details of marines spreading across the town. How long before they learned that the *Ami* had been there in the guise of the *Isabelle*? How long before they knew a Scotsman had gone ashore?

How long before they turned to her for answers?

How long before she knew the answer she could give them?

She gazed at the sea and saw Alex's face, his body braced against the wind and his strong arms steering a ship that weighed tons. He had done it with such ease and confidence, and even pure joy. She had felt that joy, standing next to him, feeling the same rhythm of the sea, the dance of the ship across the waves, the fresh breeze against her skin. She had felt wonderful, full of a kind of power she'd never known before.

Was it all a myth, a fancy that could not last?

A tear trickled down her cheek. Duty. Honor. Desire. Hope. Love. Need. All the important emotions.

All of them conflicting.

Where was Alex? *Not the captain. Not the pirate. Alex.* Alex with whom she had made love. Who had made her believe that she was so much more than a plain woman who deserved nothing but loneliness.

What would happen if she went with David Murray? If she mothered his children and gave birth to others?

Her head hurt. Pounded with decisions she did not know how to make. Alex did not care about her. But she had given him her heart. How could she give less to David Murray, or did he care whether she had a heart to give him?

Did Alex even have a heart?

She brushed that thought aside quickly. Or course he did. She had seen it in the way he looked at the children. How many had he brought out of Scotland at the risk of his own life?

She was not included in that small charmed circle. She was a Campbell and no matter what she did, she would always be a Campbell to them.

Yet he had desired her, even treated her with respect.

She did not know how long she sat there, staring at the

sea that had both imprisoned and liberated her. It would not be long before David Murray arrived to take her to supper. Perhaps she could learn more about him.

She knew that the decision she had to make should not rest on the character of the man, but on the character of herself.

Meg and Robin. She saw the children in her mind's eye. How could she go without seeing them again, without finishing the book she'd been reading to Meg, without teaching her the joys and agonies of being a female, without showing Robin there was a softer side to life? What if they lost the one person who had protected them? What if they lost Alex?

She'd vowed to remain with the children, to help them, to provide for their physical needs as well as those of their hearts and souls.

She felt a keening noise coming from her throat. She tried to stifle it, but she knew she was not entirely successful.

Think! Do not let emotions rule everything else. What is most important to you? It is your life. No one else's.

And suddenly she knew.

Mickey met Burke in the mule shed in back of Burke's lodging. "I cannot get to her," he said. "The British are everywhere, asking questions."

"I know," Burke said. "They have been here and at the tavern." He spat. "Someone told them they had seen a gringo in this area. I do not believe whoever said the words will live long."

That sounded reasonable to Mickey. He did not like anyone who interfered in someone else's business, particularly for profit. Greed made a man untrustworthy. "What do you plan to do?"

"The captain should have returned today. Something has delayed him. Tomas has gone off to look for them."

"Tomas?"

"The man who guided the captain to the meeting place with the *bandeirantes*. He returned early. His wife had a child two days ago. It cries all the time, and he was ready to leave again."

"I don't like this," Mickey said. "The British do not look like they are leaving soon and some toff has moved into the inn. I heard one of the Brits saying he is Lady Jenna's . . . intended."

Burke grimaced. "An English toff. She deserves better than that."

They exchanged glances. Neither of them had thought much about the Campbell lass other than with the hatred they'd directed toward a Scottish clan that had sided with the bloody British. Not at least until she had helped the captain in Martinique and nursed young Meg back to health. Disdain had slowly turned into guarded respect.

They had also both seen the way the captain's eyes had returned to her every time he thought no one was looking. It had become a matter of speculation among the crew.

"We cannot let that happen," Burke said to the man he disliked.

"Nay," said Mickey, who returned the feeling.

"If she disappears now, the British will turn Vitória inside out."

"Aye. We have to wait until we know where the captain is."

"Keep an eye on her," Burke ordered.

Mickey bristled. "I do not take orders from you." Then he smiled. "But I planned to do it anyway."

Burke's expression was grim. "I hate waiting. If only . . ."

"We do not know where he is. All we can do is wait. I suppose this bandit, or whatever he is, knows what will happen if he betrays us."

"I ha' made that clear," Burke assured him.

"I can find you here?"

"Aye. I will let you know if there is any word."

Mickey hesitated. He wasn't sure how much he could trust Burke. But then the captain trusted him completely. He nodded. "I will be around the hotel, looking drunk." He paused. "Our lady will not be getting on that ship."

Whenever Alex thought he might survive the shaking, the fierce fever, then the racking cold, the attacks started again.

He was barely conscious of Marco and the priest. The priest, whose name Alex still did not know, used his robes to help dry the sweat, and his own blanket to cover him when the chills replaced the burning heat. He urged on Alex spoonfuls of water mixed with some kind of bark and made him drink it. Cinchona, the priest had called it. It was so vile it was all he could do to swallow it.

The priest even prayed over Alex.

That, Alex thought, was an exercise in futility. Alex no longer believed in God. If He was a benevolent being, He had forsaken certain of His children long ago. If He wasn't, then Alex saw no reason for entreaties.

He wanted only a woman with hair streaked with gold and eyes the color of the sea. He wanted to hear her voice singing a sweet song, and he wanted to see a smile on her face.

He should not want that at all. A groan ripped from his throat, and he tried to contain it. He'd learned about the importance of silence. Even in this lonely place, and despite the weakness that claimed his body, part of him clung to caution.

It rained, the water filtering through the heavy growth and soaking all their supplies. When the sun emerged, the forest literally steamed. Yet still he shivered so hard he could not talk. He knew he mumbled something, but he couldn't understand it. After what seemed like hours, the shaking subsided, but he knew it was only a matter of time before the fever returned. Perhaps he could take advantage of that small window of time.

"I can walk," he told the priest. He was grateful to the man even though he no longer believed in a kind God. Perhaps he liked the priest because he was unlike any Alex had met. He was a thief, too, but a thief on behalf of his people. Alex had half expected him to disappear along with the other *bandeirante*. They could have taken his gold and the diamonds he'd purchased. They would not have the lasting relationship they wanted, but it would be more than they had had.

The priest looked at him doubtfully. He had already carved a walking stick for him, but now he offered a hand burned brown and calloused. Marco and the other, silent *bandeirante* had gone ahead, chopping out a path. Taking the priest's hand, Alex rose unsteadily, then leaned against a tree, trying to get his balance. Bloody hell, but he was weak.

He had to get back. The *Ami* should be there, and it could not wait for him indefinitely.

He took a step, then another. If only he could travel a fair distance before the chills and fever returned.

He would reach Vitória or die trying.

But the journey seemed endless. The land did not change in his eyes. The rich green that had fascinated him on the trip into the interior now seemed to reach out and clutch him, holding him back. The vividly colored flowers seemed too brilliant, even deadly.

It started to grow dark and the priest stopped. Alex felt the onslaught of fever again. He knew now it would be followed by the chills and the shaking. He hadn't been able to eat anything, not with the bark mixture he'd forced down his throat. His stomach felt sick and his vision was blurred.

"I am not going to die," he mumbled, more to himself than to the priest. "The bloody English couldn't do it. Not . . . ready."

The priest leaned over him. "Senhor?"

Alex could not answer.

•   •   •

Jenna dressed carefully in her good dress, wishing that she had Celia to help her. Instead, she twisted and turned to button the back of her dress, then brushed her hair until it shone.

She had not Celia's skill with her hair. Celia with one twist could pile her hair into a knot at the back and allow a curl to drop alongside her face. Jenna could most certainly put her hair in a knot but it always looked messy and unkempt. Instead she put on a cap over her hair, allowing it to fall free. She bit her lips and pinched her cheeks.

She was ready for David Murray when he appeared. She had hoped, nay, prayed, she would hear something from Mickey or Burke or, even better, from Alex. But there had been nothing. But then the inn had been filled with British soldiers. She had strained to hear something, anything, but there had been no news.

Perhaps Mr. Murray would have news. But she would have to be careful to hide her interest, and the reason for it. If anyone believed she had been a willing accomplice, she too would be subject to penalties.

David Murray arrived, looking very much the prosperous gentleman. He wore tan breeches with a shirt trimmed with lace, a sky blue waistcoat, and a white cravat. His hair was powdered and pulled back in a queue.

He smiled as he studied her as much as she had studied him. "You look lovely," he said.

She curtsied. "Thank you."

He offered her his arm. "I have arranged for a corner table."

Jenna wished she did not feel so guilty, that she could enjoy a normal supper with an obvious gentleman. She couldn't. She wanted supper with an outlaw.

"The weather is very warm," she said once she was seated.

"It is in Barbados, too," her companion commented.

"Tell me of your home."

"It is dryer than Vitória," he said. "But beautiful. I think you will like it."

He was assuming—quite naturally—that she would marry him as planned.

"And your plantation?"

"I grow sugar. It's made mostly into rum. South Run overlooks the Caribbean and we get the sea breeze most of the time."

Sugar. That meant slaves. But then she'd always known he must have some.

She shivered.

"Are you cold?"

"No. I was just thinking of . . ."

"I am sorry. I feel responsible. If you had not been coming to meet me, nothing would have happened. You would be safe back in Scotland."

And hiding in her room. A virgin. Unloved, unwanted.

She tried to smile. "I do not regret anything," she said. She started to say she had learned to love the sea, but she had already said that the sea made her sick. Those lies, again. They always came back to haunt her.

"You are a brave woman," he said.

She shook her head. "Nay. I had little choice."

But she had. She could have escaped in Martinique. She had made a decision then.

"I did not intend to keep reminding you of what happened," he said apologetically. "And I was able to keep the lieutenant from questioning you. I told him you knew nothing, that you had been locked in a cabin the entire time. The other passengers were able to give descriptions."

"Thank you," she said again. How many times had she said that?

He was silent for a few moments. "If it is not . . . too soon, I thought we could wed here."

Jenna stilled. "You do not know me," she said feebly.

"I admit I was not totally enthusiastic about wedding someone I had never met," he said slowly. "But my grandfather, who arranged the marriage with your father, assured me you were kind and intelligent, that you would make a good wife and mother. You are more than that."

She was very conscious of the lump in her throat growing larger. "There are no marriageable women in Barbados?" she asked finally.

"They marry young," he said. "I had no desire for a girl of fourteen or fifteen. I wanted someone educated to teach the children, and I suppose I wanted someone who had lived in England."

"I am Scottish," she reminded him.

"Aye, but your family is Campbell."

There it was again. Her name. A curse to some.

But not to David Murray. His very kindness convinced her of that. How could she cheat him? Lie to him? She was sure he believed she was a virgin. A decent woman. An honorable woman.

The silence stretched between them.

"Will you consent to a marriage here?" he asked.

"No," she said sadly. "I had planned to try to get to know you in Barbados, to see whether we suit before a wedding. It is too soon." She started to say, particularly now, implying that the last weeks had been too terror-filled for her to make decisions. But she could not lie to him. If he had been demanding of every detail of the past weeks, she could have lied. But his very patience made it impossible.

He looked disappointed, but he nodded.

"How long have you been in Barbados?" she asked.

"Fifteen years," he said.

"How did you happen to go there?"

He shrugged. "You would hear, sooner or later. I was involved in a duel. I killed a man. I was a third son, and an embarrassment. My father gave me a sum of money and said he never wanted to see me again. He put me on the first ship out of London. It happened to be bound for Barbados."

"And you turned it into a plantation."

"Not without a lot of work," he said.

"And your wife? Was she from Barbados?"

He hesitated, and she felt unease in him. Discomfort. As if he, too, was withholding information.

She was learning about secrets and lies. She wondered if she too avoided a glance, or hesitated a moment too long.

He flushed under her scrutiny.

Why did he want to marry her so suddenly?

She studied him. She had seen venality in faces. Greed. Ruthlessness. She did not see it in him. But then did he see a pirate's light-of-love in her? Obviously not.

"No," he finally said. "She was from Martinique."

She knew her eyes must have widened. "French?"

"Yes."

Her eyes lowered to the food that had just been delivered to the table. None of it looked familiar. But she was hungry. She had not realized how much until this very moment. Her mind had been occupied by other matters. And now it was an excuse as well. She did not want to like this man.

She did. He was hiding something. She recognized that. But she was hiding something too, and she did not think that made her a particularly evil person.

She tasted some meat that had been spiced far beyond anything she had tasted in Scotland or on the *Ami* or in Martinique. The fire roared down her throat and she grabbed the goblet of wine that had been put in front of her.

He picked up his knife and started to eat.

Oddly enough, the silence between them was not awkward. He was an easy man to be with; easier, in fact, than the captain.

Unfortunately, she had found she no longer valued easy or comfortable. She wanted the electricity that flashed between a man and woman, the storm that made every part of her quiver inside at the thought of him. She wanted to feel the way she had felt in the captain's arms, as if she had come home. She knew him now, perhaps better than he knew himself. She knew the way he hid his feelings, and she knew the raw courage with which he defended those for whom he felt responsible, the fierce loyalty he invoked in others.

She looked up and saw Mr. Murray's gaze on her. She met it directly, amazed at herself for doing so.

She never would have done that a year ago.

She never *could* have done that a year ago.

Hours later, David Murray returned her to her room. He hesitated at the door, then lifted her hand and kissed it.

"I hope you will reconsider," he said.

She did not have to ask him about what. He meant his proposal for an immediate marriage.

She could do nothing until she knew what had happened to Alex Malfour or whatever his name was. Until she told David Murray everything, and he had reciprocated. Probably not even then. How could she ever settle for less now that she had known glory?

It was dark outside now. She saw one British patrol on the street, and no more.

She waited an hour. Then another. She braided her hair. Considered changing into the sailor's clothing, but then she would have no excuse at all if seen. This way, she could say she needed some air. Just some air.

That, at least, would be the truth. She felt she was suffocating by not knowing what had happened, by the intricate verbal dance she'd just performed with David Murray. She knew she would go mad without knowing something.

Midnight. It had to be long after midnight.

Mickey would be out there someplace. He would not have deserted her.

She waited another hour. The streets were completely quiet now. No British marines anywhere.

She opened the door and looked out. The corridors were quiet. She wondered which room David Murray occupied, though it made no difference.

Jenna gathered her skirts around her and her slippers made little sound as she fled down the corridor, then the stairs. The gentleman who manned the desk was nodding in a chair. She moved through the hall to the back door and quietly opened it. A half-moon and stars lit the alley outside.

She stood in the shadows there, trying to get her bearings, hoping against hope that Mickey would suddenly appear.

Mickey or someone else.

She pressed her back against the wall of the building, more lonely than she ever thought she could be, even in her worst moments. Apprehension had filled her these last few hours. She had thought about the captain, and somehow she knew he was in trouble.

She tried to tell herself it was only her imagination.

Yet she couldn't throw it off.

A shadow. Then a form materialized from behind a building.

"I have been waiting for you," Burke said. Not Mickey. Burke. He was supposed to be with the captain.

"How did you know I could come?"

"I knew," he said with assurance.

"Where is the captain?"

"I just heard. He is still in the forest. He is ill."

Her heart dropped. "I will come with you."

He gave her what anyone else would consider a grimace. She knew it to be the slightest hint of a smile.

"I just need to get a few things."

"Aye," he replied simply.

She turned around and ran into the inn, then slowed to tread more silently up the stairs. She reached the top, only to find herself face-to-face with David Murray.

Chapter Twenty-four

His face was in the shadows, lit only by an oil lamp from the hall. He wore no waistcoat and his shirt was open at the neck. His eyes were questioning. "My lady?"

"I needed some air," she explained.

"You were talking to someone?"

"Just a sailor."

He glanced around the hall. The doors were all closed tight. "May I come into your room?"

She froze. What if he told the lieutenant and his marines that he had seen her sneaking out to meet someone? What if he kept her here? What if Burke came up to find her when she did not appear?

"I am very tired," she said. "Perhaps tomorrow."

"If I were a gentleman, I would agree," he said. "But I have not always been one, and I need the truth."

"The truth?"

He had opened the door to her room, and by his very movements he herded her inside. He also brought the oil lamp inside.

"You need not fear me, my lady. But neither do I wish to

spend my life trying to save someone who does not want to be saved."

She wanted to flee. Alex was deathly ill somewhere, and perhaps she could help him.

"I am not sure what you mean," she said instead.

"You did not appear to be a terrified hostage."

"I am a Scot. I do not terrify easily."

"Apparently not," he said, "if you go out at night and meet a sailor, and not one from the British ship."

"What do you want, sir?"

"I do not want to covet a woman already taken. Are you taken Lady Jeanette?"

"I am betrothed to you."

"I think we both understood that . . . we might not suit."

"And we do not suit?"

"I believe we could. If you have not already given your heart to someone else."

"And if I have?"

"I will understand." His steady brown eyes probed her.

"Why?"

He went to the window. "You asked me why I could not take a bride on Barbados. There was a reason. My wife was French. She was also a quadroon. A free woman but, in the eyes of society on the island, tainted. That is why I had to look elsewhere for a wife. No family on the island will consider a match."

"And your grandfather?"

"He did not know about Simone." He turned back to her. "I knew you might leave when you heard."

"Nay," she said. "Not for that reason."

"My children need someone who will love them. They told me you liked children. I had hoped . . ."

Jenna looked at his earnest face. She thought then she could trust him. She had to trust him. She had to leave or Burke would either leave on his own, or come after her.

"I must go," she said. "I am sorry, but someone I care about needs me."

He smiled slightly. "I feared that. The captain of the *Ami*?"

She did not answer.

"I know French quite well because of my wife. I had heard that he was with a woman with light brown hair and sea-colored eyes. And she did not seem to be a prisoner. I do not think the lieutenant received the same information I did."

"Like you, the captain has children," she said. "He saved ten of them in Scotland and is looking after several of them. They need him."

"And you? Do they need you as well?"

"I do not know if they need *me*," she said honestly. "But they need someone."

"My grandfather was right. You would have made a good wife. But one can not help whom they love. I know that as well as anyone."

She smiled. "I think you do. If circumstances were different, I would accept your proposal and gladly so. But I cannot."

"You are sure it is what you want?"

"Aye."

"I am sorry about that," he said.

"You will not say anything to the British?"

"I owe them nothing," he said.

"You owe me nothing, either. You came all this way to . . . save me."

"It was selfish. You were my last chance. At least on Barbados." He hesitated. "And you are kind enough to be honest. I have loved deeply. I would not take that away from you."

"You can still find someone in England."

"It was not a good idea," he said. "My children will suffer as long as we remain on Barbados. It is time to go somewhere else. Perhaps then we can find someone who will love them."

"And you," she said. "If I had met you first . . ."

"I do not think so, Jeanette. You cannot force love." He turned back toward the door. *"Bonne chance,"* he said, and left. He was not French, but the French expression seemed more meaningful and poignant than any other would be.

She stared at the closed door, wishing for that small bit of time that she could have loved such a good man. She would have been content.

But she had gone beyond contentment with Alex. She had to follow her heart. If she did not, she would wonder and regret all her life. She might be making a terrible mistake, but she could not settle for less than love now.

Her heart was with Alex. She had given all of it to him in Martinique.

And he was ill.

She looked around the room, gathered a few belongings and said a prayer. *Please let David Murray be what he seems to be.* Would he keep his word? Or could she be leading the authorities to Alex?

Jenna opened the door. No one was in the corridor, which was now dark because the oil lamp remained in her room. She turned back and blew it out, then made her way past the doors, wondering which one belonged to David Murray. Was he still there?

She made it down the stairs and saw no one. She opened the door to the back and slipped out. Immediately Burke stepped next to her. "I did not think you would come. I was going to go."

"I was delayed. Someone saw us."

Burke took his dagger out of his belt. "What room?"

"Nay," she said. "He will say nothing."

"How do you know?"

"I know. And I will not tell you what room he is in."

He gave her a fierce look.

"We do not have time to argue," she said.

With an angry look, he pivoted around, leaving her to follow. They stayed to the shadows but moved swiftly through the streets until they reached the shacks on the outskirts.

There they met Mickey and a dark, swarthy man who said nothing as they arrived, merely turned away and started walking. They all silently followed him until they reached water. The swarthy man gestured them to get into a canoe. Mickey went first, and the small vessel swayed back and forth until she thought it would tip over. Finally it settled, and with Mickey's help she stepped inside. Then Burke entered and finally their silent companion, who took the middle seat and started paddling.

Jenna kept looking back over her shoulder, expecting to see British soldiers behind them, but there was only silence.

David Murray had kept his word.

Alex drank more of the bark. It did not seem to help. The alternating chills and fever continued to ravage his body.

"It takes time to work, senhor," the priest said.

Alex did not know how much time he had. Each day he felt life ebb from him. Even a few steps exhausted him. His life had become a series of nightmares. He was haunted by Culloden, by those few moments of slaughter. His friends falling under cannon, the agony of his own wounds, the sounds of the dying.

The trees faded into one another, seeming like a shroud closing in around him. The incessant rain was like drumbeats, a sound he'd never wanted to hear again.

"I will . . . not make the . . . ship," he said.

"Tomas will tell them what happened and that you will be late," the priest said.

"They cannot stay there."

The priest said nothing.

"Will you see that the diamonds get to my people?" he said. "There are children."

"You have told me about them, senhor. It is why I have stayed with you. I did not know at first whether you were a good man. I think you are."

Chills racked Alex's body, and his teeth chattered so hard he could not respond.

The priest covered him but the covering was wet and did nothing to warm him. It was too wet to start a fire.

He was barely conscious of a noise. That he was conscious at all was comforting. That he was *barely* conscious was terrifying.

He tried to turn, but the shaking had seized his body again. His vision was blurry and his ears seemed stuffed with some substance.

"The captain?"

He heard the soft but determined voice as if from a great distance. A dream. It had to be a dream.

Jenna Campbell was at sea. Miles away.

Perhaps he was hallucinating again.

But then he saw her face. It was blurred, just as everything was blurred, but he saw the sea-colored eyes, and felt the touch of her hand. It was warm on his icy body. "Alex," she said.

He tried to concentrate. She *was* here. He felt, saw, and heard her, even if it was as if through a tunnel. "Jenna?"

"Aye, Captain," she said, and he thought he detected both concern and wry humor in her voice. "You cannot get rid of me."

He knew now—with every fiber of his weary body—that he didn't want to get rid of her. He had never wanted to get rid of her.

"The . . . *Ami*?"

"Safe," she said. "She sailed to an island south of here to wait for you. It is said to be isolated."

"The English . . ."

"In Vitória now, but we—Burke and Mickey and myself—got away safely."

"Burke . . . good. But how . . ."

"Do not try to speak," she said. "We have brought some blankets and found something to keep the rain off you. Rest. Just rest."

She sat back, her hand on his cheek, and started to sing a soft song, just as she had sung for Meg. Burke appeared and piled several blankets on him and covered them with an oil-cloth. He nodded to Burke, then closed his eyes.

He was so tired.

Jenna was frightened. Frightened for him. So frightened that she forgot her own discomfort: the clothes plastered against her skin, the leeches that clung to her body, the insects that attacked in swarms. Her hair was tangled with some of those same insects and sweat and dirt. Her legs ached from traveling through rough terrain, and her arms were cut by all manner of foliage.

But that was nothing compared to the captain's condition.

Burke had been told he was ill, but she'd not imagined how ill he was. Even through the sun bronze of his face, he looked pallid under thick black bristles of a beard. His body was shaking so hard that she feared it would break.

She had talked to the priest, and he'd told her what he had been giving him.

"Can you not give him more?"

"Not without killing him," he replied in poor English.

She swallowed and knelt again next to him, holding his hand tight in hers, trying to give him some of her body's warmth.

"What is it?"

The priest shook his head. "The sweating sickness. I've seen other Europeans get it. I only know that the bark of our cinchona tree helps the illness. It is exported to other countries."

"How long has he had it?"

"Four days."

"Has it gotten better?"

"No, but it takes time."

"What else can we do?"

"Just try to keep him warm. The chills ravage his body."

She looked down at him. "Go away," she said. "All of you. Leave me alone with him."

"Nay," Burke said.

But the priest was looking at her. "*Sim*," he said, darting a glance at the other three Europeans. "You want him to live?" he asked Burke when the man started to protest.

Burke looked at her hard, then seemed to understand. "We will not be far away."

The priest gave her a leather pouch. "I have pounded the bark. Mix it with water and give it to him when the sun goes down, then at dawn." He pointed his hand at the pistol, lying beside Alex. "Fire it if you need us."

Then he faded through the woods with a silent stranger. Burke, Tomas—the man who had guided her small party— as well as Marco and Mickey reluctantly followed them.

She checked the blankets. They were quickly drying now that the rain had stopped. She piled them on Alex, then lay next to him, putting her arms around him and trying to warm his body with her own.

She felt every shiver, every shake of his body, and held him even closer, willing her strength into him.

"It will be all right," she whispered. "I will not let anything happen to you."

Then she started to hum.

After several moments, the shaking subsided slightly. His body relaxed slowly and in minutes he seemed to fall asleep. The shivers did not stop, and she continued to hold him.

He wouldn't die. She would not let him.

The shaking gradually faded.

Alex was still shivering but the violence was gone. He felt drained, too weak to do more than lie there, absorbing the warmth of Jenna's body. Her hands had relaxed, and he knew she was sleeping. He feared if he moved, she would wake.

What had brought her here? How did she get here? And what kind of danger was she in? Burke would look after her. Probably Mickey would also, though he did not know him as well as Burke. What if she got the same illness he had?

Neither the priest nor Marco nor their guide had come down with this. But he could not take the chance.

He put a hand to her cheek. It was soft. Warm. He was struck by the fact that she had left safety to come to warn him, to be with him. She had done it in Martinique, but he had thought it had been something spontaneous then, and for the children.

Why? He was certainly no prize. God knew he was probably the least of all prizes. Especially now. His hand went to his thickly stubbled beard. His skin was caked with dirt and sweat. He could not even move a hand without supreme effort.

Yet she had slid in next to him, using her body to warm him. He tried to move. He was so damnably weak, and he was suddenly burning up.

The fever was better than the chills, but not much. The fever did not bring the shaking. He craved water.

A groan was forced from his throat, and he felt her stir.

Her eyes opened. Those beautiful blue green eyes that always so disconcerted him. They looked worried.

"Alex?"

His name had never sounded quite as lyrical before.

She touched his face, almost drawing back from the heat. "You are hot."

"The illness . . . does that," he said. "You should not be near me. You might get it, too."

"I've been kidnapped by a pirate. Nothing scares me."

He gave her a weak grin.

She shifted away from him and rose to her feet. He watched as she added water with the same mixture the priest had used. She was dressed in sailor's garb, a rope holding up her trousers and a shirt falling over her breasts. Her hair was uncovered, twisted into a long braid that fell over her shoulder. Though she dressed the part, no one could think her a man.

She was obviously unconscious of her appeal as she concentrated on preparing the potion. He dreaded taking it. The taste was so bad it was all he could do to keep it down. And his stomach was empty.

"Burke?"

"He and the others went a small distance away. They are close enough to hear, but I thought . . ."

He remembered waking next to her, her body entwined with his, that her body had warmed his. But he did not know—had not known—that they had been left alone. For her modesty? Or did the priest believe she could care for him better than he could?

"They are all right? The children? The crew?"

He had asked before. He did not remember. "Safe," she assured him. "The *Ami* left before the British came."

He looked up at her blankly.

"Peace has been declared," she said.

"You can go . . . home, then."

"Nay," she said. "No longer."

He tried to absorb that, but no thought remained in his mind long. He closed his eyes. He couldn't remember when he had been so tired.

But then she was urging him to drink, pressing a cup to his lips. He opened his eyes and tried to push it away. "You must drink it," she said softly.

Something kept echoing in his mind. "You said you couldn't go home. No . . . longer, you said. Why?"

"Drink and I will tell you."

He drank, fighting not to bring it back up again. She held his head up. He could not even do that.

That fact shamed him. He drank what he could, then fastened his gaze on her. "Why can you not go back?"

"Mr. Murray was in Vitória," she said. "He came with the British frigate to rescue me."

He tried to understand her words. They made no sense. "How . . . ?"

"Your friend the governor, I suppose. He or someone on the island had heard Brazil mentioned. The British arrived and are prowling the coast. David Murray decided to come with them."

"Then why did you not go with him? Or was he . . ." He left the words unsaid, but the implication hung in the air. Was he unsuitable?

"In fact, he is very nice. Even kind. He did not try to stop me from coming to you."

He questioned her with a glance.

"I told him I could not marry him."

He tried to understand, but his consciousness was fading in and out. He tried to imagine the encounter between a man who had come to rescue his bride only to discover she did not need rescuing.

Why had she risked everything to warn him? Mickey could have done that. Or Burke.

Meg. It must be for Meg.

God, but he was hot. He had wished an hour ago for heat, but now it was burning him up inside.

He couldn't think any longer. Couldn't reason.

He closed his eyes and hoped the foul mixture he'd just consumed worked.

The priest returned at dusk.

He spoke again in poor Spanish as he squatted beside Alex.

"The fever has ebbed," Jenna said. "Will the shivering return?"

"It has been three days since he started taking the bark," he said. "It should begin to work."

"And if it does not?"

"Then it is God's will."

"It wouldn't be my will," she said angrily. "There must be something else we can do."

"You are not Catholic?" he asked.

"Nay."

"And the captain?"

"I do not know for sure, but he is Jacobite," she said. "Does it make a difference?"

"It could," he said wearily. "I must know if I should give—"

She suddenly understood. "No," she said. "No."

"Then pray, senhorita. He does not have much strength left."

"Food. Is there anything he can eat?" She grasped for a piece of hope. Any hope.

"Tomas is hunting. If he finds anything, we can make a broth."

"And Burke?"

The priest smiled. "He is very devoted to your captain. It is all we can do to keep him away."

"He has been with him for years."

"Then I will send him to you. I thought you wanted privacy."

"He will want Burke," she said.

"So be it; I will send him."

She watched him leave, then sat next to Alex. He seemed to be breathing easier, but was that just wishful thinking? She touched his skin. It still felt hot to her. She wanted to bathe him with the water available in the jug, but that might wake him. He needed sleep more than he needed to be clean.

The sun sank lower, and the air started to cool. Still, she did not move. She wanted to be there if he needed her. Burke appeared, seemingly out of nowhere, carrying something wrapped in cloth. He nodded to her and sat down.

She was surprised that he said nothing. No bluster. No questions. Perhaps that indicated, more than anything could, how serious Alex's condition was.

Dark settled around them, pitch black, since not even moonlight filtered through the heavy foliage. Jenna changed position slightly, but stayed where she was. So did Burke.

At some point, she went to sleep. She wakened in the thick, almost sodden air. Each time it took her a few seconds to realize where she was. And she would look down at the shadow that was Alex, and touch him lightly so as not to wake him while making sure he was still there.

His body was still warm, but not as feverishly hot as it had been. The chills had not returned.

Please let him get well.

One time she heard Burke moving about and felt his gaze on her though she saw nothing but shadows. He did not say anything and yet there was a quiet but strong understanding between the two of them. They did not need words.

Then her eyes closed again.

She woke to a gray dawn stretching across the sky. Burke was sleeping not far away. She looked down, and found Alex staring up at her. She touched his forehead. Still slightly warm but nothing like earlier.

He caught her hand. "You should not be here," he said.

"I could not stay away."

His dark eyes had more life in them than hours ago. "I do not want you to get ill. You should leave."

"No."

His lips twisted into a small smile. "Have you always been this stubborn?"

"Nay," she replied. "Just since I met you. You seem to bring it out of me."

He sighed, and she knew it took every ounce of his strength to even talk. Still, he looked better than he had.

"Can you eat?"

"Aye," he said; then looking a little surprised, he said again, "Aye."

"Then you are getting better."

"It was your warmth last night," he said.

"You remember that?"

"Aye," he said slowly. "I felt your warmth coming into me. You would not let me go."

She swallowed hard.

He moved and she saw him wince. She took his hand and held it tight. She felt the pressure of his fingers against hers, and the pressure comforted her. There was strength left in his body.

"Burke brought something last night. I think the priest sent it."

He gave her a weak grin. "Then I am not so sure I am hungry after all."

She touched his cheek. "Aye, you are." She gently untangled her fingers from his and directed her attention to Burke. "You brought food?"

He grimaced. "Some might say so." He unwrapped something and handed it to her.

It was some kind of hard bread along with a strip of cooked meat. She wondered if it was snake, but she was not going to ask. Instead, she returned to the captain's side and offered it to him. He took it and chewed slowly, each bite obviously an effort.

She watched him force one bite after another. Each seemed to take more strength than he had but he tried until his hand fell to his side.

"Some water?"

"Aye."

She cradled his head with her arm, holding it high enough to allow him to drink better. He gulped it down.

"How . . . how did you get here?"

"I walked," she said simply.

He chuckled. It was a weak chuckle, but a chuckle, nonetheless.

"You do feel better," she observed with satisfaction.

"Aye, but then I could not have felt worse," he said.

"I noticed," she said. "I was worried about you."

"You should worry about yourself, lass."

She smiled at the word he chose. There was an odd intimacy in it, an admission perhaps of all the small—and large—steps they had taken together.

"I do," she assured him. "But it seems your life and . . . health is important to my own."

He flinched. "This Murray . . . you did not like him?"

"I liked him very much," she said.

"He blamed you—"

"Nay, he blamed me for nothing."

"Then why . . . ?"

"I told him I loved someone else."

She saw the information register in his face. "You cannot."

"One does not choose whom they love or do not love," she said.

He closed his eyes. He was denying her words. Refusing to accept them. After a moment, he opened them again. "Where are we?"

"We are a day away from Vitória," she said. "Your . . . companions doubt the British can track us. But they are taking precautions."

"Burke?"

"He's here."

"The money?"

"He has it," she assured him.

He sighed wearily as if he had exhausted all his strength in those few questions.

"Rest," she said.

"We have to get back to the ship."

At least it was "we" now, Jenna thought. "Not yet. Get some rest, and we will start tomorrow." She took his hand in hers, surprised that his fingers tightened around hers.

But he was weak. Ill.

Tomorrow? When he gained strength?

She would not let herself think that he would not touch her when fully returned to himself. That he again would become the loner that he seemed to take such pride in.

At the moment, she did not care. All she wanted was to see those blue eyes fill with the light and stubbornness and curiosity that had so attracted her. She wanted to see him stride impatiently across the jungle paths to the deck of his ship.

She would sacrifice anything to see that happen.

Chapter Twenty-five

The chills returned. Alex shivered, but they were not followed this time by the violent shaking. The cycle that had so racked him was changing, the intensity fading.

He woke to find Jenna sleeping in his arms again, and tried to keep from moving. Her warmth seeped through their clothes and it was life-giving to him.

But more than her body warmth was life-giving.

She made him want to live, to fight to live.

Even in the dirty, muddy trousers and shirt she wore, her hair gathered into a braid that fell over her shoulder, she looked beautiful. Even with the weakness that sapped his body, he felt a surge of desire deep within him. He would have believed that impossible a few days ago.

He wanted her in so many ways. He'd been startled to see her, but then not completely surprised. That was the most amazing thing of all. He had come to expect the unexpected from her.

Inside, she was every bit the adventurer that he was, and knowing that she had sacrificed marriage and a family and security for him was humbling.

He just was not sure that he could give her what she wanted, what she needed, what she deserved.

He did not know whether he could ever stop running, ever stop trying to wreak vengeance on the British. And now that a peace treaty had been reached, he would be hunted across the British empire.

She deserved more than that.

She stirred, sleepy eyes opening and looking at him, comprehension slowly dawning, then they lit with delight. She raised one of her hands to touch his face.

Too late, he thought of the danger involved. "You should not be so close, lass," he said. "I would not want you to get this illness."

"You are better," she said. "And the priest said it does not spread from one person to another."

He shivered slightly, but it was nothing like the cold he'd felt before. "I am not so sure of that," he said. But the fingers of his right hand found hers, and wrapped around them.

"You should have gone with the Englishman," he said. "You would be safe. From the British, from this forest, from illness."

"But my heart wouldn't be safe," she said softly, uncertainty in her eyes, her voice.

He had no reassurance for her. He could never have reassurance for her. He'd given up on his own life months ago, even years ago. It was not self-pity but awareness that he was a marked man, in more ways than one. He'd been scarred on his face and leg, and in his heart. He did not think he could ever care for someone as much as Jenna should be cared for. Protected. Loved. He had blocked out feelings for so long that he did not know how to feel any longer. He felt a thousand years old, and he did not know how long it might be before he totally lost the use of his leg. A French doctor had said . . .

"Your heart would be safer elsewhere," he said.

"It doesn't understand that," she replied.

"You can go back. You've given me the message. One of the *bandeirantes* will take you. You can live well and have many children."

"Mr. Murray has some problems of his own," she said. "He may not be there long."

He tried to understand that. From what little he knew, her prospective husband was a wealthy plantation owner, wellborn and well situated.

"His wife was a quadroon," she said. "He—and his children—are not accepted in Barbados."

He was stunned. He knew what the word meant. He knew what it would mean in English society, even the English society on a faraway island. No wonder Murray had wanted a bride he'd never met, or one who had never met him.

"Your luck is none too good, my lady." He could not keep a cool note from his voice. So that was the reason she had come for him. The marriage planned for her was unsuitable. At least the man was honest enough to explain it.

She withdrew her hand from his grasp and moved away. "Do you think that is why I came to you? Because he'd married a quadroon?"

"It was not exactly what you had expected, was it?" He wanted to think the worst of her. He did not want to think she would have come all this way just for him. He did not want that.

Fire lit her eyes. She was clearly furious.

"Nay," she said. "It was not what I had expected. I had not expected to like him. But I did. I had not expected to admire him, but I do. He had the courage to marry the woman he loved. He had the fortitude to take the censure of his neighbors to raise his children alone after she died. He did not let fear rule his life. Which makes Mr. Murray a far better man than you."

He felt the contempt in her voice and it was far worse than the illness that had so recently plagued his body. He wanted to see joy in her expression again.

I had not expected to like him. The Englishman could offer her more than he could. And there were children.

Jenna loved children.

"Why did you come here?" He thought he had asked the question before, but the previous hours were a haze in his mind. Had he asked or had he dreamed?

"I told you, I had to let you know about the peace treaty. I feared you would walk into their arms."

"Mickey could have done that."

"Mickey could not have gotten to Vitória on his own," she said coolly. "The *Ami* could not return without being endangered. The Portuguese trader that brought me did so because I was a woman in need."

He felt loss at the distance she—or had it been himself—put between them. He had hurt her with his implied accusation. Hadn't he meant to do that? Was not that the best? Would the Englishman not be the best for her, particularly if she liked him?

She did not like *him* at the moment.

He closed his eyes. It was best to leave it here. She could still go back. She could still have a future.

When the priest returned, he looked at a sleeping Alex and nodded. "He is better. Good. We must go," he said.

Jenna looked at him. "The British?"

"Aye, with Portuguese officials who are none too happy at the prospect of losing some of *their* diamonds. Tomas has been watching several miles down the trail."

"He is not strong enough yet."

"He must go," the priest said again.

"He can do it," Burke said.

"They are not far behind," the priest warned.

She started to lean over but Burke reached Alex first. "I will get him ready," he said curtly.

Jenna wondered why she heard hostility in his voice. She did not think he had heard their earlier conversation, or had he? Had he, too, believed she was fleeing a marriage because of the man's children?

But now was no time to argue. If the British caught Alex, he would hang. She knew that.

She watched helplessly as he shook Alex awake, as Alex opened his eyes. His gaze went to Burke, then to her, and finally to the priest. "Something is wrong."

"I thought we were safe," she said.

The priest shrugged. "Someone said something they should not have said. I will find out when I return."

David Murray was her first thought. He knew she was meeting someone. He must have guessed it was the privateer captain.

But she could not quite believe that of him. He could have stopped her then and there. He could have sent soldiers after her before she reached the forest.

Alex's eyes were asking the same question.

"Nay," she said.

He did not question the protest. Instead, he tried to rise. He had been cool a moment earlier, but just the effort of trying to stand made his forehead bead with perspiration. A groan ripped from his throat as he placed an arm around Burke's shoulder. "I can . . . make it," he told the priest.

The priest nodded.

"Can they really find us in here?" Jenna asked.

"They have trackers, too, senhorita. Tomas can try to cover our tracks but we must move swiftly."

She started to protest. Alex did not appear as if he could go two steps, much less across a dense forest.

"We can go by canoe much of the way," the priest said. "Then we can lose them."

Alex turned to her. "You can stay here. They will find you."

"Along with the snakes and jaguars and other animals," she said. "Nay."

He looked frustrated. "You can say you escaped."

She gave him a disgusted look, then turned around. "Father, I'm ready."

He looked from her to Alex. "Captain?"

"Aye, I can make it," he said.

The priest nodded, then started walking. Alex took his arm away from Burke and motioned toward a stick on the ground. Burke picked it up and handed it to him, and Alex leaned heavily on it. He took a step and stayed on his feet. Just barely but he managed. She allowed him and Burke to go first, then followed.

They reached a river within an hour. Alex saw two canoes as they approached the wide expanse of water. If they had any farther to go, he would not have made it. As it was, he was using the very last of his strength.

He was hot again. Very hot, and his face was dripping. He knew by now it was a prelude to the chills.

He also knew that when they reached the river, the danger would be great, even without his illness. There were fierce rapids, even fiercer fish that could tear a piece of meat into shreds within minutes. Alligators.

Why hadn't she agreed to wait for their pursuers? He had hoped that his behavior would have made her do so.

There were two canoes, canoes that he remembered they had used earlier. He had lost all sense of time and place in the past several days. It seemed they had been walking forever. He leaned against a tree, but his gaze went around their small group. Their guide was as impassive as ever. Mickey was grumpy as always, and Burke . . . well, he was Burke, wary and always watching both his back and Alex's.

And then there was Jenna. When he had first seen her a month ago, he would never have conceived of her tramping through the jungle in trousers and shirt that were too large. Because of the heat, she had tied the shirt around her waist. Her face was smudged with dirt, but her eyes were as bright as he had ever seen them as they surveyed the expanse of the river.

She truly loved adventure.

But had he destroyed her life as he had destroyed his own by siding with a prince he knew could not win? His heart had lead him to fight. It had been his brain that had told him a rebellion was fruitless. He was trying to listen to his brain again. He was trying to ignore his heart.

With assistance, he stepped into one of the canoes and sat in its bow.

Jenna sat at the other end. Tomas and the priest took the paddles. Burke, Mickey, Marco, and the silent guide took the second canoe.

The sun was overhead as they glided into the river and headed downstream. Mosquitos and other insects were thick. His clothes had dried on him but now they were wet again and had stiffened with dirt. He looked at Jenna. Her gaze was not on him but the trees. She exclaimed as she saw something and pointed it out to him. A parrot. He'd seen many in the past days, but this must be her first. He had to smile at the sheer delight of her exclamation.

If anything happened to her, it would be his doing. He wondered whether he could live with that knowledge.

Jenna had watched as Alex settled painfully into the end of the canoe, careful not to rock it. She had taken the priest's hand and stepped gingerly into the boat. It seemed very fragile and unsteady to her. Still, there seemed no choice.

But in moments, she lost some of her fear and looked along the banks of the river. She saw a lazing alligator, the heavy growth of trees, even chattering monkeys. Then a vividly colored bird scolded them for disturbing him.

She had noticed little on their journey from Vitória. The way had been difficult and it had been all she could do to keep up with the others, to bear the heat and the insects. But now she could look to her heart's content, enchanted by what she saw.

Often she would catch Alex watching her with bemusement and something else in his eyes. He no longer had the ability to veil them as he had had when she'd first met him. She saw flashes of desire there, even though she knew she must be the worst-looking female in the world.

A tiny seed of satisfaction settled in her. He was not as indifferent as he wanted her to believe.

She turned back to gaze at the unfamiliar and exotically beautiful if often treacherous forest. She felt as if her heart was in the same forest.

Over the past hours, she had been alternately furious at and in awe of Alex. She saw the moisture gather on his brows and face, heard the hard breathing, saw the agony with which he took every step, yet he never asked to rest. It was that part of him that had so attracted her. Most of the men she'd met in her old life were dandies or officers in impeccable red coats who preened and bragged incessantly.

She did not approve of violence, but she did respect courage, and Alex had displayed it over and over again.

They traveled throughout the day until evening, then drew up to a sandy bank. The priest warned her not to go close to the water. She watched Burke help Alex step from the canoe. She wanted to give him her own hand, but she feared it would be rebuffed.

He gave her a weak yet devil-may-care smile as he leaned against a tree and watched the others establish a site, chopping down enough foliage for them to move around. No fire, though.

She felt helpless, not sure what to do. Despite his smile, she knew he was keeping distance between them as he'd done since Martinique. She did not know whether he really believed the accusation he'd made earlier about her not wanting the Englishman because he'd married a quadroon, or whether it had been one of his shields to keep from being involved.

She felt a sudden need for some privacy. She also

wanted to wash the clothes she was wearing, but that would mean going toward the river. She looked at it, and saw nothing that should keep her from it.

Jenna looked at the priest, then headed outside the circle.

"Senhorita?"

"I need some privacy," she said.

"Do not go beyond the sound of our voices," he said.

"Aye." She did not look at Alex as she left. Months ago, she would have been mortified to have been in this position. But after the past few weeks, she'd accepted the fact that everyone had the same needs and it made no sense to be embarrassed by it.

She went a short distance but the voices were still loud enough to be obtrusive. Too near. She took a few more steps. She could still hear voices though they were more faint. She heard the buzz of insects and felt something on her arm. She looked down and saw a leech on her arm. She'd had several before and knew she couldn't take it off herself.

She took care of her needs, her ears straining to hear the voices. Just as she was pulling up her trousers, she felt something fall on her. Thick and huge. She screamed as a giant snake began to wrap itself around her.

The moment Alex heard Jenna scream, he struggled to his feet, pulling his knife from its sheath. Burke was on his feet also, as was Tomas and their guide. Alex grabbed the guide's machete as he ran toward the sound.

She was just outside their small clearing, a huge snake wrapping itself around her. Her eyes were wide and terrified. More terrified than he had ever seen them. The snake's head was close to hers. Too close. Any swing of the machete might also hurt her.

She screamed again and he knew he could not wait. He was a swordsman. The machete was more awkward, but he had no choice. He only hoped the strength he suddenly felt was true strength.

He went straight for her and, with a prayer he hadn't uttered in years, raised the machete and took off the snake's head with one swing. It took every ounce of strength he didn't think he had. Only fear made it possible. The remainder of the snake fell, writhing, on the ground. He threw the machete down and grabbed Jenna, folding his arms around her shaking body.

He held her tight. Her clothes had been splattered with blood from the snake. He took her hand and led her away, back to where they had left their belongings.

Alex couldn't even imagine the horror. It would have horrified *him*. He had seen snakes, come close to an alligator, caught a disease, but the thought of that snake, especially it wrapping around her, was more terrifying than facing Cumberland's cannon. And she would not have undergone the experience if it were not for him.

He ran his fingers through her hair. "I'm sorry," he said.

She leaned against him. His head lowered and he touched her face with his lips, first around her eyes, then across her cheeks. He knew his own hands were shaking and not from the disease that had so invaded his body.

His heart cracked as she looked up at him, her blue green eyes slightly glazed, her legs unsteady.

It had been involved before. He'd liked her, admired her, wanted her. Yet she hadn't breeched the barriers he'd erected against caring and letting someone care about him. Now they were crumbling like a riverbank in a flood. She walked into trouble. She ran into danger. She waltzed into disaster. She'd done it all for him.

Dear God, how he wanted to protect her. How was he going to do that in the pitiful state he was in? The blow to the snake had been luck. Luck driven by desperation such as he'd never known before, not even the Culloden. He couldn't do it again. Right now, he wondered how he was even keeping on his feet.

She felt so good in his arms. So right. She tasted like heaven as his lips dusted her face with featherlike kisses.

He swayed. Weakness buckled his legs, folded him to the ground, taking Jenna with him. He moved so she would land on top of him. When her gaze met his, the glazed look was gone. Instead, a trace of mischief sparkled in those startling eyes. "We are a good pair," she said. "Neither of us can stand."

Pair. It had a seductive sound to it. Seductive in more ways than one. He moved slightly, turning her around.

She seemed suddenly to be aware of her own appearance, the blood and grime of the jungle on her clothing. And of his own sorry state. "Did I hurt you when I landed on you?"

"Nay, lass. Not in that way."

She looked down at her clothes. "I should wash."

"Aye."

"You, too," she said.

Only then did he realize he hadn't escaped the blood.

"I did not know there were snakes that big."

"I have heard of them," he said, "but I have never seen one until now."

"Thank you," she said.

He shrugged. "If I hadn't killed it, one of the others would have." But the rawness in his voice belied his shrug. So did the hand that clasped hers. "You can still wait for the British . . ."

She put a finger to his mouth. "Nay. I have cast my lot with you even if you . . . do not want me."

Do not want me. If she only knew.

He could not let her go. He should. But he couldn't. Dear God, she had come so close to dying.

His hand brushed her hair back from her face, resting for a moment on her cheek.

"Senhorita?" The priest had returned.

She moved then, rolling over and sitting up in one movement.

"We have brought you some water to wash," the priest said.

"It will take a great deal."

"*Sim*, for both you and the senhor."

"No more snakes?" she asked.

"I think not," he said in his broken Spanish. "Perhaps next time you should not go so far."

"I did not go very far at all."

"In this forest, even a few steps can be too many, senhorita."

He stooped beside Alex, a twinkle in his eyes. "But I sense everything is now all right."

Alex did not think so at all. He thought of the other snakes in the forest, the alligators in the river, the flesh-eating fish, the "bad air" illness he had. He did know one thing. If they ever reached the *Ami,* he would make sure he never stepped foot in Brazil again. He had aged twenty years in the last few moments.

She reached for one of the jugs of water Tomas had brought them and tore off a piece of her trousers. She wiped her face clean, then tore off another piece and did the same for him. Alex knew he should move away, or insist that she use all the water for herself, but her touch was so light, the gesture so tender, he could not move, could not resist, could not say nay. He was so tired. The cycle of fever, chills, and shakes had been gone for longer than at any time since its onset, but he was still infernally weak.

It was dark when Jenna finished. Mickey and the *bandeirantes* had made repeated trips to the river for water, then disappeared while she changed into a dress and washed the sailor's clothing she'd been wearing. She hung them up on a branch and hoped they would be dry the next day. She did the same with Alex's shirt.

She saw only shapes. They had no fire because smoke might lead any pursuers to them. Her eyes had become accustomed to the deep gloom of the forest where there was only a glimpse of a moon and a few stars directly over-head.

She'd needed to keep busy to keep from thinking about what had happened earlier. She could still feel the tightness around her body, the horror of the snake.

Jenna did not want to be alone. Physically alone. Even the presence of seven men nearby did nothing to ease the trembling despite her attempts to ignore it. She did not want anyone else to see how frightened she was. How frightened she still was. She did not think she would ever regard this forest benignly again.

She moved next to Alex. But she couldn't reach out again. She had been rebuffed before. He had taken her in his arms, but that was in reaction. Now he'd had time to build his defenses again.

And she did not want his pity.

Still, she needed the sense of safety she always felt with him. To her surprise, he pulled her close to him. He didn't say anything. He just held her close.

The trembling subsided. The horror started to fade.

She felt safe again.

But for how long?

Chapter Twenty-six

She screamed. The snake was twisting itself around her, tightening its body and squeezing the breath out of her. She flailed out, but it just kept wrapping around her. . . .

Her hand were seized, imprisoned. Her panic intensified until she heard soft murmurings and felt lips touching her face.

"It's all right, love." She heard the softness of his words, felt his protectiveness as he wrapped his arms around her. His body tightened against hers.

He was shirtless, and her hands reached out for him, touching the warmth of his skin. He was alive. She was alive, and she needed to feel every bit of that life. She was completely clothed, yet their bodies sought each other even through the layers of cloth. She felt him growing hard beneath his trousers and her body remembered how he had felt weeks ago in Martinique. Heat puddled inside her.

Despite his body being weakened by the illness, his warmth and need comforted her, even as it sparked fires inside. His lips caressed her face, then her lips, and they were clinging together, both with their own need. If she hadn't been fully clothed . . .

But she was, and he was weakened from his illness, and there were other people around and . . .

The passion was there, the need was there, the celebration of being alive. He parted his lips and she parted hers, and his tongue began a lazy seduction. Her fingers played with his back and she felt him grow rigid.

She wanted him. She needed him even more.

Their kiss deepened, his lips rough and demanding and as desperate as her own. She wanted to whisper that she loved him, but she feared that would cause him to move away, and she did not want that. She wanted him with her, against her. In her. She wanted his heat and passion and power.

Her body pressed closer to his.

Then nothing mattered, not the other sleeping bodies in the clearing, nor the silent guardian who was sitting on an incline, watching the river. Not the future nor the past. Nothing mattered except Alex.

Under the rough blanket, she unbuttoned his trousers, and felt him pull up her dress and the one petticoat she wore. She wasn't wearing a corset. She moved closer to him.

His fingers fondled and teased, and then he entered her. It wasn't the wild, exultant joining of weeks ago, but there was an intensity as well as gentleness that bespoke of care and longing and sweetness. She swallowed her sounds of pleasure and rejoiced in the living and belonging and in the tenderness evident in his every touch. She felt his seed flowing through her, the warmth of it, and then the shudders of pleasure.

He fell back and she snuggled next to him, her head on his chest, where she heard the sound of his heartbeat as she slowly fell asleep.

• • •

The sun woke Alex. His arms were still around Jenna and she was sleeping. He wanted to brush hair from her eyes but he did not want to wake her.

She'd had a bad night. She'd awakened screaming, her hands batting at him. No, not at him. At the snake. He had calmed her, murmured soft words in her ear, comforted her. And then . . . then . . .

She had finally gone to sleep again. His body had continued to respond to her closeness. He swore at himself. She was too vulnerable.

So was he.

He was her refuge now. Perhaps she was his, too. He hadn't wanted it. He had not even expected it. Yet somehow she had become more important to him than any person before. He had loved his family, doted on his younger sister, cared deeply about the children he'd found, but he'd never felt one with anyone before. Jenna had, quite simply, become part of his heart and soul.

But was that the best thing for her? It was, he knew now, the best thing for him.

He felt her stir, then she opened her eyes and gave him a sleepy smile. "Thank you," she said quite formally, even as she stretched out and part of her body rubbed against part of his. He felt himself responding again.

He was better. No fever. No chills. He swallowed hard, afraid to really hope they might be gone for good. He knew, though, that the British were not gone, nor were they likely to be.

He had to get Jenna to safety. To the *Ami,* and then they would find a haven.

He smelled something roasting and looked around. A small fire was blazing. It was covered by a wood brace and leaves to dilute the smoke. Pieces of meat had been skewered over the flames.

He brushed hair from her face—it had worked itself loose from the braid she wore—and straightened her clothing as best he could.

He ran his hand down her arm. "You are going to be hot."

"I planned to wear the trousers again," she said. "Perhaps they are dry now." Her eyes lit in a face colored by the sun. "I'm beginning to discover the advantages of being a male. I will truly hate to go back to wearing dresses and corsets and stockings and petticoats."

She was making light of yesterday. He grinned. "You look a lot better in trousers than most men."

She looked at him suspiciously. "Really?"

He leaned over and kissed her forehead. "Really," he confirmed.

"I must look terrible. My hair . . . my face. My mother said ladies always protected their faces."

"And they look pale and unappealing," he said.

She looked surprised. But then she always had when he'd offered a compliment. Now he wished he'd offered more. He suspected she had received very few.

But now was no time to linger. Tomas was tending the fire. The priest had piled up everything else, other than their clothing, near the clearing's edge. They were obviously ready to go, and were lingering only to eat. Alex took his arms from her and sat up. "I think they are ready to go as soon as we eat," he said.

She rose, her dress wrinkled and soiled, partly, he knew, because of their lovemaking last night. She looked at the meat on the fire and wrinkled her nose in a way he remembered. Snake! Nothing was wasted here. He wondered whether she could eat it.

She looked toward the forest, her eyes clouding. She needed another moment of privacy, and he understood completely. "This time I'm going with you," he said.

She appeared to consider which would be the worst: the lack of modesty or being in the forest alone. The latter won. She nodded.

He leaned toward her, speaking so softly she knew no

one else could hear. "I will never ever let anything happen to you."

How could he do that if he abandoned her once they reached the coast and the *Ami?*

She asked no questions, though. Instead, she took the clothes hanging on a branch, investigated them thoroughly, then headed for a tree. More than a week on land, and she still had the lolling gait of a seaman.

He longed for the rolling deck of a ship, for the new, fresh breeze and skies unshielded by trees so thick you felt you could not breathe.

He followed and when she stopped, he gazed around, looking for anything that might present a danger. He saw nothing. He nodded his head, then turned around, averting his gaze. Other than a monkey jumping from one tree to another, their movements seemed to have stilled all other living creatures.

Then she was next to him and she held out her hand to him. He looked at it for a moment, then took it and held her close. She touched his cheek. "The illness has gone away."

"For the moment," he said. "The priest said it can come back at any time. It could even hide for years, then recur." He heard the emptiness in his own voice.

She looked at him. "I love you," she said simply.

He stilled. A muscle jerked in his throat. He'd known it. He knew she was not the kind of woman who would sleep with a man unless she did. Or thought she did. He'd kept telling himself it had only been the danger and adventure. He could do that no longer.

"You should despise me," he said. "You never would have been in such danger yesterday were it not for me. You wouldn't be in this place."

"I came here on my own," she said simply as she pressed her fingers to his mouth to quiet his self-condemnation. "I make my own decisions."

"You did not make them when I took your ship."

"Nay. But all the others were mine."

"I am a wanderer, lass."

"It may be that I am, too."

"It has been only a few months. Being a fugitive becomes old. You do not make decisions. Decisions are made for you."

"There are places to go."

"Not now."

"Aye. I have heard that the American colonies are a vast place. You can get easily lost."

"You also need a sound body."

"I think you have a very sound body," she said with a smile.

He grinned despite himself. She kept surprising him. She would never be boring. Or predictable.

"You see what you want to see."

"I see someone who can do whatever must be done," she said. "Someone with honor and courage and strength. Burke said you could have escaped Scotland long before you did if you had not continued to pick up children."

"Burke said that?"

"Aye. He told me you always got yourself in trouble and I should have nothing to do with you."

"That sounds more like him."

"He cares about you."

"He cares about his own hide," he said, surprised that Burke said anything at all. But his own words were a lie. Burke had had many opportunities to leave him, and he would probably have fared better by doing so. Burke was as loyal as any man alive. This discussion was going nowhere, though. He could not let it go anywhere.

"We should go back. They will be getting impatient."

"That means we have to eat."

"Aye."

She shuddered slightly. "I am not sure that I can."

"There is hard bread, too."

"I like that much better."

Any other woman would be screaming rather than looking a little smug at finding a solution to the problem. He
found himself smiling again. And not just on the outside.

They paddled down the river for three more days, then the
men carried the two canoes over land and started down another waterway. Even Alex helped. He'd not had a relapse
since the snake episode.

Jenna thought it was willpower. She had discovered by
now that he had an iron will and steely control. He was like
that with her, too. Since that night when she needed him so
badly, he'd very carefully drawn a line between them. She
would catch him watching her, and every once in a while
he would hold out a hand to help her in and out of a canoe,
or when she tripped, but mostly he kept the distance he'd
always tried to keep.

Not that there was time to indulge in anything other
than survival. The priest was confident they had lost
their pursuers, but they must know that Alex's ship had
to be somewhere along the coast. Their big problem was
reaching the *Ami* before the ship was discovered by the
British.

The priest knew the island pinpointed by Mickey and
agreed upon by Claude. They knew that much depended
on Claude. He could just return to France, reporting to
their sponsor that he had been chased by a British frigate.
He could then keep the captain's share of the prize. There
was that, and there was also the chance that the British
would find the ship. That would leave the five of them in
a country where they would be hunted by both Portuguese
authorities who looked unfavorably upon smuggling, and
the British who would like nothing better than to find the
pirate and any of his friends.

Alex seemed to gain strength every day, although when
they made camp each evening he limped badly. She knew
every step was a mammoth effort. It hurt her to watch as

he grimaced when he folded his legs when they took a brief rest.

They slept only during the deepest hours of night. She'd had one nightmare—again the snake—and Alex had held her until she slept. She had awakened alone.

She said no more about love. She knew he viewed the future with skepticism, but she'd said what she had to say and did not intend to inflict her hopes or needs on him. She'd almost died that day, and she was not going to leave the world without making him realize someone could—would—love him.

The only thing she could do now was try to avoid being a burden to either him or anyone else. Except for the snake, she ate what they gave her, tried never to complain, and washed their clothes when the priest said it was safe. She thought often of her life in Scotland. Servants had done everything. She had never washed a piece of clothing in her life.

Now she would not return to that kind of useless life for anything. She felt valued here. Liked for what she was doing, not for her bloodline, or wealth, or position.

"How much farther?" Alex asked.

"Another week," the priest said. "We have to stay in the forest, and that slows us."

Jenna already knew that. The priest had told her the coast was patrolled and the mountains to the west were often well-traveled by treasure hunters and planters. That left them to hack their way through overgrown trails. A mile took far longer to traverse in the jungle than in the cool Scottish hills.

They built a small fire and cooked river fish. Then, exhausted, Alex lay down and was asleep within minutes. Jenna remained awake, too tired to sleep, too emotionally drained to rest. The others in their party made it nearly impossible for any kind of intimacy, even if Alex would allow it. He made sure they were never alone. Even when he accompanied her for her brief bouts of needed privacy, they did not venture out of earshot.

She did not know how long she sat, unwilling to lie down. She feared the nightmares and the questions about the future that haunted her. She wanted to stand and wander, to be by herself for just a few moments, but she was not a fool. A few feet outside of where they were and she could become lost forever, or worse.

A star appeared directly above. It appeared alone, the others hidden by the tree cover above. And even that lone light winked on and off as clouds drifted across the sky. She watched as they grew heavier, eclipsing the star altogether. The air grew dense, and she felt the moisture in the air. It would rain tonight.

She sighed and lay down. She might as well try to get some sleep before it came.

"Put the paddle down, senhor," the priest shouted to Alex over the noise of the rushing water.

Alex took his paddle from the water as Tomas and the priest continued to guide the canoe through ever more rugged rapids. He knew he wasn't as skilled enough to be of help, nor did he have the strength of the other two men.

Water sloshed into the canoe even as they were assaulted by rain above. The rain had tortured them for the last three days, coming in torrents, then suddenly stopping. Steam rose from the forest, making it nearly impossible to breathe.

After the river, there were clear trails, according to the priest. Once they disembarked this time, they would have two days' walking, then he knew a fisherman who would take them to where the *Ami* lay waiting for them.

Alex hoped. He prayed—something he hadn't done in a very long time.

Jenna's clothes were splattered with mud from getting in and out of the canoe and walking in mud that sometimes sucked at her ankles. Her hair was pulled back into a braid but wet tendrils clung to her face. She looked wretched. She looked glorious.

The rapids became fiercer and the two men paddling moved in a quick, sure rhythm, spitting out words to each other, words he could not understand. Jenna clutched the sides of the canoe. Her face paled as the white water became more and more vicious.

The canoe behind carried Burke and Mickey and the tight-lipped guide.

Tomas and the priest steered the canoe clear of some rocks. Suddenly, the canoe dipped as the water fell beneath them. It hit some rocks and Alex flew into the air as it turned over. Even as he was pushed under the water, horror struck him. Jenna could not swim. She'd admitted that to him several days ago.

He struggled to the surface. He saw two other heads in the foaming water. He did not see Jenna.

Alex took several strokes, fighting a whirlpool beneath the small fall, then swam forward. No Jenna. He dove underwater and then he saw her. She was caught in the whirlpool, her arms frantically clawing the water.

He grabbed her and pulled her up to the surface. She fought him, and he put an arm around her and dragged her along with him. He headed for the banks as the current pulled and tugged and tried to drag him back underwater.

Finally she stopped struggling, and he was able to get to the bank. He laid her on the ground. She coughed up water and he turned her over. More water erupted, then she stuttered, "The . . . others?"

He looked around. They had been swept downstream. He saw the canoe downstream, tumbling along in the water. Then he saw Tomas helping the priest. The other canoe was still upright and heading for the bank.

"All alive," he said.

The breath seemed to go out of her body then. She lay motionless. He touched her neck. The pulse was throbbing. Exhaustion. Shock.

He sat beside her as the others reached them. He nodded to let them know she was all right.

But she wasn't all right. She would never be all right again. Not after what she had gone through during the past few days, weeks, months.

One thing he knew for sure now. He was her Jonah.

Chapter Twenty-seven

They remained on the bank through the night. Tomas was able to retrieve the overturned canoe, but they lost Jenna's bag of possessions, including her dresses, change of clothes, and what money she had.

She regretted that, but not too much. She was alive, and that was no small thing.

Nor was it any small thing that again it was the captain—Alex—who had saved her.

She'd been sick for a while. She'd swallowed a great deal of water, and it took time for the panic to fade. She could not get over the queasiness, the pain in her stomach.

Alex looked even sicker than she did. She'd heard him curse and knew it was aimed at himself. "Ah, Jenna," he said then. "If anything had happened . . ."

"You didn't let it," she said.

"Almost," he said. "I almost didn't see you down there."

He looked so miserable. "I do . . . have a tendency for getting into trouble, I fear."

He did not answer but she knew he continued to blame

himself and that only drove him farther and farther from her.

Marco and Tomas started a fire and she huddled close to it, willing her clothes to dry. Everyone but Alex filtered away on various errands or perhaps to leave them alone.

She wanted to reach out and take his hand. Instead, she put her arms around her knees and huddled next to the fire.

He was not going to take her in his arms. That much was clear. But perhaps she could learn something more about him, anything that would help her understand him. She knew, of course, that he was Scottish, that he had fought at Culloden, that he had protected a band of children for nearly a year. She still did not know his true name.

And as long as she did not, she would not know him, would not know how to find him, or what made him what he was, or how to reach anyone who cared about him. She thought how terrible it would be if he simply vanished from her life, and she'd have no way to know whether he was alive or dead.

And with him, directness always worked best.

She watched him trying not to watch her. "You said you have a sister," she said.

His gaze met hers. "Aye."

"Where is she?"

"In Scotland."

"No one else?"

"Nay, they died not long before Culloden. My sister was already married." He looked at her for a long moment, then he added, "To a Campbell."

"A Campbell," she whispered.

"Aye, a branch of your family. His name was Alasdair." His voice was cold again.

She searched her memory. She had heard, though, of a scandal. Alasdair was a distant cousin who had died last year. His wife had been accused of murder, but then found innocent by no less a personage than the Duke of Cumberland himself. "Leslie," she said. "Janet Leslie."

"Aye. A Campbell nearly killed her."

She could not breathe for a moment. She'd known, of course, that he'd hated the Campbells, but she'd believed it was the disdain of a Jacobite for a clan who allied itself with the English. She had not known it was so much more than that.

"Is that why . . . ?"

"That is why another one of your cousins accused her of murder."

"There are a lot of Campbells," she said softly.

"Aye, they are a plague on this earth," he said bitterly.

Jenna bit her lip. Now she knew why he had never quite trusted her, why he had kept so much to himself.

His eyes had hardened as he told the tale, but suddenly he reached out and took her hand. "I should not have blamed you for something you knew nothing about."

But he had, and he might again. And, aye, she did know something about the ruthlessness of her father, of the other Campbells. She had heard them plotting to wipe out all the Jacobites in Scotland. But she had been a lass and could do nothing.

Or could she? If she had but spoken up . . .

"Nay," he said as if knowing her thoughts. "You could have done nothing."

She blinked back tears that had not fallen throughout the trek. Not when she was attacked by the snake. Not when she almost drowned. Not even when she feared for *Alex's* life. One of her family nearly killed his sister, and another accused her of murder. Because she was a Jacobite? No wonder he hated her family.

His hand tightened around hers. She looked up at him. His beard had grown, and he looked like a bandit. His clothes were drying but were wet enough that they stuck to a body grown lean during his illness. His hair was also darker with moisture and those piercing dark blue eyes were filled with an intensity she had not seen before.

"My sister remarried," he said after a moment. "The

man also sided with the English at Culloden but I've never met a better man. I came very close to killing him. In fact, I wounded him so badly he hovered between life and death."

"He lived?"

"Aye, he lived, and not because of my doing. I judged him without knowing him."

It was an apology, and yet distance was still between them. His anger was still there too, though it was not aimed at her. He was a very complicated man who was full of contradictions. She wondered whether she would ever understand him as well as he seemed to read her thoughts.

"She is happy then?"

"Aye," he said, then lapsed into silence.

"Good," she said.

He was silent for a few moments. "Are you always so honest and forthright?"

"Nay. I used to hide in the shadows."

"Because of the birthmark."

"Aye. And I was plain."

"You are anything but plain, Jenna. You are the bonniest lass I know."

She looked down at her soiled clothes and felt the heaviness of her hair clinging to her face. Self-consciously, she pushed it back. "Nay," she said. "You are still ill."

"I do not know if I can ever get over the anger, lass. I've turned into a thief. I almost murdered a man who did not deserve it. I allowed hate to color everything. I have become my enemy."

With those words, Jenna suddenly knew the battle ahead. The enemy was no longer her family. It was not that she was a Campbell. It was a self-loathing that went far deeper.

Her fingers wound around his and brought it to her lips. "And the good things?" she asked. "The children? The men who would do anything for you?"

"Saving the children was a way to strike back at the English," he said. "Don't turn it into something else."

But it had been something else. Would he ever realize it? Or believe he was worth loving?

They reached the coast five days later. Tomas had been able to retrieve the second canoe. It had taken all of Jenna's courage to step back in, but she knew they could not walk through the forest to the coast. It would take them weeks.

Nothing else could happen, she told herself. And nothing else did.

Not even a kiss. Not a moment of affection. Nothing. Instead Alex drove himself mercilessly. The fever struck him again, but he wanted Burke to look after him. She watched him suffer through such chills that she thought he might rock the earth, but he still flinched whenever she neared him.

The priest had taken her aside. "It is best for him that you stay away," he said.

She had looked at him with misery but knew that he was right. Alex grew worse when she tried to do something to help him. He was able to travel again the next day, the medicine working small wonders.

Alex Leslie. She now knew his name but it made no difference. He trusted her, but he did not trust himself, and that seemed an even worse burden for him to carry. He had undertaken this venture thinking he would probably die. And he had not cared.

She did not know what to do to change his feelings. She could only look at him, knowing that each furlong they traveled brought them closer to a departure she did not want. Because he did not feel he had a future? Because he did not think he had anything to offer? Or was it still her name?

Jenna was a realist. She could look after herself. She'd left most of her jewelry aboard the *Ami*. The few pieces she had brought with her in the event of emergency had now disappeared down the river. If they did not reach the *Ami*, she would be penniless. She would also be unable to return home. Rumors would live with her throughout her life. She knew the misery of a birthmark. The shame of being a fallen woman would make her position untenable.

And Meg and Robin? The thought of the children had kept her going these past five days. She made up stories she could tell the lass, including descriptions of the parrots and flowers that so enchanted her.

When they finally reached the mouth of the river just before dusk, she asked whether she could use the water to wash her hair and her clothes.

"Stay close to the bank," the priest said. "Tomas and I will keep watch."

She had no soap, but just rinsing out her hair and her clothes made her feel better. The trousers and shirt had been clinging to her body, and she wore them into water that looked almost as muddy as she already was.

To her surprise, Alex came in with her. The chills had stopped yesterday, but his clothes, like hers, were caked with sweat that seemed to attract insects.

She kept an eye out for alligators, but the priest said they would be unlikely to see them here. Still, there was always the danger of snakes. She was not sure whether Alex had come in to bathe himself or to watch over her.

Jenna wondered whether she was making things worse.

But at least she did not think anything else could happen. In the past two months or so, she had survived cannon fire, a storm at sea, a giant snake, and rapids. Perhaps she was just becoming numb to it all.

She stayed close to shore and did the best she could. The priest produced a small bar of lye soap, and she scrubbed and scrubbed, then handed it to Alex. Then, reluctant to linger in the water, she climbed up on the shore and watched him soap, then dive into the water. She remembered the strength of his arms when he'd pulled her from the river, but it had been only three days since his last attack.

He finally came out, shaking his hair. He took off his shirt and she saw the scars again. He was thinner than he had been, but color had returned to his face. He looked wild and restless and dangerous.

They decided to rest overnight. They would have to move away from the river, according to the priest, since there was river traffic. That also meant there would be no fire tonight. Their clothes would have to dry on their bodies. No fish tonight, either, unless they ate it raw, and Jenna was not that hungry.

She sat next to Alex, praying that it would not be cold tonight.

"How many more days?" he asked the priest.

"We should reach a village tomorrow night. A fishing boat can sail you to the island. A day. No more."

"My thanks for all your help," Alex said, knowing the words were inadequate. They could have taken the diamonds and the money at any time. Instead, they had placed themselves in danger for him and his friends.

"You can repay us by returning. My people need your help."

Alex hesitated. He was not going to lie to this man, and now he had personal business to settle before he could do anything else. "Someone will. You have my word on it."

The priest frowned. "I thought . . ."

"I have people I must get to safety first," Alex said. "With the treaty, I—and they—could be hunted. But I have a partner in France who is eager for a steady source of diamonds, and Claude, my first mate, and Marco . . ." He looked toward Marco in question, and the man nodded. "And Marco speaks your language. He will be back." He suddenly smiled, his teeth white through the darkness of the new whiskers. "And you never know when I might appear."

The priest nodded.

"We will finish our business tomorrow?" Alex asked.

"If you still have the funds."

"Burke has the gold," Alex said. "Thank God he was in the second canoe."

The priest raised one thick eyebrow, but said nothing else. Instead, he offered Alex some of his prepared mixture. "I will give you some of the powder to take when you leave."

"Obrigado," Alex said.

"De nada," the priest said in reply to his words of thanks. "You are learning Portuguese," the priest said.

Alex nodded. "Where will we find you again?"

"Through Tomas in Vitória or the fisherman to whom I am taking you. Either of them can find me. Tomas has gone ahead to the village. He will bring some mules for you and your lady."

His lady. If only . . . If only the sun did not disappear at night.

The priest disappeared then through the forest. He seemed at one with it, and had no fear of its dangers.

Jenna shivered and wished for a comb, but that too had been lost when the canoe had tipped over. Instead, she combed her hair with her fingers.

"I think I want to do what Meg did," she said.

"And what's that, lass?"

"Cut if off."

He looked stunned. "Nay, lass. It is lovely."

"Not now."

"We will be back to the ship soon. Then you can wash it all you want."

"And then what?"

"It's not safe to go directly back to France," he said. "The British will be expecting that and probably patrolling its coast now that there is peace."

She watched his face, waiting for him to continue.

"I've been thinking about going to Louisiana. It's in

southern America. Once there, we can make enough changes in the *Ami* to get her—and the diamonds—back to France."

"And you? Will you go back then?"

"Nay, I think not. The other children are settled in good homes. I will send some money back for them, but I think Robin and Meg will be safer, and happier, in New Orleans. It's French, but a long reach from London."

"And me?"

His eyes darkened. Or perhaps it was the nightfall that made them seem to glitter.

"You can still go to Barbados," he offered.

"I think not," she said coolly. "I would rather be a governess or—"

"Nay," he said. "You would not make a good servant. You are too stubborn. You would be dismissed in a day."

"It was what I planned if Mr. Murray and I did not suit."

"'Twas not a very practical plan."

"I did not used to be stubborn. You seem to inspire it."

"No one could tame you," he said, his eyes sparking with something she had not seen for much too long. Five days, to be truthful. "I will give you whatever you need to establish yourself. You can go to Boston or Philadelphia. New York."

Jenna was insulted. "Nay. I need nothing from you," she said.

Obviously reluctant, he hesitated again. "What if I employed you to care for the children?"

"In New Orleans?"

"Aye. I can visit there."

"Visit?"

"Aye."

But he would not stay. Because she would be there. He did not have to say that. He would give up the children—and a safe haven—to ensure that she and the children were safe.

"I will think about it."

"Before we reach the ship," he said. Not a question but a demand.

"Aye."

He unwound himself and stood. Without looking back, he limped out of sight.

She had been outraged. Alex knew that. He should have never offered her money, but he wanted to make certain she would be safe. Keeping her with the children would assure that. And she would be good for them, and them for her.

He did not know why he'd waited to make that particular proposition. He'd wanted to give her choices. Opportunities. He should have known she would accept none of them. Except possibly for the last one.

And that would be both hell and heaven for him.

No matter how hard he tried, he could not believe he would ever be good for her. He had lost his soul, had become everything that he hated. And that did not even address his physical problems, nor the fact that his face was marked for life. He could never go on British territory without risking his life and that of anyone with him.

He had to settle the matter before he saw Meg and Robin again. He had to know that they and Jenna would be safe. Perhaps once that happened he could continue the diamond smuggling himself, rather than turn it over to Claude.

But first she had to agree.

At dawn, two men in white shirts and trousers appeared with three mules.

The priest bestowed a self-satisfied smile on them. "One for the captain, one for his lady, and one for me," he said. "We will make better time."

Jenna thought heaven had just opened. Her shoes were wet and in tatters and she had several blisters she'd tried to hide. The mules, while rather pitiful compared to her father's fine horses, were as grand to her as the grandest of his prized steeds.

Alex saw her expression and even he grinned. He went over to her and interlocked his fingers to help her mount. She put her hand on his shoulder. Felt its strength. He was so unaware of it. Unaware of his basic decency. Unaware of his core power. And nothing she could say would convince him of that. Raw longing made her hand linger.

He did not pull away. Instead, he took her hand. "There is not another woman alive like you." It wasn't said in an "I have to have you" tone but more with regret.

She did not know what she should say. Or maybe she did. She just did not think he would accept it. So she merely removed her hand to the mule's shoulder. At the moment, she saw a lot in common between the animal and man.

Alex looked at the fishing boat with trepidation. It looked as flimsy as the canoes that had overturned.

He avoided Jenna's gaze. He did not want to see fear again. God knew she had experienced enough fear in these past few months to turn anyone else into a raving madwoman.

The ship obviously leaked. It had a shallow draft, and its sails were small and tattered. One good wind and they would all go to the bottom of the sea.

It smelled of rotten fish.

But then, probably, so did he.

"My ship?"

"There are a hundred islands around here, and many hidden bays," the priest said. "It has always been the pirate's sanctuary. My friends know most of them. They can find your ship. Unfortunately I must stay here. I become very ill aboard ship." He took out a bag from his robe. "The remainder of the diamonds."

Alex opened the bag and poured the contents into his hand. A rainbow of colors. Blue. Gray. Green. Amber.

"Jenna."

She had been talking to Mickey, but went immediately to him and looked at the contents in his palm. She picked up one blue stone that caught the rays of the sun and it glimmered. It was magnificent.

She dropped it back in his hand.

"Nay," he said. "It is yours. You have earned it."

"But it belongs to all the crew."

"It will be part of my share, and you have done as much—if not more—than any crew member. We would still be in Martinique were it not for you."

"Keep it for me," she said.

His gaze held hers. "I will."

He turned to Burke, and nodded. The man took a pouch that had been tied around his waist and covered by a now ragged shirt. He tossed it to the priest, who dropped it into the folds of his robe.

"You are not going to count it?"

"Is it necessary, senhor?"

"Nay."

"Then it is done. There are more stones like this."

Alex did not doubt that for a moment. He had stopped wondering at the resources at the priest's fingertips. He seemed to claim uncommon loyalty, but then he would. He had no riches himself, and his one concern seemed to be buying the freedom of others. A little smuggling was apparently justified for the good it accomplished. He was beginning to revise his opinion of godliness.

"You will pray for this ship?" he asked with more than a little irony.

"I would not lose my means to an end," the priest replied wryly.

"That is enough for me," Alex said. "Jenna?"

He already knew the answer.

"It is enough for me, too," she said, and held out her hand for help in boarding. This time it was to Marco she turned, not to Alex.

He should have been gratified. Wasn't it what he wanted?

He hoped he wasn't glowering on the outside as much as he was on the inside.

One day in the leaking boat hadn't sounded too bad to Jenna. But then she'd discovered that nothing about this adventure was easy.

There was no shelter. The boat smelled terrible and it lumbered through the calm sea like she imagined an elephant would. Each dip made her think there would not be a rise. But surprisingly, the boat continued to surface again, water spraying all its occupants.

The boat, which she certainly did not consider a ship, bobbed and wove past small patches of land. She hoped each would be the last, even though it meant she had to make decisions she did not want to make. Fishermen with nets kept watch, but all they saw were other small fishing vessels.

What if the *Ami* was gone? No, the *Isabelle,* as it was now named. But it would always be the *Ami* to her, just as she thought it would always be to Alex. What if it had been captured? Or had headed back to France, believing that they were dead or imprisoned?

Alex stared straight ahead, his stance restless, his gaze constantly sweeping the sea. He still had the weeks'-old beard. It was thick and bristly and yet it added to his attraction. Untamed. Unconquered. He was both and always would be.

A shout came from above. It was in Portuguese and she did not understand the word, yet she knew the meaning.

A ship had been sighted. Curiosity, even trepidation, urged her toward Alex. He was peering out in the direction a crewman was pointing.

"The British?" she asked.

He listened closely to the chatter above. He could make

out some words. Not all. He caught enough to understand it was a Portuguese government vessel.

The diamonds aboard could convict them all. *If,* that was, they were not turned over to the British.

"We cannot outrun them," he said.

"How far?"

"An hour away. Not much more."

The crew of the boat was frantically working what sails there were.

Her heart thumped so hard she thought Alex would hear it. They had come so far . . .

She turned to Marco.

He gave her a wicked, delighted grin. He seemed to enjoy trouble. "Do not worry, lady. When they are not fishing, they are smuggling."

But the speck she had barely been able to see grew larger and larger.

The fishing boat headed directly for a ribbon of water that ran between two islands. But it was like a hare and a tortoise, and the fishing boat was very definitely the tortoise. She watched as the hare gained on them. Then there was a shot that splashed just short of the ship. She was becoming accustomed to the sound.

Alex gave her a quick look. There was no place on this boat to hide. No way he could protect her here. They could not surrender. The lives of the fishermen were as much at risk as their own.

Instead, Alex grabbed some lines and helped turn the ship in the wind.

Another shot. Water splashed up and drenched her. They passed between the islands. The wind caught the sails but it also caught those of the larger ship. Still another shot landed only feet from the ship.

Alex gave the ropes to someone else, and turned toward her, clasping her tight in his arms as if he could guard her from a cannonball. She leaned into his embrace, feeling the comfort in it, the protectiveness. He leaned his head against her hair, whispering to her, but she could not hear for the rapid speech of the crew.

She heard an elated· shout, then another, and looked back at the pursuing ship. The shrinking figures had abandoned the cannon as the ship came to a complete stop. Even from the distance, she heard a crashing sound as the ship hit a reef and foundered.

Alex looked down at her and released an indrawn breath. Then he leaned down and kissed her.

His arms tightened as if he would never let her go as their small craft lumbered to safety.

Chapter Twenty-eight

Alex felt a heave of relief as its tall masts of the *Ami* came into sight, the ship anchored in a protected harbor on the leeward side of a large island.

Sailors were lined on deck and when they saw him, they waved and shouted. Robin and Meg had huge grins on their faces, and his heart raced. It really was a good feeling to be missed. Claude and Hamish both saluted.

He assisted Jenna aboard and watched as she gave both children huge hugs. Even Robin submitted to it with an abashed smile. "I missed you both," she said in a voice that left no question of her sincerity. The children beamed.

Then she turned to Celia, who had been watching with a wary expression until she saw the hugs and the smile on Jenna's face. She visibly relaxed and, in turn, received a big hug.

Alex watched the tableau with bemusement. They all belonged together. They were a family. Jenna and Meg and Robin. Even Celia.

Then the children broke away and came over to him. Robin put out a hand in a gentlemanly fashion. "I am pleased you are safe, sir."

Meg stood before him. "Me, too."

But there was not the exuberance of their greeting with Jenna. There was affection, to be sure, probably even love, but also a reserve. That reserve hurt.

And yet he knew he had cultivated it. He had instilled it in them, afraid of his own feelings, of an involvement of the heart.

He stooped down and put an arm around Meg. "Your hair is growing out," he said, damning himself for thinking of nothing better to say.

It seemed sufficient to Meg, though. She broke out in a wide smile and hugged him hard. It was the first time she had done that, and he felt as if he had just grown two feet taller, as if his heart had opened for the first time.

Then he put an arm around Rob, saw the surprise followed by delight in the boy's eyes.

Two sets of arms wound around him, and he had never felt so whole.

He finally untangled himself, understanding for the first time that he had been a coward, afraid to love or accept love, and perhaps the latter was the most difficult of all. He had thought he was being strong, when he was really being weak. It would continue to be difficult for him. One did not change overnight.

He stood and greeted the others, particularly Claude who had waited so faithfully. Then he asked Claude for some coins. The small craft was still bobbing alongside the *Ami,* but obviously ready to leave. He asked them to wait until Claude returned with a small pouch of coins. Alex then climbed back down to the fishing boat. He clasped hands with the fishermen who had risked their lives for him and rewarded them with gold coins from the cabin.

They grinned at the unexpected bonus, nodded their heads, and took his outstretched hand as he said good-bye to them.

Once he climbed back aboard, the sails were unfurled and the ship slid from its anchorage on a course they hoped would let them evade the British and the Portuguese. He felt immense relief as well as the exhilaration as he always felt at sea.

The children—and Jenna—watched with him at the railing until the small boat disappeared.

Then Jenna looked down at herself, the soiled clothing, the hair tied back but knotted and dirty. "I think I will wash my hair and change clothes." She turned and fled down the hatchway, Celia trailing behind her.

Alex waited until they had clear seas, then went down to the first mate's cabin he was sharing with Claude. He too needed to do something about his current state. Burke appeared and Alex asked him to take some water to Jenna, then to bring some to him. Burke, he added wryly, might want to do the same.

Burke grimaced and disappeared. Alex wondered whether they would exhaust the water supply among the lot of them.

Alex was in the officers' mess, playing with a deck of cards, when Jenna appeared.

"I'm hungry," she said, surprised to see him there. She had expected him to be on deck. She, in the meantime, was hungry for anything that was available.

He rose. He had shaved and the good side of his face looked incredibly handsome. He was wearing a white flowing shirt tucked into a pair of trousers that hung more loosely than usual around his long legs. Her own dress, one she'd brought from London, was equally as loose.

She felt dowdy with a dress that no longer fit and wet, albeit clean, hair that she had braided.

But when he looked at her, she knew immediately he saw another Jenna, a Jenna that was pretty and desired.

"Cards?" she asked as she looked down at his hands.

"Aye. A deck my brother-in-law gave me."

There was a peculiar look in his eyes. One she had

never seen before. He seemed to be working out a puzzle in his own mind.

He turned away from her. He placed a card faceup. A jack of spades.

He smiled in a strange way. "Does that mean anything to you?"

"Aye," she said. "The Black Knave legend. The man who saved Jacobites and tormented the British. He disappeared, but then returned." Then her eyes widened. "Not you . . . ?"

"Nay. I was recuperating from wounds. But I knew of him."

"My father feared him."

"Like my brother-in-law, he fought with Cumberland and was sickened by it. He later married a Jacobite."

"He still lives?"

"Aye."

"Where?"

"In America."

"I thought he had been killed."

"That is what he wanted everyone to believe."

The fact that he told her that much showed a trust she'd not felt before. She wanted to ask more. She wanted to ask why and how he knew what he did. She sensed there was far more to the story than he'd said, but there was also a reason he was telling her this now.

She held her breath.

"I'll always be a fugitive."

"I know."

"I have a restless streak."

"I know."

"I like the sea."

"So do I."

He was arguing with himself, but something had happened on the deck of the fishing boat earlier. When he had clasped her, protecting her against iron cannonballs, his reserve had melted. He'd told her then—wordlessly—that she meant far more to him than he'd ever wanted her to know.

She had felt it in the way his lips pressed against her hair, in the grip with which he held her.

"I do not know if I can ever stay in one place."

"Then I will go with you."

"I have killed people."

"I know." She touched his hands. "But always in a good cause."

"Nay. There was a time I just wanted to kill."

She stepped closer to him. Her fingers touched his coal black hair, then ran down the scar. "Do you know how much you have given me?" she asked.

"Trouble. Fear. Danger."

"Belief in myself. And that is far more important than anything else."

She saw a muscle throb in his throat.

"Let me make my own decisions," she whispered. "Until now, everyone has made them for me. The greatest thing you can do for me is let me make this one."

He turned over the heart queen. "That was what my brother-in-law called my sister."

Heart queen. It was oddly whimsical. Another story?

One day she might hear it all. But now all she wanted was a happy ending to her own story. She still wasn't sure she had one.

She took the deck from him and thumbed through it. She finally placed the diamond king faceup.

"My sister called me that," he said.

"I think I would like her."

"You would. You both have heart." He rose to his feet. "I would not like to harm that heart."

"You can do that only by ignoring it."

He looked down at her. The heart under discussion started beating rapidly.

He had looked at her with passion, with longing, with

lust. He had never looked at her quite like this before. With
love he did not try to disguise.

"I can promise you little, except that I will try."

"That is all anyone can promise."

He chuckled. "You always surprise me, Lady Jenna."

"I'm not a lady any longer. I do not want to be."

"You are always a lady, Jenna. Even when you dress in
trousers and are half-drowned. The problem is I'm no gentleman."

"I always thought gentlemen were overrated."

His arm went around her and she leaned against him,
her head against his heart. She thought it might be beating
as loud as her own.

"I might be very bad for you."

He was still arguing with himself. But at least he was
doing that. It was promising.

She looked up at him, and his lips met hers. They were
gentle at first, then demanding, and she met his kiss with
all the passion and love and need that had been building
during these months. She opened her mouth to his breath
and it became hers. She listened to his heart and it beat in
tandem with her own.

She felt his surrender.

Or was it his triumph?

The *Ami* neared New Orleans. It had taken nearly two
weeks, but they had avoided the major shipping lanes.

As they neared the Mississippi and started up its mouth,
Alex wrapped his arm around Jenna. Meg peered ahead
while Robin helped with trimming the sails. "We can sell
the *Ami* here, buy a smaller trading ship for the Portuguese
trips," he said. "The Comte de Rochemont should be
pleased with his diamonds. I should have enough from my
share to buy property and start a shipping company."

He had mentioned New Orleans before, but he had not
actually made a decision. He'd wanted these days with her.

He'd wanted to make sure that once imminent danger was gone, she would feel the same.

That he would feel the same, that he could really give her a life, that his own fears would not destroy her.

But he'd let something go that afternoon when he'd looked at the cards. Other men had experienced the same demons he had, and had made something exceptional of their lives. Perhaps he could, too. At least, he could give it a chance. For both of them.

First, though, he would have to fulfill his obligation to Etienne, who had given him an opportunity to forge a life of his own. He would propose a partnership of sorts—a shipping company for trade between France and New Orleans with perhaps a few stops along the Brazilian coast. Claude had already said he would continue the smuggling. He, too, had developed a sense of adventure, and in a few trips, he could be a very wealthy man.

Alex's share of their privateering and the diamonds would give him enough to build a company.

During the journey to New Orleans, he'd wondered whether he could be happy in one place. He hadn't been even when Scotland was at peace before the ill-fated rebellion. But then perhaps he had been looking for what he had now found. A family.

It had taken him time to get used to the idea. He had given it up long ago, and it had taken that moment on the fishing boat when a cannon had nearly killed Jenna yet again that he realized love was worth taking the chance of loss. She had taken so many risks for him. How could he do less?

He wanted to protect her. He had to protect her. He loved her with every fiber of his being.

The Forbes cousins—Rory and Neil—had taken the gamble. They had risked everything to save others, then were still able to love and build futures. Had he less courage than them? Had he been wrong in depriving Jenna of deciding her own life?

Jenna looked up at him. It was the first of October and the air was cool and crisp. The wide river was lined with trees. No alligators or huge snakes anywhere.

His gaze met hers, saw the questions. They had made love the first night at sea again, the night after he had stared at the bloody cards for hours.

It had been even more glorious, more passionate, more magical than the night in Martinique. Knowledge added a new depth of intimacy. The relief of certain safety after weeks of terror and anxiety had removed the desperation, giving them time to learn about each other in the sharing of love.

They had touched with wonder, and trembled with the depth of their need. He had not been able to slow his movements, not when she welcomed him so completely.

But the next time, it had been seductively slow and easy, their bodies moving together in a sensuous dance as they explored each other, and kissed lazily, and then exploded with passion.

From then on, they'd shared the same bed. . . .

And now she felt natural in his arms. She was his refuge.

His home.

She looked up at him with the excitement he'd come to recognize. She was ready to embrace this new life as much as she had embraced him in the night. Her face was rosy with the sun, her sea-colored eyes brimming with vitality, her body braced against the wind and any troubles that might confront her.

By the saints, but he loved her.

More wondrous still, she loved him.

"Will you marry me when we reach New Orleans?" he asked. "Meg and Robin need a family."

"And you? Do you need a family?"

"Aye."

"Is that all?"

He smiled slowly. "You are going to make me say it, aren't you, lass?"

She waited, her brows raised in challenge.

He touched a curl that was blowing in the wind, then his fingers moved to her cheek.

"Nay, that is not all, lass. I love you. I love all that you are. I have for a long time. I just—"

She raised up on her toes and halted the sentence with her lips.

And answered him.

$\mathcal{E}$pilogue

New Orleans, Nine Years Later

Her heart swelling, Jenna waited at the altar as Meg came down the aisle of the Catholic church, to stand beside her, then clasp hands with Robin.

Robin looked incredibly handsome in his wedding clothes with a tender yet beaming smile spread across his face.

Alex stood beside him, the perfect side of his face in her view. He looked magnificent, but then he always looked that way, no matter her view. The area around his eyes crinkled frequently now with humor rather than bitterness. It crinkled in that appealing way now as tenderness radiated from his face. He had waited for this day for a long time.

His family. Her family. *Their family.*

Meg and Robin were as much a part of it as were eight-year-old Rory, six-year-old Sarah, and four-year-old Alexandria. There would be another addition in six months. Jenna hoped for another lad to balance their brood, but any bairn would make them happy.

Alex had been made for fatherhood. She'd known it almost from the first weeks of their meeting, but he'd per-

fected protecting his heart then. Once those walls had tumbled, he'd embraced life and love and family with the same
fierceness he'd once used to deny them. Oh, he'd had a
few setbacks—morose times when he'd feared life was too
good and designed only to take back what it had given. But
in the succeeding years, as one healthy child followed another, as laughter—and even tears—had filled their town
house in New Orleans, those moments had faded while his
smile broadened.

He'd been uncommonly successful. The diamonds had
given them seed money, and subsequent voyages to
Brazil—an effort financed by himself, Etienne in France,
and Claude—had made them all rich. Alex had built a
shipping company that now had seven ships trading
throughout the world.

She had gone on one voyage with him, but that had
been the one and only adventure they'd shared outside
Louisiana. It was before they had children. Their adventures now were the children and the business. Someday,
perhaps, when the children were grown, she and Alex
would go adventuring again.

She turned and looked back. Rory Forbes and his wife,
Bethia, were there. Jenna knew the stories now. How Rory
Forbes had been the Black Knave in Scotland, a mysteri-
ous man who spirited Jacobites out of Scotland under
Cumberland's nose. How the legend had continued with
Neil Forbes, who was still in Scotland and married to
Alex's sister. Neil had helped Alex, Meg, and Robin es-
cape Scotland.

Neil had written Rory and Bethia about the connection
to Alex and his new wife. They had become friends
through letters, then the Forbes had decided to visit the
Malfours, the name Alex and Jenna continued to use.
Robin, in fact, had spent a year in Virginia, working with
Rory's stables; he'd wanted to raise horses himself, and
Rory had been his mentor.

"We are gathered in the sight of God," the priest began.

Alex looked at her and winked.

Memories flooded her. Their own quick wedding in New Orleans and the lovely night afterward. The house they had bought in Beinville. The wedding of Celia and Burke, who remained with them as companion and butler.

Then the birth of their children. The first had been hard and long, but Alex had never left her side despite the outrage of the doctor. Then the easier births of their two daughters. She would never forget the way Alex had looked at them, wonder in his eyes and tenderness in his touch.

And now there was another on the way, and he was ecstatic.

Her eyes moved from the older Rory—friend—to young Rory, who sat next to his namesake. The latter looked just as Alex probably had as a lad, except he had lighter eyes, more like her own. He had his father's dark hair and crooked smile and sense of adventure.

His sister sat next to him. Sarah. Quiet and shy and bookish, just as her mother had been. She had a small birthmark of her own. A mark of great good fortune, Jenna told her. Her own birthmark, after all, had brought her Alex.

And young Alexandria. She had all of both her parents' sense of adventure. Bold and bright, she was all energy and mischief.

Jenna loved them with all her heart, just as she loved Robin and Meg who were as much hers as the children she actually birthed.

And now she watched as the two made their vows and promises, and her heart sang.

The ceremony finished and they exchanged a kiss long enough that it drew arched eyebrows. Then they turned to Alex and her and gave them blinding smiles.

Meg mouthed the words "I love you both," before sweeping down the aisle.

Alex took her hand. "Thank you," he said softly.

His heart was in his eyes. It said so much. "We did well, didn't we?" she replied.

"Aye," he said, his eyes roaming over her figure, which was beginning to change. "Four more weddings to go."

She grinned. "Are you sure only four?"

"Nay," he said. "With you, anything is possible."

"With *us,* anything is possible," she corrected.

And then he kissed her and she knew it was true.